Birth of a
Queen

TJ Lee

DEDICATION

To women everywhere. Our crowns may be tarnished, lopsided, missing pieces, or even invisible, but you were each born with a crown. You are all queens.

We birthed them, and we raised them. Many of them forget that they are nothing without us, it's our job to remind them!

Prologue

Grace

"Dude? What the hell? Why'd you shoot me?" Scott yelled from the couch in the other room.

"Gee. I don't know. Maybe it's because you just stole *my* car, nitwit." Justin answered, with an eye roll no doubt.

"Children, if you can't behave, then you don't get to play." I laughed at the tone Layla used as she playfully scolded the boys.

Things had certainly been different since Carter brought us to Mojave.

On the one hand, we were open for business, like every day. As though to demonstrate my mental point, my eyes floated up to Rachel, who was serving her second vamp of the night, at the table. As long as they played nice, and didn't get greedy, Carter let some of his men have an all-access pass to his house.

To everyone except Todd and I anyway. Carter didn't let them touch us.

We knew that going in though, we knew that was how it would be. We just didn't know what else was going to happen.

On the other hand, while Los Angeles still had no power, everywhere else did. It was kind of nice to live in the modern age again. Carter had even been kind enough to choose a house that was not only large enough to hold all seven of us, but also came fully stocked to serve our needs. In other words, the boys had plenty of video games to play. Many of which some of us had never been able to play before.

Some of us, like Todd and myself, had never even *played* a video game before. Thanks to a lovely thing called the Foster System.

"Hey, Gracey. What ya cooking?" I felt the soft hand grip my waist as the man himself leaned over my shoulder.

We'd only been in Mojave for a little less than a week, but Todd had already settled nicely into the new role, our new way of life. He was calmer than ever before. He even seemed more relaxed than he was in our last foster home. Which was where we met for the first time, sort of. We did go to the same high school before that, just never spoke much to each other.

"Spaghetti. It's not much, but it's something at least." I could feel him watching me. He knew my mind was elsewhere as I stirred the ground beef I was frying.

The other great thing about our new home. Carter made sure we had more than enough food for our needs. We were now eating three square meals a day and had all the snacks we wanted. If it weren't for being on-call vampire chew toys, this life would be awesome. I could sort of understand why Todd was chill here, even with the vampires, this place was better than living with Pinky and the Brain (his terms of endearment for our last wardens).

Raya had offered to take my turn to make dinner tonight, they all knew my mind was constantly on the move, ever since the drones showed up. My visions were spotty at best, but I could feel something coming. It was that dark, ominous feeling you got when a movie turned to that slow dark music to build suspense.

Up until yesterday afternoon (which was like last night for us since we lived on a vampire schedule) we had only ever seen the drones policing the streets, terrorist style. If you stepped one foot out of line, it was your last step. I never realized they would also be used to send messages to the "New California Republic."

At least now the others knew what Curtis' voice sounded like. I only knew because of the visions I had had over the last few months.

Curtis was a vampire, one of the worst. A few months ago, he led a systematic, and successful, attack on California. Roads and buildings were bombed, vampires slaughtered thousands in their beds. Cities burned. And a wall around the state swiftly followed.

According to Curtis' message, he was now in charge. San Francisco, San Diego, and Los Angeles were going to be the vampire cities. The only humans allowed were the donors. All humans left in those cities would be shipped off to the smaller cities. A census of every human was to be taken, and jobs assigned.

I worried for Carrie. She was a human friend of ours from the city. Well, actually, as we just found out, she was a pure-blooded witch. Turned out I was a witch too, not pure like her though, thankfully. The purer the blood the stronger the call our blood had to the vamps.

One of her mates, Deacon, was technically the Vampire Prince. Both of her mates were Vampire Borns, a more natural type of vampire. They were born vampires. The others, referred to as Nightwalkers, were created.

Curtis was Deacon's enemy. And Carrie was the Vampire Born's first chance in centuries at having another child. A son, of course, as a curse from a thousand years ago killed all their females and kept them from birthing more. It wasn't exactly safe for a human, or a witch, to give birth to a vampire. But my vision showed that both her and the boy would survive.

Curtis was my target. When all this went down, I had visions of what we needed to do for us to survive. Todd and I created a group, a harem of sorts. Those visions led us to Deacon, who ran a bar in LA, these days catering mostly to vamps. Through him, we met Carter, who became one of our regulars. Carter was in charge of securing the wall in our region.

My vision said he would take me to Curtis.

With Deacon's help, Todd made contact with the U.S. government, a Captain in the human Army sitting just on the other side of the wall. We now had a burner phone, so we could send any information we found directly to them.

Now, I just needed to become Curtis' favorite pet, so I could hear things.

My eyes suddenly glazed over, as what I had been waiting for finally came. Todd, recognizing the signs, took the spatula from my hands and turned off the stove.

"We've got incoming." He hollered out to the rest of our makeshift family. In the distance I could hear the tv being turned off, and footsteps running to join us.

The first vision hit.

Deacon and Carrie were coming, they were approaching the wall, preparing to go through the gate. Only, the gate was no longer there. Carter and his men were ordered to block it up two days after we arrived. Deacon's truck stopped when they saw it. After a few minutes, they started driving again.

Carter and his men stopped him at the nonexistent gate.

“Where you going, Deac? You shouldn’t be out here right now.”
“Open the gate, Carter.”

“Can’t do that. We’re under orders. What’s wrong? Why are you trying to run?” Carter could tell something was off. His men began gathering, preparing for a fight.

Deacon looked at Carrie, her powers were to read intent and being able to know a lie when she heard it. Deacon nodded at whatever she said.

“Sorry, Carter.” He backed up and then swung around.

I could see them driving along the wall for a few hours, trying to find another way out. By the time they reached where the next gate should have been, an army of vamps was waiting for them. In order to keep Carrie safe, Deacon had to surrender. The war would be over, and not in our favor.

The next vision hit right after, the alternative play.

This time, Carter didn’t go out on the defensive, this time, he went out in concern. They get out of the truck. Carter begged them to get to shelter before the sun finished coming up. Carrie climbed on Deacon’s back, and he jumped the wall. They were met by the human army, taken by them. I watched, waiting. The signs of their path continuing were there, just not the details.

I focused on the difference between the visions. How was I to get them to jump?

And there it was. I was with Carter in the second one.

I blinked my eyes, clearing the fog away, and looked at the clock. It was already past five. I had a little over an hour until Sunrise.

“I have to go. Now.” I ran to the bedroom to grab my shoes, not paying attention to the people following.

"What happened? What did you see?" Todd asked as he chased after me. He at least knew better than to stop me.

"Deacon and Carrie are on the run. If I don't get to that gate before them, they are screwed."

"Do you need us to come with you?" Raya asked with concern, she looked up to the older witch like she was an older sister of sorts. Raya and Carrie had been together during the first wave of attacks.

She stepped to Todd's side as I slipped my last shoe on. Carter had been gracious enough to give us free reign in a Walmart the night after we got here. It had been a long time since I had a decent pair of shoes.

"No, just me. I need to lay the groundwork to knock Carter off balance, and to nudge Deacon in the right direction."

"Which is?"

"Up." I ran around them and headed for the door, grabbing the keys to a jeep we had use of. "I'll be back, stay here."

Chapter 1

Grace

"Hey, pussy cat. What are you doing out here?" Carter grinned as I pulled up to where he kept a tent for an office. The moon shined off his nearly bald head.

They typically worked 24-hour shifts and needed protection during the day. It wasn't technically a tent, more like one of those collapsible roof things I'd seen people use at the park, with dark tarps hanging down the sides.

I ran straight at him and jumped on his chest, knowing he responded better to this. Once my legs were tightly wrapped around his waist I leaned back and looked at him.

"I missed you." I pushed out my lower lip in a pout. "You were gone when I woke up and hadn't been back."

"Awe, kitty, you know I have to work." Carter loved it when Todd and I acted like we were more attached to him then he was to us. Vampires, no matter the brand, were territorial and possessive. And men in general were ego maniacs.

I bit my lip and pretended to fight a grin. "That's why I thought I could come visit you. I knew you were on duty all night, so I thought maybe you could use a little snack." I tightened my grip on his neck and moved in a little closer. "Is it okay that I came?"

The whites of his eyes began to glow, a low growl coming from him at the same time. Man, he was so easy to manipulate.

Carter carried me to the makeshift wall and pressed my back against it, all the while, releasing his other beast. We learned a long time ago to mentally check out while the vamps fed and did whatever else they wanted. If we let our minds get involved, it didn't work out so well.

It wasn't just the blood the vampires craved. It was the chemicals *in* our blood. Certain activities were known to heighten our production of those chemicals. Something vampire bodies had difficulty doing.

If our minds were too involved then our bodies wouldn't react the right way, nor would they create those chemicals. In order to survive, we needed them too.

I was almost 18, and I had basically handed myself over to the vampires as a plaything. The adult's plan to take out the vampires was to go to war and fight back. While that probably worked for most wars, it wouldn't for this one. Their typical type of spies would never be able to slide into Curtis' entourage.

Vampires thought of humans as nothing more than pets. So, that was the part we played. We were young, we were healthy, and we were overlooked.

"Thank you, kitty. You can come visit me anytime you want. I'm surprised you didn't bring Todd with you."

I looked down, pretending to be shy. My eyes landed on the blood that was still dripping down my chest. Carter liked to watch his artwork for a bit after he was done feeding.

"I snuck out. I wanted you all to myself for a change."

Carter barked out a laugh, then leaned down and licked the blood off me. Not in the right spot for his saliva to heal me, more like around it. And only just enough to clean off some of the blood dripping down. I gave him a soft moan, as it was in a delicate spot, and it helped sell my reason for being there.

"Can I stay for a little bit? I'm not ready to leave you yet." Playing into his ego was always a winner. And a little tiring, to be honest.

Carter reacted immediately, he set me down and pushed me to the ground. We had played him at Deac's bar for weeks before he finally brought us back with him. I knew what he wanted, and I knew what would get him to let me stay for a while.

A few minutes later, he finally sealed my chest and then led me back to his tent. I barely stepped foot inside before Carter heard something in the distance. Nightwalker hearing wasn't as good as the Vampire Borns, but it was still better than mine.

I stopped with him and looked in the same direction he was. "Isn't that Deacon's truck? Why is he all the way out here?"

"I don't know, kitty. Maybe he needed more supplies?"

"The gate is closed, Carter."

"Yeah, but not everyone knows that." His eyes scrunched, looking at the passengers closer. "He's got Carrie with him. He never takes Carrie outside of the bar. Something is very wrong with this. Is he trying to run?" The closer the truck got; the more defensive Carter became.

Now for the real reason why I came out. "Carter, the sun is going to be up soon. It's not safe. We need to get him inside."

Carter glanced up at the sky, which was already a smidge lighter. He mumbled a curse and half ran to where Deacon was stopping the truck.

"What are you doing here, Deac? Didn't you get the message from Curtis?"

"No, but I heard about it from my customers. Why'd you block the gate?"

"Orders. I don't ask, I just follow. Why are you here?" He looked up at the sky again and shook his head. "Forget it. Come with me to safety, you can explain once we are undercover. This has got to be the stupidest thing I have ever seen you do." Carter took a few steps back toward me as Deacon and Carrie climbed out of the car.

I could see Deacon whispering something to her before they got out. They didn't come our way though, instead they both walked to the front of his truck.

"You coming or what?" I hadn't ever heard Carter's voice shake like that before. He was close enough to the tent that he would get back inside before the sun came up, so he wasn't worried about himself. He was only worried about his friend.

I took a few steps forward, drawing Deacon and Carrie's attention. Carrie gave me that look, the same one she did when I saw them in the bar last, with Deacon's hand on her stomach, the happy little couple that just found out she was pregnant. She was silently asking me to look into the future again. This time I already had.

My eyes shot toward the wall and then to Deacon, and I nodded minimally. Deacon nodded back, understanding my meaning. I gave my friend a small farewell smile.

"Deacon! Come on! Your little mate can catch up with Gracey inside. Let's go." Carter ran backward further as the sun broke over the mountains, his hand slid protectively behind my back as he reached safety.

“Don’t think so, Carter. I’m sorry to do this to you. You’ve been a good friend for many decades. I’m glad you are doing well. But it’s time I stop hiding. It’s time to take care of my mate and unborn son. It’s time to take my place at my father’s side.”

Deacon squatted down in front of Carrie, his eyes on me, seeking confirmation. I nodded just a smidge again. Yes, this was the right path. I wished I could warn them about what they were going to run into on the other side of the wall, but there was no way to do that. Nor was I sure if I was supposed to.

Once upon a time, I shared everything I saw with my friends. Carrie taught me not too. She was the first witch I had ever met. That I knew of anyway. Her mom had my same power, so Carrie was able to give me a few pieces of advice before Carter took us away. I liked the older witch and wished we had had more time together.

“What the hell are you talking about, man? Curtis ain’t gonna care about your human mate, or her kid. Just get over here bef… oh… holy…” Carter was cut off as the sun hit Deacon and Carrie like a spotlight on a stage.

Carter jumped back, cursing, expecting to see his longtime friend begin to burn.

Deacon turned his face toward the sun, a soft smile playing on his lips. Carrie tightened her arms around her mate’s neck, locking her legs around his waist. Not one of the many vampires in the tent with us said a word, beyond their first colorful ones anyway. My favorite was the “bloody, hell” that was said in a very thick English accent. It kind of reminded me of the way Ron Weasley always said it in the movies.

We were pretty sure the last owners of Carter’s house were Potter fans. They had one whole room dedicated to it. I had never read the books before. Or seen the movies. Hadn’t thought I would like them. I was wrong. Rachel and I burned through them all in the short time we’d been there.

“I guess there are a few things I didn’t tell you. And she isn't a human. She’s a witch. And I’m not your typical vampire. You need to brush up on your history, Carter.” Deacon backed up a few more paces, the sun lightening his path with its rays. “Thanks for the laughs, my friend.”

I held my breath as Deacon ran faster than any of the other vampires I had seen so far. They had been nearly a block away from the wall when they started. Within a blink of an eye, he was jumping. We all watched as he pushed off the top with one foot, keeping them over the barbed wires, and then they were gone.

It took all of five seconds before chaos ensued. “What the hell was that?” was repeated over and over again, with variations in the words used. Hell was probably the tamest.

One vampire in particular was still staring at where Deacon had disappeared from, his jaw open.

“Well, I’ll be. I heard the stories, but I never believed them.” Ah, so that was Ron Weasley. Except blonde and evil. Soo… Draco Malfoy, then?

Carter spun on his heel, stepping over to the English bloke. “What stories? Do you know how he was able to stand in the sun like that? Was it his age?”

The vamp blinked and brought his attention back to Carter, he blinked again then straightened his back like a good little soldier realizing his commanding officer was talking to him.

“No, sir. When I was human I was told stories about a vampire race that could withstand the sun, sir. They were supposed to be stronger and faster, and dying out because of a curse, sir. They aren’t like us, they are born, not created. They once ruled the vampires. Sir.”

Carter's mouth opened and closed, not sure how to respond. He slowly pulled his phone out of his pocket, tapping the screen a few times, then put it to his ear.

"Lucas? Carter. Have you ever heard of a vampire being able to withstand the sun?"

Carter's back stiffened as he listened to the other man speak. Carter whispered a curse again as he started pacing in the tent. He was like a caged animal.

"I've been walking this earth for over a hundred years. How have I never known this before?!... Yeah, well, looks like it's time someone starts teaching history the right way… Yeah, that's right, we've got 'em. Well, we did. I just watched one jump the freaking wall with his mate."

Carter's face paled, making him look more like the mythical version that movies always made vampires out to be.

"He's here already? I thought he wasn't coming for a few more days?... Y… yes, sir. We'll be ready, sir." Carter hung up his phone and looked around at everyone, but not seeing anyone.

"Who's coming, sir?" Someone asked from a corner.

"Curtis. He'll be here soon." Carter's eyes swept to me. "Grace, get back to the house. Make sure the place is straightened up. From what I just heard; Curtis is not going to be happy when he gets here. I might need your little friends to help sooth him."

I stepped closer, raising a hand to his chest, the same way I'd seen Carrie do to her two mates when they got upset. Watching her had been good for many lessons.

"If that is what you wish. Are you sure you don't want me to stay here with you? You look like you could use some soothing yourself." I wanted to see Curtis. I needed to see him. This was my chance. Possibly the only one I would get.

Carter leaned down and kissed me, almost like a lover would.

Well, maybe. I was basing that off Carrie and her mates, too. They were the only real loving relationship I had ever seen. It was obvious that they weren't just possessive of her the way Carter was of us. They worshipped the ground that witch walked on.

"Thank you, kitty. I wish you could stay longer, but this is no place for a pet right now. You can take care of me later. It's a good thing you brought so many friends along for the ride. Curtis likes to have his pick." He swatted my butt and grinned when I leaned against him and purred. "Go along home now, kitty."

I pouted one more time and walked back to the jeep. It took some effort, but I managed to keep my pace steady, knowing he was watching me carefully. I looked back at the tent as I climbed in, and sure enough, Carter's eyes were glued to me. I stuck the tip of my finger in my mouth and gave him a small smile. I giggled when his eyes sparked.

I ran into the house fifteen minutes later. Everyone should have been getting ready for bed, instead they were all sitting on the couches in the living room, waiting for me to report back. As soon as I ran through the door, all six of my friends, my family, stood up.

"Deacon and Carrie jumped the wall, in the sun. The words out. Curtis is coming."

"Are they going to be safe?" Layla cut through the talking that ensued. She was just as attached to Carrie as her twin was.

Then again, maybe we all were in a way. Carrie had this big sister aura to her. You couldn't help but feel protected in her presence. Like you innately knew she had your back and wouldn't lead you astray.

"I think so. I wasn't able to get a clear picture of what would happen next, but it was the best alternative."

"Is this it then? Curtis is coming. Is this our chance?" Todd was brimming with adrenaline.

We'd been planning this for months. It started with him and I, the night Ryley broke into our foster home, and we heard him mention Curtis' name. That was when the visions of my destiny started.

"I think so. I need a clearer view though. The sun just came up. That gives us a few hours. Everyone needs to rest up. Carter said he was bringing Curtis by later. He said Curtis would need soothing after this. He also said Curtis liked to have choices, which he will certainly have a variety of with us. I want everyone up and dressed before nightfall."

With nods, they broke up and went to their separate rooms. When we were in the shelter, we naturally slipped into pairings, which carried over into the apartment we shared after. We kept those pairings when we came here. We never discussed it; it just sort of happened.

I believed we paired off with who we were most comfortable with.

I was surprised by some of the pairings. Justin and Rachel were the youngest, both fifteen. Justin looked like a generic Cali boy, just like Todd. Blonde hair and blue eyes. Rachel had that gorgeous dark skin with black hair that could be braided for weeks at a time.

Then came the twins, Raya, and Layla, at sixteen. They were very clearly Native American beauties. Todd and I were seventeen. I was maybe a shade darker than him with black hair and purple tips.

Last came Scott, who was eighteen. I hadn't the courage to ask him what he was mixed with yet, but he reminded me of milk chocolate.

As I told them, Curtis had would a variety of choices with us.

At first, the twins had been eyeing Scott and Todd like a piece of meat. Rachel and Raya had been the most innocent of all of us.

Which I always found ironic since Raya and her sister had the most perverted minds.

Todd and I had always been a pair, at least since the vampires first attacked. Before that we just provided comfort to each other on a as needed basis. We both went to the same school, and eventually lived in the same foster home. He was there, easy access, and always willing.

I expected Rachel and Justin to unite, but somehow, Rachel ended up with Scott. He was nearly as possessive of her as Todd was of me. One would think Justin lucked out when the twins gravitated toward him, but Layla learned, during our prep sessions in the shelter, that she preferred a different anatomy. She bounced around but always went back to her sister and Justin.

Sleep refused to come to me. My mind was restless with what was to come. I let Todd help me burn some of the excess energy off, like I always did. But lately, I felt like I was as into it with him as I was with Carter. It was all just part of the job.

Unfortunately, I knew it wasn't the same for him. He still talked about hiding me away from the world after all this was over, just the two of us. At one time, I liked the sound of that. For some reason, that had changed for me.

Ever since Todd came back with the burner phone, I had been getting flashes of a large man in army fatigues. And then flashes of a large black wolf with a deep purple tint. Each time, my heart would pick up the pace. I didn't understand it, and I didn't know who it was. But it had changed me, somehow.

I wasn't sure how I felt about that either.

I looked at the clock, seeing it was barely eight in the morning and sighed. It was hard to tell time with the sun blocking blinds Carter had up all over the room. It might as well be midnight with how dark it was in our bedroom.

I rolled over to the side and pulled out the phone I kept hidden under the mattress. I pushed the power button and slid it under the pillow so the sound would not wake Todd. He never had problems sleeping lately. Even when Carter was between us.

I slowly counted to thirty, then pulled it back out. I clicked on the message app, then the one thread we had on there - the Army Captain who was our contact.

Me: C is on the way.

It was a few minutes before the response came in. He was always pretty quick in getting back to me, knowing I rarely had much time.

Hill: What happened? I haven't heard from you in a while. Is everything alright?

I smiled. The good Captain did not like our plan, but it was already approved by his higher ups. I'd only messaged him twice before this. The first being when I got the phone, to thank him for his help. The second was when we arrived in Mojave. From the tone of each message, he was a bit of a worrywart.

Me: We've been good. We have more food and entertainment here than we did in LA. Oddly, we feel safer here. Everyone knows we belong to Carter.
Me: D jumped the wall. I had a vision. He was going to be met by guns from your people. Why aren't you there?
Hill: I got called away. How many vamps saw him?
Me: All of them. The sun was up.

I never met the man, but I was pretty sure he was cursing up a storm right then. Todd had told us how Hill knew what Deacon really was already. And that he was wicked strong. I didn't know if he was one of them, or something else entirely, but he knew enough to help.

Hill: Is that why C is coming?

Me: Yes. Carter called someone named Lucas. He didn't even know about vamps like D. C was already in LA. He wasn't supposed to be here for a few more days.
Hill: What happens now?

Me: I'm not sure. Everything is splotchy. I can't get a clear read. Carter says he is bringing C by later. I think this is my chance.

I could practically hear his sigh. He was dreading this. I was sure he was. Again, I didn't know how I knew. I just did.

Hill: Are you sure you want to do this? I can get you out. All of you.
Me: The gate is sealed, and with C coming, their numbers will go up over here. This is the only way.
Hill: Fine. Get some sleep. Let me know what happens.
Me: Thank you.

I turned the phone off and slid it back under the bed. I felt calmer now, which was odd, but whatever. At least I could finally fall asleep.

Chapter 2

Deacon

"I think I'm going to be sick."

I laughed softly at my Angel.

She carefully lowered her feet to the ground, but kept her grip on my shirt, steadying herself. I looked up just as a dozen rifles were cocked, all pointing at us.

"Who the hell are you and how did you get over that wall?" A deep voice barked out.

"My name is Deacon. Where is Captain Hill? I need to speak with him."

"Captain Hill was needed elsewhere. I'm his replacement. And I believe you still haven't answered one of my questions."

"I jumped. Now, if you'll excuse me. I need to get my pregnant wife to a hotel. It's been a long night for both of us." I started to walk forward, but a rifle with a silver dagger on the end blocked my path. “I see someone taught you how to deal with vampires. I’ll save you the trouble,” I pointed at the new ornament, “that won’t work on me. Look at the sky gentlemen, the sun is up. I’m obviously not one of them.”

“Then what are you? That was some jump.” The new Captain pointed out… again.

I sighed, wishing Grace had been able to give us a little more to go on. “I think we need to take this to your office, sir.”

The Captain eyed me carefully, then nodded before doing an about face and marching off. The men with the guns shepherded us after him. We were led back to the same building that Hill had kindly let Todd and I wait in on my last trip out here.

It was nothing more than a two room, easy up cabin. Obviously it had been thrown together in haste. Along the wall of the main room, a lobby of sorts, sat a table with bottles of water and a basket of granola bars. As well as one of those coffee pots that made one cup at a time. I had one in my bar. It just hadn’t been used as much recently. Not since the Nightwalkers became my main patrons. Coffee wasn’t really their thing. Or ours, actually.

On the opposite side of the room, were two couches, which looked like they came from a yard sale, arranged in an L shape. In front of that was a small round coffee table. It was in even worse shape.

The Captain stepped into the room, followed by one other soldier (he looked like his ancestors had come from South of the Border), who closed the door behind them. I ignored them both and pulled my mate to the couch.

“Sit, rest.” I told her, before walking away.

“Now, as I was saying...”

I lifted a hand to cut the Captain off, without saying a word to him.

I picked up one of the bottles of water and two granola bars. One was a Nature's Valley Honey Oat pack, and the other was a chocolate covered Chewy. I sat down on the table in front of Carrie and handed her the water first.

"Are you still feeling sick?"

She smirked and shook her head. "I'm fine, Deacon. Really."

She lifted a hand to tap my chest, a silent reminder that I could feel everything she could. Well, everything about her anyway. I wished I could ask her what she felt from the Captain, what his intent was.

Instead, I closed my eyes and rested my head against hers, trying to fish out her feelings. She was calm, a little nervous, but otherwise fine. Carrie wasn't feeling any immediate threats from them then. I kissed her head once and stood up.

"Eat. And drink the water." Her eyes shrank to glare at me, so I softened my tone. "Please?"

With a huff she picked up the water and leaned back into the couch. I turned and met the curious eyes of the Captain. Since she didn't seem scared, I would play nice. For now.

"My apologies, Captain. As I said, my wife is pregnant. It is still early on, and with all the stress of the last few days, I worry."

He looked my mate over again, and then looked at me. "How did you jump that wall?"

"Quite simple, I ran, and then I jumped. As I said."

"No human could jump that wall. We've had many men try to climb it, just to be shot as they worked their way over the barbed wires. How did you? With the vampires right there no less?"

I clapped my hands softly, rubbing them together, before spreading my arms out to my sides. “I don’t know what you are expecting to hear, Captain. I run - well - *ran* a bar in LA. After the vampires took over, I brought in donors, humans willing to let them feed. For a fee of course. This helped keep many vamps from hunting at night. It also gave my wife and I a bit of protection. As well as all those who worked for me. After we heard the announcement on the drones, the one telling everyone of Curtis’ plans, I knew it was time to leave. We just found out that my wife is pregnant, and I was not going to risk my unborn child’s life while we waited to be rescued. We got to what we thought was the gate, just before sunrise. The vampire in charge is one of my regulars, in fact he convinced some of my donors to come back with him last week.”

At the mention of the teenagers, the Captain’s eyes creased just a bit. He was aware of them, but I doubted he knew much beyond that.

“I was able to talk to him just long enough for the sun to push them all undercover, then I hightailed it over. A man can accomplish a great many things when he is trying to protect the ones he loves.”

The Captain scoffed. “My men told me that you have been here before, for supplies. So, I believe the bar story. But I still don’t believe how you got over that wall. No human could have jumped that. Extra adrenaline or not. You both will wait here, while I call in and see what they want me to do with you.” He walked into the other room without another word, thankfully taking his lap dog with him.

I sighed and sank onto the couch next to my mate, pulling her into me. “If this was the better option, I’m not sure I want to know what would have happened if we kept driving.” I kissed her head as she turned into me. “Do you feel anything from him?”

“Caution. He is wary of you, I think. How are you? Do you need to feed?”

I looked down at her beautiful blue eyes. “I can wait, Angel. I am more worried about you.” I chuckled as she rolled said beautiful blue eyes.

She gently tugged at my black hair, still mostly contained in a rubber band on the back of my neck. “You didn’t have time to feed last night, then you had to jump that wall. And who knows what will happen next. The last thing we need is for you to go through withdrawals again.”

I laughed harder and kissed her creased forehead, as she wasn’t happy with me for laughing at her. “If we had been in a high-powered situation, instead of in the bar, surrounded by the scent of so many people’s arousal, it would not have happened.” I exhaled, all the amusement dying out of me. “You do have a point though. I don’t know when we will have the time later so I can do this without freaking the humans out. And I worry that Curtis will be ready to jump that wall by nightfall. I’m sure he already knows I am here. However, I will only feed if you let me feed you. We need to keep your body strong for the baby. I will not lose you.”

I swallowed the laugh at the way her eyes lit up. She was as addicted to my blood as I was to hers. Which was common, and why it was rare to trade blood with anyone but a mate. I bit into my wrist and held it up to her.

“You first, Angel.” She leaned forward, greedily latching onto me. Her eyes rolled to the back of her head, her hand reaching lower for me. “Uh, uh, Angel. We don’t have time for that right now.”

She whimpered and gripped my arm with both hands. I struggled to keep my free one off her.

I gave her another minute, knowing we didn’t have long, then pulled away. Her eyes sparked with need, not happy that I cut her off so soon. I laughed and slowly leaned in, kissing her softly first.

Her body shook a moment later, as my fangs broke the skin on her neck.

It wasn't long before I had her on my lap, my hand inside her jeans. She was at least aware enough to bite her tongue to keep from yelling out. A few minutes later, I licked her neck slowly, taking in the last drops, and wiping away the evidence of what I really was. She collapsed against me with a sigh.

"How come you can play with your food, but I can't play with mine?"

I chuckled at her pout and held her close to me.

"You didn't give me much of a choice, Angel. Your blood was already so worked up, I nearly lost complete control over myself. If you had been in one of your skirts, I would have done more. I know you would not have appreciated one of them coming out with your pants on the floor."

She sighed into me, a small yawn coming out of her. "No, I wouldn't have. Thank you. I think."

I chuckled softly. "Lay down, Angel. Take a nap. I have a feeling we will be here for a while."

With another yawn, she spread out across the couch, her head in my lap, and immediately fell asleep. I ran my fingers through her hair once, before I carefully lifted enough to slide my hands into my back pocket, searching for my phone. Colton needed to know what happened.

Only, my pocket was empty.

I silently cursed my stupidity for leaving it in the truck. With a disappointed groan, I pushed my hearing out. I had heard the Captain make the call when he first left the room, but he must have been told they would call him back. Since then, it had been just him and this other man talking about us. Thankfully, it didn't sound like I had missed anything.

"We could just let them go, sir. He wasn't a threat before. I don't know why he would be now."

"Because I don't trust him. No one could have jumped that high. He didn't climb any part of it either. One minute the top of the wall was empty and the next he was standing there, jumping again. It doesn't make sense. Something isn't right."

"If it wasn't for the sun, I would have assumed he was a vampire."

The Captain huffed. "As would I. For all we know, he is something else entirely. Who knows what else is hiding in the shadows?"

"If he was with them, why would he be running?"

"He could be a spy, or a decoy."

"And his pregnant wife?"

"Psh, we don't know that either of those things are true. It could all be part of his cover."

"Last time he was here, he told the guard that he and the boy with him had to go back. They couldn't run. The vamps had an eye on his wife. His story has not changed."

"That doesn't make it true."

The other room grew silent, with the exception of papers turning and fingers tapping on keyboards. After a few hours, the Captain sent his lackey back out.

"I am going to collect the Captain's lunch. Would either of you care for anything?" The lackey kept his voice soft when he saw my sleeping Angel.

"If you wouldn't mind, that would be good, thank you." I nodded my thanks as well. Carrie needed to eat, and maybe it would set them at ease more if they saw me eat with her.

Another twenty minutes passed, and the man returned with a tray filled with three plates. He set two plates on the table in front of us, and then took the tray into the office with him. The plates held club sandwiches. One with potato chips on the side, and the other, a garden salad. I huffed a small laugh, grateful that he kept her needs in mind.

As I raised my food to take a bite, I heard the phone ring inside the office. Maintaining my nonchalant mood, just in case someone walked in, I took the bite while eavesdropping.

"Captain Miles… Yes, sir. Thank you for getting back to me. We have a situation on hand that I need your clearance for… No, sir. We have had no fighting. But we do have a man that jumped the wall from their side, with a woman on his back… Yes, sir, the sun was up… No, sir. All he says is that he was anxious to get his pregnant wife out of there… No, sir. He claims it was adrenaline. They are being detained, sir. My aid says the wife has fallen asleep… Deacon, sir. Says he ran a bar. My men remember him coming for supplies a few weeks ago. He had the boy with him… Yes, sir. *That* boy."

I couldn't help but wonder if they were already in touch with Grace and Todd. She seemed to be a thorough little half witch, or maybe it was quarter witch. Her scent was much fainter than Carrie's.

"Where, sir?... Yes, sir. I will arrange a team and head out. We should be there around midnight, sir." Captain Miles hung up the phone.

It was quiet in the inner office, with the exception of chewing. I was listening so intently that I was barely aware of my own eating.

I anxiously waited for him to speak again, to give me more information. I was sure they were taking us somewhere. I just wasn't sure where that was exactly. And why it would take so long to get there.

"Reyes?"

"Yes, sir?" The aide asked, well, more like yelled.

"Get a squad together. We need to escort Deacon and his wife to General Brooks in Phoenix."

"Are you going with them, sir?"

"Yes. The General is anxious to talk to the man himself. He sounded excited at the prospect. There is more going on than what we have been told. The General has been in meetings with the President and a few others since last night, I know that much. He was almost giddy by the time we got off the phone."

Colton and my father were supposed to be at that meeting. That meant the General knew what I was. I'd been around long enough to know how men like him thought. He wouldn't be giddy if he were preparing to turn me over to my father.

No, he'd want to use Carrie and me to motivate my father to whatever the human government wanted. We weren't safe. I was tempted to pick up my mate and run. But then what would we do? If they shot at us, I would risk her and our son. Neither was a risk I was willing to take.

Why did I leave my phone in the truck?

"Make sure the men we leave behind are prepared for anything. They need to be on alert. This could all be some kind of distraction."

"Yes, sir. What time do you want the squad ready to head out?"

"1630."

A moment later the door opened. Reyes glanced down at the couch and cracked a smile.

"She's still asleep?"

I forced out a small chuckle, like I wasn't worried in the slightest, or making plans to run. "We waited until the bar closed last night, trying to sneak away in the night. She slept a little in the truck, but it wasn't peaceful."

"How far along is she?"

"Not long, she's still in the first trimester. Her family has difficulty carrying to full term though, so we are being overly cautious. I don't want to lose them both. Whatever keeps her calm."

Reyes nodded. "My wife had two miscarriages and had severe bleeding when our daughter was finally born. I understand the fear. Is this your first?"

"Yes. Her mother, grandmother, for generations, it has never been easy. We don't know why. She lost her mother many years ago. With things as they are, we haven't been able to have her seen. I didn't even know where to start looking for a doctor in that mess. I was hoping to get her seen as soon as we got settled somewhere. I hadn't planned on them sealing the gate. Do you know when they did that?"

"A few days ago. We just sat here and watched too. We were commanded to stand down. No one knows what is going on. We only know about Curtis' message because he was kind enough to send one of our own drones over the wall to inform us. We shot it down, of course."

I chuckled. "Of course."

"I will be back to check on you both soon. Let me know if she needs anything else."

"Thank you, I appreciate the help. Oh, do you know what time it is? It seems I left my phone in my truck when we ran."

He turned his wrist and looked at his watch. "It's almost two now."

"That late already?" I scrunched my eyebrows in concern. More time had gone by than I expected.

"If you'll excuse me."

I just nodded my head, my own thoughts swimming.

"Curtis knows we are here by now, doesn't he?" A soft voice pulled me out of my thoughts.

I looked down and saw my Angel looking up at me. Her fears swam through my chest like a dark cloud. "Yes, I'm sure he does. He may already be working his way towards the wall. If he isn't there already."

"Even with the sun up?"

"Yes, he has many ways to get around."

"How old is he? Is he older than you?"

"I don't know exactly how old he is. But I do know that he is older than Colton. Not by much, I'm sure. I remember him begging my father to come out of hiding, many times. He has always claimed that we should take our right to rule back. Curtis was disgusted with hiding more than anyone else was."

"What do we do now? What's going to happen?"

"I heard the Captain on the phone." I brushed her hair with my fingers again, knowing my touch would help calm her nerves. "He has been instructed to take us to Phoenix. The President is there… They want to talk to me."

Her eyes lit as she sat up. "Is Colton there? Will he help us?"

I chuckled and pulled her into my side. "Do you miss him, my angel?" She elbowed me to cover up her blush. Our group mating was still new to her. "It's okay. I miss him too. He is part of us now, it's natural. You don't need to be ashamed of it."

"I'm not ashamed of it. I just… I don't know. When we aren't together every day, it starts to feel weird again. When we are, it feels normal. But yes, I do miss him. It has been too long since we've seen him. I hope he's safe."

"I'm sure he is. His message last night said he would meet us on the road." I wanted to promise her that we would see him soon, that we would be reunited with our other mate, but I didn't want to get her hopes up. "Lunch came while you were sleeping. Eat, please."

She must have been hungry, for once she didn't give me an attitude about being bossy. Technically, she did miss breakfast though. I kept brushing my fingers through her blonde hair as she ate, keeping myself calm more than her. When she finished, I moved her onto my lap and held her close. The only time I let go of her was when she went on a hunt for the bathroom.

Unfortunately, there wasn't one in the makeshift building.

I walked to the front door and opened it carefully, two guards stood on each side. The one to my right, the direction the door opened, looked at me like he wasn't sure what to do. We weren't technically prisoners, but we weren't guests either.

"Is there a bathroom nearby that my wife could use?"

He made eye contact with his partner, then nodded. "I'll take her."

I pulled her out by the hand and started with them. His partner stopped me by placing the side of his gun to my chest. "Only her."

"No. I need him with me. Please." Carrie pleaded with the man.

“What’s the matter?” Reyes, who was standing not far off, jogged over when he heard her.

“Carrie needs to use the bathroom, but they refuse to let me go with her. We need to stay together.”

“We can’t let you. Our orders are to keep you inside.” Reyes pointed to a small blue shed looking thing next door. Carrie looked over and grimaced. “You can stay right here and watch, but you are not going with her.”

I looked at Carrie, waiting for her to decide. She smiled when she looked back. I felt no fear, not even anxiety. She must not have felt any ill intent from them.

“Alright, but I’m watching.” I didn’t like the idea of her walking away from me with armed men.

“You don’t trust anyone do you?” Reyes asked, his eyes on me, while mine were on my mate and the soldier. I could still see him in my peripheral though.

“Very few people. You have to understand. When the vampires first attacked, they kept coming for her. I already had it in with a few of them. Bars and clubs have always been popular with vampires.” I laughed when he gave me an incredulous look. “The night life in big cities was a prime time for them to come out of hiding. I’m a businessman, I hired a few donors and took advantage of the opportunity. When it became obvious that they were targeting my wife, I made the deal to keep us protected. It took some time, but eventually the message spread. She and I both struggle with separation. We came too close too many times to it being permanent. As I said before, I couldn’t let her stay there any longer. I’ve heard the stories about Curtis. For some reason, my wife smells sweet and tempting to them all. I didn’t trust that he wouldn’t try to take her from me.” At least I was able to be mostly honest with the man.

We were silent for the next few minutes as we waited for them to come back. I probably would have been pacing had I not been able to feel Carrie. Even still, I sighed when she walked back over so I could put my arm around her again.

We had barely stepped two feet back into the waiting room when the Captain finally came out of the inner office.

“Sergeant?”

Reyes snapped to attention, the two guards with him.

“Yes, sir?”

“Are the men ready to leave?”

“Yes, sir. We have two Humvees gassing up now, sir. We will be ready to roll in a few minutes.”

“Good, make sure those left behind are on alert. We just received word that Curtis is on the other side of that wall. Or he will be shortly.” The Captain’s greedy eyes landed on me. “Want to save us some trouble and tell us why he randomly showed up on the same day you jumped the wall?”

“Not especially, no. But I will tell you this. If Curtis is coming, you need to get all your men out of here. You will lose every man you have on this side. They will either be killed or kept as donors. Vampires cannot create testosterone on their own.” I made a point of looking around the compound, there were nearly a hundred men stationed there. “I see a lot of men filled to the brim with it.”

Captain Miles chuckled, like I was a child telling a ridiculous joke that made no sense. “We are well prepared to defend our base, I assure you.”

The anxiety began to bleed through my mate, and her body shook with fear. I just wished I knew who she was more scared of, Curtis or the Captain.

Before I could think of any other reason for him to save his men, the two trucks pulled up.

Reyes put a hand between my mate and I, earning himself a growl. “Remove your hand.” I warned him.

“You are not riding in the same vehicle as your *wife.*” The Captain sneered. “We will have each of you in a truck.”

I snarled as Reyes began pulling her away again. “I will be with her the whole time. She will be safe with me, I promise.”

I flicked my eyes to him, and then to Carrie. She closed her eyes and took a deep breath. Her body filled with peace.

“It’s alright, Deacon. He means me no harm.”

I tipped my chin to the captain. “And him?”

She studied him, the others watched her warily. “He has not yet decided. Let me assure you, Captain. We are not your enemy.” Her voice was methodical, almost hypnotizing. And just the right blend to make the man relax.

Suddenly, her eyes widened, and fear shocked through her system. “But Curtis does. We need to run. Now.”

Thankfully, Reyes was smart enough not to doubt, just listen. We both spun and ran to the trucks. I clenched my jaw as Carrie was set into the truck behind me.

We all flinched when a loud boom was heard, and the earth shook from the force. The pause was brief before we jumped into action.

While our escorts loaded into the trucks behind us, the remaining soldiers took up position around the gate and walls. By the time we were pulling away, the gate was crashing down. I looked through the window in time to see a dozen men covered in black from head to toe, with not even their eyes shining through, run through the new opening.

“Step on it, private.” I told the driver, who didn’t even think about who was giving the orders, he just followed them.

I spun in my seat, praying the other truck did the same. Every vamp running through the gate headed straight toward us, bypassing all the soldiers trying to shoot at them.

I watched in horror as they grew closer to the truck carrying my mate. Her fear spiked as one of the covered Nightwalkers jumped on top of her ride.

I heard her fear filled scream over all the other noise.

“I am the Prince of the Vampire Borns. My father was meeting with the President this week. My race are born vampires, we are not created. We maintain our humanity. Curtis is a rebel. If you want to ensure our help with the fight against him. You will *not* let them lay a hand on my mate. If she gets so much as one scratch on her, I can guarantee me, and all of my clan, will join ranks with him.” I growled to the Captain in the front seat. “We are not hindered by the sun as they are. We are stronger, faster, and have many more talents than them. You do *not* want to go against us.”

The soldier sitting next to me cursed. Not waiting for orders, he just popped through the sunroof and started shooting. I wanted to jump out of the truck and run to my mate, but I feared that would slow us down even more.

I watched as Reyes rolled his window down and threw a live grenade at the swarm of vampires chasing them. It was quite effective. From the other side of the truck, two more were thrown. Soon, their truck caught up to ours, losing the runners.

Unfortunately, the Nightwalker still stood on top of them, as comfortable with the speed as he would be on a surfboard.

I pulled the soldier in the sunroof down. “Give me your dagger.” I commanded, my voice even.

The kid just stared at me in shock, his eyes going between my open palm and my face, my eyes glowed with the fire burning through my veins, testifying as to what I really was. When he didn’t move, someone else did. Cold hard metal hit my hand. I looked up and saw the Captain looking at me. I nodded my thanks once, and stood up, pushing through the hole in the top.

I turned my body and looked at my enemy. The wind from the speeding trucks blew my hair back, causing many loose strands to fall back from the tie holding the bulk of it. His eyes met mine and he laughed.

“I almost didn’t believe it. When Lucas called and told me the Little Prince had surfaced, I had to see for myself. For hours I’ve been listening to Carter pleading with me to understand why he let you get away and how he never knew who you were. I can’t really blame him, your people have hidden themselves so well, even their own blood has forgotten they exist.”

“They are not my blood.”

“No. I don’t suppose they are. But I heard a rumor that there is someone else who is.” He bent over, bracing himself on his knees, then lowered his head, looking down at the truck beneath him. “I heard you found a pet of your own and managed to do what no one else has in centuries.” He made a show of taking a big breath as he straightened back up, making sure I knew what he was doing. “Utterly divine. Tell me, does she taste as good as she smells?”

I kept my face passive, not letting him see the fury I was feeling. Every ounce of panic that my mate felt, built the fire in my veins higher and higher. Instead of answering I slowly lifted my hand to the rim of the car.

Curtis took my silence the way I knew he would, as though I were too scared to speak. As soon as his head tipped back to laugh, I acted.

With one quick flick, the dagger flew across the gap between our trucks. It landed right on target. Curtis froze, his balance giving way, and fell off the truck. Cheers and shouts erupted from both groups. The trucks started to slow, and I dropped back down.

“Don’t stop, go as fast as you can. Captain, you need a new weapons dealer. That dagger was not pure silver. He is stunned, no more. The rest of his men will catch up shortly. They do not have my speed, nor will they want to face me without him. As long as we keep moving, we will be safe.”

The Private driving pushed his foot all the way down again, while the Captain relayed the message through the radio.

“You know I still have to take you in, right? I am under orders to deliver you to the General.”

“You do what you have to, Captain. And I will do what I have too.” I told him flatly, my eyes facing out the windshield, my mind focused on the feelings from my mate. She had been in shock, then happy, then the anxiety began to creep in again. I doubted any of this was good for our unborn son.

Chapter 3

Colton

We had been stuck in the same deadlock for hours, neither side willing to bend. The U.S. President wanted to wipe out all of the vampires. We just wanted to end the war and secure our freedoms. King Dominic knew there was no way the Nightwalkers would be willing to step into the shadows again.

Our secret was already out. What was the point in hiding anymore?

Many of our own clan were tired of hiding. If we were not careful, they would side with Curtis. Something he had been trying to achieve for centuries.

Besides me, there were four others assigned to protect our King. Most were older than me. I was still considered to be the higher-ranking officer though. A position I inherited when my father decided to retire.

He went cliche, he moved to a condo in Boca Raton, Florida. Which was why I was called to come. It was my job. A job that hadn't really called for much over the years.

I didn't so much as flinch when I felt my phone vibrate. I almost didn't check it. Before a few weeks ago, I wouldn't have.

Now, I had something, someone... s, that I feared for.

I pulled the phone out of my pocket, and the King raised an eyebrow at me. He knew that was out of character.

Deac: Just got word, Curtis is on way. We are leaving.

My heart stopped. For the second time in my long life, fear ran through my veins. I took a few steps back, allowing the man behind me to take my place.

Me: Head for Vegas
Deac: Is it safe? She has a bun in the oven.
Me: What??? When did that happen?

My head spun. How? I'd only been gone for a week! My heart immediately warmed.

Carrie was carrying our son.

Deac: The day you left. It's a long story that will have to wait.
Me: Vegas. She carries the royal line. That is the ONLY place she will be safe. I will try to meet you along the road. Stay safe. That baby is partly mine too.
Deac: Must you share all the good things in my life with me?
Me: Yes.

I bit back the laugh that threatened to break through. I knew he wouldn't be mad. On the contrary, he would be laughing. I knew Deacon as well as I knew myself. We'd been together for nearly half a millennium.

He started as my charge when he was barely reaching manhood.

Then he became my best friend.

Now, he was my mate. Well, one of them anyways.

Carrie changed everything. I hardly paid any attention to her when he first brought her into the bar. I tried to name her scent for him, but I couldn't. Then I left. When I went back to the bar a few weeks later, showing up with the sun, he was waiting. Seeing as I had told him I was coming.

It wasn't hard for us to sneak over that wall in unpopulated areas.

It was always a relief to see each other again. Vampire Borns were not solitary creatures. We were social, we craved affection and companionship. No matter the form it came in.

Then I saw Carrie come out of the bedroom, wearing small shorts and a small shirt, her hair all a mess. Her innocence shined through her eyes. Her entire being called for me to protect her. For the first time in over four hundred years, I was jealous of my friend.

I experienced so many new emotions since that day.

When Deacon said his marking wasn't enough, that the others were still drawn to her, I couldn't resist. I thought he'd laugh at my idea to double team her. Let them all think she was with both of us. Instead, I saw the thrill in his eyes, the hunger. It sparked my own fires.

The moment my hands touched her skin for the first time, I knew I was never going to want to stop.

Little by little, she adjusted to my touch, willingly accepting it. Then Victor got his hands on her. That was my first experience with true fear. It wasn't fear for her life, either. By the time I even knew something was wrong, she was already safe.

No, it was fear that Deacon would never let me touch her again. It was just the opposite though. We comforted her together. And we'd all been together ever since.

Now, I feared for not just their lives, but the life of our son. While he may not carry my blood in his veins, he would still be mine as well. We were a solid unit. Nothing could tear us apart.

I chose to stay in the back of the room, my emotions running rampant through me.

My attention was caught, when a woman walked into the room, dressed professionally, her dark brown hair pulled into a bun. She leaned down into one of the generals' ears and whispered. As no one else was talking at the moment, every Vampire Born in the room was able to hear her.

"Sir, you have a call from Captain Miles at the Mojave gate. He says it's important."

The General frowned. "Tell him I will call him back in a bit."

"Yes, sir." She turned and left, and the talking started again.

Mojave gate? That was where Deacon was supposed to go. I pulled my phone out again, no messages.

Me: Deac? Where are you? What's going on?

Half an hour later I tried again. Still no response.

"What if we gave you all property? You can build your own city. Have your own space." The General offered. His voice was a mix of tired and frustrated.

King Dominic laughed. "Right. And as soon as we got settled you all would drop a nuclear bomb on us. We are not stupid, General. Every one of us has been around longer than all of you. Hell, All your ages don't even add up to half of one of my men." A few eyes widened. "We've seen all the tricks. We've been fighting this war longer than you have. Now that Curtis is somewhat in the open, it will be easier. We can do this ourselves. But we would rather make this a group effort. In addition, you need your people to see you as the hero, as the men who rescued them from a monster. I bet that would go over well with your constituents."

Not for the first time, I noticed a certain soldier shift his weight uncomfortably. I had my eye on this one. I didn't understand why he stood in the back. He should be seated at the table. An alpha wolf belonged at this table. It wasn't just humans and vampires involved with this mess. If we were able to be in the open again, then he should be fighting to get his people back in as well.

I looked down at a buzz from my phone, sighing with relief when I saw Deacon's name pop up. It was short lived.

Deac: Is this Colton?
Me: Yes
Deac: It's Carter. Look, I had to call him. I didn't know what else to do. Deac is my friend, but he jumped a wall…in the SUN!!! What the hell, man? It wasn't until after I heard Curtis was coming himself that I realized there was more to this.
Me: Carrie?
Deac: Was on his back. Look, I don't know what's going on over there, but I do know he hasn't left yet. We have spy holes in the wall. Deac was taken into a building by gun point.

I cursed silently to myself. I looked at the time, it was nearing lunch time. We'd been in this room for almost twelve hours.

Me: Do you know the plan?
Deac: No. I just know Curtis is coming and he is bringing his own team in.
Me: I will take it from here. Thank you. Do yourself a favor, get out while you can. Curtis is not after what is best for vampires, he is only after power. Be prepared, he may take it out on you.
Deac: That's what I'm afraid of. But unlike Deac, I'm trapped by the sun. Curtis has a way of traveling during the day, I don't know how.

I huffed. I did. Sadly, I remembered Curtis very well. I remembered a time when he would laugh. I remembered a time when he was actually a decent guy. Then the kingdom fell. And then he turned sour, very sour.

Me: Did you take the teenagers home with you yet?

I couldn't believe I was going to say this.

Deac: Yes. Not long after you left. Why?
Me: Give Curtis an all-access pass.
Deac: I was already going to let him have the other five.
Me: No. ALL of them. I know you don't want to, but that little kitty of yours is your ace in the hole, your get out of jail free card. By all means, keep the boy, but let Curtis have the girl.
Me: Stop pouting, you're too old for that crap.

I slid my phone away, laughing to myself at what I was sure was Carter throwing a hissy fit. I walked up carefully to my King and bent down to his ear.

"I need to speak with you… concerning your son, your highness." Yeah, that last part got his attention.

Deacon hadn't seen his father in almost a hundred years. Children were so rare, it didn't matter how old they got, we held them dear.

The King's eyes sparked, his eyes glowing just long enough to make everyone else in the room gasp and jump backward.

"My apologies. I think now would be a good time to break for lunch."

Nobody questioned his taking charge, they were all too scared. He stood up and stepped into a corner of the room.

"Tyson, Clint, stay close enough to the President and General, I want to know what is going on in Mojave." He waited until they were gone, then turned back to me.

"What about my son?"

"Deacon messaged me a few hours ago, Curtis was headed for LA, he told me he was leaving. I haven't heard from him since. Moments ago, Carter, a Nightwalker who was a regular in the bar, messaged me with Deacon's phone. He said Deacon jumped the wall, in the sunlight. Carter was confused, he may be a century old, but he knew nothing of our existence. As any good soldier, he called his superior. He said they've been watching the human army camp on the other side. They are holding Deacon, in Mojave."

"I don't understand. Why is Deacon being so reckless? Why doesn't he just run from the humans? Surely he could have at least hidden himself until nightfall?"

I scratched my jaw awkwardly. "There is something that we have not told you, your majesty." I bowed my head, the guilt for keeping secrets from my king beginning to weigh on me. "Not long after Curtis started the assault, a woman screamed for help in the alley. Deacon rescued her. Her scent calls to all of us, more so to your son. He offered her protection. In time, he could no longer fight his urges." I raised my head again so he could see the truth in my eyes. "Your son met his fated mate, my Lord."

The King sucked in his breath. Surprise was written all over his face. I grimaced, knowing I had one more bomb to drop on him.

"In his message earlier, Deacon told me that she now carries his son."

The King's shocked face slowly morphed into a smile. "Is this true? Will there really be another heir?" I saw the moment the other fears began to set in. "They mated? Fully mated?"

"Yes, my Lord."

"So, when she goes, she will take my only son with her?" This time it was barely a whisper. No father wanted to outlive his son.

"We think she is strong enough, my King. She is a pure-blooded witch. I haven't spoken to them about it yet, but I do know that

Deacon has been feeding her his blood since the day she showed up. He marked her every night for over a month to keep the Nightwalkers at bay before they even mated. I've seen first-hand how his blood has healed her, strengthened her. But that is a concern for another day. The human army has both of them. Deacon will not run with her if there is a chance of Carrie and his son getting hurt."

"We need to get to them. These negotiations are not going as well as I'd hoped they would. Otherwise, I would ask them to just hand them over. I worry if they know of his value, of *her* value, they will keep them hostage. They don't know it yet, but they have our entire race by the balls."

The wolf shuffled back into the conference room, his eyes darting around the room before he came to us. "Deacon's in trouble. The little spy messaged me this morning. Curtis is coming."

"Yes, Carter told me the same thing."

"Did he say why Deacon felt it necessary to jump a twelve-foot wall with the sun shining on him?"

I was slightly impressed with the protectiveness the wolf was demonstrating for my mate. "When you met Deacon, did he tell you who he was?"

The alpha wolf shook his head. "No. I know what he is. I know he runs a bar. And I know he has a mate. That's it. Why? Who is he?" His eyes jumped between the King and I, realizing there was more.

"My son, my only son." The King stated firmly.

The wolf cursed and closed his eyes.

"That's not the main reason he jumped." I added. "His mate is pregnant." The wolf's eyes shot open again. I was glad I wasn't going to have to explain that to him. "Carter said the human army has them. Did the little witch say whether this was good or bad?"

"No. That is all I know. She is going to make her move on Curtis though."

I nodded. I figured as much, as well. "I told Carter to give her to him. He is very fond of the little witch and her boyfriend. But handing her over may be the only thing that saves Carter's life. He's been around Deacon for decades. Then he just stood there and watched him jump."

Clint came back in and stood close, there was something he needed to say but wasn't sure he could in mixed company.

"Go ahead, Clint." It seemed the King trusted the Alpha already.

"I listened in as the General returned that call. They had a man jump their wall after sunrise, he carried a woman on his back. He claims she is his wife, sir. The Captain at the gate is holding them. He does not know what to think."

"What did the General say?"

"To bring them to Phoenix. They have a holding cell they are going to keep them in. I stayed long enough to listen to their plans. They assume he is one of ours, but the girl is not, since she was on his back. They will use her to get him to cooperate."

I growled deeply, an automatic response to my mates being in danger. All eyes turned to me.

"They did not say a name though." He finished, still watching me carefully.

"That was Prince Deacon and his mate." Clint's eyes shot back to the King. "His *pregnant* mate."

That one word made me proud again. But my anger over their captivity was taking control. I felt the fire burning in my eyes, and the growl vibrating my chest. I was barely aware of the King's hand on my shoulder.

"Colton. What are you not telling me? I know they are your friends, but you normally have better control than this."

"*My* mates," was all I could get out.

The wolf was slightly confused. The others were not.

"Awe. That explains it." The King turned to the confused wolf. "They welcomed him into their mating, quite normal in our world. This is good. My daughter-in-law and grandson will have extra protection now. Not that they needed it. We will all protect the future heir. It has been some time since we had a baby in our clan. Clint, gather the others. Alpha wolf? Where do your people stand with all this?"

"We have not yet decided. I need to meet with the other Alphas. My pack and I will stand with you. It would be nice to use my wolf in a fight once in a while. My being here is purely coincidental. After the little spy made first contact, they brought me in. As they are young, and I am the only one they have met, the General believes they will trust me more."

"That wasn't a coincidence. The little witch had a vision. If Deacon had gone alone, as planned, he would have been seen by the others, driving home during the day. Curtis would have taken Carrie, and we believe he would have had hidden Deacon somewhere. Curtis would have won the war. The little witch came to us. She told us of her visions. Carrie's mother held the same power and was able to give her guidance. That was when we learned of her plans. It seems sending the boy to drive Deacon home placed every one of our species in the right place." I explained in detail, trying to focus on anything but my mates being held against their will.

"Interesting theory, one I will surely pass on to the others. I need to get back. Good luck." The alpha wolf bowed his head toward the King in respect, which was returned, and left.

"We need to go back to the house you cleared for us, collect our things, and get to my son and his family."

As though it were a command, the others walked back in. Without a word, the King stalked out of the conference room, us in his wake. He walked down the hall, exuding power, as he buttoned his suit coat back up. Our King was a man on a mission. A father on a mission.

Hell, a *grandfather* on a mission.

The only time he stopped was when we came across the General standing in a corridor of the building that had been cleared out for the meeting.

"It seems we are at an impasse. We will be leaving now. When you realize that we will get further together, call us." He snapped his fingers and Tyson leaned forward with a business card. "Have a good day, gentlemen."

Mike and I passed the King as he put his sunglasses on, and led the way out the doors, the King walking in the center of us.

The house I had chosen was twenty minutes away and sat in the middle of an empty field. There were motion detector lights surrounding the property, starting at a gate placed 100 yards from the house.

While everyone quickly packed their bags, I grabbed a set of books and photo albums I had previously set aside. Along with a few smaller items that looked important.

"When you brought us here last week, I thought it was an odd choice. A little out in the open for someone as safety conscious as you. As I took in all the precautions, I accepted it. I've watched you, wondering when you became interested in taking things from the humans. You never struck me as the scavenger type. But after what you revealed today, and that load you have there, I have to wonder if you know the previous inhabitants of this home." The

King leaned against the doorframe, his arms folded across his chest, a knowing look on his face. His mannerisms reminded me of the friend and mate I left behind.

"Yes, my Lord. This is where Carrie grew up. As I said, she is a pure-blooded witch. From what we have been able to pull from her, it seems like her family has been hunted for generations. Nearly every death had bite marks. She was not meant to be in Los Angeles. She had gone to visit her boyfriend at the time. Thankfully, he was not alone, and she left, as he was killed that same night. She had a few horrific days before Deacon found her. She was trapped in a city that was not her home. I thought she might like some of her belongings, her memories."

"You love her then?"

"Very much so, my Lord. I am very grateful to your son for inviting me to join them."

"And how does she feel? I knew a few witches in my time. They can be stubborn. And evil at the drop of a hat."

I grinned. "Carrie is the most stubborn woman I have ever met. She keeps us both on our toes. But she is far from evil, your majesty. No matter how hard Deacon tries, she will always be pure and innocent." The King threw his head back and laughed. He knew his son well. "You need not worry. We are a united mating."

Our conversation was interrupted with the buzz of my phone on the dresser top. All amusement left the King's face.

Deac: Curtis is here. He has a dozen men with him, all of them are completely covered. They mean to go after Deac with the sun up. We have seen movement from the humans, preparations for them to leave, but it has not happened yet. He is waiting for them to be leaving, he wants to hit them on the road.

I relayed the message, and we were all out the door minutes later. We had traveled to the meeting in one of the black Explorers that we originally brought with us, but now we were taking both. While we had no plans to return, I hoped one day we could let our mate return to her home, at least to visit.

The sun was setting when I got the next message.

Deac: They got away. Curtis was just carried in, only half his men returned. He had a dagger in his chest, but it was not pure silver. Curtis paid for the shipment to be mixed up before it made it to the soldiers.
Deac: I almost want to run.
Me: Sacrifice your pet. It is your only chance to survive another day.
Me: Get rid of this phone ASAP, if it is found on you, you will be killed.

"They escaped from Curtis. Carter did not know the details, but Curtis was found with a dagger in his chest. Unfortunately, Curtis had already managed to swap out all the silver daggers that they received. It wasn't pure silver. Which I'm sure Deacon knew before he threw it."

"What makes you think it was Deacon if you don't know the details?" Clint glanced at me from the driver's seat.

I frowned at him from my seat beside him.

"I doubt it was the humans." The King chuckled. "We will ask when we get to them."

All was silent for another hour, until the King spoke again. "I hear large trucks. Do you?"

"Yes. They are further up. Sounds like Army Humvees. Pull over. It's probably them." I commanded.

Chapter 4

Deacon

"My mate is scared and anxious. Will you please pull over, so I can calm her down? It is not good for the baby." It had been hours since the battle with Curtis and I could still feel her turmoil.

The Captain huffed. "Thought you said she was your wife?"

I kept *most* of the frustrated growl internal. "Mate and spouse are the same thing. Vampires mate, humans marry. Please. Let me go to her."

He turned and gave me an irritated look. "How in the world would you know how she feels?"

I grinned at him. I found that I enjoyed irritating the man. It made the time pass faster. "Magic, my dear Captain. You are going to be running into it a lot, I suggest you get used to it. Now…"

"We are not pulling over!"

As if to emphasize his point, the Private hit the brakes so hard the truck swerved.

"What the hell are you doing, private?"

"L… L… Look, sir." The kid lifted a shaky finger to the middle of the road.

While I could see the six figures perfectly in the dark, to the humans, they would be little more than shadows.

The Captain stepped out of the truck, leaving his door open. The soldiers on both sides of me kept their makeshift bayonets pointed at me. I scoffed but otherwise played nice. My angel was still trapped inside the other truck. The daggers and guns wouldn't hurt me, but they would certainly hurt her.

"We are on government business. You need to clear the road immediately."

"You have something that belongs to us. Two of them actually. We will leave when they are released."

I closed my eyes and sighed. He came.

I wasn't a fool, I knew he would protect me, but I wasn't his priority either. Which was the main reason I agreed to welcome him. The other reasons were just benefits.

"I am under orders by the United States President to deliver my cargo to him. And him alone."

"Captain, you saw what I can do on my own. Do you really want to come up against more? Against my soldiers?" I called out to him.

I heard the light chuckles reach back to me. I doubted the humans did though.

The Captain leaned into the truck and picked up the radio. He gave me a patronizing smirk as he lifted it to his moving lips.

"Sergeant. Bring her out, keep your gun on her."

I wasn't the only one growling when he added the last bit. Two hands rapidly appeared on Colton's shoulders, holding him back.

I heard doors open from behind us, but the angle we were turned in made it difficult for me to see her.

"I said, let go of me… now." Carrie growled out.

I felt a sliver of fear, but mostly determination coming from her. The soldier pushed her forward enough that I could see them. My eyes zeroed in on the gun at her back. My fire blazed through my veins.

Game over.

I elbowed both soldiers next to me in the head, at the same time, knocking them both out. Then I swung my legs up to the left and kicked the door off the truck, it flew at least twenty feet away.

"Let her go, Captain. I told you what would happen if you harmed her."

"Get back in the truck, Deacon. No one will get hurt as long as everyone does what they are told. I am taking both of you in, just as I was told." To his credit, I couldn't even smell fear coming from him.

I stepped to walk around the truck and the soldier pressed his handgun into her side, hard enough to make her yell out in pain. The fear flooding through her fueled my anger even more. I glanced at Colton, who had his eyes trained only on Carrie.

I spun back to the Captain as the hands restraining Colton disappeared. At the same moment, I pushed off the ground with a snarl and landed right behind the Captain, turning his head before my feet even hit the ground.

I turned in time to see Carrie fall against Colton's chest, crying. The human with the gun lay at his feet. It had all happened so fast that the human soldiers were stunned. I ran to my angel and wrapped my arms around her.

"Are you alright, sweetheart? Did they hurt you?" Colton asked as he patted her up and down, checking her sides for wounds.

She gave an odd laugh that was also a cry. "I'm okay. *We're* okay. I promise."

I laid my head against hers, soaking in her scent. I wasn't fazed by the sounds of the guns being calked or the men beginning to surround us.

"Reyes, call your men off. Let us leave in peace."

"I can't do that, Deacon. You just killed our Captain and a Corporal."

I sighed and looked over at him. I nodded in the direction of our clansmen. Colton picked up our mate one second and set her in the middle of them the next, completely covered by my clan. Surprisingly, my father stood in the front.

Reyes' surprised curse was parroted many times.

"What would you do if someone held your pregnant wife at gunpoint? Would you sit there and wait to see if they actually did it? You all saw me take down Curtis with a flick of my wrist. Check your supplies by the way, the Captain obviously won't be doing it. That dagger was not made of pure silver, I'm willing to bet your others aren't either."

The soldiers with daggers looked at them incredulously.

I started walking slowly backward. "The men you left behind need you. Call this in and tell them the vampires did it. Tell them whatever you want. But I warned him. I warned you all. You hurt her; you will take on our whole clan. Go home, Sergeant."

I kept my backward pace slow, my hands out in front of me. The soldiers watched until Reyes commanded them to load up. A few ran around and grabbed the bodies, then they were gone, leaving nothing but dust and a broken door behind.

I spun and ran the rest of the way to my mates. After hugging them for a brief moment, I felt a hand on my shoulder. I looked up and saw my father. The only change since I'd last seen him was a slight graying of his hair. We weren't completely immortal, we did age, it just took a couple thousand years.

Well, after our original development at any rate. In the early years, we aged the same as any other species.

I let him pull me into a hug, feeling extremely grateful that they all came. "Hello, father."

"Son. I hear you've been keeping secrets from me." He tried to keep his tone firm, but he was too amused for it to pass.

I grinned as I pulled away. "My apologies, father. I can be a little overprotective when it comes to my angel."

A sexy little snort came from behind me. "A little?"

I turned and gave her a playful glare as Colton barked out a laugh. She poked him in the stomach.

"Why are you laughing? You're just as bad! I swear. It's angel, you didn't finish your food. Sweetheart, drink more water. Angel, you need more sleep. Sweetheart, stay behind the bar away from any living breathing person in the world."

The others all laughed hard at her attempt to mimic us. She folded her arms and huffed. Clearly annoyed with all of us.

Colton kissed her cheek. "I missed you. You both had me worried."

Her scowl softened. I went in for the kill.

I brushed my nose along her neck, leaving small kisses. "You know it's only because we love you. It's our job to protect you."

Her growl was more of a whimper this time. "I hate you both."

We both chuckled. The others continued laughing like hyenas.

"Are you going to introduce me to my daughter-in-law some time tonight?" My father was clearly still amused as well but was keeping his composure.

I sighed and stepped to my angel's left side, since Colton was already planted on her right. With my right hand on her back, I introduced them.

"Father. This is Carrie, my fated mate and the mother of my unborn son. I assume Colton already told you all this of course."

"Well, somebody had to. It's a pleasure to meet you, Carrie. We are honored to welcome you into our clan." My father sniffed deeply, causing a chain reaction. When one sniffed, everybody else always had to join the party. "I understand now why the Nightwalkers are all attracted to you. Your scent. I know it from somewhere. From long ago."

"It's the blood of her ancestors, father. At least, we think so. It was them that cursed our clan." I admitted carefully, not sure how the rest would react, especially as more than one in attendance lost a mate that night. We never understood how they were able to survive, when the one their soul was sealed too, did not.

"Yes. That's it. I remember now. There was a coven not far from our borders who smelled so sweetly." My father must have caught the small scent of panic from Carrie. He smiled softly and put a hand on her cheek. "Have no fear, child. Even those of us who were there would not blame you. We blame only two people. The witch that cast the curse, and the vampire who betrayed her. My father banished him from the royal courts the day after. No one has seen or heard from the witch since then."

"Is she still alive?" Colton and I both smirked at her surprise.

My father shrugged, raising his hands. "No one knows. We are told they were fully mated, which means if one is alive then so is the other. But that is enough for tonight. Let's get in the cars and go home, shall we? At the risk of sounding like your overprotective mates, you do need your rest. Unlike them, I have seen the toll our seed can take on a female that is not of vampire descent."

"Did they hurt you, angel? Do you need me to heal you?"

"No, Reyes was true to his word. No one touched me. Not until the end. Reyes had planned to bring me out, but the other one just grabbed my arm and yanked on me."

The cars were close enough that we reached there quickly, even at her pace.

Without a word, my father sat in the front with Clint, the rest climbed into the other car. I walked around to the other side, giving Colton a minute with her. He held the door but didn't let her get far before he kissed her.

I laughed at her surprised squeak. She should have known it was coming. When he finally released her, she scooted into the middle and sat between us, a slight blush to her cheeks.

When my father saw it he laughed again. Mumbling to himself. "Pure and innocent indeed."

Carrie didn't catch it, but I did. I looked at Colton and he just shrugged with a grin. Looked like he told my father quite a bit.

It wasn't long before her head was on my shoulder, and her breathing slowed. Colton lifted her feet while I lowered her head to my lap. Once she was settled I bit into my wrist and then put it against her lips.

In the beginning, I had to coax her to drink in her sleep, now it was second nature. I ran my fingers through her hair, watching Colton's fingers glide up and down her jean clad leg.

It wasn't long before her grip on me loosened, telling me she was deep under. I sealed my wrist and laid my hand over her stomach. Colton set his hand next to mine, his pinky finger slid under mine and folded them together.

"I thought she said she didn't need healing tonight?"

I looked up at my father, his concerned eyes were on her through the mirror in his sun visor.

"She would have said that no matter what. I felt her fear the whole ride. Whether they hurt her or just scared her, I know not. Either way she needs to sleep. Drinking in her sleep pushes her further under." I answered his question softly.

"She'll be mad at you in the morning. You know she said not to do that anymore." Colton reminded me with a smirk.

I shrugged and looked out the window. "She will and then she will get over it. Besides, even the psychic witch agreed. In both futures she saw Carrie and the baby healthy. She wouldn't tell us what the differences were. She only confirmed that whatever the plan was, to keep it up. This was our plan."

"Were you trying to get her pregnant? It took years with your mother."

"No, we weren't. Carrie is different. She feels our heat when we release. She can even tell the minute differences between Colton and myself. I could feel her that night, she was building again, and I was only holding her. She said she could still feel my seed moving inside her. She knew what she needed, and we fed into that. Somehow she knew we needed to trade blood again. I feared we were going to either kill her or change her, but she wouldn't let me stop. She was burning up all night, but by the morning, the fever was gone, and she was back to normal. She can still feel him, like a small bubble of fire." I turned to face my father. "Did mother ever say anything about that? Any of the breeders?"

"No. But then, she fought the whole way. I don't know that she would have told me if she knew she needed more."

"My mate was a witch. She said it was warm, but that was all." Clint added sadly. "We weren't fated though. She never felt my seed attach. We rarely traded blood, we didn't feel the need to, beyond passion of course. Maybe those few times are why she made it as long as she did. If I had known, I would have done it every day."

"If you were mated, how did you not die with her?" I had never heard Colton speak so softly to anyone besides Carrie.

It was a good question too. Clint's mate had been one of the few left alive that night. Of course, since it was only the vampire females that had been killed.

"We never traded blood at the same time. It was always one after the other, therefore, we never fully mated. At the time, there was still a lot of prejudice against the mixed mates. Most weren't as harsh to the fated pairs, chosen was different though. Especially after the curse hit. She thought she could prove herself to the clan first, by giving me a child. Proving she was worthy. Then we would seal ourselves to each other. I felt the pain of sorrow when she left me but taking care of our son helped nurse my wounds."

"Where is Kenny, these days?" I asked.

Clint laughed softly. "He lives on the beach in Florida. He spends his days surfing. He still has so much of his mother in him. She loved sitting on the beach, her feet buried in the sand."

The car fell into silence, everyone lost to their own thoughts. I noticed movement and looked down. Colton was still gliding his fingers on her legs. He smiled when he caught my eye.

“I see why you prefer the skirts. This is quite aggravating.”

I barked out one laugh. With my free hand, I slid her shirt out from under our joined hands, letting them fall onto her bare skin. Then I reached over and flipped the button on her jeans. I slowly pushed the zipper down and folded the sides.

Colton’s fingers slid up higher. Very carefully, enjoying every inch, he slid his hand inside. He closed his eyes and sighed. I laughed softly.

“Feel better?”

“Much. I never felt so scared as when I didn’t hear back from you.”

“I didn’t realize I had left my phone in the truck until I went to message you from the human base. How did you know where to find us?”

“Carter found your phone. He reported back to Lucas as soon as you jumped. It wasn’t until after he heard that Curtis was coming that he realized why you ran. I still don’t think he knows the whole story. Clint also listened in to the conversation between the general and the captain. We put it together from there.”

“Curtis is going to kill him once he heals.”

“Yeah, what happened? Carter said something about a dagger in his chest.” I laughed at Clint’s shocked interruption and told them the story of how we got out of there.

“If only it had been pure silver, this would all be over.” My father sighed sadly.

He almost never spoke about Curtis, but considering their ages, I often wondered if they knew each other at one point in time.

Reliving the fear of Curtis on top of my angel's truck like that was hard. I ended up following Colton's example, just in the Northern regions. I went from her collar, down. Making sure she stayed covered.

Chapter 5

Grace

I fell into a deep sleep after messaging with Hill. Deeper than I'd ever been before. The dream was more realistic than any I'd ever had before too.

I walked through a deep forest for what felt like hours. The trees were so thick, I could touch them on each side as I walked, using them to keep my balance on the uneven, rocky terrain. The only light came when the wind blew the leaves in the trees, giving the sun a chance to break through.

From a distance, I heard a waterfall. I felt a pull to go toward it. Not knowing what else to do, I allowed the pull to guide me.

When I finally arrived, I saw a woman, not much older than myself, sitting in a small crevice of a large stone, her feet dangling in the water. She had long black hair and wore a thin cotton dress. On her right hand sat a dark green ribbon, tied around her wrist.

"I've been waiting for you, Grace." While she didn't look old, her voice sounded like that of someone who had seen more days than they cared too. Someone who knew more than they wanted too.

"Who are you? Where am I?"

"Who I am isn't important right now. As for where you are, well, you are asleep, in your bed. I've been waiting for you to visit me here. It's been a long time since anyone has visited with me."

"Why am I here?"

"Because you have chosen to walk the path, the path that no one else would have walked. You are brave, young one. Much braver than I was at your age." She pushed herself up to a standing position. "Because of this, I am going to help you."

"How? How can you help me?"

"I am going to make it so that you don't need to take your friends any further on this journey with you. And I am going to tell you the trick to getting Curtis' attention from the first moment he sees you."

"But the visions said I would need my friends. They were clearly shown with me."

"I know. I saw the same things a long time ago. I knew this day would come. I promised myself that if you were brave enough to walk this path, then I would be too. There is a way that you can do this and set your friends free. Are you willing to continue alone? To leave them all behind? I warn you, there will be times that this path seems harder, rougher, scarier. And it will be. But you will be more fruitful following this one."

I swallowed. I didn't want them to get hurt, but they gave me strength. "*All* of them?"

She walked around a large stone and came closer. "Yes, dear. *All* of them. Even Todd. I know it's hard to lose one's family, to lose the one we hold dearest. But either you set them free now, or you will watch some of them die later. "

A silent tear slipped from my eye. I always feared that we wouldn't all make it out of this. "If I follow your advice, will they all survive?"

She smiled softly and nodded her head. "Yes, child. Whether you realize it or not, you have already created a path for them to get free. Others have been helping lay it as well."

I heard a voice calling my name from a great distance.

The woman looked frustrated. "We don't have much time. What is your choice, Grace?"

"Save my friends. Tell me how to get Curtis on my own." I whispered quickly, desperately. I would not let them die, not if I could help it.

She was close enough now that she placed her hand on my cheek. I gasped as the vision shook through me. The swimming pool in the backyard. The waterfall. I saw myself standing under it, completely naked, as though I were showering. Curtis was standing on the edge of the pool, watching me. I turned and smiled, reaching out a hand, an offer.

An offer he would not be able to ignore.

I blinked as she stepped away again. The voice got louder. It was Todd, calling my name.

"That's it? That's all I have to do? Something so simple?"

The dream woman gave a sardonic laugh. "Nothing is ever so simple. But yes, that is all you have to do. That one… simple move, and you will land yourself in the lion's lair. Go now. Your time is short. Do not tell your friends. Remember what your sister told you. Not everything is meant to be shared."

"Sister? I don't have a sister."

"All witches are sisters. We are never alone. Family will see you through." Both her and her voice faded.

A second later, I gasped for air and shot out of bed.

"Hey, hey. You alright? You scared me when you wouldn't wake up." Todd sounded relieved as he pulled me into his arms. "Was it a vision?"

I tried to answer but choked on all the air I had taken in instead. I nodded as I cleared my throat. "Yes. yes. I know what I need to do."

"What is it?"

I shook my head. "I can't say. Remember what Carrie said? Not everything should be shared. Besides, I only saw myself this time." And one very strange lady.

I never trusted the words of strangers before, but she didn't feel like a stranger to me. It reminded me of the way I always felt around Carrie, from day one. Maybe the strange lady was another witch. And like she said, we were all family.

"What time is it?" I asked Todd as I looked around the room. Stupid curtains.

"Nearly sundown. A lot has happened since you fell asleep. We don't really know anything, but there has been a lot of activity out there." He scooted off the bed and helped me up. "Come on. The others are waiting."

I nodded and took his hand, letting him lead me out of the room. Scott had made pancakes for everyone, and they were all eating at the table. I sat down, watching each of them carefully. If the dream lady was right, I was going to be leaving them all soon. I was going to miss my friends.

A morbid part of me couldn't help but wonder which ones I would have lost had we kept going the way we were.

I jumped, startled, when Todd set a plate down in front of me.

"Are you sure you don't want to talk about that vision?"

"What vision? Did you see something else? You said earlier Curtis was coming. Do you know what we need to do?" Rachel asked in one breath.

I smiled softly, she was nervous and anxious to get this moving already. We all were. "Yes. I know what *I* need to do. You all just continue like normal. It is me that has to do this one. Only me."

They seemed confused but accepted it. They had far too much faith in my ability. Not once had they ever taunted me because of it or made me feel different. I was going to miss them so much. I still didn't understand what the dream lady meant by this path being harder.

Was it because I would be alone?

Was it because I was going to have to leave them behind?

Would they feel like I abandoned them? Betrayed them?

As long as they were still alive to do so, I wouldn't care if they hated me for the rest of their lives.

After our evening breakfast, they all went their separate ways to get ready. I showered, making sure I was smooth and as ready as I could be. The sun was nearly down when I left the bathroom. I didn't know a timeline, just the dark, and tonight.

I didn't bother with clothes. I just walked out of the room in nothing but a towel.

"I'm going for a swim." I told them. Todd stood up, a grin on his face. I held my hand up. "Alone. All of you need to stay inside."

He frowned slightly but sat back down.

I gave him what I hoped would be a reassuring smile, then went outside. I left the towel on one of the chairs and walked into the water. I swam around a few times, hoping to burn off some of my nervous energy, then stood near the waterfall, waiting.

Thankfully, it wasn't long before I heard voices.

"Lay him over here on one of these chairs. Slowly, slowly. There we go." Carter directed the other vampires, nervous, scared, and frantic. He didn't even notice me.

"Why did you insist on us coming here, Carter?" Another man spat on the floor. "We need to get him on the chopper and back to the city. He has a harem full of humans he will need to call for when we take the dagger out. We need to replenish his blood as soon as it comes out."

"Yes, Lucas. I know. I told you. I have a house full of donors that he can use. Do you really want to leave him in this vulnerable position for much longer? That dagger may not be pure silver, but it has to hurt like hell."

"Will you two shut up already?" Curtis snarled from the chair.

I heard him sniff. Then sniff again.

That was my cue.

I quietly slid under the water and closed my eyes.

"What's that smell? I know that smell."

I turned just enough to be able to see Carter look my way, and then a sad, but resigned look took over his face. He waved a hand at me, pulling the attention of the two others.

"That's Grace, your Lordship. One of my donors that I was telling you about."

Curtis groaned painfully as he sat up. I closed my eyes and dipped my head back, letting the water roll through my hair. His next groan was much louder, almost like a yell. I opened my eyes, reminding myself to slow down my actions, and saw him breathing heavily, a bloodied dagger now in his hand, his chest pouring out blood.

My eyes caught movement in the window, the others were watching.

Curtis pushed to stand, both Lucas and Carter jumped in to help. He swatted them away, his eyes only on me. I mentally took a deep breath, then lifted my hand. Curtis gave a small chuckle and began taking his clothes off. I lowered my hand but stayed right where I was, as I waited for him to come to me.

As soon as he was clear, he held onto the rail and began the trip down into the water. My eyes widened as I saw what was in store for me. This vampire was taller and wider than the others. He was even wider than Colton. His dark brown hair was a little on the shaggy side, like he had just taken a hat or a mask off.

His laughter deepened when he saw my reaction. I bit my lip and looked down as if I was feeling shy.

At the bottom of the steps, he lowered into the water and swam the rest of the way, his eyes never wavering from me.

I felt like I was in the middle of a swamp, watching the hungry alligator stalk me. As he got closer, he stood back up and just stared down at me. I stepped back into the falling water, holding my hand up again.

His hand slid into mine slowly, and then up my arm. It made its way up to my shoulder, and then down my back. As it slid down, he pushed me closer. I closed my eyes, and let my body respond the way it naturally would.

Because, seriously, if this man were still human, I would be on that like white on rice.

I gave a small yelp, when his very large hand squeezed my butt. He laughed and then began sniffing my neck like I was an expensive bottle of wine. I could see why Carrie always liked it when Deacon did that. I let the small needy whimper out, just like I had seen her do. His reaction was immediate.

He lifted me up with one hand, bracing me against the rock wall as he went right in. Fangs and all. The curse word that flew out of my mouth was not what I had planned. Which was alright, he seemed to like that.

I was barely aware of the other two leaving. I was sure Carter was headed to Todd, probably moping. Lucas probably went to one, or two, of the others.

I lost count of how many times my body reacted to the large man in the water with me. I had no idea how much time passed. I did know that I was getting weaker the longer it continued. My arms, which had been exploring his very large muscles, started to fall. My eyes were starting to close when he finally released my neck.

"Hold on, little darling. I'm not quite done with you yet." He may not have bitten me again, but he sure did a lot of other things.

My body grew more and more weary, from both the loss of blood and the massive amounts of energy he burned from me. I had a feeling that the only thing keeping me awake at that point was the heat that kept rushing through me. It wasn't hot, mostly just warm. A soothing warmth at that. Like a blanket taken straight out of the dryer.

Curtis finally stopped moving, and just held me up. My eyes moved down to his chest, where the hole had once been. There wasn't even a scar. Without thinking, I lifted my hand and lightly rubbed it. He hummed happily.

"How? I… I've never…"

"You ain't never seen someone heal before, little darling?" I shook my head, and then groaned. The movement made me dizzy. "This is why I always keep at least one witch in my harem. Witch's blood can heal." He leaned down and whispered in my ear. "Just don't go around telling everybody that. Keep it our little secret."

"W…w…witch? B… but I'm not a…a.."

He laughed harder. And louder. "You didn't know you were a witch?"

I shook my head again. And nearly fainted from just that. He cursed again and I felt him shifting. My eyes were having a hard time opening back up again until something thick and warm hit my lips. My eyes shot open, and I tried to pull my head away. He growled and pressed his wrist to my lips harder.

"Be a good little witch and drink your medicine. I'm not ready for you to leave just yet."

I couldn't help it. My reaction was purely instinctual.

I pressed my lips closed and tried to fight back. At least until he pinched my butt *really* hard. I yelped and jumped away from his hand. My mouth opened just enough that he was able to shove his wrist in further.

I whimpered as his blood began dripping down my throat.

"There we go. Now, it won't heal you, but it will keep you from dying on me. I won't usually take that much from you, but that little princeling left me in pretty bad shape with that dagger. Right through the heart." His voice was dripping with menace by the time he finished speaking.

Wow, go Deacon.

My tongue reacted to the liquid dropping on it, it bounced up and swiped his wrist. Oddly, his blood tasted more like hot chocolate than actual blood. It was warm, creamy, and soothing. I flicked my tongue up again and watched his eyes roll back.

Interesting.

I did it again, only this time slower. He growled and started moving other parts again. Before I knew it, I was full out sucking on him, and digging my nails into his arms. Now this, I wouldn't mind getting used to.

Chapter 6

Grace

A few minutes later Curtis ripped his wrist away and started kissing me. It was still some time before he finished. Again. He laughed at my expression after.

"I take it no one has fed you before?"

I leaned my head back, shaking it slowly against the faux rock that the waterfall was coming from.

"Good. That means no one else can claim you. Your name is Grace right?"

"Ya huh." I was still a little breathless.

He chuckled again. "Who do you belong to, Grace?" I gave him a confused look. "Are you someone's pet or just a donor?"

"Um, well. Carter calls me his special kitty."

"Hmmm, that's perfect. He needs to be punished for letting the princeling go, but he is a good soldier. Maybe I'll just deprive him of his favorite pet."

I pretended to hide my smile. "Does that mean I belong to you now?"

He sniffed my neck again and hummed. "Yes. You are my kitty now."

I leaned forward, pressing my chest to his so I could whisper in his ear. "Whatever you wish… master."

He groaned and popped his neck.

And I just found what would work on him. Faster than I thought I would too. Certainly, faster than I had with Carter.

The waterfall poured over us as he carried me through it again and out of the pool, then laid me down on the chair. He came with me of course. I was surprised neither I nor the chair broke from the force he used. Or his weight. Curtis was well endowed in many ways.

"You are going to be a good little kitty, aren't you?" I nodded and purred. "Maybe even my favorite one. I haven't changed out my harem in a while."

Touchdown. And she scores!

I hated sports but the boys had been playing a lot of football on the gaming thing inside.

Curtis stood up, then used my towel to dry us both off. He pulled his pants on, then slid his bloodied shirt over me. He then took my hand and had to practically help me walk back inside.

Carter was sitting on the couch, Todd next to him. Lucas was on the other couch, one twin on his lap, the other sitting on his right side. The others were all stationed on the floor, where they could see everything perfectly. It must have been a Lucas thing. They had never sat like that before.

“Lucas, call the others in, they need to feed before they leave. Carter, you messed up.”

“Yes, sir.” I actually felt a little bad for him. He sounded so weak and pathetic.

“Do you know how you messed up?”

“By not staying informed and letting one of your enemies both live in your territory and then escape.”

Curtis sat on a chair and pulled me onto his lap. “Please, tell me. How long have you known Deacon?”

Carter swallowed. “About 70 years, sir.”

Lucas whistled. “How did you go that long and not know what he was?”

“I never knew there was another type of vampire out there. He said his smell was different because he was so old.” Carter shrugged. “I was only about 20 or 30 at the time.”

Curtis huffed. “Tell me about Deacon.”

Carter scratched his jaw with one hand, his other fell back on Todd. He gave Curtis a bit of an odd look, like he was confused but too scared to say anything. “There really isn’t much to tell. For the last 50 years or so he’s been running a bar in LA. Always had decent cuts for us in the evening. Once the humans started hiding, he opened the whole bar to us. He always had a talent for finding the good ones.”

I waited, worried he would spill where he found us. How would Curtis take that?

"Anyway, for the last few months it's just been him and his mates running the bar."

Todd barely covered his sigh of relief by turning it into something else.

"Mates?" Curtis growled.

Carter's hand moved faster, he looked more than a little scared now. Poor Todd.

"Ye...yes, sir. There was Colton, he's been around for a while, coming in and out. They didn't seem more than friends until Carrie came along."

And now it was the twins having to hide their reactions, lovely. We were going to be so screwed if they kept this up.

"Carrie? He had a female mate? Where is she?" Uh oh, Curtis was tensing up big time.

Todd's eyes flashed down, trying to hint, reminding me what to do next. I could have honestly slapped myself. I reached behind me and flipped the button on the black cargo-like pants he was wearing. Carefully, I slid in. I ended up having to pull him all the way out, there was just no room for that sucker to get bigger inside his pants.

Curtis immediately started to relax again.

"She went with him. He had her on his back. Deac said he didn't want her anywhere near you. I mean, I was a little confused at first, but then I remembered how many vamps kept trying to take her from him. Pretty sure that was why he let Colton mate with them and all. With both of their scents on her, you could barely get her normal scent. I mean, up until she got pregnant that is." Carter's face clouded over. "I still don't understand that one. He talked like it was his, but that doesn't make sense."

Curtis was really getting worked up now. He looked like he was about to go on a killing spree. With Carter being the first victim. Then most likely us. I slid off his lap and went to my knees, which he seemed to appreciate, judging by the grip on my hair.

"Pregnant? Prince Deacon's mate is pregnant?" He growled out.

Carter's swallow was loud enough for everyone to hear. Todd was even louder as Carter was basically taking it out on him. Curtis stopped talking for a minute, his focus solely on me.

Apparently there was a lot more to Curtis than everybody else, and I didn't just mean his physical size. I had a feeling I now knew what it felt like to be waterboarded. I had a lot of colorful names I wanted to shout at him when he wouldn't let me up.

I stayed down there for a minute needing to catch my breath. And my sanity.

Curtis slowly dragged a finger under my chin and lifted it up to look at him. He wiped my mouth with his thumb, an amused expression on his face.

"You're lucky I don't kill you right now, Carter. You're lucky you are more valuable to me as a leader than a foot soldier. You were also very lucky the day you found this treasure. I can see why she became one of your favorites. Where did you find her?"

"They all snuck out of the shelter they were living in one night, bored. I offered them better living conditions." I didn't need to see his face to know Carter was pouting.

Good story. I could work with that.

"Hmm." Curtis looked around at all my friends, watching each of them carefully.

Rachel was smart and had one hand on each of the two boys on her sides, acting as though this whole thing had turned them on and they didn't want to be left out. Curtis chuckled when he saw them.

"Some very good little pets." His eyes came back down to me.

I needed his attention to stay on me. So, I sucked it up and leaned forward enough to lick up, my eyes still on his.

When he didn't budge, I took that as permission to continue. I wasn't ready for another load of him, pretty sure I wouldn't be eating for a while. So, I licked my way up slowly. Pulling the shirt off as I went, until I reached his neck. I slid into place and sucked on his neck.

"Did you train her or was she always this hungry?"

Carter's voice managed to sound even poutier. "She was already like this."

"I can see why she was a favorite then." He hummed again, letting me do everything. Then took over. It was over much faster that way. "Still can use a little training though."

I laid against his chest, letting him pet my hair and butt. Holy crapsicles was I tired.

"I can't just let you go without a punishment, Carter. You let my main rival, the biggest threat to my reign, jump a wall. So, here's what I am going to do..." He paused for dramatic effect. "I'm going to relieve you of your favorite toy. If you mess up again, I will take them all."

Lucas was the one pouting this time. "Why can't we take more now? You know how much I love twins!"

Curtis laughed so loud, I jumped. "I know you do, but you wear them out so fast. How long did the last pair live? A week? No. But you can have Candice as a consolation prize. I won't be needing her anymore. I got myself a new little witch to play with."

"Witch?"

Curtis tskd. "We need to work on educating our young ones better. Yes, Carter. This little treasure you found is a witch. I knew it from the first moment I smelled her. Have you never smelled a witch before?"

"Up until this morning, I hadn't thought so."

Curtis tensed up again. I wanted to cry. I placed a hand on his neck and rubbed it softly. I hadn't even officially started as his *pet* yet and I was already exhausted.

"Who?"

"Um. Carrie? I mean, that's what Deac said anyway. Grace smells like her a little bit, but Carrie's is so much stronger. No one knew what it was, but everyone flocked to her."

"So, the Little Prince That Could mated himself to a pure blood. No wonder he risked so much to save her." Curtis snapped his fingers and shook his head. "That's right. Lucas, why didn't you remind me that we heard all this, this afternoon?"

Lucas wasn't even paying attention. At least not to the conversation going on around him. Layla and Raya were both sitting on his lap now, proving they had some warped things going on in their heads. I mean, we'd all done that too each other, but they were sisters, for crying out loud!

Curtis chuckled. "That hit really messed with me. I must have lost more blood than I realized. I even taunted him over it right before he threw the dagger. She did smell good. Hmm."

Curtis leaned back in the chair, one arm over the armrest, the other moving along my back absentmindedly. I was actually starting to feel like a cat, with the way they forgot we could hear everything, and then pet us like we were only there for their comfort.

"How often did you go to this bar?"

"Um, before I found these guys, about once a week. Most everybody cycled through his bar though."

"How often would you say he marked his mate?"

I could hear Carter licking his lips, one of his nervous ticks. "Even before he mated her, his scent only ever seemed to get stronger, never weaker. So maybe every day. I heard he missed a day or two once and nearly lost it in the middle of the bar."

"And how long ago did you scent the fetus?"

I chanced a glance at Carter on the couch, the poor vamp was practically shaking. He let go of Todd and leaned back, Todd knew what that meant. He fell to his knees and helped Carter out.

"A week, maybe two."

"How did she look?"

"Fine, even this morning, I saw no difference."

Curtis laughed. He even smacked my butt because he was so happy. "He figured out the secret. Even back in the day, the breeders would be sick from day one." His eyes came back to me, studying me. I wasn't sure I liked that look. "Go fetch your things, little witch. We need to head out." He smacked me again, and I giggled as I got up and ran to the bedroom.

I quickly pulled the phone out and turned it on while I got dressed. I kept one ear on the hall for any noise. Thankfully, by the time I was dressed in a small sleeveless dress, one I had worn to the bar a few times, the phone was running.

Me: No time. 1 and done. I'm in. The others are staying. Not everyone would have made it. Please get them out.

I didn't even wait for Hill to respond. I sent it and immediately shut the phone back off. I stuck it inside one of my tennis shoes and buried them in the bag with everything else.

I jumped and spun when the door opened. My sigh of relief was very loud when I saw it was only Rachel.

"I only have a minute. I had to ask permission to use the bathroom." She whispered, coming over to give me a hug. "What the hell happened? I thought we were all supposed to go?"

"The vision changed. It was clear. Either it was this way, or someone would die. Did you hear what he said about Lucas and the twins? I contacted Hill. I told him to get you guys out. Please make sure Todd goes when the time comes." That was my fear. That he would refuse to leave until this was over.

Rachel sighed and stepped back toward the door. "I'll do my best. Curtis' other men are gonna be here any minute. Good luck, girl."

"You too, tell everyone goodbye for me, and thank you."

She nodded once and sauntered down the hall as the front door opened again. I gave her a minute so it wouldn't look like we had been together.

Curtis was talking to someone near the counter, leaning against it. His eyes turned to me as soon as he smelled me coming. A predatory grin spread across his face. He grabbed my hand and pulled me toward the door.

I lost my battle of wills and looked back at the room. Carter was now feeding from Todd, whose eyes were on me. The others had all been picked up by someone, as the room had already tripled in vampires.

I gave one small sad wave.

Lucas was outside waiting, still pouting about not getting to keep the twins. Curtis seemed pretty happy, considering Deacon and Carrie got away, and he had been stabbed in the heart. I yelped when he cheerfully swiped my feet out from under me and then took off running.

What seemed like only seconds later, we were near the gate, walking up to a helicopter. Two minutes later, we were in the air.

I remembered seeing the fires, the rioting, the complete and utter chaos that had surrounded us those first few days. But I had chosen to focus on my own survival. My friends' survival. I never imagined what the city must have looked like as a whole. Maybe it only looked so bad because the towns we flew over first looked normal.

But Los Angeles did not.

The towers that once stood majestic in the sky were either missing or were a waterfall of stone. I had only ever seen my side of the destruction, I never realized just how bad it actually was. The city looked like Armageddon had come.

In a way, it had. For us it had anyway. Now it was all about surviving.

I jumped when I felt Curtis' large thick hand on my thigh. Both he and his friend laughed.

"Did you send the message?" Curtis asked, his voice laced with a sudden undercurrent of anger.

"Yes. O'Doyle was still following them. I had Renegade run the dagger to him. The message will be received by morning."

"Good. We will not attack the princeling right away. Let him have time to think he is safe."

"He never wanted to rule. He never wanted to hide. I don't understand why he didn't just stay and join you. If he was going to leave, why didn't he do it before? It would have been easier for him."

"You're right, he never wanted this. I don't think he ever cared about his royal responsibilities. If he had stayed in his bar and told me he had no interest in any of it. I probably would have let him be, despite the past. What changed was his mate. His pregnant mate. In order to protect her, he had to come out of hiding. Now we shall see how willing he is to take up the mantle he was born too."

"Do you think they will follow?"

Curtis grunted. "That I'm not sure about. You know the few I have been able to remain in contact with over the years were tired of hiding. I was working on swaying them to join our side. I would have reinstated them to where they once were. But now? Now they have a pregnant female, one who may actually survive. They have a Queen again. Deacon never liked hiding in those caves either. In his youth, he was very open about it. Only time will tell what happens."

They were quiet for a time, just long enough for me to start dozing off, then their next words hit me. I fought to keep the state I was in, not wanting to ruin the moment.

"How far have the northern regions made it with the new wall?"

"Not nearly as fast as you had it going before. Those areas are solid and set in stone, literally. Not even Deacon would be able to jump those, nor climb. I checked in with the crews this morning. The Oregon border is officially sealed. With the exception of the hidden path. They have reached as far south as Lake Tahoe, where they will leave the next path. The Mexican border was sealed before we started. All we have left is the line in between. We plan about two more paths in those."

Curtis' hand squeezed and slid up my thigh, pushing my dress higher. "Good. When the humans finish, give them the choice. They can make the change or live in a feeding center. They will not be free to sell us out."

I kept my eyes closed, my breathing steady, as I felt the top of my dress be lowered to my stomach. Thankfully, I'd already grown accustomed to that type of thing, so it wasn't as hard. I may have pretended to sleep through Carter a few times.

"She is a beautiful specimen." Lucas sounded like he was staring at a buffet, and he was starving. "What do you plan on doing with her? I still get Candice, right?"

Curtis chuckled. "Yes. I was losing interest in her anyway. Training her took too long and wasn't worth it in the end. I have many plans for this little witch. She won't need as much training. Just look at the way she lays there."

"Hmm. I can't tell if she is asleep, or if she is just being obedient." Lucas huffed in slight annoyance. Someone obviously didn't like not knowing something.

"Maybe a little bit of both. I did take a lot of blood from her earlier. If I hadn't fed her, she would have died."

"You fed her? That's not something you normally do."

"No. She reminds me of someone, someone I met a long time ago. From the moment I saw her I planned on keeping her, knowing it would hurt Carter was just a bonus. I was tempted to bring them all. I need a harem in LA. I don't feel like dragging them around to every city."

"Then why didn't we?" Now Lucas sounded like a disappointed toddler.

"Honestly? I don't know."

Curtis slid one hand under my head and another under my butt, slowly moving me until I was lying flat on the seat, my feet in his lap. Of course, he also used that opportunity to push the bottom of my dress up, the only part of me that was covered now was my stomach.

“We may go back and get them later, we’ll see. It wasn’t completely Carter’s fault after all. We stopped teaching our young about our history. I didn’t want them looking for the royals to follow after, not like they once did.”

I heard Lucas give a low whimper and lick his lips, as Curtis’ hands inspected me.

“You will do well to keep your hands off her, old friend.”

Lucas chuckled. “Have I ever stepped out of bounds?”

Now it was Curtis who was laughing. “No. You know your limits.” I couldn’t help the flinch as Curtis’ hand inspected inside of me. I heard a zipper come from across the seating area, Curtis’ laugh grew louder now. “Enjoying the show?”

“Apparently, yes. I’m not sure if I want you to wake her up so I can see more, or if I want you to keep going with what you are doing.”

“Tell you what. Since you did sacrifice your twins for me, why don’t you tell me what you want to see, and I will do what I can.”

Was Lucas whimpering or was he giggling? “How close can I get?”

Before I knew it, I felt his hot breath on my thigh, as he got a really good close up. It was harder to play dead at some points, especially when Lucas wanted to see more traditional movements. He really had some interesting fetishes.

“What does she taste like?”

Curtis slid back out of me and sat down at my feet again, his hand taking up residence where it had been before.

"Perfect. Come here and you can taste her off me."

They were both grunting at my feet, the harder Lucas was, the harder Curtis was on me. I could feel the helicopter lowering us down to the ground. The shock of bumping the earth must have pushed Curtis over the edge.

I heard Lucas drop to the floor of the helicopter. "Heaven. Absolute heaven. I wish Candice and the others were here already, I am in quite the state now."

"Stand up, I'll take care of it."

"Bless you." Lucas sounded like a beggar on the streets after getting some money.

I heard the doors open while Lucas shifted. I felt his boot slide under my legs and felt the pressure of him moving back and forth. Curtis apparently couldn't do us both at the same time, so I got a reprieve.

Lucas barely stumbled out a thank you as he fell away from our bench. So far this place was shaping up to be worse than Carter's house.

"Did you bring dessert, my Lord?" A new voice asked greedily.

"Not for you. Spread the word, this one is mine and only mine. Touch her and die. Is the house ready?"

"Yes, sir." The new vamp answered with a gulp. "We had a cleaning crew come through yesterday."

Curtis was not so gentle this time as he pulled me off the bench and threw me over his shoulder. He kept me somewhat balanced with one hand on my still bare butt cheeks.

"The little witch will be in the room next to me. I don't want her with the rest of the harem."

"Yes, sir. There is an adjoining room connected to yours. It connects through the master bath. The previous owners used it as a nursery at one time. That is, if you don't mind sharing the bathroom with your donor."

"I don't. I will especially enjoy watching her when she is in the shower."

Their steps were quick as they walked towards the house. I cracked my eyes open and saw the ground was getting lighter. The sun was beginning to rise. I closed them again as soon as we stepped through the patio doors, having caught a glimpse of a pool. We must have landed in the backyard.

We climbed many stairs before turning down a hall. I was pretty sure I had a bruised rib or two by that point.

"This room here is yours, sir. And right through here, is the extra one for your donor." A different voice told him. This one sounded more reserved, more subservient. "The rest of the harem will be on the previous floor, when you select them."

"Wonderful, and the rest of my council? When will they be arriving? We do have room for them here, yes?"

"Yes, my Lord. There are ten rooms in this house, and a guest house in the back with three more. Your councilmen will be arriving just after sundown. They said they will take the day helicopter, so they could leave earlier."

"Good, you are excused."

"Thank you, sir. Sleep well."

Was this guy a butler? He sounded like a butler. Was he human or vamp?

"Charles?" Curtis spun around, making me a little sick.

"Yes, sir?" The possible butler's voice sounded a bit further away.

"Go see Lucas. He needs to feed."

Human then. And back up dinner.

"Yes, sir. And you?"

Curtis rubbed my butt. "I already ate, thank you."

"As you wish, sir." A door closed in the distance, most likely Charles closing Curtis' door.

Curtis slowly slid me off his shoulder, cradling me against him, as he carried me to the bed. He was gentler now, as he laid me down. He slowly pulled the dress off me, then my shoes.

I expected him to leave, not lay down next to me. His missing clothes weren't a surprise though.

He grazed my cheek with the back of his fingers. I turned toward him and let out a small sigh.

"I hope I didn't hurt you."

Crap, did he know I was awake?

"I don't want to hurt you, but I can't let my men know that. For now, they have to think you are nothing more than my little witch donor. I will protect you from them. The way I failed to protect her. I wish I could say these things to you while you are awake, but I don't want you to take advantage of me."

No, don't stop talking. This was good stuff. Give me everything I need to know. The sooner the better.

When he didn't say anymore, I snuggled further into his chest, giving another small sigh.

"You look so much like her. You smell like her, too. Partially anyway. I will take care of you. As long as you continue to behave and give me no reasons to punish you. No one else will ever touch you." His hand slid to my stomach, of course he had to travel over the mountains first. "If your body behaves, you will give me what I need to win over the royals."

He was quiet long enough that I started to fall asleep for real. This had to have been the longest night of my life. I was just far enough gone that a small whimper slipped out when he got up. Despite the demon infested pillow, I had been warm and comfortable.

Chapter 7

Deacon

By the time we reached my father's property outside Vegas, the hour was closer to morning than night. I helped Colton slide Carrie more fully onto his lap, and he lifted her out of the car with him. Tyson led us toward a suite at the end of the 4th floor hall.

"Do you require one room or two?" He asked with a knowing grin.

I laughed. "One room is fine. Thank you." I held the door as Colton carried our mate into the room. I locked the door behind us and followed them in.

Colton was already on his knees beside the bed, one hand on her cheek, his head resting lightly against her forehead. I knelt down next to him and put my arm around him.

"Clint told us of their plans for both of you. I was ready to slaughter them all. That was how your father knew about my part. I've never been so scared in my life, Deacon. I never should have left either of you."

“What difference would it have made? If you hadn’t been with my father and the others, they never would have known. We would have ended up killing a whole squad of human soldiers, and possibly still lost her. I’m sorry you were scared, but this was the best way for it to end. For us to get free.”

I rubbed a hand on his back before standing up. “Come, I know what you need. It’s what we both need, after today.” I started stripping my clothes, and then working on my angel’s. Colton kissed her head one more time before taking care of his own.

I crawled up next to Carrie, kissing her softly as I paved my way to her luscious neck. I knew when Colton had possessed our mate’s body, even in her deep sleep, she couldn't help but react. I inhaled her scent, waiting for it to hit the right moment, then I slid my fangs in. Colton’s hands were on me, mine were on her.

When I released her neck, I rolled to my back. Colton leaned down and took care of us all at the same time. As his body stuttered, he cursed at himself.

“Deacon, I’m sorry. I wasn’t thinking clearly.”

I waved at him limply, my eyes closing. “My seed is already attached and growing. There is no place for yours to go. We’re good.” I jumped when something wet hit me again. Then I laughed.

Someone was very happy about thc change and wanted to show their appreciation.

It was sometime later before we both crawled up to lay next to our mate, laying kisses on her cheeks, and passed out, one arm each across her.

A few hours later, I woke up to feeling her in my chest. When I opened my eyes, I saw Colton watching us both. He grinned, and I laughed. He was feeling playful this morning. Carrie’s eyes were starting to blink open, right as both our hands enveloped her mountains.

She was barely getting her breath back - more than a few minutes later - when she finally spoke. "Not that I am complaining, but when did the rules change?"

Colton laughed and nuzzled her neck. "I had a desperate need for you last night. I lost control."

At first she was confused, having no memory of that. I tried to slowly slide off the bed. I shouldn't have gone slow. She picked up my pillow and threw it at me. I got a good tongue lashing, until I kissed her to shut her up.

We were all enjoying the very large shower, sometime later, when someone knocked on the door. Colton grabbed a towel and grumbled all the way there. I pushed my mate against the wall and lifted her leg. The joys of being the prince.

I didn't notice Colton had come back until I set her back down. I tipped my head to the side. "Why are you staying out there? What happened?"

"Colton? What's wrong?" Carrie walked over to him, placing a hand on his bare chest, looking at his face that was slightly paler than normal.

"The King went to his favorite club last night. He told his aide that seeing us altogether like that made him hungry, and not just for blood. His body was delivered this morning. His head was in a separate box. A dagger in his chest."

Carrie gasped, covering her mouth. Colton pulled her against his chest, his eyes meeting mine.

"The dagger had Curtis' blood on it still."

Chapter 8

Carrie

I stood by my mate's side, holding his hand. We solemnly watched as the flames engulfed his father's body. The higher the flames rose, the tighter his grip became. When my fingers couldn't take the pressure anymore, I pulled my hand out and wrapped my arms around him.

Deacon shifted me to be in front of him, and held me close, his hands resting over our baby.

It had only been two days since we arrived. Two days since his father was killed. We didn't know how Curtis found him, only that he did. We waited this long for the funeral, in order to give more of the clan members a chance to come and say goodbye.

The property surrounding the house was huge. We had nearly two hundred Vampire Borns out there, and we still had room. And I was the only chick. Talk about feeling out of place.

Before the fire had been lit, Deacon spoke to them all.

"My father ruled our clan for 457 years. He took over when his father was killed, the day that the humans fought back. Now he leaves because of events from that day. Curtis was never happy with how my father responded. He was new to ruling. His father was gone. Most of the elders were gone. He felt the responsibility to carry on the line, and to protect his people. The other day was the first time I saw my father in many years. Too many years." He took a deep breath, steadying himself.

"We take our long lives for granted. We don't feel the passage of time the way the humans do. I regret that. I regret that I did not talk to him more. He spent his last days trying to negotiate with the human president so we can stay free. Stay in the open. So, we can live real lives once again. He left the safety of his home because he wanted to celebrate the good news we brought him."

Deacon stopped and looked at me, seeking permission. I nodded. I was good with whatever he needed to help him during his time of mourning.

"Even though he died a gruesome death, I have to believe that he died happy in the knowledge that I not only found my fated mate…" he paused while letting the shock subside, "but that she also carries the first of the next generation of Vampire Borns."

Deacon chuckled when all we could hear was the crickets, and vampires sniffing the air.

Then the cheers went up, sounding like a cannon blast. Deacon let them have a minute, as he softly kissed my hand, then raised his hand and they calmed down.

"Curtis has already been made aware of this information. That was why he came after us. And he will keep coming after us. He has always thirsted for power. I have made no secret of my desires to not rule. I'll be honest. I loved my little bar in LA, especially with my mates by my side. But Curtis saw fit to change all of that. We all want to be free. We all want to stop hiding who we are. It gets old faster than we do."

A few chuckled at his lame joke. I just rolled my eyes, shaking my head.

"I will continue with what my father started. I will fight for our clan on both fronts. I will find a way to rid this world of the evil that plagues us once and for all, and I will find a way for us to remain in the open." He took a deep breath. "In order for me to do that, I am going to need your help. I need to know that you are not only by my side, but that you will protect the future of our clan."

For a moment, I thought I missed something. Each of the men crossed their right arm over their chest and sank to one knee.

They were obviously showing their fealty.

Was it too early to claim pregnancy brain?

"Thank you, my brothers. Now, before we start planning the war to come, we must first give my father his royal farewell." He looked to the side and Colton stepped forward with a lit torch.

Deacon took the torch in one hand, his other still holding onto me, and lowered it to the pyre his father laid on.

When the time passed, and the fire burned itself out - faster than I expected - Tyson collected the King's ashes. Colton approached Deacon again. This time, it was Deacon that fell to one knee.

"As the General of the Royal Born Army, it is my pleasure and duty to crown you King of the Vampire Borns. Do you, Prince Deacon, promise to protect and lead your people?"

Deacon swallowed. "Yes."

I could feel his fear and panic through our mating link. He never wanted to step up and be the King. Not because he was lazy, as many probably thought, but because he was too afraid of failing them all.

Colton lowered the thin gold crown onto his head. "As your people, we accept your promises, we accept your leadership, and we promise to have your back and follow your counsel. Things are not the same as they once were. We don't know what the future will bring us, but we trust that you will have our best interests at heart. Rise, King Deacon of the Vampire Borns."

As soon as Deacon stood up, Colton, and every other vampire, took a knee again. A moment later they were up.

Colton chuckled awkwardly. "So, it has been far too long since we had a queen. It seems her crown may have been buried with her."

"You know what? I am all good with that. I've never been the tiara kind of girl anyway." Lots of deep chuckles floated around the yard.

"Stop being ridiculous, sweetheart. We discussed it, and you do need something to set you apart."

"You mean, besides being the only girl in a sea of men?"

The chuckles just kept on rolling. Even Deacon was laughing at me.

Colton rolled his eyes, something only we could see from this angle. "You're ruining this, you know *that* right?"

I scowled at him, as he pulled out a long rectangular box from his back pocket. He opened it, revealing a gorgeous necklace. In the middle of the white gold chain, rested a medallion. It was a V, with a crown made of Ivy sitting on top, the hands of the letter supporting it. The crown looked very similar to the one Deacon now wore.

"This is the royal crest." Deacon explained, as Colton placed the necklace around my neck.

Once the necklace was in place, Deacon reached into his pocket and pulled out a thick ring, bearing the same symbol.

"I found this in my father's safe. It has not been worn for many centuries. Not since we went into hiding. I think, with us officially stepping out, it is time to bring back a few of the old ways." He turned to Colton. "I would appreciate it, old friend, my mate," everyone laughed, including them, "if you would continue your post of General. My father had faith in you, even when you followed me all over the globe in my effort to hide from responsibility. You covered for me when I may have slipped just a little bit when I saw someone hitting on my mate."

"It was a wink, Deac." Colton teased. "You lost it over a wink."

"For some reason, I expected a royal ceremony to be more formal. I should have known better when y'all showed up in jeans." I shook my head at their childish behavior.

"That's what happens when we have no females to keep us in line!" Someone yelled.

Deacon nodded and pointed at the crowd. "That's very true. See, angel, just like with the bar, we're all just a bunch of toddlers. You will feel like you are right back in your classroom."

I elbowed him. He laughed, put his arm around me and turned back to Colton.

"As I was saying. Colton, will you please continue to be the General of the Royal Born Army? I must warn you; they are a little disorganized after centuries of downtime."

Colton chuckled and held his hand up for Deacon to slide the ring on his finger.

"Hey, Deac! Aren't you supposed to put the ring on your female mate's finger?"

Both Colton and Deacon flipped the loudmouth off.

“It will be my honor, my Lord.” Colton bowed reverently, and everyone cheered.

“There is actual food in the house, please, help yourselves. If you want anything a little more on the red side, you're on your own.” Deacon laughed at the playful groans.

He and Colton had debated over finding donors. As it was the traditional way to end ceremonies and funerals, but that was a long time ago. They no longer had villages full of people willing to be the open bar anymore.

Inside the large house was a ballroom-like place. Deacon led me to a table at the front of the room, and onto a small platform, raising us above the crowd. Colton appeared by my side a few minutes later, a plate filled with roasted chicken, mashed potatoes, and large heaping of salad. He then took up his position standing behind us.

I argued with them over that, the day before, when we were overseeing the set up. But apparently it was Colton’s traditional place. Formally speaking, he was the General. Deacon was now the King, and I somehow went from a newbie Kindergarten teacher to Queen of the vampires.

I really needed to check in with my best friend, Clarise, back home. She was going to die.

The rest of the clan sat at the three very long tables that ran the length and width of the room. They were shaped in a U, with our table stationed at the opening, only slightly higher. It wasn’t hard to imagine how things were back then.

I pictured Victorian Era clothes, and humans lying across the tables while the vampires talked and ate. Not much different than the bar really.

At least these guys looked like they had a few more manners.

All of them made their way up to us at some point. Some shared their stories about Deacon's dad, or times of old. Many teased Colton for finally nailing down Deacon. And every one of them expressed their welcome and gratitude toward me.

I was pretty sure they all thought I was going to die in nine months.

The first time I yawned, Deacon insisted it was time for me to go to bed. Unfortunately, Colton had to stay to monitor the rest of them. Or babysit, as he put it.

I let Deacon lead me back to the room, where he made sure to feed us both. He was getting better at control until we were both done. Unless Colton was with us, then he had an outlet. As long as it wasn't aimed at me, we didn't have the torturous pleasure of the blood lust. Deacon did say that as soon as this war was over, we were going to spend an entire weekend in that lust. I wanted to argue, but there was no point, he could both smell and feel what the idea of that was doing to me.

I was just about asleep when Colton came in. He slid into the bed and started kissing my back. Next thing I knew, we were all awake. With one less rule to follow in the bedroom, he was one happy vampire.

Deacon was sticking firm on the no blood rule. They both were. I didn't mind. It made sense that there would be one thing set aside for my fated mate only.

One of the last thoughts running through my mind as I fell asleep was a comment someone had made when they came to our table. They feared what would happen when I died in childbirth, taking Deacon with me. Deacon promised him that we had figured out a way to keep me alive, and strong. He even had the man study me.

Apparently he was really, really old and had been involved with the breeders. Clint eventually came up and promised him that I was already light years stronger than his own mate had been.

Still, I couldn't help but wish there was a guarantee that I would survive to raise my son. And if I did die, a way to not take Deacon with me. Our son would need his father. Our people needed him.

One minute I was listening to my mates whisper over me, the next, I was sitting on the edge of a small lake, hidden in a forest. There was a beautiful waterfall not far off. When I looked closer, I saw that there was someone standing under it. I closed my eyes quickly and turned my back to them, the moment I realized they were bathing.

"You can open your eyes now, Carrie. I apologize, I was not expecting you yet."

I opened them carefully and saw a fully clothed woman with long black hair sitting next to me.

"Uh, hi. Who are you?"

The woman chuckled again. "Who I am is of no consequence. I am here to guide you. Unlike your sister, you don't need me as much. You just need me to point you in the right direction."

"I'm sorry. Sister? I don't have a sister."

The woman sighed sadly. "Yes, she said the same thing. The state of the world today saddens me. I hope your journey to fix it works out. That is why I am helping you. Your job now is to not only lead the vampires back into the open but help guide all of us back out. Witches and shifters along with them. Your sister witches need guidance. Too many have turned to the dark arts. Too many have been persecuted by the world for what they are. Too many hide from their talents."

Her eyes pointedly met mine. I looked down sheepishly.

"Unlike your sister witch, you had the guidance of your parents. They set an example for you. They taught you. But you let the world block your view. I have already set your sister on her path. She was scared but she succeeded. She has landed herself in the den of the lion. Now you must do your part so she can survive.'

"Oh! You're talking about Grace!" My excitement dimmed fairly quickly. "Ooo, does that mean they are with Curtis now?"

"Only Grace is. She sacrificed herself to save the rest. She took the harder road, leaving them behind. Her path will now turn in ways she never saw coming. Whatever you hear, whatever you see, remember, she is only playing her role. She will need you to have faith in her, to trust her, when very few will. You both share the blood of the witches, she is your sister, she was sent to you for your guidance. They will all need you before this darkness lifts."

I felt a tingling sensation on my thighs that made me laugh. The woman laughed with me.

"Your time is nearly up. You did not have to accept the two mates, that was not part of your path, but I have seen how it will help you in the end. Which is why I am here. You need to go back into the past. You need to refresh your mind of the lessons your mom taught you. Within those lessons, you will find a way to not only strengthen your bonds, but you will also strengthen your mates, *and* grant the wish you made before you fell asleep."

"Wish? What wish?" Dang, she was gone, and that sensation was climbing higher.

Chapter 9

Carrie

My eyes flew open as the sensation turned to fire, fire that was spreading through my body. I looked around, trying to get my bearings as my breathing evened out.

A very large man was on his knees, one of my legs over his shoulder, another man stood next to him. I laughed when the familiarity of the scene sunk in.

"Seriously? I'm starting to wonder if you two were always sleeping together and I joined you."

They broke apart and started laughing. "No, angel. While we did share a woman from time to time, we did not do this on a regular basis. Very rarely was it just the two of us. And that was usually because we had needs that needed to be met. Remember, no women in our clan."

Deacon slid on top of me, while Colton slid out. "We came together because of you, sweetheart. You made up the difference. Our love for you turned our friendship into more. Now, it's not just about need, it's about want."

I watched as Colton reached down and pumped Deacon against me. Deacon devoured me at the same time. Yet, my eyes couldn't leave what they were doing. Colton noticed this first. He used his other hand and lined himself up with Deacon. I watched as my mates connected right over me.

"You feel it, sweetheart? You feel the burning need when you watch the two you love together?" Deacon's voice was actually a little on the shaky side.

I nodded, oh yeah, I was feeling it alright. Course I was also feeling Deacon's desires in my heart too, it was becoming very overwhelming. Colton kept teasing my body with Deacon's. Deacon kept teasing me with his tongue, and right when I didn't think I would be able to take it anymore, Colton finally let Deacon slide all the way in. It didn't take much more for any of us.

Deacon practically collapsed on top of me. Colton barely made it to my right side before falling over.

"Did you two sleep at all?"

They both laughed. "Angel. You were asleep for maybe five minutes."

"Really? Wow, that dream/vision thingy felt like it was so much longer."

"Vision?" Colton sat up, the General on alert. "What happened?"

"Well, one minute I was listening to you two girls gossip, then I was sitting next to a lake or river, or whatever, in the middle of a forest." I was from the desert. I didn't know the difference between the various bodies of water. Except the ocean. That one I did know.

"There was this woman, who, now that I think about it, looked a lot like Grace." I gave them a quick rundown of what she said. "I don't know exactly what she means about going back to the past though."

"I think I do." Colton stood up and walked to the other side of the room, all his glory just hanging about. I licked my lips, making Deacon laugh.

"Laugh it up mister, I'm not the only one having these thoughts. That line goes both ways, *and* I can feel you poking into my side."

He laughed some more and kissed my cheek.

"Keep it up you two and I'll sleep in shorts tonight."

We both frowned at Colton. Who laughed as he carried a large box over to the bed.

"Yeah, see you can't say that, and then lift heavy objects while naked." I told him.

Colton just shook his head at us, Deacon's hand was already absently drawing circles on me. And Colton had no way of hiding what that view was doing to him.

"What's in the box?" I asked, trying to refocus all three of us. They were no help. "Colton!"

He jumped and shook his head.

"Right. So, I was going to tell you about this when we first got here, but things haven't exactly gone according to plan. When Dominic asked me to find him a safe house for the meeting in Phoenix, I could only think of one place."

"You stayed in my house?" I grimaced. "Did I leave a messy kitchen? I couldn't remember if I had done the dishes first. Oh, how bad did the fridge stink?"

"It was all fine. Your friend Clarise cleaned it out, she told you that, remember?"

I sighed and laid back down. "Oh, yeah. I forgot. Carry on."

"Anyway, I wasn't sure when it would be safe enough to take you back there again to visit, so I grabbed a few things." He moved the box to the floor and pushed it aside. "I brought a bunch of knickknacks, and what I am hoping are old journals from your mom and ancestors."

Colton crawled to my side again, his lips landing right on top of Deacon's fingers, his tongue joining the party.

"You can look through them tomorrow. I don't think you are in the right headspace to go through it now, and it's already late." His words were mumbled from the blockage.

I whimpered. "So not my fault."

They both started kissing my neck and moving in synchronization. I reached both hands down to try and do my part, but they must have been on the same wavelength or something. They each caught a hand and held it over my head. Before I knew it, they were going south together.

I slept so deep after that, that you would have thought someone drugged me with their blood in my sleep again.

Color me surprised when I woke up alone the next morning. That never happened. It was one of those unspoken rules. At least one of them was always around.

I could feel sadness coming from Deacon, an intense sadness. It was so strong that I started to tear up.

I could hear the shower running, so I tip-toed over and snuck a peek. Sure enough, my two mates were in the shower together.

I half expected to catch them messing around, because let's face it, vampires were horny like 24/7. It was a good thing that Deacon fed me his blood every night. Without his extra strength, I would never be able to keep up with them.

I had no idea how long they had been there, I was thinking not long, because I doubted either of them would have left me alone for so long. No matter the circumstances.

Deacon had his head bowed under the water; his long black hair ran down the sides of his head from the pressure of the water. The shower heads from the walls were blasting into their sides.

I was very confused the first time we used the shower.

For one, you could fit like ten people in there. Two, there was no door or curtain, just an opening in the wall, kind of like a narrow doorway. And three, who needs shower heads all over the walls?

I guess if you had ten people showering in there it would come in handy. Aaaand… I never wanted to think about why they decided to do that again.

Colton stood behind Deacon, his hands massaging his shoulders, every now and then he would lean down and place a soft kiss on his back.

"What troubles you, my King?"

Yeah, that title was going to take some getting used to.

"What doesn't, Colton?" He huffed in exasperation. "In my arrogance, I hid from my father, from the world, for a century. I barely had five minutes with the man and then he was gone. I haven't even started yet, and I can already understand why he chose to hide our people. If it wasn't for the Nightwalkers, I'd probably let them stay that way."

His huff was more on the sarcastic side as he lifted his head, staring at the wall in front of him.

"For 300 years, I nagged him to let us be free. To let me outside. He finally relented, he let me go with you to put down an uprising that Curtis caused. And I never came home. I stayed out in the world. I don't deserve to be their King."

I opened my mouth to argue, but Colton beat me to it. "That is why you are the right man for the job. You don't want it. You don't want the glory. You don't want the title. You've been out in the world. You know what we need. You've been among the Nightwalkers. You know how they work. Between you and Carrie, we can unite all the magical beings in a way they have never been before."

I watched, and felt, as a shudder ran through my mate. He was reacting to not only Colton's words, but to what he was doing. It wasn't just his shoulders he was rubbing anymore. Colton had slowly worked his right hand around to the front.

"Let the tension out, my Lord. Right there." Colton spoke softly, coaxing Deacon.

I leaned against the wall, my legs feeling shaky. I heard Deacon give a sound I knew all too well. Sure enough, when I opened my eyes again, I watched Colton moving more than just his hand.

When Deacon's hand came up, I stepped forward and took it. Colton removed his hand and pulled me in for a long kiss. Deacon followed after. Then I knelt in the shower and finished what Colton had started.

Colton stepped out of the shower, giving us a few minutes. Deacon held me under the water, his head on mine.

"How long were you there?"

"Long enough. You can talk to me, you know. I have no idea what I am doing here, either. Four months ago, I was finger painting with five-year-olds, and now I'm expected to guide all the witches and help you unite everyone. My mom tried to teach me, and I ignored her. I have my moments. When they come, I know you are always there for me. Let me do the same. Please?"

He nodded and kissed my head. "I'm sorry. It all just got to me for a minute. I was lying there, watching you both sleep, and everything just sank in on me. I couldn't breathe anymore. I had to escape. So, I came in here," he huffed, "and you both followed me."

"It's your fault. You wanted two mates. You can kiss alone time goodbye. I had to kiss mine goodbye the second I stepped into your bar. Creeper."

He chuckled softly and tapped my nose with his, trying to get me to tilt back so he could kiss me. I smiled and shook my head, then held him close to me. He pouted but held me tight.

"Mates are not just for physical fun. We're partners. You lean on us. We lean on you. Don't hide your feelings from me, not that you can, but still. Please, Deacon, don't shut us out." I felt him nod. "No, I want to hear it. Promise me, Deacon. Promise you will talk to us, let us help you carry this weight."

This time his sigh sounded almost like a laugh. I pushed off him, taking a step back, getting irritated with him.

"How would you feel if you woke up and I was not in the room, but you could feel my sadness? If you found me trying to wash it away, and hide it from you? Would you let it go?"

He frowned. "I have felt your sadness. When I left to go get supplies with Todd. The pain nearly tore me apart. I almost canceled the whole trip. But I knew you had Colton, and I trusted him to take care of you."

My lip trembled. He still wasn't promising. Nor did he plan too. I let myself wallow in the disappointment, the sadness, I let it all bleed through my link to him.

He grimaced and rubbed his chest. "Angel…" I started to walk away, moving my arm back when he tried to grab me. "Fine, I promise, just please don't walk away from me. I get it, alright. I understand your point. Feeling this… and you moving away… I get it. Please come back."

I fell into his chest and cried softly while he continued.

"I promise I won't hide it anymore. I'll talk to you." I felt his head lift off mine. "Both of you." I heard a small chuckle and knew that Colton had come back in. "Just had to leave me with the big guns, huh?"

"Eh. Figured she would make the point better than I could." I heard his little smirk, and then his feet as he started walking on the wet tile.

I giggled when his arms wrapped around both of us.

"And here I thought she would always be the softer touch and you would come in with the heavy hand."

"Nah, I just softened you up for her to do the low blow."

I swear Colton picked his words for a reason. I slid out of their grips. "Do you two *ever* think of anything else?"

I barely made it out of the shower before two large hands lifted me up. I was on the bed before the scream even passed my lips.

Chapter 10

Deacon

I was starting to think this whole two mates thing was a bad idea. I had only been thinking about the fun times, not the serious ones, when I first offered it. Although, in my defense, I took my fun times very seriously.

Colton may not be able to feel what I feel, but he certainly had known me long enough that he could read me like a book. I wasn't in the shower for five minutes before he came in. I was so caught up in my own sorrow and fear that I hadn't realized Carrie was there. Not until her own desires were as strong as my own, and she was only watching.

I wanted to protect them both from this. I thought, if she was asleep, I could take a moment to let the fear run through me. Let my anxieties out instead of being bottled up all the time. I thought I could do it and save her the pain and the worry.

My angel had a soft heart, she cared for so many. I didn't want her to feel what I felt right then.

I didn't want to promise, because I knew I would not be able to keep that promise. I would always protect my angel first.

Then she moved away, she wouldn't even let me touch her. I felt her disappointment in me, her sadness that I was going to hide from her again. She proved why it hurt her so badly. And I didn't like it one bit.

The idea of her hurting, and her not letting me help her, hurt worse than everything I had felt moments before. I made the promise, and I would do my best to keep it.

Colton and I laughed as I threw her on the bed. She liked to complain about our constant needs, but she enjoyed it as much as we did.

"I'm sorry." I told them both again, as we laid quietly in the bed.

"Never again. We are supposed to be a team." My angel yawned and burrowed into my chest like a gopher.

Colton and I both laughed.

"I need to get up, it is nearly noon already. I am meeting with those who your grandfather used as officers before. We are going to reorganize. First though, we need to search for the others."

I made to stand up with him, but Carrie's little arm wrapped around my waist and held me tight. I had scared her good with my words and my thoughtless actions.

"Stay, my King. She needs you more. She may not be far along by human standards, but she is not carrying a human child. I will let you know if we need you."

Colton walked over to the closet and dressed quickly. Before he left, he came around to us. He leaned over me and kissed our, now sleeping, mate's head. Then came to me.

A few weeks ago, when he left us at the bar for the last time, I teased him about not kissing me goodbye as well. That was the first time we had ever kissed. We had done many other things, things that were just about need. But not kissed.

Since he feared losing us, Colton seemed to have no more reservations. I didn't get a kiss on the head before he left. He kissed me slowly, letting me feel how worried he too had been about me this morning. Colton was never one to talk about emotions, but he was always good at displaying them. When I began to turn to him he pulled away with a low growl.

"I will see you later." He stepped away, making me laugh quietly as he readjusted his pants.

I let my angel sleep in my arms for a while before I woke her. And I didn't let her out of the bed until her stomach growled.

I escorted her to the kitchen, holding her hand tight in mine. There were still many vampires roaming around. When they all had first started showing up, Carrie worried about having enough beds. We had to remind her that wouldn't be a problem. It wasn't like any of them were opposed to sharing with others. Nor did we really have to sleep every night.

She was eating a sandwich, laughing with Clint over a story from when I was younger, when my phone rang. I kissed her temple and stepped outside to answer it.

"Hill." I greeted the Alpha. "This is a surprise."

"I heard about your father. You have my condolences."

"Thank you. But that's not why you're calling."

"No. Although it is why I am calling you instead of him. I have contacted the other Alphas. Most of their packs have been living in small towns together. My pack is a military pack. Unfortunately, more than a few of them were on the bases in California. I have had no contact with them. The other alphas agreed to send their fighters. We are in this with you."

I had to quickly remind myself that I was a King now and dancing for joy would not look right.

"Thank you, Alpha. That is wonderful news. From what I have heard, the negotiations with the humans was not going well. If I were to call another meeting, would you be willing to sit in? Did you all vote on an alpha to represent your people?"

I turned around, noticing the room had gone quiet. They were all listening in to my side of the conversation.

Hello, spotlight. My name is Deacon. I've been hiding from you for just shy of a century.

Guess I might as well get used to it.

Hill snorted, gaining my attention again. "It seems they all agreed, unanimously I might add… on me. My pack deals with the human government the most. I am not even close to being the oldest, but they still wanted me. I will sit with you. It seems our time in the shadows has ended as well. The General has relocated to Carson City. The Nightwalkers have reached nearly halfway on their new walls."

"What new walls?"

"They've been building walls of cement, nearly twenty feet tall, right over the previous wall of rubble. The forces on the Oregon border claim it appeared overnight. We have no idea how it happened either. It was like someone stopped time, and when it restarted, the wall was there. Do you know any witches that can stop time?"

"Not personally, and it has been years since I've heard of anyone having that power. Who is building the wall this time?"

"Human construction companies mostly, but they are guarded by the vampires. They work in three shifts. The men say the vampires are dressed like ninjas."

"Yeah, when they chased us in Mojave they were wearing something like that. The material would have to be very thick for it to protect them. It seems Curtis had planned more thoroughly for his invasion then I originally thought." I used to think it had been messy and unorganized.

"Oh, and I heard from your little spy a few days ago."

"What did she say?"

"That she is now with Curtis, but she left her friends behind. I thought they were all going?"

My eyes met Carrie's, her head tilted, probably noticing my confusion. "So did I. Unless the vision changed."

Hill sighed. "She said no one would have made it. I think she means they would not have survived. She also asked for me to get them out."

I pinched the bridge of my nose. "I told them in the beginning that it was too dangerous to tango with Curtis. I am not surprised that part of the vision changed. I doubt they let her leave easily. Todd especially will be struggling. We do need to get them out before he tries something stupid." I was going to end the call when I remembered Carrie's dream. "Something has changed. Something big. Carrie had a dream last night, not something she usually gets. The witch in her dream told her to not lose faith in…" I carefully looked around the room, men I had known my whole life, but hadn't seen most of them in a century, "you know who. To the world it will look like she was against us, but that wasn't true. Whatever is happening, whatever role she thought she would be playing has changed. I doubt you will hear from her very often, and no matter what we do hear or see, we have to keep faith in her. If we don't, we may lose her for real."

"What do I tell the General?"

"Whatever she tells you. We have to play it out. If you don't follow through, her vision will change, and we won't know what we did until it's over, for the good or the bad."

"And if they start thinking she is against us? They will assume everything is a trap."

"Then you let me know. We will do what he will not."

"Right. Fine. I will wait until the meeting to reveal myself to the General. So, you will need to schedule it."

I grinned. Chicken. "Send me the number. I will have Colton schedule it, General to General."

Hill whistled. "You are organizing."

"Yes. It is time. I suggest you all do the same."

"Let me know the time and place."

I laughed. "Why? Isn't he keeping you close as well?"

Hill chuckled. "Yes and no. I am not with him now. I am cleaning up the mess you left behind in Mojave."

Well, that soured my mood. "How bad is it?"

"Not as bad as I expected. Curtis and his men were after you. For the most part they ignored the soldiers. I am trying to plan out an extraction for the kids. The gate hasn't been resealed yet. I want to move fast, just in case."

I looked around the kitchen, which was holding a little more than a dozen men now. "You know what? Wait for us."

"You want in?" He sounded surprised.

"What better way to prove to the humans that we can work together, than for us to actually work together? I bet your wolf wouldn't mind taking part either."

Hill full out laughed. "I think I can work with that. I will call the local pack, too. The wall is cutting into their territory. I'm not the only one who is missing members."

I nodded and stood straight, the others straightening as well, reacting to my change in demeanor. "Good. Plan it. We will be there tonight."

"Attack at sunrise?"

"Yes, when they are at their most vulnerable."

"See you then." We both hung up. Carrie stood up and walked to me.

"What about the kids? What changed? Are they safe?"

I cupped her cheek and tried to soothe her. "They are fine. But a few things have changed." I looked up at Clint. "Get me Colton."

"Yes, sir." He stood and walked out of the room.

I turned back to Carrie. "She left them all behind. She said they wouldn't have lived. She wants us to get them out. So, we will."

"My Lord?" Colton came in, his eyes checking us over to make sure we were both fine.

"I spoke to Hill. The shifters are coming out of hiding. All of them."

Cheers went up around the room, and more started walking in. We may have a big kitchen, but if anymore came in it would be a tight fit. I still wasn't sure who all we could trust, so I left out most of the conversation.

"I need a team for a rescue mission. Select them and meet me in the conference room." He knew there was a lot I wasn't saying, but he also knew I had a reason for it.

Twenty minutes later. We met in the conference room. Colton had chosen a dozen men. The four that had been with him and my father when they rescued us, and eight more. I waited while Carrie walked the room, getting a feel for each of them. She tried to get a read on everyone at the party the night before, but this wasn't an exact science we were working with.

She came back around to me, nodded once, and sat down. I stood up, they were all watching her, confused.

"My mate has the power to sense intent and lies. I apologize for any offense, but we have to be careful. Curtis may have spies, just like we do."

I explained what we were going to be doing, and who we were rescuing. I didn't tell them about Grace though.

"This is a good chance for us to prove to the humans that we can all work together, that not all of us are as evil as Curtis. As of now, they want to kill us all. Captain Hill, the Alpha of an Army pack is planning this little get together. He and a few of his men will join us, in wolf form. We need to leave soon. We attack at dawn."

One man at the end of the long table jumped out of his seat with his arms raised like he scored a touchdown.

"Yes!" Steve shouted. "Sorry." He blushed as he quickly sat back down. "It'll be nice to let loose. I had a few shifter friends back in the day, we used to race."

I smiled. "I'm sure they are excited too. They live among humans about as well as we do. Their wolves have to stay hidden most of the time." I turned it over to Colton, letting him organize it all. When we got to Mojave, it would be him running it with Hill.

"Are you coming as well, your majesty?" Steve asked.

"Yes. At least this time." I looked at Carrie, who gave me a challenging look. I sighed. "We both will be. The kids we are rescuing are friends of your Queen. They know a lot about her and what she can do. They need our protection."

I felt the gratitude coming from her, along with relief. I'd take that over what happened this morning, any day of the week.

An hour later, Colton's search teams left. We left half an hour after them. The sun was still up, so we were fairly certain we had no Nightwalker tails.

Just like before, we drove in three SUVs. We let the four search teams borrow a few of the others. Colton drove our car, while my angel and I sat in the middle row. We only had fifteen people, but we wanted the extra space in case we brought any more back. I figured we might need to drop the kids off somewhere after.

Apparently once my father had left the caves, finally, he did so in style. It wasn't like they had gone without comfort in the caves. He had tried to make them feel comfortable. But a cave was still a cave.

Three hours later, Colton pulled up into a rest area, a mile from our destination. It was probably once a popular hiking area. From the dust on everything, no one had been there in a while.

"What are we doing?" Carrie asked softly, looking out the window.

"Carter said they have holes in the wall that they use to watch the human army. Plus, if the gate is not sealed, they will see us pulling up. They will know to prepare, and possibly even call Curtis." Colton explained.

"So, we are sneaking in then." It was more a confirmation to herself than asking us.

Everyone unloaded and geared up. Modern technology was a wonderful thing. Bullet proof vests would help cushion us against the paralyzing reaction we had to silver daggers. They also had many places to carry daggers of our own.

Colton approached Carrie with one.

“I thought I wasn’t fighting?” She eyed the vest like it might bite her if she touched it.

“You’re not. This is just in case. Deacon, you should feed before we go as well. The stronger you are, the safer you both will be.”

I put on a dramatic act. “Fine.”

My angel giggled as she tilted her head. For someone who didn’t like voyeurism, she was trying pretty hard to reach for my zipper. I pulled away after only a few minutes and kissed her head.

“Later, angel.”

She pouted. Colton and I both laughed.

Once both our vests were in place, I squatted down, allowing her to climb onto my back again. As soon as she was settled, we all ran the last mile. We were on the base three minutes later. Well, Carrie and I were. The rest were a few minutes behind us.

“Where can I get me a fated mate?” Tyson made the others laugh.

“Don’t know, but you can’t have mine. I already have to share her with him, and he is greedy enough.” I threw my thumb over my shoulder at Colton as Carrie slid down. His hand swung down the moment she moved away and smacked my butt.

My jaw dropped. Colton spanked me!

“It was your idea. Live with it.” The others thought it was quite funny. I found it as something else entirely.

"Sounds like a party over here." Captain Hill walked around the building we were behind, wearing nothing but a pair of athletic pants that had snap buttons running down both sides. "Can anyone join or is it just for the royal vamps?"

I held my hand up and he took it. "Nice to see you, Hill. You look like you are ready to play."

He stretched his arms out in front of him and rotated his neck. "My wolf was feeling anxious, we needed a run. You have good timing. The human squad going with us are just turning in for the night. As well as the two wolves. Everyone else is performing business as usual. I will warn the guards on duty when we are ready to go."

"And the local pack?"

"Their Alpha was able to contact them, they had moved further inward, hiding their scents among the humans. They will be here just after dawn. We go in, they come out."

"Why are they trying to hide their scent?" Carrie asked.

"You remember how we talked about the chemicals humans create and vampires can't?" She nodded, so I continued. "Well, shifters carry testosterone on a regular basis. The more dominant they are, the more they have."

Her eyes widened in both shock and worry. "The Nightwalkers would bleed them dry."

"Yes and no. I have not been able to contact any of the ones who were stationed at the various bases in California. We're talking at least two dozen warrior shifters. If Curtis is smart, he will keep them on lockdown. They won't kill them. At least not yet. If a big battle comes, they will be passed around to all the top fighters. Which they probably wouldn't survive. Now, why don't you all follow me? I have a back door you can use to get into the main building." Hill turned and we followed.

We spread out and got comfortable in the same drab waiting area Carrie and I had been in less than a week before. I grinned, a little later, when a man walked out of the inner office, his eyes darting to all of us, settling on my mate and me. I was sitting on the couch, her head in my lap. Colton was sitting at the other end, rubbing her feet.

I laughed when Reyes cursed. “This is who you brought in to help?” He turned back to the other room and Hill stepped out. Who looked at us, and then back to him. And shrugged. “Lovely. Just lovely.”

“Awe, and here I thought you and I had become friends.”

Carrie lifted a hand and smacked me in the chest.

“If you hadn’t murdered my CO, that might have happened.”

“If he hadn’t put a gun on my mate and threatened to kill her, I wouldn’t have had too.” The air in the room thickened as my men went into a hunch from their various positions in the room and growled deeply. I lifted a hand to calm them. “I told you. I would rather we work together. We are here to help. Besides, those kids belong to my mate and me. They worked for me. I promised to protect them, and here I am.”

“Sergeant, you are going to have to swallow a lot of pride and past beliefs before this mission is over. It would be best if you started with an open mind, trust me.” Hill patted his shoulder, then went back inside his office.

Reyes grimaced, then looked at Carrie. “Are you hungry? Just because I have a beef with him doesn’t mean I want to risk you or your baby.”

“If you have veggies and ranch, I would love it. Thank you. Oh! And chocolate ice cream.”

Even Reyes laughed.

"Cravings kick in already?"

"It has been a long time since a new generation of our clan was born, we aren't really sure of the timeline. But yes, it seems so." Colton rubbed up her leg, making her sigh. "We look forward to some of the others."

Carrie lifted a foot just enough to kick him in the inner thigh.

"Keep it up and next time I move higher." She warned him.

Reyes laughed and went to go get her food. After she ate, she fell asleep on the couch, more content than the last time we were there. I was sure that had more to do with both of us holding her than anything else. She seemed most at ease these days when we were both with her.

As night fully fell, the others retreated to the back to spar and warm up. They trickled out little by little, eventually leaving the three of us alone. Hill had already gone to his tent to sleep for a few hours.

I had my head back, laying against the wall, my left hand stroking my mate's neck, my right rested over her stomach. I rolled my head to Colton, when I felt his fingers slowly lift mine, folding them together, over our unborn son. That was when it hit me. We never held hands before my angel came either. We had shied away from anything that felt too intimate. But now, we did it naturally, as though we had been doing it all along.

"You should stay behind with our Queen. You should not be going into danger."

"This is my fight, too."

"Yes, but we need you safe."

"I will not hide, Colton. The time for hiding is over. If I am not willing to fight, then why should the others be?"

“I wasn’t referring to the rest of the clan.” He squeezed my hand with his own.

My face softened. “And we don’t need you safe? How is it fair if we keep putting you in danger to protect us?”

He released my hand and carefully slid closer, trying not to wake our mate. I closed my eyes when his palm touched my cheek.

“It has been, and always will be, my job to protect you. My reasons why may have changed, but it doesn’t change my duty. Besides, if we lose you, we lose her. And our son.”

I gave him a playful scowl. “So that's what it is. You just want me alive, so you don’t lose her. Tsk, and here I thought you…” I chuckled as he cut me off with a kiss.

He rested his head against mine and we were silent for a minute.

“Why did we never do that sooner?” I asked him, because seriously…why?

“Do what?”

“Kiss. Before a few weeks ago, we never did that. We’ve done pretty much everything else possible, but not that.”

Colton tipped his head to the side, thinking about it. “I never really thought about it before. I don’t know. It was more of a joke that day, just a way to shut you up since you had to tease me for kissing her. I think it was all just business before, not intimacy. Not until she came into our lives. Then, that kiss, I don’t know, something changed.”

“I almost wish we had done it sooner. All these years we’ve been together.”

Colton laughed softly. His nose bumping mine. I tried to kiss him again and he moved away.

"Such a spoiled prince."

"Such an ornery bas…" I laughed again, he just liked cutting me off.

"Definitely should have tried this sooner. It's the best way to shut you up."

I opened my mouth to argue, and he did it again, laughing.

Moving very slowly, Colton laid Carrie's feet on the couch. He opened his jeans and placed one leg over our mate, and braced one hand on the wall, the other behind my head. I had one hand on him, and one hand down my other mate's shirt. I could feel she was waking up, but by now she enjoyed watching as much as playing.

I knew she was fully awake when she rolled over and got on her knees. Before Colton finished he went behind her, pulling those atrocious pants down for her. We really needed to buy her more dresses.

It wasn't long before she fell back asleep, not even letting me zip up first. Colton slid back under her, keeping her pants open, and scooting closer to me. He slid one hand in each of our pants. So, I put one of mine in his, and one in her shirt.

We didn't so much as blink an eye when the others started coming back in. Not that our eyes were open, Colton really did like kissing now.

I made sure her hair covered her before I finished enjoying my mates. Her jeans didn't fare as well. When we finally turned back to the room, we had to stifle laughs.

I loved being a vampire. I loved the fact that we weren't as reserved, or moral, as the humans put it.

Why hide the good stuff?

“The Queen hasn’t allowed us to molest her in public like that yet, no one tell her you saw anything.” I whispered.

“Nice try, but I appreciate it anyway. I am just going to keep my eyes closed and pretend you both weren’t inside my clothes in a room full of people.” She murmured. Colton and I high fived. “I hate you both.”

“We love you, too. Now, I suggest you keep your eyes closed, sweetheart. Or you’ll feel like you are back in the bar… with no women.”

I snorted at Colton.

It wasn’t long before she was back asleep. See, I knew she would start getting over it eventually. She just had to keep her eyes closed.

Chapter 11

Deacon

An hour before dawn, Hill walked in, choked, and stepped back out. Reyes walked in, sniffed, grimaced, and then looked confused at his Captain.

"Sorry, need a minute. Smells like a brothel in there." Hill was gasping for air and trying not to laugh. He was being a tad overly dramatic. Nothing had happened for the last few hours. The smell was nearly gone.

Carrie stretched, then quickly fixed her shirt before giving me the stink eye. I just winked at her. "I kept you covered. Someone else didn't." I glanced at Colton and her still opened jeans.

"Nobody can see anything." He whined.

She quickly stood up and zipped up. "I repeat, I hate you both. At the rate you two go, I'll pop out one kid, just to start baking another."

“If you manage that, we will all bow down and worship the ground you walk on, my Lady.” Tyson added from the corner he and Clint were in.

Carrie blushed.

“Something you learn about Vampires of any race,” Hill stepped back in and patted Reyes on the shoulder, “they have no shame.”

“Shifters aren’t the same?” Carrie sat between Colton and me.

Reyes’ eyes widened slightly. Colton and I both already had our hands on her legs.

Hill patted him roughly again. “No. We are somewhere in between. We didn’t broadcast it, but that curse that hit you all seems to have affected us as well. We do still have a few females born with the ability to shift, but it is rare. Many of those females have more than one mate, as well.”

Reyes’ eyes shot to Hill, confusion, and wariness bled through him.

“I take it you haven’t told him yet.”

Hill just shook his head to answer my question, grinning at his friend. I kissed my angel’s head and stood up.

“We should probably get this started then. Your men will need a minute to adjust to the world they didn’t know they were living in.”

As the rest of our men stood up, tucking themselves back in - Reyes was going to have a coronary before this day was over - Colton kissed Carrie’s head and stood up as well. We picked up our gear and began putting it back on.

We filed out the back door, where the two other shifters were waiting in the same type of pants Hill was wearing. The human squad chosen to go with us stood there looking confused. Probably at our appearance and because three of their own were clearly out of uniform.

“Alright, most of you don’t know what we are about to do. I have kept it that way for a reason. Simply put, we are crossing that gate, taking out some Nightwalkers, rescuing any humans we can, and getting our butts back over to our side as fast as possible.”

One soldier raised his hand and Hill nodded. “What’s a Nightwalker, sir?”

Hill turned to me, so I took over. He walked over to his two pack members and the three of them backed up for space. Their wolves would need more than the human side did.

“A Nightwalker is a vampire that is created. They can only walk at night because the sun will fry them. We,” I pointed at my clansmen around me, “are the Vampire Borns. We were born vampires. We are faster, stronger, have better hearing, and we *can* walk in the sun.”

“We’re better looking too.”

I rolled my eyes as Colton slapped Steve on the back of the head.

“Is that why you were able to jump the wall with the sun up?”

“Yes.” I cleared my throat awkwardly, and my angel took my hand. “I am also the King of the vampires. Curtis, the vamp behind all this chaos, is a rebel. We’ve been in hiding for many centuries. He created an army and made the mistake of not telling them who we are. We are the royals, at one time, they worked for us. We are the only ones who can bring them to heel. Therefore, we are joining the battle. And we are bringing the other magical creatures with us. You are the first humans to learn of this, and that’s because you will be fighting by our side today. My mate here is a witch, a pure blooded one. And she carries the first generation of our clan to be born in over 400 years.” I wanted to laugh at the way they stepped away from my angel. "Don't worry, as long as you don't lie to us or have evil intentions, she will leave you alone. Now, there is one other magical creature that is among us. Captain?"

Hill's eyes changed from their normal brown to a dark black, his voice took on a second layer, making it deeper and more gravely. "No matter what you see, I am still your superior officer."

As one, all three men jumped in the air, doing backflips, and landed on four furry feet. Their shifts had been perfectly synchronized.

Every human ran a few more steps backward and cursed.

"Show off." Colton grumbled.

Jealous? A growly voice ran through all our heads. Carrie gasped.

"Alpha wolves have the power to project their thoughts into everyone in their pack's minds. Their pack can relay messages that way as well, as long as both parties are in wolf form. But only some Alphas have the power to send it to all, no matter the species. *If* he is powerful enough." I nodded my head. "It's an honor to be in the presence of one so strong, Captain."

Thank you. Now. Here is the plan. Smitty, your team will handle the Nightwalkers. They will be hiding in their tents. Shoot off a few grenades at each one. Walker, you, and your team see what you can do about blowing more holes in that wall. Deacon, I will leave searching the houses to you, you can cover more ground faster than we can. One wolf will stay with the soldiers, myself and the other will come with you. If we find more than the kids, we will steal a car and bring them over. Reyes, it is your job to protect Carrie. We are using this mission to prove to the higher ups that we can all work together. So far they only know about the Vampire Borns. The President refused to work with them. The sun will be up in a few minutes, when that happens, we will sneak up on both sides of the wall. Walker, your team will take down that gate.

The soldiers went to attention and saluted. Colton and I both kissed our mate one more time.

"Reyes, I'm trusting you. She told me you tried to keep her from getting hurt the other day. It's not just me that will go on a rage this time. The Vampire Borns all know we have a pregnant Queen. It's been far too long since we've had either of those."

"Yeah, got it. End of the world if anything happens to her. Come, my Queen, let's get you some breakfast and then move you out of the open." He offered her his arm, like a gentleman.

Carrie gave us one last sad wave, blowing us a kiss, then walked off with him.

"She will be fine, my Lord." Colton whispered, rubbing one of my shoulders. "Let's go get those kids."

I blinked my eyes and turned to follow him.

We broke into one line, and hid along the wall of the building, the side that would be cast into shadow when the sun rose. Hunkered down next to us were the three wolves. Hill's was pitch black with a bit of purple sparkling through, it reminded me of Grace's black hair with the purple tips. The one behind him was tawny, and the last was gray. The Alpha was the biggest, which was normal. He was just above my waist and thick enough that it would be difficult to wrap both arms around him to break a rib that way.

When the sun began to break, brightening the valley floor, Walker aimed a grenade launcher and shot it four times, twice to each side of the chain link gate. It fell with a loud crash, followed by the sounds of men running over it. We waited long enough for the wolves to take the lead, then we shot off.

In minutes we were in a neighborhood. My men split in half, taking different sides of the street. A drone came zooming between two houses, toward us. Colton lifted a gun from his thigh and shot it down with one shot. We didn't bother with going inside any of these houses. There were enough of us, along with the wolves, that we would smell anyone in the area.

By the third street, Colton had taken out three more drones. I skidded to a stop when I caught a whiff of human blood, and one Nightwalker. My head snapped to the left, Colton and Hill ran in front. This door we did break down. The sounds of it cracking and falling were drowned out by the screams of three females. I stepped around the two overprotective men in front of me and sauntered into the house.

"Good morning. I heard someone needed a lift out of here." I grinned at the shocked faces in front of me.

"Deacon?"

"Colton?"

"Is Carrie alright?"

"Is that a wolf?!"

I laughed. "Yes, Carrie is fine. She is currently waiting anxiously for you all on the other side of the wall. And that wolf is a shifter. Captain Hill to be specific. I see everyone but Todd. I'm guessing he is in the other room with…" I sniffed again and laughed. "Carter. Fitting." I passed by them and went down the hall, leaving Colton to start pulling them all together.

I opened the door quietly to the dark room, then leaned against the door frame. I figured I would be nice and wait a minute. When the two fell to the bed, I flipped the light on. And started clapping.

"Not as good of a show as my mates put on, but still, not bad."

"Deacon? What are you doing here? Curtis will kill you *and* me if he finds out!" Carter jumped off the bed. Todd just sat there, staring at me.

"We don't have much time. Todd, grab your things. Your little witch girlfriend told us it was time to rescue you."

"No. I'm staying. I will find my way to get to her."

I sighed and rubbed the side of my head. "Sorry, kid. The vision has changed. All I know, is that some, if not all of you, would have died, which is why she went alone. You know Grace better than I do. She told Hill that you guys needed to get out, so we are here to get you out."

Todd grumbled as he pushed off the bed. He slid into a pair of shorts he picked up off the floor and walked over to a closet.

"Wait… what? What visions? And how did you know she was a witch?" Carter looked like he was about to lose it.

"I know because I smelled her. Honestly, what do your creators teach you? We are in a bit of a hurry, so save me some time. How many humans are in the area?"

"None. It's just us." Todd answered as he put his backpack over his right shoulder. "What's going to happen to Carter? Curtis basically said he would kill him if he screwed up again, and I am pretty sure this is worse than just you jumping a wall."

"Awe, sweet, you grew a soft spot for him." I playfully put a hand over my heart like I was touched.

Todd just shrugged and looked away.

"Any chance, you guys can take me with you? Guarding a wall wasn't exactly what I had in mind when I signed up for this gig. And any chances I had of moving up got blown sky high last time you came through." Carter pleaded pathetically, finally reaching down for his pants. He wasn't as fun to look at as my mate either.

I debated his request for a minute, he could come in handy. "Are you willing to switch sides?" I held up a finger to stop him from answering. “Keep in mind, my angel is an even stronger witch than Grace. She can tell when you lie, and your intent.”

“I’d rather work for you, Deac. I’ve known you longer. I’d rather not go back into hiding, but I also don’t want to die. I did what Colton said, I let Curtis take the girl.” Todd’s head snapped up to him. “Sorry, pup. I didn’t want to let her go either, but we both know it’s what saved me.”

Todd frowned but nodded.

“Fine, but how do we get you out of here? The sun just came up.”

“We stored your truck in the garage. He can hide in the front with a blanket over him like you did.” Todd was more eager to get this clown out than I thought he would be. I studied him and he shrugged. “He grew on me, alright?”

I chuckled and walked back out. “Colton, we’ve got an extra!”

Colton saw Carter behind me. His only response was to huff and shake his head with amusement. The others were all ready to go.

“Is Grace safe? Is she alright?” Rachel asked, her eyes pleading.

“Last we heard, yes. But it's been a few days. Carrie had a dream, something has changed. Grace’s position is not one we expected. Not that we even know what that means, we just know that it has. Anyone have the keys to my truck?” Scott threw them at me. “Awesome. Didn’t think I would ever see this baby again.”

“You all are sure no one else is around?” Colton verified.

“Yes. We’ve searched pretty much everywhere. Had to do something during the day besides play video games.” Raya shrugged.

“Then go load up in the back of the truck, make sure Carter is nice and covered.” I turned to Hill and Colton. “I’ll drive them out, you two can run on my sides if you want. We will collect the others as we go."

Fifteen minutes later, we drew close to what used to be the gate. A good portion of the wall was missing as well now. Nearly half a mile. Maybe more soon, it wasn't looking too sturdy. It was beginning to resemble a row of dominoes.

"All the walls are being fortified. They just hadn't gotten this far yet." Colton reminded me.

"Someone needs to let the humans know. They have about twelve hours to get out of here."

Word has been spread to the human police. That's all we can do for now. If we had more time to plan, we could have had more soldiers here.

We waited near the gate, as three vans and two trucks pulled up. The three wolves ran to them, ran circles around them, and then zoomed through the gate. The vans followed after.

"Guess the other pack is here." Steve stated, unnecessarily.

"Let's go, your Queen is anxious for our return." I rubbed a sore spot right over my heart. "It's like I can feel her pacing and stomping her foot."

Colton chuckled. "Shall we see who gets to greet her first?"

He winked and took off. I stepped on the gas. Carter laughed from the floor as I growled expletives.

Sure enough, Colton had her wrapped in his arms when I pulled the truck as close as I could to the building. They broke apart and he laughed. At least she elbowed him.

"That was cheating, and you know it." I told him. Carrie ran over to me and jumped on me. "Hi, angel." She kissed me hard, holding my face with her hands. "I brought you some presents, want to see?"

She kissed me again then jumped off with a squeal and ran to hug the teenagers she had practically adopted.

Todd helped Carter stay under the blanket until they got inside. All the soldiers were standing around now, watching the three very large wolves. Their faces showed a mix of confusion and wariness. The wolves just stood in the middle of the compound until Reyes came running over with their pants from earlier.

"I wasn't sure, but I thought you might like these." He set them down carefully and backed away slowly, like the wolves might bite him if he moved too fast.

Hill's growl was playful and turned into a human laugh as he shifted and grabbed his pants. "It's still me in there. I'm not going to bite you. And even if I did, nothing would happen… except maybe a little bleeding." He ignored the cursing, gasps, and yells from his subordinates.

A door to the van in the front of their caravan opened and a woman came walking out. "Alpha, we appreciate your help." She showed him her neck and bowed to him. "But do you mind if we join the rest of our pack now. We have many pups that miss their parents. They attended the human school and could not get home."

"Yes. Your pack waits for you. And welcome home, female."

In her excitement, she jumped on him and kissed his cheek, then ran back to her van. Soon, all the new cars were gone.

We could hear more cars in the distance though. People were running.

"You are going to have more visitors soon, Alpha." I warned him.

"My men will direct them, let's get inside and talk to the kids."

Carrie had already herded them all inside, and even had a spread of food ready for them. Carter was hovering not that far off, his eyes on my men as we stepped in. I heard him sniff the air a few times and huff.

"So that smell had nothing to do with age, then? I figured as much after speaking with Curtis, but I guess I still hoped."

I laughed as I walked over and pulled him in for a hug. "No, these men are from my clan, they are just like me, although all of them are older. Believe it or not, I am the youngest in my clan. Clint over there is, what 1500?"

"1638, your highness."

More than one of the humans in the room were cursing under their breaths. Even Carter's eyes were bugging out.

"Carter? What now? Are you working with us, or are you going on your own again?" Carrie asked him.

Carter looked at her and then shivered in a bit of fear. She laughed.

"I told Deacon that I would be on your side. Whatever he needs."

We all watched Carrie, waiting.

Carter visibly melted with relief when she nodded and turned back to the twins.

"What about you all? Do you have anywhere we can take you? Any family?"

"No." Layla shook her head. "None of us have anyone. All of us only had family in Cali. Can't we come with you? You know the government will separate us and put us in foster care. Well, except Scott. And Todd."

Carrie looked up at the latter. "My 18th birthday was a few days ago."

Carter grinned and chuckled like he was remembering something. Todd looked at him and blushed. Guess they spent it together.

My angel looked at me, pleading. They followed her gaze. What was that I said about her *practically* adopting them? Guess she was going to make it official in her own way.

"Please, Deacon? We can still be donors if you need us. You know we don't mind." Rachel practically begged.

"I wouldn't mind if they came back with us, my King." Steve popped in, winking at the kids. The others echoed his statement.

I sighed. "Fine, but just so you know, I have hundreds of clan members, so you better make sure you pay attention. If you tell them you need a few days, they will listen."

"Umm, Deac. Please tell me you aren't still at the house in Vegas." Carter spoke up cautiously.

"We are, why?"

Carter's curse was mumbled as he rubbed a hand over his face and freshly shaved head. He wasn't completely bald but was close enough. "You're going to want to move, like now. Curtis had you all followed. As soon as the dagger was out, Lucas sent it with another man, under orders to join the vamp who was following you. I'm guessing they stayed with you all the way to wherever."

"That's how they knew where to find your father." Colton said somberly. "We need to move houses. The house in the Rockies should be safe."

I scowled at him. "We are not hiding in caves."

"Your father had a home built after you left." Colton cleared his throat. "Just in case you decided to come home, my Lord."

Ouch, that hurt.

My angel felt that dagger with me. A tear slipped out and she reached for my hand. "That sounds perfect then, Colton. Call the staff we left behind. Tell them to pack up as fast as possible. And to leave before the sun goes down. I'm assuming they know where it is?"

I swallowed the lump of sadness in my throat, while my angel gave instructions.

"Where in the Rockies?" Hill stepped closer.

"Near Grand Junction." Colton answered for me, reading my face while my angel read my heart.

"The Rockies pack can swing by and make sure the place is safe, they are located near there. I can call them."

"That would be wonderful, thank you, Captain." Carrie answered before turning to the kids. "Well, looks like we have a long drive ahead of us. Why don't you all use the bathroom now, so we don't have to stop for a while. It's right out front and to the right. Clint, Tyson, and Robert, will you please go get our cars. We might as well load up from here. The rest of you, go with Sergeant Reyes and see if they need help directing the refugees."

Without argument, everyone dispersed, leaving us and Carter alone. My angel stood up and wrapped her arms around me. Colton sent a message to the staff, then went over to Carter and started getting any information he could out of him.

I buried my face in my Angel's neck and let her comfort me, just as I promised I would. It was easier to do than I thought it would be.

Chapter 12

Colton

I spoke to Carter for nearly an hour, bleeding him dry for every detail since Deacon jumped the wall. Some of it was unnecessary, but I didn't want to trust his opinion on what was important and what wasn't.

That, and I wanted to give Carrie time to comfort Deacon.

I purposely kept that information from him all these years. I was waiting for him to show signs of wanting to return home. I didn't want him to think he had to go back, just because his father built him a house.

Deacon had been happy for the last century. These last few months with Carrie were beyond that. He would have ended up leaving the bar, regardless of Carrie's involvement. But without her, he would have been bitter about it. Not now though.

Carter stressed having followed my advice, and letting Curtis take the witch from him. I let him think he had a choice. After hearing the story, it was all the witch's doing, not Carter's.

I wondered though. Did she know why the waterfall would affect Curtis like it did?

Why did he nearly drain her?

How did he heal so fast from a dagger in the heart?

So many questions I had now, but no one around who would know the answers. Maybe I could speak with some of the others when they returned. Which reminded me, I should send a message to the search teams we sent out. They needed to direct those they found to Colorado now.

After Dominic died, we had contacted everyone we could. The ones who didn't shy away from technology anyway. There were many that preferred to live off the grid, so to speak.

I stepped away from Carter, who seemed grateful to be out of the spotlight, and sent the messages. They all replied quickly.

With everyone warned, I pulled up the map app on my phone and began plotting out routes. It had been a good deal of time since I went to the house in the Rockies. Plus, I didn't want to risk Curtis following us again. If we drove only during the day, we limited those chances. We wouldn't take a straight path either.

Once I settled on a route, I made reservations for five bedrooms at a hotel about halfway there. One for my mates and me. Three with two queen size beds, for those with us. And the last, for the housing staff, whenever they arrived. I was sure no one would mind doubling, or even tripling up, in the beds. It wasn't uncommon.

Vampires craved companionship, wherever it would come from. Speaking of companionship.

"Carter, the back of the building is under constant shade from the buildings and the trees. Stretch your legs, we are only driving during the day." I pointed to the back door.

Carter grimaced. “Yeah, that’s probably a good idea.” He opened the back door a pinch, looked out carefully, then stepped out.

I walked back to my mates, who were sitting on the couch, Carrie on Deacon’s lap. She lifted her legs and I slid under them, sitting by his side. We were in nearly the same position we had been in last night.

“Everything planned out?” Deacon asked solemnly.

“Yes.” I gripped the back of his neck with my large palm and brought his head over, kissing his forehead. He grumbled. Carrie giggled. “How are you?”

Deacon huffed. I knew his annoyance was just an act though. “Better now. It was just a shock. I chose to stay away from home for stupid, childish reasons. I missed a lot of time with my father. But I am grateful for the time we did have.”

“You had many centuries together. I wish I had had that much with my parents. It doesn’t matter how much time we had with them. It is never enough. He knew you loved him though. Parents always know.” Carrie tucked her head into his neck.

I moved my hand to wrap around his shoulders, my other hand gripped tightly to Carrie’s thighs. She rolled her eyes at me. Deacon and I both chuckled.

“Did you plan everything out?” Deacon asked me again, his free hand, the one not wrapped around our mates back, held my leg that was next to him. He sounded better, so I gave him more than a one word answer this time.

“Yes. We will drive to Flagstaff today. I made reservations at a Holiday Inn there. We can sleep, meet up with the staff, and then continue on the next day to the new place.”

“Why not just drive straight there? Won’t this take longer?” Carrie asked softly.

I lifted my hand and stroked the back of her head, playing with her beautiful blonde hair for a moment, before putting it back on her thigh.

“This gives us more time to watch for a tail. I also want to avoid driving at night, to cut down on the possibilities. I’m taking every precaution I can.”

She nodded and closed her eyes with a small, tired sigh.

“Are you alright, sweetheart?”

She laughed softly. “I’m fine.”

“She’s tired.” Deacon added with a low growl.

“That doesn’t mean I’m not fine.”

Deacon growled again, this time more playfully. We both laughed at him.

“We should start moving soon. With this many humans in our group, we will need to stop more often.”

“If you are ready to leave, then why is your hand moving northward?” Carrie opened her eyes and glared at me.

“I said we should. I did not say I was ready to. Besides, my hand isn’t the only one moving off a leg.” I glanced down to my lap, where my zipper was sliding down. A shiver ran through me as Deacon’s hand made contact.

I leaned my head on the wall, my eyes closed, and my own hand sliding into place on Carrie. I heard Deacon’s zipper next and chuckled. The idea of each of us handling each other pushed me further on. It didn’t take long, not that it ever did with my mates.

A few minutes later, we stepped out onto the front porch. We walked with Carrie to the port-a-potties, giving her a minute. When they saw us, our men signaled the humans, and they all gathered around our cars.

“Where’s Carter?” Todd asked, looking around to the side of the building.

“In the back. Grab the tarp and go get him.”

The kid didn’t even question me, he just did as I told him. Five minutes later, with Carter hunched under a large tarp, he returned.

We now had four vehicles. The three SUVs and Deacon’s truck. We came with fifteen of us, and we were now leaving with twenty-two. The truck was going to be needed.

“Clint, Tyson, and I, will drive the SUVs. Steve, you mind driving Deacon’s truck?”

“Nope.” He held a hand up and Deacon tossed him the keys.

He lifted an eyebrow and Layla shrugged, stepping over to join him.

I chuckled. “Alright. We’ll take Carter in the SUV with us. Richard as well.”

“I’m with Carter. I can make sure the tarp stays over him.”

Deacon laughed quietly at my side, causing Todd to blush a little again.

“Fine. The rest of you, split in half, and load up the other two SUVs.”

Richard helped Todd get Carter into the back, before climbing into the front passenger seat. Deacon then helped Carrie into the middle row.

I watched the others, making sure everyone got loaded up. Scott and Rachel went to the middle car. Justin and Raya went to the back one. I was honestly surprised. I had expected them all to try and ride together. Our other ten men split up, five in each car.

Deacon and I said farewell to Hill and loaded in, both of us feeling better with the knowledge that no one was being left behind.

We stopped a little after noon, to get lunch for the humans. Then again an hour later, Carrie had to use the restroom, again.

Deacon took her inside a Walmart, while everyone else waited in the cars. The others had a tighter fit, getting in and out wasn't easy. At least that was how Carrie excused it. I was pretty sure they were all plenty comfortable. At least our men were. They hadn't had willing females in a while. It only took one glance at the truck to confirm my suspicions. The second we parked, Layla was moving to Steve's lap, letting him sink into her in every way possible. I did a quick check at the other cars, making sure we were all close and safe.

I wasn't even paying attention to the actions in my own vehicle, until Richard whimpered and shifted in his seat.

I looked over at him and laughed as he released himself from the prison known as pants. There was a time when they weren't so constricting. Modern technology wasn't always such a good thing.

"You alright over there?"

He huffed then looked over at me, his eyes roving up and down my body. "How tightly are you bound in your mating?"

I gave one loud laugh. "Too tight. You're on your own."

He cursed and looked to the back. My eyes followed him. Todd had shifted so he was stretched across the back seat, his bottom half was covered by the tarp. He had his head against the side window, his face giving everything away.

I hadn't noticed the sounds before, or the scent filling the car. Guess I had gotten used to blocking all of that out when I helped Deacon in the bar. Especially over the last few months. While we both would have loved to participate in certain activities, Carrie refused. Unlike Deacon, I didn't expect that to change, nor did I care as much.

"Think they'd mind one more?" Richard's eyes were still locked on them in the back, his reaction to their shared arousal scent hanging from his clothes.

Todd lifted a hand and answered the question with an inviting wave. Within seconds, the middle seat was folded, and Richard was leaning over Todd's head, which had graciously lowered to relieve him of his problem.

Now that my brain was fully aware of the scent, and the actions, I was beginning to have my own problems. I stepped out of the car and leaned against my closed door. I whimpered quietly, debating on stepping further away so I couldn't hear them. I forgot how loud Richard could be. It may have been a few hundred years, but there was a time I didn't say no to his propositions.

I never really thought about it much, but somewhere along the way, Deacon became the only man I engaged in anything with. I used human women from time to time, but never my own people. Only Deacon. They just stopped appealing to me. I started spending more and more time away from our clansmen, and more time with Deacon. Even when we both still lived with the clan, I spent most of my time with him.

The first time we shared was when we first started traveling. It was his first time trying for an heir. The woman he had picked worshiped him like a god. But he quickly grew bored with her. He thought for sure she would be strong enough to last full term, which was the only reason he kept trying. One night, he knew she was expecting him, but he didn't have the ambition to go.

"Why don't you just pick another, my Prince?" I asked him, not for the first time. He was such a whiner.

He hmphed and fell onto the bed. I sat next to him. He turned his head to look at me, then he really started looking at me.

"What?" I asked with one eyebrow up. He was cooking something up.

"My problem with Patricia is that she no longer appeals to me. I fear that I will not be able to do the deed needed to be done to get her pregnant."

"Again, why don't you pick another woman?" Duh.

"Because this one is strong and healthy. It is not just about appeal, but also about her ability to actually bear the child."

I sighed and leaned back on the headboard of his bed. "What can I do to help, my Lord?"

His grin grew wicked. I knew he had a plan. He was just waiting for me to bite. "Come with me. Help me."

"Help you how?"

"You know how. Get me to the point I need to be at. You help me get there, then I can plant my seeds in her soil."

I guffawed at his analogy. Ah to be young again. "You never participated with any of the males at home before. Why now?"

He shrugged and jumped off the bed, already assuming my answer. "They don't appeal to me either."

I stood and followed him to the door. "And I do?"

We had only done it a few times when he was younger and curious. He grew up around it but hadn't tried it. I offered to help, he accepted. When he was in need, and couldn't get relief elsewhere, I helped him out. He was always kind enough to return the favor.

Deacon scratched his head awkwardly. He had only recently started growing out his hair, it now reached past his ears.

"You are my friend, Colton. You don't treat me like I am still a child. Now, are you going to help me or not?"

I bowed my head to him slightly. "I am at your service, for whatever you need, my Prince."

He laughed and led us out the door. Patricia was both somewhat offended and somewhat excited by the prospect of the two of us. I hardly touched her. I wasn't there for her. Deacon reacted quickly to my touch, we also continued on longer than we needed to. She wasn't the only one that he planted seed in. After that night, he gave up on her.

He often lost appeal to the women he chose and had to call for my aide. A few times I randomly picked women for us to use together. I hadn't thought about it until Richard asked for help, but Deacon was the only vampire I'd been with in nearly two centuries.

Well, male ones anyway. The female Nightwalkers were occasionally a bit of fun. They had a ruthlessness to them that soaked into all aspects of their lives.

I shouldn't have let my mind wander into the past, and my history with Deacon. Mix that with the sounds Richard was making, and I was in quite the state. My jeans turned into a jail cell of their own, and that zipper wasn't helping. The slightest rub from it was liable to set me off.

I was saved when I finally saw my two mates walking back, Deacon had one hand around our pregnant mate, and a large bag in his other. He raised an eyebrow at me, then laughed as Richard's groans reached his ears. Carrie just looked at us, confused.

As soon as they were close enough, I grabbed them both. I placed Carrie right between us and crashed my lips to Deacon's. It wasn't long before he pushed me against the car, both of us feeling up the glue that kept us all together. Our lips soon separated and took possession of different sides of her neck.

Once we were all satisfied, and I was relaxed again, we helped her fix her clothes. Then we fixed our own. She cared more than we did. And her goods were only for our viewing pleasure.

"Dare I ask where all that came from?" She asked breathlessly, perfectly content in letting us redress her.

"Not my fault, they started it." I threw a thumb toward the back of our car.

"And what? You saw them and thought you would like some midday fun?"

Deacon chuckled and slid his arm around her waist. "It's the scent, angel. When it reaches a certain point, our bodies react. You know how much we depend on our sense of smell for things."

"Yes, but it didn't bother you this bad in the bar."

"It was more spread out then. Besides, we did do things in the bar, you just limited what we could do. And then we attacked you after closing." I kissed her softly. "Confined spaces make it harder to ignore. Richard ended up having to join them."

She thought about this hard, her face almost in a scowl, but not quite. Then she nodded and opened the back door. She didn't even put her foot all the way in before she rocked backward, nearly falling on Deacon.

"Angel, what's wrong?" Deacon was worried and beginning to panic.

"That smell. What is that smell?"

I pressed my lips together, trying not to laugh as she practically moaned with pleasure.

Deacon sniffed again. "The sweet one?"

Carrie's eyes closed and her body sank into his. "Yes." She licked her lips, and sniffed deeper, slower. "It makes me feel… I'm not sure I can describe it."

I stepped in front of her and slid my hand back into her pants and between her thighs, feeling the warmth. "You don't need to, sweetheart. This is what we were just talking about." Her hips desperately moved against my hand.

"How am I able to smell it now? I never have before."

Deacon's hand slid down the front of her shirt, which was tented up. "We told you, it's a more confined space this time, mixed with the pregnancy hormones, angel. Your sense of smell is increasing. As is your reaction to them."

She moaned as we helped her through it. "It's too soon. I'm not even a month along yet."

Deacon held that part of her up for me and I bent down to do what he couldn't from behind. While my teeth were busy, he answered her questions.

"You are growing a supernatural baby. We don't know the timeline. It has been too long. When we get home, we can do some research. Maybe your mother's books have answers."

Carrie didn't speak again until we finished helping her out. The door had been left open, so the car aired out some. When she came back to her senses, she blushed and buried her head in my chest.

"No saying you hate us this time, sweetheart." I laughed when she hit my chest. "If we hadn't done it, which nobody saw by the way, you would have eventually ended up straddling Deacon in the car. And everyone would have seen that."

She nodded, whimpering at the same time.

"What did you guys buy? I thought this was just a bathroom stop?"

"She was cold, so I got her a blanket for the rest of the trip. It will only get colder the closer we get. Once we get to Colorado, she will need warmer clothes." Deacon set the bag down inside.

I frowned. I hadn't thought of that.

We climbed back in the car and started on the road again. I glanced at Richard, who was back in his seat, and chuckled. His face was more relaxed now.

"Feeling better?"

He sighed dramatically and patted his lap. "Much. Sorry about that."

I looked in the rearview mirror when I heard the low, possessive growl.

"Why is he sorry, exactly?"

Carrie laughed and patted Deacon's chest, trying to calm him. Richard gulped.

"He doesn't need to be. It was an honest question. All he asked was how tight our bond was. Then he joined them in the back. At least he had enough common sense to ask instead of only assuming. Calm down."

"My apologies, your highness. I heard the rumors, but that is all. I will make sure the others know as well." Richard was practically begging for forgiveness for his honest question.

Carrie tipped up and whispered in Deacon's ear, something the two of us up front, and Carter in the back, could hear perfectly. It was all reassurances and reminders of our loyalty to each other. He could be such a hot head sometimes. And more possessive than most.

Some mornings I fully expected to wake up back in that bar, sleeping alone. The whole thing being a dream. It wasn't in Deacon's nature to share.

We drove the last two hours in silence. Well, mostly silence. Carter must have been really bored trapped under that tarp. Carrie struggled again but wouldn't let Deacon do anything about it. We were all shifting uncomfortably by the time Todd rolled over and got on his own knees.

Thankfully, we were pulling up to the hotel right about that time. The four of us practically jumped out of the SUV, gasping for air.

"Maybe we should take the truck tomorrow? Just the three of us." Carrie whispered, jumping up and down, shaking her arms out.

"You should probably stop jumping like that, angel." Deacon's eyes were following every movement of her chest.

"Why?"

"Because you weren't the only one trying to keep it together in there. And the way you are moving… I'm about ready to take you right here, where everyone will be watching."

I laughed at how fast she stopped and stepped away from him. Deacon's chuckle darkened as he hunched down, ready to chase and pounce. Her step away was a challenge. Judging by the way her eyes widened, Carrie knew it too.

I put a hand on his shoulder, gripping it tight. "Soon, mate. Soon." I saw the darkened flames of Deacon's fire brimming in his eyes as he turned to me. It was my turn to gulp. He was barely on the edge.

"A few more minutes, my Lord. Deep breaths. While she would cave to you, she would also be very mad at you when it was over."

Deacon blinked a few times, the fire dimming to a controllable level, and straightened back up. He lifted one hand and Carrie took it with a sigh.

"I'm going to go check us in."

She nodded at me as Deacon pulled her into his chest, holding tight. His way of begging for her forgiveness for his lack of control.

Carrie knew what he needed. She always did. She knew his predator side needed to come out. As soon as the hotel room door was open, she took off running. She barely made it the ten feet to the bed before he caught her, but the small chase had been enough.

I sat in one of the recliners and enjoyed the show, giving him time to claim his fated mate and settle his predatory side back down. When he was ready, he lifted a hand to me, and I joined them.

Around midnight, Carrie's dinner dishes empty and sitting to the side, Deacon gave her the nourishment that only he could provide, and then drank what he needed. I held them both for the few minutes it took. I then happily helped them burn off the aftereffects.

Carrie yawned and gripped my waist tighter. She snuggled into my chest, with Deacon pressed behind her. "When was the last time you fed, Colton?"

I tilted my head to the right. I hadn't actually thought about it. "A while, I guess."

"You need to feed soon. We need you strong as well." Deacon told me somberly. I could hear a touch of guilt from him. He got to feed from our mate. I could not.

“I’m fine.” I tried to argue. I got two scowls back. I shook my head with an amused huff. “Fine. I will use one of the kids tomorrow. Would that make you both happy?”

“Use Layla. She doesn’t care much for guys and won’t try anything.” Carrie’s eyes were already closed again, a smile playing on her lips.

Deacon and I both laughed quietly.

I bent down to kiss the top of her head. “Whatever my Queen wishes.”

She had just fallen asleep when a heavy fist knocked on the door.

Deacon started to get up, knowing I had purposely not vacated her premises yet. I didn’t get her blood, so he could deal with letting me have a little longer in there. I waved him off and slowly vacated her playground. She frowned, but her eyes did not open. I could have let him go, so she and I could stay as we were, but I wasn’t sure who was there.

I bent down to the peep hole in the door and relaxed. I opened the door, not caring about my state of undress, or the liquid that was still coating me.

“Bryant. I was beginning to worry. Did you all just arrive?”

He bowed slightly, something he didn’t have to do since I was only the General. However, seeing as I was mated to the King and Queen, the older vampires felt the need for more respect.

“Yes, my Lord.” He lifted a small backpack. “You asked that we bring this to you, instead of putting it in the moving trucks.”

I smiled and took it. “Yes, thank you. This will make the Queen very happy in the morning. Did all go well with the packing and getting here.”

"Yes. However…" He appeared to be wary as he looked up and down the hall.

I stepped back, opening the door the rest of the way, and waited while he came inside.

Deacon covered Carrie with a blanket, and sat up, listening in. Bryant bowed slightly toward the bed, then gave me his attention again.

"A few minutes ago, one of the perimeter alarms was triggered. I pulled up one of the gate cameras and watched as a dozen men approached the house… They torched it." He lifted his phone, the camera still on. The entire house was engulfed in flames.

"Was everyone gone?"

"Yes. The house was empty, save for the basic furniture. The files, all the important things, are downstairs in the truck." I closed my eyes and rubbed my hand down my face. "What would you have us do now, General Colton?"

I opened my eyes again, my hand still on my chin. "The front desk has a key to a room for you all. Get some rest. We are meeting in the dining hall at breakfast."

Bryant lifted an eyebrow at me. Since when did we care about breakfast?

"The humans we rescued requested coming home with us. They were donors for us in the bar. They are also friends of our Queen. They offered to continue that role. They will need to eat before we leave, as will the Queen. Her pregnancy is moving faster than we expected."

"It has been far too long, but I do believe that is normal. We have many histories of our people. When we arrive, we can research it."

I could hear Deacon sigh at the same time I did. “That would be wonderful. Thank you, Bryant. Now. Go. Sleep. I will need you to lead the way tomorrow. It has been more than a few decades since I was last there.”

He bowed again and walked out of the room. I locked the door behind him and turned around. Deacon was already standing at the other end of the small hallway, leaning against the divider between the bathroom/closet area, and the rest of the room.

“What troubles you?”

I leaned against the door, letting my head fall back. “It was close, too close. If Carter hadn’t told us, then we would have gone straight back to Vegas. We all would have been sleeping when Curtis took his revenge.”

“You think that’s what this was?”

“Yes. I see no other reason why he would attack now. Not if he knew where we were all along.” I sighed and pinched my nose.

I opened my eyes when I heard his heavy footsteps on the carpet coming closer.

“What else is bothering you?” I huffed and shook my head. “I know you just as well as you know me.”

I grunted. “I am feeling guilty.”

That surprised him. “For what?”

“I should have paid better attention after we rescued the two of you. That is my job and I failed. I was so caught up in my own relief that I got too relaxed. Too comfortable.” I closed my eyes again and turned away from him in shame.

“Hey. None of that.” He put both hands on my face and turned me back to him, much in the way I’d seen him do to Carrie. “You weren't the only one there. Nor were you the one who actually had to fight Curtis back. No one caught on. No one noticed. It didn't even cross our minds that he knew where the house was, even after he killed my father."

"Yes, but…" I chuckled. Deacon pulled my move to shut me up.

"You were right. That is very effective."

I didn't let him keep talking. He was right, we should have done this long ago. The only thing better than kissing Deacon was kissing Carrie.

We stayed where we were, not wanting to disturb our pregnant mate. We had worn her out enough for one evening.

Chapter 13

Grace

When I opened my eyes again, they were crusted over, my body was stiff as a board, and I *really* had to pee.

I looked around the room, getting a good look at it for the first time. It wasn't a large room per se, but it was large enough for a double size bed, a dresser, and a small closet. There were two doors. One to the bathroom that supposedly connected mine and Curtis' rooms, and the other, probably to the hall. On the right side, I saw a large window, with a bench under it. The bench had a small door on the seat, revealing a cubby inside which was filled with blankets and sheets. I looked out the window curiously, and saw the pool, then grass, then the ocean.

Off to one side, I could barely see the beginning of another building. The guest house, maybe?

Near that, sat two helicopters. One we had flown in on. The other looked more military, the only windows being the front ones that the pilots used. Curtis' council must have gotten here early then because the sun was barely beginning to set. I had to wonder if they were still sitting inside the helicopter, protected from the sun, waiting for it to be safe to come inside the house.

I walked over and debated which door led to the bathroom. I hadn't yet gotten dressed, since I wasn't sure where my bag was and my need for the bathroom was gaining by the second.

One of the doors was on a flat wall. The other was on a wall that was at an angle and pushed out more. Taking my chances, I opened the latter.

Score!

Woah.

This had to be the fanciest, and the largest, bathroom I had ever seen. Perks of being a spy I guess.

There was no door leading to the master suite, it was wide open. I took a quick peek and saw that Curtis was still sleeping.

Not wanting to disturb him, and praying he wasn't the kind to watch a girl pee, I tiptoed to a small door next to the pool size tub. I sighed with relief at the sight of porcelain. I was even more relieved after a gallon of pee came out of me.

The shower looked too tempting to ignore. I carefully slid the glass door open and stepped inside. We could have fit half our little group in there if we wanted too. It wouldn't have been the first time we showered together. All we had in the shelter was the locker room showers. With the creepy manager sneaking around, we chose to stick together at those times. It was also where Todd realized he had a thing for doing things in the open.

I stood under the hot water, letting it massage my sore muscles. They felt like I hadn't moved in days.

I jumped, startled, when two large hands landed on my shoulders and started rubbing them.

"You slept a long time. You had me worried."

I lifted my head and looked over my shoulder. Curtis' black hair was just long enough to stick up when in a mess, and he had black fuzz all over his jaw.

"How long did I sleep?"

"Two days."

"Two days?" I spun around to face him as my voice echoed around the shower.

My eyes widened as I took all of him in again. They jumped back up to his face and I felt the blush rise for real. I obviously hadn't thought it all the way through before I turned to face him.

His chuckle was low and deep as his hands slid down my back until they were low enough to grip me. He took that last step, making it impossible for even air to be between us. I swallowed the whimper when something far from small pressed against me.

"Yes. It's not often I see humans sleep for so long."

"I never have before. Why didn't you wake me?" I glanced around the bathroom, my brain beginning to function again, finally. "Where are we anyway? Last thing I remember was flying over the desert."

"We are at my home in this region. As for why I didn't wake you, well, I did take a lot of blood from you and your body shut down to begin replenishing it. We will have to make sure you drink plenty of water and eat only healthy food today."

I nodded slowly, like that made sense. It didn't. How could I sleep for two days? How much did I miss? I cursed at myself for slacking off.

Curtis brought a hand forward and lifted my chin up.

"You did nothing wrong. I can smell the panic rising within you. Why are you afraid?"

I wasn't really sure how to answer that one. I chewed on my lip and looked down, trying to buy time until I could think of the best response. Probably not the best place to look.

Was there nothing small about this vamp?

"Are you afraid I will punish you?"

I nodded. Sure, let's go with that. Curtis pushed me through the water and against the wall, his very thick thigh coming between my legs.

"I will not punish you for something so simple. I expect you to take care of your body. I expect you to stay healthy. If you really feel that bad about it though, you are welcome to make it up to me. I will never complain when you wish to take care of my needs."

Good to know.

I looked up at him again, then glanced down, like I was asking permission. He just laughed and moved his leg, while getting a grip of my hair. He coaxed me many times, calling me his little witch over and over again.

Curtis stood back a few minutes later and watched as I washed my hair and body. Someone had stocked up the shower with more than just men's soap. Of which I was very grateful. I stood under the water longer, letting the water soothe my aching muscles, and enjoying the few minutes of respite.

I hadn't thought about the effect waterfalls had on him though. Oops.

He turned off the water and lifted me up. Curtis had much better balance in the shower than Todd did. He did a lot of things better than Todd and Carter. I also wasn't having to remind myself to shut my brain down so he would get the reactions he wanted. He was such a big man that I had no room left for rational thought.

I was going to have to be more careful than I originally expected.

I was surprised when he lowered me back down and opened the shower. “You aren’t going to feed from me?”

“Not for a while, no. I took too much the other day. I needed it, yes, but it nearly killed you.” He handed me a folded towel off a shelf. “How often did Carter feed from you?”

“Every day. Never as long as you did, of course. But he fed from both Todd and me every day. Sometimes twice a day.”

Curtis frowned in disappointment. “He is turning into a glutton. You do taste divine, but that is no excuse. We do not need to drink blood that often.”

“In the beginning, it wasn’t as often. He would visit us near the shelter every few days. We didn’t like it there, so we asked to go with him. He promised to take care of us.” I shrugged. “We had more food, heat, and real beds with him. That was when he started to feed more.”

I started to wrap my towel around me, but he took it back with a grin. Now I knew. I walked into my room, and he followed.

“Do you know where my bag is?”

“Closet. Did Carter share you with the others?”

I shook my head as I pushed the folding doors to the small hole in the wall open. My bag lay on the floor, unopened. I carefully pulled the tennis shoes out and set them in a corner of the closet, out of immediate sight. I stepped back out, with the bag, and walked over to the dresser to unpack as I dressed.

"Me, no. We convinced him to bring our friends along so they could serve the others. Most of the humans in that area left or died in the bombings. The wall guards did not have easy access to food sources. I'm afraid it is too much for my friends to handle."

"We are sectioning off food centers wherever most of the vampires will be. Typically, the lower ranks don't have their own pets. They will have access to the centers though."

I nodded, pausing as I pulled pants out to put in a drawer. "Do you have a preference for what I wear? Carter only had certain times he cared. Given, I don't have much."

I turned part way to look at Curtis, he was sitting on my bed, leaning back on his hands. His only answer was a grin.

He wanted me to guess.

I pretended to hide a shy smile as I turned back. I pulled out the checkered skirt and matching crop top I once took out of an empty house, right before starting at the bar. He watched as I slid them on. The top was designed to look almost like a bow.

"You aren't in the desert anymore. It is colder outside here."

I shrugged and carried my now empty bag to the closet and dropped it on top of the shoes. "Like I said, I don't have much. Am I allowed to go outside? Or walk around the house? I've never been to the beach before."

He raised one incredulous eye at me. "You lived in LA, yet you've never been to the beach?"

I shrugged again and walked closer to him. I hadn't really thought about what I would tell him regarding my life. I never thought he'd ask. Carter certainly never had.

"My mom was a drunk who made money selling herself, and conning people with her fake psychic abilities. After one of her marks killed her, I went into foster care. They weren't much better."

Curtis leaned forward, trying to hide the eagerness in his eyes. "Your mom was psychic?"

Oops. Good going, Grace.

I snorted in derision. "No, she knew she had no real gift. Which is probably why the mark killed her. She never made much from it, mostly because she targeted the desperate."

"What about you? Have you ever seen the future?" He was watching me very closely now.

Something in my eyes had him practically jumping off the bed and backing me into the wall. He sniffed again, going down deep into my neck.

"You're scared again. What has you so scared, little witch?"

I probably looked like a fish. Why did I mention my mom's stupid act? I could have left that part out!

"What have you seen?" A stupid traitorous tear slipped out of my eye. He licked it off, his tongue moving slowly. "I will only punish you when you do not listen and do as I say."

"I don't see much, just flashes, pictures really. They've never made sense to me. I didn't even realize they were anything until…"

"Until what little witch?"

I closed my eyes just for a minute, begging for guidance here. Flash one, I tell him about Carrie, and then things aren't so great for me and my friends. Flash two. I tell him something else. He would try to use me, but he would keep me even closer. I could see myself in many different cities with him.

Curtain two it was then.

"Until we met Carter. I kept seeing images of him. And then he was there."

"Interesting. Have you seen anything else?"

I chewed on my lip, not having to act nervous at all. I was completely terrified. His hand slid up and down my arm, as though he were trying to comfort me.

"Yes. You. I saw an image of you."

"What about me, little witch?"

"I don't know. I told you. I don't understand these things. I was always afraid to say anything to people." I let my tone turn defensive. "What was I supposed to say? Hi! My name is Grace, my mother was a known con, but I saw a building blow up in my head." I scoffed. "I have always tried to ignore them. I thought I was crazy. I heard Carter mention your name a few days ago, and then images of you started popping into my head. And then there you were, standing by the poolside. I didn't even know I was a witch until you said something, and I still don't know what that means."

For once the tears were completely real, I was terrified of what would happen next. Yes, I saw it, but I didn't want him to know the full strength of my abilities.

Why the hell couldn't someone else have been the spy instead of me?

Why couldn't I have escaped with my friends?

Curtis cupped both my cheeks in his hands, his eyes danced with delight. "Have no fear, little witch. I will not ridicule you. You are back among your own people again, the magical people. I've known a few psychic witches in my time. I will guide you and help you. All I ask is that you obey me in return. I will protect you."

I had a huge lump in my throat, so my voice cracked. "What about when you visit the other regions? I heard your announcement through the drones. You are always going to be on the move. People have never been nice to me. They always knew I was different." That wasn't a far stretch of the truth.

His lips were actually quite soft against mine. "No one will ever dare touch you again. You will come everywhere with me. You will be my secret weapon until we get what we want."

I sniffled, my eyes went to his lips as he moved away, and he smiled. "What do we want?"

"For humans to take their rightful place at our feet. The magical beings once ruled this land, we will do so again. And you will help me. You *will* help me. That is why you kept seeing me. You were meant to rule by my side."

Say what now? "I thought I was your pet? I don't have very much witch's blood in me."

He shook his head slowly. "You have more power than many of the full-blooded witches I have met. We will let them all believe that you are nothing more than a pet, but when I get my throne, I will need a Queen by my side. One who can see ahead, one who will do my bidding," his hand slid down to my stomach, "and one that will bear my heir."

"But… I thought…"

He lifted one finger to my lips. "The time has not yet come to tell all our secrets, my queen." His lips were not so soft this time.

Queen? He wanted me to be his queen????

Chapter 14

Grace

"I have another meeting with my council this evening, you are coming with me. When it is over, you will come back and rest. A meal will be brought to you." Curtis informed me as he slid me back down to the floor.

I was sure this was going to become a regular thing if he planned on getting me pregnant. Thankfully I still had the IUD in. What do you know? Mom actually did something right for me. That was a first.

"Whatever you wish, master." I purred, earning a small growl. Curtis pulled me to his room roughly, and I giggled. And internally rolled my eyes.

The eye roll was important to help me remember who I was. I couldn't let myself get sucked into this. I mean, holy crap. Curtis was way hotter than Carter and Todd, combined. Hell, he was *bigger* than the two combined. He also knew what he was doing, and he did it very well.

And, come on, who wouldn't want to be told she was going to be a queen?

And there might be a really small part of me that wanted revenge on all the bullies when I was a kid. Not enough to want world domination though. I think.

He let go of me as we stepped into his room, moved to his dresser, and pulled out clothes. And something that looked like a dog collar. I blinked and stumbled back in surprise at the speed he dressed at.

Even when Carter was in a hurry he wasn't that fast. I had only seen one other vampire do that. I was sure the other could too, I just never saw it.

Curtis was not a Nightwalker.

No wonder he was keen to impregnate me. He had a smirk on his face as he walked back to me at a normal pace, thankfully.

"When you go places with me, you must wear this. At least for now. When I announce you as my Queen, then you can take it off. For now, they must see you as my pet. No one can know what we truly are. If you have a vision, then you must tell me without alerting the others. Do you understand?"

I nodded. "I think so. I am not your pet, but I must act like it until the right time?" He had no idea how true that was.

"Yes, my little witch." He lifted the collar up and snapped it around my neck. It was black and had small spikes on it. A thin leash was attached to the back of it.

I closed my eyes and hummed. He chuckled. "Do you like toys, my Queen?"

I felt his teeth scrape along my jaw, and I shivered.

"I've never tried them… my King."

I yelped when I was suddenly airborne and landing on the bed. His pants were gone faster than they were put on.

"Say it again." He commanded as he lowered himself onto me, his hand rotating slowly, wrapping the leash around his wrist.

Note to self, he really liked to be called King.

Half an hour later, he led me down the hall. His hand was on my butt possessively, the leash in his other hand. We entered a room with half a dozen vampires sitting at a table. They all stood when we came in.

"Look who has finally woken up." Lucas grinned, winking at me.

I scowled back at him, making the others laugh.

"Yes, as I said. I took a lot of blood from her. I assume you have made Candice comfortable by now?" Curtis pushed me closer to the table.

"She is right where I want her. Thank you again, my Lord, for your generosity." Lucas bowed to him.

I didn't want to know what that meant.

"Good, first order of business. Timothy, do you have the instrument I need?"

A vampire with long blonde hair, making him look like an Elf from Lord of the Rings, reached down to the floor, and picked up a bag that looked like a black, old school doctor's bag.

"Right here. Just as requested."

"Good, are we ready then?"

The others moved their chairs out of the way and stood three to each side. Curtis looked at me with a grin, picked me up and sat me on the table.

“Lay down, little witch.”

I lowered myself down, a bit apprehensively, knowing I had no other option. My heart raced, and I knew they could all smell my fear. Their grins widened, proving me correct.

“Now, now, little witch, no need to be scared.” It sounded like Curtis was taunting me. Which didn’t exactly help me much.

With a flick of his fingers, they all grabbed me. Lucas held my head, and the others held my arms and legs. Curtis walked around to the bag and pulled out what looked like a pair of really long tweezers.

“Pull her to the edge. Spread her legs and bend her knees.”

I screamed as I was yanked down roughly until my butt was nearly off the edge. I could barely see Curtis when he sat down in the only remaining chair.

“As long as you lay still, little witch, this won’t hurt at all.”

No matter how hard I tried, I couldn’t stop how hard I was shaking. I had no idea what they were gonna do.

The shaking slowed when I felt something unexpected, but welcome, considering the options. My eyes rolled to the back of my head, and my hips moved against the warm tongue. I looked down and saw the top of Curtis’ head between my thighs.

Each of the vampires in the room had glowing yellow eyes, and hungry looks on their faces. I let the shockwave he caused run through me, each of my limbs relaxing as it passed.

“Much better, kitty.” Curtis said softly.

I just hummed in return and then flinched when I felt something thin, cold, and hard move inside me. I squeaked when it pinched me, and nearly cried out as I felt something being roughly removed from inside me.

"And there it is. Just as I thought." Curtis announced triumphantly. "You can let her go now. Sit up, little witch."

I carefully pushed myself up and tried to figure out what he was holding. It was small, and somewhat white. But it also looked like it had melted.

"What is that?"

Curtis chuckled and tossed it into a trash can nearby. Then did the grossest thing ever and licked the tweezers like a popsicle stick.

"That, little witch, was all that was left of your IUD. When was it put in?"

"Um. I'm not sure, five years ago maybe. My mother insisted on it when I hit puberty. She died not much later. And the doctor who put it in seemed a bit sketchy. I don't even know if it is on my medical records. Did it always look like that?"

Curtis laughed again, unzipping his pants, and stepping up to me. "No, I melted it with my fire. I thought it would have fallen out by now, I got tired of waiting."

He nodded to the vamps standing next to him, they came around and grabbed my legs again, holding them up while Curtis went in with his own tool this time.

"Tell me what is going on in the Northern Region. Did you complete the census?"

He was seriously going to talk business, while taking care of… business?

Holding myself up was proving difficult, so I said screw it and laid back down. My top soon popped off and Curtis's hands were all that was covering me.

When he finished, he sat down and pulled me onto his lap, facing out towards the others. My legs were on either side of him, and I laid against his chest.

I closed my eyes, and for the first time, felt grateful the others hadn't come. Todd would have lost it for sure. I listened carefully as they spoke, waiting for them to say something to make all this worth it.

Suddenly, a flash ran through my mind. It only came with one, no accompanying alternatives. Deacon, Colton, and many others were running down the streets of Mojave. Todd covered Carter with a blanket in the truck. The wall became a lot smaller, the gate a lot bigger. Three wolves changed into men. Good looking men.

My friends were safe, that much I knew. I could also use some of this to prove my worth to Curtis. I turned my head to his ear and whispered, "let me turn around."

Without a second thought, he released me, and I stood up. Then straddled him again, this time facing him. His pants were still open - he had still been hanging out, rubbing against me.

I sank onto him, then rocked closer, leaning in again. "I had a flash." Curtis stopped talking as I barely breathed the words to keep the others from hearing, he covered it with moves of his own. "Part of the wall is missing. Mojave I think." I helped him finish from there.

"When was the last time anyone spoke to Carter?" He asked the room.

"Not since we were there a few days ago, why?" Lucas answered.

"Call them. Now." He commanded. He was getting mad and taking it out on my butt. He fixed my top, finally, when he was done. "I'm taking her back to the room. I expect someone to have gotten a hold of them before I return.

He pulled on my leash and made me walk faster. He didn't speak until we were in my room again. He unclipped the collar, set it on the dresser, and started taking my clothes off.

"Tell me what you saw." He commanded, pushing me onto the bed, face first.

"That was it." I gasped out as he slammed back into me. "I just saw a giant hole in the wall. It looked like the desert one in Mojave." I couldn't help the tears from how rough he was. "D… did I do something wrong?"

"No. On the contrary, you did something right. Very right." His hand rubbed me instead of hitting me the next time, then he moved away long enough to flip me over. He licked my tears away and softened all his moves.

"In time you will learn to like the rougher stuff. I promise." He kissed my stomach before backing away. "Rest now. I will have a meal left at your door in a few minutes. No one is allowed to come in here besides me. After you rest, I will take you shopping for more clothes. My future Queen needs more than a few sets."

I bit my finger and gave him a small smile, while I slid towards the pillows. "Thank you, master." He swiftly lifted one of my legs and spanked me again. He chuckled when my eyes rolled back.

I waited until I heard his footsteps travel down the hall, then scrambled to the phone. While it powered up, I pulled my clothes back on, jumped back in the bed, and laid under the covers, with the phone half under the pillow. I was met with a few missed messages.

Hill: What do you mean you're with him? What happened?

Hill: Fine, we have a plan to get your friends out. Stay safe.

Breathing a sigh of relief that they were soon to be out of harm's way now, far from Curtis' reach, I responded to the worrywart.

Me: Sorry, I am told I slept for two days. Don't ask, you don't want to know.

His response came so fast, he had to be waiting by the phone. I allowed myself one small laugh. It seemed true to his character.

Hill: You're right, I probably don't. How are you?
Me: No worse for the wear. So far he isn't so bad.
Me: They know where Deacon lives in Vegas.
Hill: We heard. Carter came with the kids.

I felt lighter. Good, I was worried Carter would be killed after this. He was a vamp I didn't mind so much.

Me: I don't have much time. There are secret doors in the walls, the new ones.
Hill: Where?
Me: Don't know yet. It was too vague.
Hill: Carrie had a dream. She was told your position changed. What happened?

Carrie had a dream? Did she see that weird lady too?

Me: A lot. No time to explain. Where are my friends?
Hill: They left with Deacon. They begged too.

I laughed quietly to myself. Of course, they would. There was a knock at my door, probably meaning my food was here.

Me: Gotta go. Will only msg when can. TTYL.
Hill: Good Luck.

I shut the phone off and a piece of the flash from earlier returned. It was a closer look at one of the men that had been a wolf. It was the same man I had been seeing regularly since Todd got the phone.

I received a flash of him every time I talked to Hill. I thought it might be him, mostly because it was all that made sense.

No one was in the hall when I opened the door, so I comfortably collected a tray with two covered plates, a bottle of water, and a glass of milk. I closed the door with my foot, smiling at the mouthwatering aroma coming from my hands.

I set it on the bed, then sat in front of it, my legs folding under me. I slowly lifted the larger lid off its plate. I licked my lips dramatically. Lying in front of me was basically food porn. A large slice of steak, juice still running from it. Next to it was a pile of mashed potatoes, and a double serving of steamed broccoli. The last was not exactly a favorite of mine, but I knew well enough that I needed to eat it. And not just because my body needed the vitamins.

I picked up the smaller cover and giggled with glee. A very large slice of chocolate cake, with chocolate frosting, and strawberry filling in the middle.

Ten minutes later, I set the tray aside and lay back on my pillows, the food coma quickly beginning to settle in. I was startled awake, sometime later, by a large hand on my cheek. I jumped slightly, giving off a small squeak.

"It's okay, little witch. It's just me. I am the only one with a key to our rooms. No one will ever be in here but me and you." Curtis' eyes glanced over to the empty tray, and he smiled. "I wasn't sure you would eat all of that."

I forced my body to relax back into the bed. "Normally, it would have been too much. But it has been a few days since I last ate." I couldn't help the small grin. "What happened to only eating healthy today?"

He chuckled and stood up from his heels before sitting on the bed next to me. His hand slid down to my neck.

"I don't just punish bad behavior. I like to reward good behavior too. You didn't fight me and my men earlier, nor did you question why I took that thing out of you. You also did well in only telling me about the vision. My little witch deserved a reward. Was it good?"

I licked my lips and he laughed. "Yes. I don't remember the last time I had cake. Or a fresh steak. Carter bought us food, but we had to teach ourselves how to cook it."

He stood back up and began unbuckling his pants. "I will make sure you have plenty of meat available to you. We need to keep your iron and protein levels up. The war is heating up, and I can't guarantee I won't need your blood to heal me again." I slowly rolled to my back as Curtis moved to the foot of the bed, then slowly climbed on. He grinned at me. "Such a good little witch. Shall I give you another reward?"

I bit the corner of my lip and nodded slowly, making him chuckle again. I mean, if I was going to basically be his little whore and personal blood bank, I should get something out of this. And he was *very* talented at it.

"I liked that outfit." I pouted a few minutes later. Curtis laughed from the other side of the bed. The checkered outfit now laid in shreds all over the bed and on the floor.

"I'll buy you a new one. I'll buy you anything you want."

I rolled to my side and curled into his arm, shocking him just a little. "I forgot you said we were going shopping tonight."

His hand carefully lowered to my shoulder, almost like he wasn't sure what to do next. It must have been a long time since he had any affection, if ever.

"Actually, we will have to put off the shopping trip for tonight. I need to go see the wall."

"What did Carter say when you called?"

Curtis gave out a low growl. "He didn't answer. It took some time, but we got a hold of someone else. It seems Deacon decided to come back for a visit. He came in with a mixed group of humans, Vampire Borns, and shifters… this morning." His body tensed up, and his fingers dug into my arm. "Psychic visions come *before* something happens. Yours came later. Why?"

I held my breath, trying not to freak out too much. "I don't know. I told you before. I don't know how these work. I was still sleeping this morning. Maybe it happened during a dream, and I was only remembering it." Curtis adjusted, moving to his side, lowering me to my back. "Honestly, Curtis. I told you as soon as I had it… or remembered it. Whatever."

I was full out crying and freaking out, by that point. It was the truth. I didn't know why it came late.

I guess I looked pitiful enough, because he eventually loosened his grip, sighed, and kissed my forehead.

"You're right. You told me that you don't know any of this. You wouldn't know the difference between a memory of a dream and a vision."

"I… I'll do better. I promise." I was so not the one to do this job. Day one…ish, and I was already screwing this up.

Curtis chuckled softly and pressed his lips to my head again. "We will work on it together."

I nodded, rolling to face him again, burying my face into his chest. I felt his chest shake with amusement, and his arm tightened around me. Hmmm, maybe I could help him remember how to show regular affection. Maybe I could soften him up. Not just for me, but for others.

“What was your dream vision again? Tell me what it was like.”

“It was just a picture really. Part of the wall was missing. That’s it.” I gasped, leaning back enough to look up at him. “Did Carter get killed? Are my friends alright?”

I swear I could hear the wheels turning in his mind.

“I’m not sure, love.”

Love? Oh joy, he was going to play me right back.

“My men said Deacon came storming through with the army. The soldiers threw grenades at them, while Deacon, his vampires, and a few wolves ran toward the neighborhood. The few that survived said Deacon had all the humans in the truck when he drove back out. There has been no sign of Carter.”

I sniffed again. “Will he hurt my friends? Do you think he killed Carter? He was good to us. I don’t want him to get hurt.”

Curtis rubbed a hand up and down my back softly. “I don’t know. The royals will probably use your friends as donors. They will keep them locked in a room, and only let them out when they need them. I wish I could say your friends will be treated well, but the royals are not known for their hospitality. As for Carter, Deacon will probably try to torture information out of him. Or punish him for calling me in the first place.”

I let a few more tears fall and let him act as though he was comforting me. After a few minutes, I mumbled my next question into his chest.

“What’s a shifter? And why did Deacon have wolves with him?”

Curtis snorted. "The magical community is made up of three types of magical beings. Vampires, witches," he poked my side and I giggled, "and wolf shifters. They are humans that have the power to shift into a wolf. At one point in time, we all had our own kingdoms. The humans lived with us. They worshiped us."

"What happened?"

Curtis waited so long that I wasn't so sure he would answer. Maybe I asked one to many questions.

"War. The humans revolted. Eventually all the magical kingdoms fell. It was more than a millennia ago. Most of our history has been lost."

"What are you going to do now?"

"A message has been sent to both Deacon and the humans. In the meantime, it's time to finish that wall."

We laid there quietly long enough that I started falling asleep again. I tried to think of other things I could ask, that wouldn't sound like I was digging. Unfortunately, I kept coming up blank. I jumped with a yelp again when there was a loud knock at the door. It was totally on purpose, putting forth the air of innocence and gullibility. I was *not* feeling content and comfortable.

"My Lord, it's time. The chopper is filled and ready to go." Lucas called through.

I gripped Curtis tighter. "Are you leaving me already?"

He brushed the hair away from my face and smiled softly. "No, love. You are coming with me. Remember? I said you would stay by my side all the time now."

I bit the corner of my lip and nodded my head. He kissed me softly, then told me to get dressed. I pulled out a black sleeveless maxi dress. It was a bit tight but accented all the right areas. I slipped on my heels again, then met Curtis at the door.

He clicked the collar back on, letting the back of his knuckles graze down my neck.

Chapter 15

Grace

I followed quietly behind Curtis as he led me by the leash down the hall, and then down the stairs. When we arrived at the back door, Lucas was waiting for us once again. Without a word, he opened the back door, and waited for us to pass.

He winked at me, again, earning another scowl from me. I was beginning to think he did that just to see my response. He enjoyed it too much.

Silently, we boarded the same helicopter as before. The other stayed silently on the ground. Were the others not coming with us?

"Vegas?" Curtis asked, looking at Lucas, as we raised above the house.

It looked much larger from up here. Judging by the surrounding area, I had to wonder if we were in Hollywood, or one of those other richy rich places. Did we take over a movie star's house?

That would be kinda cool. It would have been kind of ironic if that *Twilight* chick had been killed by the real deal vamps.

“Done. The men were sure it was empty though.”

Curtis gently dragged his hand down the back of my head. I turned to face him, and he did the same down my cheek with the back of his knuckle. He smiled softly, so I leaned into his embrace.

“If they did take Carter, they didn’t wait long to question him. He may have divulged that we knew they were there.”

From the corner of my eye, I could see Lucas’ eyes scrunch slightly, as he tried to follow the subtle hint Curtis was giving him. The one telling him what line he gave me. I helped him out and pouted. Lucas finally caught on. I had to close my eyes to hide the eye roll. Moron.

I swear, the bigger the egos, the smaller the brains men had.

“And the other cities?”

“They have been contacted. The attacks have already begun.”

And just like that, flashes flooded through my mind. First, the White House. Then a casino on the strip. Finally, Time’s Square. The tear slipped out on its own. Curtis wiped it without a word.

So many people were going to die tonight. And it was just the beginning. I listened as they discussed the plan for the other cities over the next few weeks. California had not been the end goal, it seemed. It had just been where they planned to make their strong hold.

Would we be back to the house in time for me to send a warning message to Hill? Surely Deacon could have his guys there? Or maybe those wolf-shifter-guys?

Unlike the last time we flew, I was left mostly alone. It was kind of nice. Curtis kept one arm around me protectively, almost like he was trying to show me some type of affection. I lapped it up like the dog I was used to being treated as.

Well, I guess I should say like the cat.

The entire ride, I kept my head on his shoulder. Pretty much giving him the same treatment. I really did appreciate the reprieve from other things. I could deal with more of this and less of that. It was a nice change of pace.

As time passed, I grew more comfortable with it. Being held without immediate expectations was something I had never experienced in my life. I kind of liked it.

I had to remind myself that Curtis was only faking it though.

This was probably getting off to a bad start. At least for me.

We disembarked as soon as the doors were opened. Unlike last time, Curtis helped me out, almost like I was a lady. Like the Queen he planned to make me. If not for the collar and leash he held, I might have felt like one.

"Are the crews here yet?" Curtis asked a vampire I recognized all too well.

From the mix of anger and confusion on his face, he remembered me just as well. When he didn't respond automatically, Curtis looked at him and growled.

"Ryley!"

Ryley jumped with a whimper and looked at him and then me again. "Sorry, sir. No. They aren't. They should be here within the hour though."

Curtis didn't miss how Ryley's eyes kept jumping to me. "Do you know my pet, Ryley?"

The weaker vampire whimpered and nodded. But he didn't respond. Curtis turned to me and raised one eyebrow.

"He found Todd and I in our foster home, during the first wave of attacks. He offered to take care of us and said he would be back. I, uh, had a *feeling* he would not have been very good at taking care of us. We went to the shelter the next morning." I didn't see a problem with Curtis knowing that. Ryley never knew of my link to Deacon and Carrie. We had purposely avoided the bar when he was going to be there.

Curtis laughed when he saw Ryley's depressed look again. He patted him roughly a few times on the shoulder.

"This is why lower ranks rarely have pets. They don't know how to maintain them." Curtis laughed again, then pulled on my leash. "Come, little kitty. Looks like we have some time to kill. I bet they have some stores around here. Looks like I can keep that promise to you after all."

I grinned at him. "Really?"

He laughed again, then yanked me to him, kissing me swiftly, before whispering in my ear.

"Anything my Queen wants, my Queen gets."

"Hmm, I do love the sound of that." I really did, too.

There was a shopping center close to where we landed. So, we walked over, his entourage following us. I didn't recognize where we were as I looked around, there was a lot more greenery here, which confused me.

"This doesn't look like Mojave."

"No. We are a little more North than that. We will head that way eventually, just not yet." Curtis lifted a hand, which I took absentmindedly, and let him help me step through the broken glass door to a clothing store.

We walked to the center, and he lifted a hand to my neck. I spun around when I felt the release of the collar.

"I don't think you will need this in here. My men will surround the stores from the outside, no one will be in here but us. Go ahead, little witch. Anything you want."

He lifted my hand and kissed it, then pulled himself onto a countertop. I was sure he could see over most of the clothing racks from there, which meant he would have an eye on me the entire time.

"Anything in particular you want?" I asked carefully.

He chuckled and shook his head. "This trip isn't about me. This is about you. What do *you* want?"

I opened to respond, then closed my mouth again. He chuckled again. I was confused – a state of mind I seemed to spend a lot of time in since Curtis took me. No one had ever asked what I wanted before. It wasn't ever about me. Yes, this whole mission was about pleasing the vampires enough to get me to right where I was. But even before that, it wasn't about what I wanted.

Not in the foster homes. Not even with my own mother.

Todd had been good to me. Carter too, as much as he was capable of, in my opinion anyway. Carter let us pick some things in Walmart, but we mostly picked things we knew the vampires would want us to wear.

This was different though. Curtis didn't even want to influence my decisions. He was just going to sit back and let me have free reign. I mean, it wasn't like we were going to have to pay for anything, but still. It also wasn't like he couldn't afford it if he wanted to. I was sure he had the money.

I just stood there, like an idiot, looking between him and the rest of the store, completely unsure what I was supposed to do. It was long enough that Curtis jumped back off the counter and sauntered up to me, putting his log-like arm around me.

"What's the matter?"

"I…" I had no clue what to say. "I've never had a choice before." I felt my cheeks heat up with the confession. I was nearly eighteen years old, and I had never had a say in what I wore, what I owned, where I lived, where I ate, anything.

"A choice in what?" Great. Even the evil vampire pitied me.

"Anything." I let out one sad laugh. "I don't even know where to start."

Curtis took my hand softly and led me to one corner. "Let's start small then. It's getting cold. So, let's look at pants." He led me over to a wall filled with folded jeans. He waved to it with one hand, and released me again, stepping away. "Take your time, love."

This time he sat on a small display table close to me. As though he was silently supporting me.

I huffed, still completely confused on what was going on. That was the last thing I expected from him. Not with the way everyone kept talking about him. Not with the reputation he had in regard to his harems and pets.

But that was the difference, wasn't it? That wasn't what he wanted me for. It had been my goal, but it was not where I ended up.

I started looking through different kinds of jeans, pulling out various styles in my size. I giggled as I tried them on right there in the middle of the store. I ignored the deep rumbles of amusement coming from behind me.

Was he enjoying me being happy?

I set a couple in one pile, and the others in another. I liked them too, but I didn't want to push my luck. When I turned back to Curtis, waiting for instructions on where to go next, he shook his head, a grin on his face.

I blinked and both piles were gone.

He stood in front of me, laughing at my confusion, then pointed at the counter, where *all* of them waited.

"Shirts next?" He asked, one hand up, waiting for mine.

I nodded, still feeling lost.

We continued like that until the counter was covered in everything from dresses, to shoes, and underwear. That last one was the only time he had an opinion. He still let me have whatever I wanted, but he did *request* a few things he liked as well.

He wasn't far from my side the entire time. Always near, as though it was a silent promise to always be with me. I didn't feel like he was hovering, or pressuring. It was more like accompanying, protecting.

And very, very confusing.

At least with how I started feeling about it.

"This is too much." I told him, my eyes on the dozen large bags his men were carrying out of the store.

Curtis kissed the side of my head softly, holding me to him. He was getting more comfortable with that type of thing. We both were it seemed.

"I told you, anything my Queen wants, she gets. When we have more time, we will swing by a jewelry store."

I gasped and looked at him. He just laughed and led me back out. By the time we made it back to the helicopters, there were more men hanging around. They looked like they had been sitting around for a bit too. These ones looked different than the others. There was something about them that set them apart, I just couldn't put my finger on it.

"Mr. Cruz. Thank you for changing your schedule and coming to this area next."

Mr. Cruz, a slightly middle-aged man, looked warily at Curtis and me. His eyes lingered on the leash between us. Oddly, I felt more comfortable once Curtis put the collar back on me. It helped me remember my place and my purpose better. A nice hard, cold, splash of reality.

"No problem, senor. I assume you are going to be leading this one?"

Curtis nodded. "Yes. Time is of the essence now. I have more men here to help, as well. The Northern crew stopped in this area. If we start here, and work down toward the South, where you just were, we should finish in no time."

"How many crews will be working?"

"Four. I want everyone to rotate shifts."

Mr. Cruz bowed slightly. "As you wish, Senor. Shall we get started, then?"

Curtis pulled me along, leading the men to where the temporary wall stood. Curtis held a hand up for me again, which I took, having no idea what was going on. Curtis put his other hand on Lucas' shoulder. Lucas then put one on Ryley, and so on. Curtis and I watched as nearly seventy men connected in some way.

Now I was really confused. Maybe I should just get used to being in this state.

Curtis looked at me and winked. "Want to see some real magic, little witch?"

I smiled back at him. "I'd love to."

The sun was just beginning to kiss the sky, a warning that all the Nightwalkers should be running for cover in the next few minutes. I was slightly worried for them.

I watched Curtis as he closed his eyes and began humming to himself. His thumb gently stroked the back of my hand, and I felt an odd sensation run through me.

A moment later, his eyes opened again, and he stared at the sky. My eyes followed his, right to where a bird sat in the sky. Its wings stayed stretched out to the sides. No pumping. No movement. The bird just floated there.

My jaw dropped when I realized it wasn't floating, it was frozen. I looked back to Curtis, who was watching me with amusement.

"Wh… what…" I wasn't even sure what I was going to ask, or how to ask it.

Curtis chuckled and pulled me into his side. "I froze time, little witch. Pretty cool little trick, right?"

I just nodded, still looking at him in amazement. My focus was broken when I heard the men start moving around. They got right to work. It was obvious none of this was new to them.

Curtis pulled me further back, getting out of the way.

"Why aren't any of us frozen too?"

"Whoever is connected to me is not affected by the spell."

Understanding dawned on me. "This is how those walls got up so fast."

"Yes. I only did part of it in the beginning. The amount of power it takes can be draining. The human workers have been building like normal since then. But after what happened in Mojave, I thought it would be best to speed things up a bit. I'm sorry to say, that means I will need to drink from you again when this is done."

I frowned at him. "You don't want to drink from me?"

His eyes widened in shock, before the amusement slid in. He turned to me, wrapping both arms around me, almost like a lover.

"It's not that I *don't* want to drink from you, love. It's that you are still healing from before. I worry about taking too much and harming you. I don't want to hurt you."

I blushed, for real again. It was the second time in a matter of hours that he made me blush naturally. Which wasn't good. He seemed to like it though. Curtis pulled me against his chest and just held me to him.

"What do we do now?" I looked up at him, wanting to learn his expressions so I could read him better.

I didn't have to learn that look in his eyes. I knew that one all too well. I had seen it in men's eyes my whole life. But for some reason, coming from Curtis, it made me blush *again.*

What the hell, Grace? Even Todd didn't make you blush this much!

"I had a tent set up for my own personal use. I'm sure we can think of ways to entertain ourselves for a time." His hand slid down my back, and onto my butt, holding me against him tightly. "With all this time on our hands, we could get started on our other plans. The sooner the better."

When he saw the confused look in my eyes, one of his hands moved forward to my stomach, rubbing it softly.

Riiight. The "let's try and impregnate Grace" plans.

I lifted onto my toes and kissed his jaw. "Whatever you wish… my King."

His look darkened and I screeched in laughter when he roughly pulled me away from the construction site.

When he said tent, I expected one similar to the set-up Carter had. I should have known better. Instead, it was a large tent, one with actual rooms. In the center area was a table and chairs. That wasn't where we stopped though. Curtis held up a curtain for me, and pulled me into another section, where an actual bed lay on the ground.

We stayed in that tent for hours. Not that we had any real way of monitoring the passage of time. The sky stayed in that early morning dawn stage, giving the workers just enough light to work with. But the sun hidden enough that the Nightwalkers were safe.

Curtis and I both slept for a good amount of time in that tent. I vaguely remembered him leaving me for a bit, and talking to others in the other room, but then he would come back. I was beginning to understand what he meant about the toll the spell took on him. He was sleeping more often than I was.

I ate about a dozen or so times, Lucas delivered the meals each time to us, before we emerged from the tent. I was amazed at what I saw. The wall in front of us was no longer made up of blocks of cement and cars. No, it was one tall piece of black stone now. Smoother than any sidewalk I had ever seen too.

Curtis left me next to Lucas for a few minutes, while he jogged up and down the wall, inspecting it. When he came back, he seemed satisfied.

"Good, clean up, then we will move onto the next mile." Curtis came back to me, pulling me into the tent again. His hand grazed over my neck softly.

"I am going to need to drink a bit after each spell. I promise not to take too much. If I do, I will feed you my own. Please tell me if you feel weak at all." He kept one eyebrow up until I nodded.

I was a little scared, remembering the pain of when he stabbed me with his fangs before. This time around though, he kissed my neck up and down first, lulling me, before slowly sinking his fangs in. The moan just slipped right on out, without permission.

His hand slid down my back, hooked around my thigh, and lifted my leg. I couldn't quite seem to help the way my body rubbed against his. Nor the way one set of my fingernails dug into his arm, or the way the other hand gripped his hair.

He drank less than Carter ever had, sealing me immediately. The slight disappointment that he was stopping already confused me.

"How are you feeling? Do you need blood?"

I bit my lip and shook my head. Just the mention of it made me remember how good it had tasted. My throat yearned for the smoothness, for the warmth.

Not a habit I should indulge.

Curtis lifted my chin, then carefully pulled my lip out of my teeth. His other hand was still holding my leg up to his waist. He wanted me to feel every devilish inch of him.

"If you need it, you should drink it, love."

"I don't *need* it." I softly confessed, making his chest rumble against me.

"Hmm, are you sure about that? It's not hard to get addicted to the taste of vampire blood. Normally, I don't feed others. But you are different. My blood will strengthen you. I almost wonder if I should start feeding you before you get pregnant. I wonder if that would prepare your body and make it easier for my seed to attach to you?"

I wasn't sure he was actually talking to me anymore. It almost sounded like he was talking to himself now.

Whatever was on his mind was wiped out when he looked at me again. Curtis slowly lowered and kissed me softly. This was definitely not what I was dreading when I planned out how to get close to him. None of this was.

An amused throat cleared from the other side of the curtain before speaking. "We are ready to move onto the next station, my Lord." Lucas told him.

Curtis sighed and released me. He opened the curtain and spoke to his friend. "Are all the men hidden from the sun?"

"Yes, sir. They are in the trucks. Mr. Cruz's men will drive us down to the next spot. I was thinking though, why don't we just try to keep the same spell up? It might be easier on you, than taking it up and down over and over again. Then we also don't have to wait for the sun to go down to start again. Or risk certain individuals finding out and trying to interfere."

Curtis turned back to me. Studying me for something. Whatever decision he came to didn't make him all that happy.

"Fine. But we are going to need plenty of food and water for Grace. I don't know what this will do to me. I've never kept it up for so long before."

Lucas bowed. "I'll make sure someone raids grocery stores along the way." He left, and Curtis dropped the curtain again.

He picked up his wrist and bit into it before raising it up to me. “Every time I drink, you will need to drink. Not much, just enough to sustain both our lives. Once this is over, I promise not to drink from you for a while.”

The frown slipped. I really needed to regain control of my body. It was misbehaving on so many levels. He chuckled softly as his wrist pressed against my lips again. It didn’t take as long for me to start drinking this time.

In the beginning, I tried to track time by how often I ate, but I lost count after half a dozen, and started drinking nearly a case of water at each stop. Any time I wasn’t eating, I was sleeping. Either that or Curtis was doing whatever he wanted to me. Even then, he was usually gentle. Most of the time that I slept, he slept with me.

True to his word, he kept me by his side. The longer this went, the longer we both slept. Our trips to monitor the building of the wall became fewer and fewer. Part of me felt guilty about not watching for the hidden gateways, but it was hard to focus on that part.

And, just as he said, every time he fed from me, I fed from him. By the time we reached the last stop, having long passed Mojave, he stopped using the collar. His reasoning was that my smell had changed. With his blood continually in my system, he had ended up marking me as his.

Whether they saw me as a pet or not, all the vampires would know that I belonged to Curtis now. It would take months of not feeding from him for the scent to fade. Or a blood transfusion.

When we exited the tent for the last time, I was tired of the dawn. I was tired of the world being frozen. I was also getting a tad bit irritable.

I stood next to Curtis and stared at where the wall from the North now connected with the wall coming from the south. Curtis closed his eyes and hummed. I sighed as I watched the sun finally break over the mountains. Even though these were nowhere near where we had been when it froze in the sky.

I screeched when I felt Curtis sag next to me. Lucas caught his other arm, and half dragged him back to our tent before the sun touched either of them. I was sure it wouldn't have affected Curtis, but I never would have been able to carry him over on my own. I also didn't know how many of the others knew he was not a Nightwalker.

Lucas practically shoved us into our room together. Curtis collapsed on the bed. Without thinking, I quickly laid next to him, and helped him roll onto his side. I even held his head up to my neck.

It didn't dawn on me until later, that I probably could have played ignorant and let him weaken right then. I excused it away by saying he was my only protection against the rest of them. It was a viable excuse. But in all reality, all I was thinking about was helping him.

I may have a slight problem on my hands. One I had not foreseen.

Curtis didn't drink nearly as much as he had after Deacon had stabbed him, but it was still enough to weaken me. He gave me more blood than ever before after that. He was nearly as worried about me as I had been about him when I almost passed out. It was kind of sweet.

The next thing I knew, we were laying in his bed, back at the house in California.

Chapter 16

Carrie

The sunlight coming through the shades was still dim when I woke up in our hotel room - the morning after we rescued the kids - to my stomach turning. I practically jumped out of bed and ran to the bathroom. With all the other random pregnancy symptoms hitting full force so early, I forgot about this one.

I could have lived without it.

With my sole focus on making it to the bathroom, I failed to notice the two large bodies following behind me. Or one of them holding my hair back.

I groaned when I finished, taking the towel floating in the air above my head.

"You didn't have to come in here with me."

I closed the lid to the toilet, and a phantom hand flushed it for me. I laid my forehead on the cool porcelain and slowed my breathing.

"Yes, we did. We will always be here when you need us." Deacon sank to his heels, releasing my hair. "No hiding. Your words. Remember?" He smirked at me.

I weakly slapped his leg in retaliation.

Another pair of large arms reached down and scooped me up and carried me back to the bed. Colton's hot chest didn't feel as good as the toilet lid had. But the rest of him was comforting. I fell back asleep, wrapped in his arms, before my head hit the pillow.

When I woke again, I was wrapped even tighter than I was before, in both sets of arms. The sun was brighter, and two voices were speaking softly over me. I smacked my lips together, the awful taste still there, and grimaced in disgust.

The sweaty chest in front of me shook, and a bottle of water appeared in front of my face. I happily took it and inhaled it.

"Better?" Deacon asked from behind me. I just nodded and laid back down, leaning against him. His chest was sweaty too.

I looked at them both, squinting at them. I sniffed the air and got exactly what I expected. It wasn't as strong as it had been in the car, but the scent was still somewhat fresh.

"He was freaking out. You had him worried. I had to comfort him, and you needed your sleep." Colton explained, with the attitude of being put out.

Deacon laughed and reached over to push him. "Me? You were the one frantically checking her pulse every few seconds!"

I rolled my eyes and shook my head as they argued over who started what. It didn't matter. I knew how it would end.

After we all got sweaty, we took showers. Much to their dismay, it had to be one at a time. This shower was too small for more than that.

"Do you feel like eating? We can always take food with us, for you to eat when you are ready. Or we can just pull over later." Colton sat across from where I was sitting on the edge of the bed, in a chair at the small table.

"I'm starving actually. I could really go for some waffles. And bacon. Ooo, and some strawberries. Do you think the hotel has all of that downstairs?"

"If they don't, we will stop at the first diner we pass." Deacon walked into the room with a towel wrapped around his waist. Colton and I both licked our lips. Deacon just laughed, grabbed his clothes, and walked back to the bathroom. "We don't have time for that." He shouted, before closing the bathroom again.

I sighed and lowered my head to the pillow again, laying on my side. "He's right. We don't. I'm too hungry."

Colton chuckled, reaching over to run his finger down my face. I swatted it away and pointed at him with a stern look. He just laughed and leaned back, his eyes glowing with a heat I knew all too well.

I hadn't finished getting dressed yet, I was lying there in only a t-shirt and underwear. The jeans were beginning to feel tight, so I was putting off wearing them. I laughed hysterically when he yanked his shirt off and dropped his pants faster than a human.

Deacon came out seconds later, still not completely dressed.

It took us nearly another half an hour before we finally headed down for food. Colton carried a backpack I hadn't noticed the day before, but I was too hungry to think much of it. I was pretty sure I would be eating that bag if they didn't give me something soon.

Everyone was waiting for us in the small dining area. Deacon escorted me to a chair, while Colton began making me a plate. Thankfully, the continental breakfast had waffle irons so we could make our own fresh waffles.

All we were missing was the strawberries. I made do with toast and strawberry jam.

"As soon as we get home, I will send someone to the store, and they will buy you all the strawberries you want." Deacon kissed my cheek.

"And whipped cream?" I laughed when his eyes sparked.

The twins, who were sitting across the table from me, laughed along with me. They were grinning ear to ear. I didn't need to hear their thoughts to know they were comparing the me now, to the me when we first met.

"Oh my gosh, y'all have to see what's going on." A hotel employee ran into the room and turned on a television hanging in a corner of two walls.

I flashed a look to Raya. She had the same panicky expression as I did. We were both remembering that day in the bus station. The manager had hurried in to turn up the tv in just the same way. Only quieter.

Deacon felt my panic and hugged me close to him.

The young girl, wearing a dark green long sleeve polo and khaki pants stepped back from the tv, a remote in her hands. After a few clicks, she landed on a news channel. A gray-haired man was speaking.

"New York is reporting their numbers to be hitting triple digits. Only slightly higher than those of DC. Vegas looks to have taken the biggest hit. Nearly two hundred dead. We received camera footage from the MGM Grand Hotel and Casino. A dozen men and women attacked every person on the Casino floor. The doors were locked, and the power turned off, keeping the elevators from running. We have chosen not to show that clip." His face was pale, telling us all we needed to know.

"While the authorities refuse to speculate, I think we all know what is going on. The vampires are no longer hiding behind their wall."

A small picture of the blown-up portion of the wall in Mojave appeared in the corner behind him.

"Yesterday morning, the military ran an offensive in Mojave, California. They blew up part of the wall and ran in to rescue whoever they could. Even after the military crossed back to this side, caravans of refugees used every minute of daylight they could and crossed over the border into safety. It seems the vampires are striking back."

I turned and looked at Deacon, guilt, and fear flooding through me.

"What did we do?" I whispered to him. I turned when I felt a gentle, and heavy, hand on my upper back.

"This was too fast. Curtis already had these plans laid. His men were already in those cities, just waiting for the order. It would have happened eventually anyway. We saved these kids, and all those humans that came out behind us. If anything, we pushed up his timeline. That is all." Colton said softly.

We turned back to the television when we heard the sounds of someone tapping a microphone. A man in his late 60s, his black hair beginning to gray, stood behind a pulpit, his face serious, but his eyes flooded with water. He sniffed, cleared his throat, and then leaned closer to the microphone.

"My fellow Americans. As the Vice President of the United States of America, it is my duty to inform you of the death of our beloved President and his family. Sometime in the middle of the night, every person within the walls of the White House was killed. We cannot state with any formal evidence who was at fault. But they were all found with marks in their necks, and arms, and… other places. All the blood was missing from their bodies. It is not within my authority to say there are such things as vampires, but whatever ails California seems to have spread across the U.S. Our President had recently been in meetings with potential allies just days before, trying to find a way to rid us of this menace. I will continue where he left off. I promise you this, we will find out who is responsible. And we will have our retribution. Anyone who has attacked our fair country in the past will attest, we do not take being attacked lying down. We will have our revenge and we will cleanse our land from their tyranny."

I ignored the rest of his speech as I began to question Deacon. "Is this going to help or hinder our drive for peace?"

"I don't know." He shrugged. He looked up at Colton. "We need to leave. Now."

We stood outside the cars a few minutes later. To my dismay, we were getting back in an SUV, not Deacon's truck. Colton walked over to me, the backpack in his hands.

"I had Bryant, and the others pull a book from the box I brought you from Phoenix. I thought it might help you pass the time in the car. I know you would rather it just be us, or at least, not Carter." Carter grunted from under the tarp as he passed beside us. Colton chuckled. "Maybe this will help.

I opened the bag and immediately recognized one of my mother's big antique books. I grinned at my mate, my vision getting blurry.

"Thank you!" I lifted an arm around his neck and kissed him soundly. "I love you."

"I love you, too, sweetheart."

Deacon was grinning when he stepped up to us. He leaned down and kissed me next. "Ready to go?"

I nodded. He looked up at Colton, who winked at him, before taking a half step back. Deacon growled. Colton laughed as he stepped forward and gave him a swift kiss too. I laughed at them both, then started to climb into the car. I stopped though and leaned out, looking at the car beside us. The twins were just starting to load in.

"Layla?" She stopped and looked back at me. "Would you do me a favor, please?"

She skipped over. "Sure, Carrie. What's up?"

Colton groaned and rolled his eyes. Deacon laughed.

"Colton can't feed from me without weakening Deacon, me, and the baby. Do you mind?"

Layla laughed. She probably already knew why I was asking her. She and Raya knew better than anybody what I went through with my ex. Hell, they were there when I found the ring he bought me, hiding in his safe. And a half naked girl in his apartment. She was dead too, but I had already learned about them 24 hours before.

"Sure. Come here, lover boy." Layla teased him as she stepped over to him, tilting her head.

"Really, sweetheart. I'm fine. I don't need to drink anytime soon."

I pursed my lips and glared at him. He sighed and picked up her wrist, avoiding any intimate contact with her. Layla giggled, not caring in the least about any of it.

As soon as he released her, he sealed her arm and silently thanked her. She winked at him and rejoined her twin, who was giggling as she watched.

Colton stepped to where I sat in the car and kissed me. "Are you happy now?"

"Now that you have taken care of your own needs, since you ignore them while you make sure Deacon, and I are good? Yes." I grinned at him. "Thank you."

He chuckled as he kissed me again, closed the door, and walked around the car to get into the driver's seat.

With that worry gone, I was free to put my focus elsewhere. I didn't even wait until everyone was situated before I opened the book titled Family History. The first page was a typical title page, with a small paragraph under the title.

The history of the Royal Witch's line. Here we mark the births, deaths, and mate bonds of our family line.

Royal Witch's Line? Why did my mom have this?

I turned a couple pages, briefly reading over the births and deaths. The dates started nearly two thousand years ago. I wondered how she found it. The book had to be very valuable.

She had always been obsessed with our histories though. I remembered her going on many trips while I was growing up. It was possible she had been hunting for this and other artifacts.

If only I hadn't pushed her away those last few years. If only I hadn't lost interest in her interests. If only… I sighed and turned another page.

It wasn't long before I started to rethink spending my time in that particular book. That changed when I finally came across more than the writings of people being born and then dying. It was the story of someone meeting their fated mate. It was sweet. And nowhere near boring like the previous entries had been.

He was a farmer on her parents' land. He had the gift of healing plants. She had the gift of making things grow.

I noticed a theme over the next few pages. The powers all matched in some way.

I quickly became engrossed in the stories that now accompanied each addition. Even how they died. I also noticed that the mates didn't always die at the same time.

Was it not the same for witches as it was for vampires?

I barely noticed the passing of time. Deacon had to pull the book out of my hands to get me to eat lunch. Once that much awareness was given to me, I also insisted on a pit stop to the bathroom.

As soon as we were on the road again, and I had eaten the whole sub he gave me, I got my book back. Such a bossy butt. Such a *royal* bossy butt.

I was more than two thirds of the way in, when a lump of folded papers slipped out. Deacon reached down and caught it before it could hit the floor. I thanked him and opened it carefully, noting that the papers were pulled from a modern-day notebook.

I gasped, putting a hand over my mouth, when I recognized the handwriting. I waved Deacon off when he tried to check on me.

Chapter 17

To my dear sweet, Carrie.

I am so sorry that it has come to this. And I am so sorry for the guilt you must have felt when you received word of our deaths. Yes, my child. I knew it was coming. I know what you are thinking. If you knew you were both going to die, why did you still go? *I tried, my child, I did. Your father and I both came up with many different plans. But it would have been worse in the long run.*

The first vision was of all three of us dying. The second, had you living. We stressed to you how important it was for you to either be on time, or not come at all for a reason. I knew you would be late, and I knew why (no, it didn't bother me because I also knew he was going to fail, and yes, I am giggling right now). I was relieved when the vision showed you not coming to the dinner at all.

Now, the hard reason. The reason we still went. In my vision, I saw another witch approaching us in the restaurant. She needs my guidance. The vision didn't tell me what it is, only that it is important. Obviously, I can't tell you what it was because, technically, it hasn't happened yet. But it is important enough that we be there for it. It is part of who we are, part of our calling.

See, there is something I never told you. I tried many times, but you were too young. And then you were turning away from our culture. How was I to tell you then? How was I to tell you that you come from a long line of Royal Witches.

Yes, my dear, sweet, girl. You are not only a witch, but you are royalty. A princess, actually. Your father and I are the coven leaders. You remember all those book club meetings I had? Well, they were actually coven meetings. Your father and I both descend from the last rulers of the Witch kingdom.

After the Witch Trials, which the shifters helped end, we broke into smaller covens. The leaders of the covens meet regularly, seeking guidance from the rightful rulers. Your father and me.

I know this probably comes as a shock to you, but maybe not as much as it once would have. When I looked further into the future, I saw why your father and I need to die when we do. If we stayed, you would have continued down the path of denial that you are currently on. However, with us gone, you let the guilt get to you. You shut yourself out. You hold to a stricter sense of duty and depend on your powers more. I am sorry that you will have to go through that, but that is the path that leads you to where you were meant to be. The path the world needs you to be on. The path your mates need you to be on.

Yes, I know about both your mates. I was a bit shocked that you of all people would go that route, but then I saw how happy the three of you will be. How safe you will be. How you will help save the world. Whatever takes you to California will never happen if we do not die.

Which brings me to what I need to tell you. I plan to put this far enough in the book that you would, hopefully, have read some of the stories, and gained many questions. I need you to be ready to hear what I have to say. Did you notice how all the powers of the mates were similar? Did you notice that not all mated pairs died together?

By now, you should know how true mates, or fated mates, in the vampire world works. Vampires are born with only half a soul; their mate holds the other half. Witches are born with a whole soul, which is why we do not suffer from low morality as they do. Sorry, I will hold my pen on my vampire issues. You don't need those right now. I'd like to say your father and I would have accepted your mates if we were around, but I'm not sure. In time, maybe?

I digress. For witches, a true mate is someone who has the accompanying power. Your father and I both work within the mind. I see the future, and he hears the present thought. That is how it works. When witches do the bonding spell, our powers become complete. When you were young, we caught glimpses of your powers. You always knew when we were placating you. And you always knew when someone close by had evil intentions.

I'll never forget when you and I went to the station to have lunch with your father one day. You were about four at the time. You were giggling and laughing with a suspect sitting next to your father's desk. But then a minute later, his partner came by, and you hid behind the suspect's legs. Later that night, your father's partner tried to kill him. The suspect, who turned into an informant, saved his life.

As you got older, and started pulling away from what we are, your powers weakened. Yes, your ability to know a lie came back last year. But your ability to know intent has not yet. I wish I could be here to help you when it does. Your grandmother had that ability. She said it was very disconcerting in the beginning.

I bring this up for more than just a trip down memory lane. I bring this up, because, Carrie, my child, my love, it is not common for a witch to have more than one power. You carry both your power and its mating power. I worried that meant you had no true mate out in the world. Our line has always stuck to their true mates, we do not settle for chosen. We persevere until we find that perfect match. We need to keep the bloodline pure. There must always be a clear line of succession for our leader.

When I had the vision of you running down a dark alley, being chased by a Nightwalker, I was terrified. Then, HE opened the door. I knew from the moment he looked at you, that this was your true mate. A Vampire Born. I don't know what his status is, or that of your other mate, but I do know, they both were meant to be yours. Whatever is coming, that is where you are meant to be.

Now, for the last question. Why did all the mating pairs not die at the same time? All this I wanted to share with you before, but you were not ready. I'm sure you know better than I on how vampires seal themselves to their mates. Ours is not so grotesque.

During times of conflict, it was tradition for the coven leaders to bind themselves to another. For one, when we bond, we share our power with our mate. (Yes, this means your father has visions too.) It is not as strong with them as it is with us (I can read minds, but not as clearly as your father can, and only if I am touching them in some way, and your father's visions are not quite as detailed as mine). The coven leaders shared their power with another, giving them strength. But the main reason they did this was to keep the leader from dying. Having a third in the mating, kept the other alive. The pain was still excruciating, but they were able to survive. The pair ruled together, so the chosen third was bonded to both of them.

You will not find that mating listed in the book. As soon as the conflict was over, the mating was dissolved. It was never told to the others, only kept within the royal court. Bonds are not something to be messed with. No one ever wanted the enemy to find out either. Imagine if they realized they could get more power through bonding?

I have no doubts that you will not only be able to carry a vampire child but survive to raise it. But I wouldn't be your mother if I didn't do everything I could to help your body be stronger and help your mates protect you better. I want you to have the best future you can.

In the back of this book, is an envelope with three dark green ribbons. The color is important, it has to resemble nature. It is also tradition for the parents of the female to bless the ribbons. Therefore, your father and I have already blessed them. He grumbled first about you choosing not only one, but TWO vampires for mates. Still, you've always had that man wrapped around your little fingers.

The three of you need to be alone, with the exception of one or two people who will help tie the ribbons. Maybe those sweet twins I saw with you. I'm glad you have been able to find friends in the chaos I see surrounding you. Anyhoo, you will create a triangle, each of you holding hands. The three ribbons are going to be tied around each connected pair. Then, you each say this phrase, starting with you, as you are the witch. Your magic is needed to start the spell.

What's mine is yours, what's yours is mine, together we make our souls combine.

Each of you say that once, and then together. Unless they have sucked you in completely to vampire culture, you will want your friends to leave before you do this. The next part is not something you want many around for. You will feel an overwhelming desire to be together. When love is involved, the feeling cannot easily be ignored.

I've seen both of your men in my visions, you must be one happy mate. They are both gorgeous. I can see how much they love you too. This spell will bind you to both of them, and them to each other. I assume they want that anyway. Vampires have loose morals. Sorry, no soap box.

I am happy to know that mother nature thought ahead and gave you both powers, instead of you sacrificing your power's mate. Your mates will have the power to tell when others are lying to them, and the intentions of others. The depth of a mate's ability to use the power fluctuates with each pairing. I imagine your true mate will have more than the chosen one will, since you have the vampire bond with him. But the other will be able to use it as well.

Don't worry about them being vampires. You are not the first mixed pair in history. Keep reading through all of our books, our histories, you will find examples of the others. There has been no change in their ability to use the witch mate's power.

If something happens to one of your mates, you will NOT die. You will survive. I do not know if one of them will die, I am just doing what I can to protect MY child. Being tied to two vampires will also make your body stronger. Keep doing whatever it is you are doing (I am purposely not looking at that).

I am having a hard time stopping this letter. It has gone on for much longer than I planned. I just can't seem to say goodbye. At this moment, you have already left to go on your date. We had a beautiful Christmas together yesterday. I had to wait to write this because I knew I would not let you go if I didn't.

I am scared. I know it will be a Nightwalker that gets us. It always is with our family. Oh, yes, that was something else I wanted to tell you. I never wanted to scare you before. There is a reason why it is always a vampire that gets us. See, witch's blood is healing to a vampire. Only the oldest know this. Those who walked the earth when our kingdoms were neighbors. When we were allies. When we had witches who volunteered to heal them.

Our pure, royal blood is sweeter, and more powerful than all others. They are drawn to our life-giving blood. That is also the reason I know you will survive when you get pregnant. Your blood will give you the strength you need to survive. Do not freak out over the typical timeline, even witch babies differ from human ones. There is no set timeline, it all depends on the magic of the parents and of their child. You took four months to grow. According to your paternal grandmother, your father took six. We believe yours was so short because you hold so much power.
Be safe, my beautiful daughter. I will forever watch over you. My spirit will guide you when it can.

We love you, more than our own lives. Remember that. This was not your fault. It was the way things were meant to be. It was our honor to be your parents.

Farewell.

Chapter 18

Carrie

I barely finished the letter before I pulled the first page to the top of the stack again and reread it. My eyes were overflowing, the tears pouring down my cheeks. My heart was filled with love and gratitude for my mother. She knew I was going to need her. And she knew what I would need most. I kept reading, not wanting to let her go just yet.

Deacon had his arm wrapped around my shoulders, his hand rubbing up and down my arm. I looked up after my second read and noticed that he was reading over my shoulder. I should be irritated about that. But I didn't have it in me.

I raised my head further, feeling more eyes on me, and met the look of my other mate. Colton was watching me through the rearview mirror, his eyes wary.

"I'm okay. It's a letter from my mom. She knew they were going to die. She wanted to say goodbye." I sniffled. "I'm not ready to talk about it yet though." I couldn't talk about it.

I laid my head on Deacon's shoulder, letting him hold me. Comfort me.

They died to not only protect me, but also to make sure I ended up where I was supposed to. Mom was right. I would not have dated Bryce for nearly as long as I had. My dad would have kicked him to the curb. If I hadn't been dating him though, I never would have gone to LA. I never would have met Deacon or Colton.

My mind spun in never-ending circles. I closed my eyes tight, trying to steady my breathing. I set the grief aside and focused on the gift they gave me. They prepared a way for me to bond to both my mates. We would all finally be equal in this.

The memory of Deacon's jealousy yesterday, when Richard had asked Colton that innocent question, ran through my mind. Bonding Colton to us should help Deacon feel better. He was sensitive to loved ones leaving right now. Understandable, after losing his father so suddenly like that.

Right now, Colton was free to leave if he wanted to, he was with us by choice. If he sealed himself to us, we would be a bonded unit. I may not be able to help them fight the war, but I could at least strengthen them. They would be able to use my powers. At least I could help in that way.

These new thoughts helped me relax enough that I was able to fall asleep. What felt like only a few minutes later, I woke to the car stopping. I sat up, one part of my brain recognized that Deacon had laid me on the seat, my head in his lap, the blanket he bought the day before laid over me. The rest of my brain was focused on the sight of the large cabin, and the smaller ones surrounding it. It was like a giant hotel, with little baby hotels all around it. A mama duck and her ducklings.

When it snowed, did it look like Santa's Village?

Would anyone get offended if I asked them to wear little Santa hats, elf ears, and clown sized booties?

Probably.

Colton opened my door and helped me out. Deacon climbed out the other side and met us in front of the car. As though they had been waiting for us, half a dozen shirtless men stepped out from a group of trees to our right. They stopped in a sort of triangular shape.

The one at the point bowed slightly to us. "Are you Queen Carrie?"

I frowned, that was not what I expected. "Um, yes?"

He chuckled, most likely at my awkwardness. "Alpha Hill asked us to check out the property for you all. We know the packs have agreed to work with the Vampire Borns, but that is not as easy for us. We will do our best." He glanced back at those with him, then turned back to me. "But for now, we feel more comfortable working with you. Our ancestors have a good history with the witches." He grimaced. "And a sketchy one with the vampires. Most of it was at least with the Nightwalkers. If your lot can bring them to heel, then we will work with you. Anyway, the only scents we could sniff out were that of dust and nature. No vampires, witches, humans, or even shifters, have been in this area for a long time. You all are safe here."

He reached his hand back and someone handed him something small. He stepped forward and gave it to me.

"This is the number for our pack Alpha. Call if you need anything."

Before I could thank him, or even ask his name, they turned and ran back into the trees.

"See, you will be the point in which all the races will stand behind." Deacon whispered. "Isn't that what the witch in your dreams said? That you will be vital in uniting the supernatural races?"

"Um, yes?"

He chuckled at my repeated response. "Come on. We need to talk."

He leaned into the car and picked up my book, the letter just barely sticking out of the top like a bookmark.

"Privately." He looked up at Colton, silently communicating how important this was.

Colton nodded and waved toward another man. This one looked older than the rest, he even had slight wrinkles around his eyes. I remembered Deacon's father saying something about age eventually getting to them. How old was this man?

"Bryant?"

"Yes, my Lord." The man bowed slightly to Colton.

"Direct the others on where everything should go. I am going to show the King and Queen to their chambers."

Bryant bowed again and stepped away.

They both took my hands, and we started walking toward the front of the massive home. The teenagers were standing around, staring at all the buildings in awe.

"We need the twins." I whispered.

Deacon nodded and called them over. They gave us curious looks but followed suit.

I was grateful when Colton brought us to a stop in front of an elevator. Our room, or chambers, was on the fourth floor again, and I wasn't in the mood for that many stairs. This place was as large as the one we had in Las Vegas. I was curious about the shower but decided I could wait to look around until later.

On the left side of our room was a large California King bed. On the right side was a sitting area. I moved there, and the others followed. I sat down and opened the back of the book, where a faded manilla envelope was taped to the binding.

“Girls, what you are about to hear can never be spoken about outside of this room. Do you understand?” I looked them dead in the eye.

“We promise.” They said it with very serious voices, no giggling or even a cracked smile about talking in unison. It seemed as though I wasn’t the only one that had changed over the last few months.

“Good. My mother left me a letter. Her visions told her that they were going to die. There was a lot that I am not going to go over right now. Towards the end, my mother left instructions on how witches seal themselves to their mates.” I opened the envelope, pulled three ribbons out and looked up at Colton. “It was common for coven leaders to bind themselves to more than one mate. Witches share their powers with their mates, and, if there is a third, it keeps the other mate alive if one were to die.”

Colton sank to his knees in front of me. “We can be sealed together?”

I smiled, feeling like my heart was going to explode with both excitement and nerves. “All three of us can be sealed together. Forever bonded.” I swallowed. “If that is what you want.”

He cursed happily, laughed, then kissed me. “Hell yes, that is what I want.”

I laughed and tipped my head toward Deacon, who was sitting on my other side. “You will be sealed to him too.”

Colton looked Deacon up and down, like he was honestly thinking it over. Deacon scowled and pushed him just hard enough to knock him off balance. Colton popped right back up and kissed our mate.

“I think I can live with that.”

“Jerk. Must you share everything good in my life?” Deacon mock scowled.

“Yes.” Colton stated firmly, somewhat breathless. We all chuckled then, the inside joke from when Deacon told him I was pregnant. “Thank you for being willing to share with me, my Lord.”

Deacon put his hand behind Colton’s head and pulled it toward his. All three of our heads were together. After a moment, Colton leaned back and cleared his throat.

“What do we do?”

“My parents blessed these ribbons for us. We need to sit in a triangle, the twins will tie these around our wrists, and then they will leave while we do the rest.” I gave them a don’t mess with me look and they giggled, finally, nodding.

I moved to an open spot on the floor and directed my mates on where to sit. We each held hands, holding tight to one another. I felt a shiver of nervous energy coming from Deacon. Mom didn’t say if we would be able to feel emotions with Colton like that. I hoped we did. I didn’t want him left out of anything.

The girls quietly tied the ribbons, kissed the top of my head, and left, locking the door behind them.

“Okay.” I took a deep breath. “You are going to repeat the words I say, after we each say them, we then say them together. Understand?”

They both nodded mutely. Colton had his own nervous energy, mixed with excitement in his eyes.

“What's mine is yours, what's yours is mine, together we make our souls combine.” I felt a pull in my chest and gasped for air. Holy cheese and crackers that hurt.

Deacon repeated my words, and then jerked. The pull on my chest got stronger. Then came Colton's turn. I felt like my heart was about to be ripped out of my chest. We waited for a beat, while we all caught our breath, then said them together. Slowly. Painfully.

"What's mine is yours… what's yours is mine… together we make… our souls combine."

That time, as the last words left our lips, I screamed. It sounded more like a groan of intense pain. Just as quickly the pain fled, and my heart warmed. The heat spread all over my body, likes flames crawling and licking me from the tip of my head, down to the tips of my toes. Then the inferno centered in my heart.

Right as I thought it was finally over, it took off, spreading once more. The heat felt like it was burning me from the inside out. The hotter it got, the more pain I felt, the tighter I held onto my mates. They were my lifeline. On some level, I could feel them going through the same thing, and I wanted to comfort them, be their lifeline as well.

It felt like we all sat there, fire burning through our veins, for hours, when in reality, it had probably only been mere minutes.

With the heat settled into my heart, slowly cooling back down, I carefully opened my eyes again. I hadn't even realized I had closed them. As I took my mates in, my heart started pounding, along with other parts of me. Both their eyes glowed deeper and brighter than ever before.

The ribbons and the clothes disappeared quickly. We didn't leave that floor for a long time. The need we all had was equal to that of the blood lust Deacon and I experienced when we traded blood during certain acts. All three of us had difficulty staying satisfied.

The scent in the air wasn't helping much either.

I passed out on the floor at some point, my body not able to handle anymore.

Chapter 19

Deacon

When my angel fell asleep, I was almost relieved. I had never been so tired in all my years. Still, this floor wouldn't be comfortable enough for her for long. I groaned as I pushed up, then slowly picked her up.

For once, Colton let me do all the work. He was still reeling from what happened. I sat on the edge of the bed, next to my mate, and let my head fall into my hands.

"I feel…" Colton started and stopped, still lying on his back on the floor.

I chuckled. I knew what he meant. I could feel them both now, too. I remembered the first time I felt my angel. It was a mind screw that was for sure.

"You feel us both."

"Yes. At least, I think that's what this is. I feel contentment, exhaustion, and then my own confusion." He rubbed his chest as though he were in pain. I lifted my head and looked toward him. "Now I feel a fluttering."

I laughed and threw a pillow at him. "The contentment is our sleeping mate. The exhaustion would be me. The confusion is you, as for the fluttering… Well, I had a moment of feeling love for you. Until you opened your mouth again."

Colton rotated his head enough to look at me. "I love you, too. Thank you for bringing me into this. I never imagined this was even possible."

I shook my head. "Neither did I. I never imagined sharing my mate with anyone. Then I saw the way you looked at her, and I felt pride. Pride in the beauty of my mate. Pride in her perfection. Pride that you desired her. I wanted to show you more of how perfect she was. Then I noticed how she responded to you. My best friend. And I felt pride again. Only this time, it was about you. Everything grew from there. I feel content as well. That feeling you get when you know everyone is safe. Everyone is home. That everything is finally as it should be."

Colton slowly rolled over and pushed himself to his knees. He was barely able to crawl toward the bed. Taking pity on him, I slid to the floor. He dropped down next to me, leaning against the bed.

"I feel the same. Like everything is the way it was always meant to be. Even though you both tried to include me, I still felt like I was on the outside. I don't feel that anymore."

Well, now I was feeling the fluttering. "I'm sorry you ever felt that way. You have always been part of this. Carrie's mom saw it. She said we were both meant to be her mates."

"That would make sense. She is going to be mad at you for reading that letter."

"No," I shook my head slowly, too tired for more than that, "she knew I was reading part of it over her shoulder in the car."

"Yes, but then you practically memorized it while she was sleeping that last hour."

I shrugged. "There are some parts in there that have not hit home for her yet. She was focused more on the goodbye and the bonding."

I could feel him struggling with his curiosity, it felt quite funny. I laughed when he caved with a sigh.

"Like what?"

"Like our mate is a Queen."

He gave me a look, like he thought I had lost it. "Deacon, babe, we already know she is a Queen. She became one when you became a King."

I chuckled softly and shook my head. "No, *dear*. She was born a Queen. She is from the Royal Witch's line. Her parents were not just any coven leaders. They were the King and Queen of the witches. Carrie was born a Princess. She just didn't know it. Her mom was limited on what she could tell her, since our mate was pulling away from the way of the witches. Remember, she stopped believing the stories for a time."

"I want to say you are messing with me somehow. But I have this weird burning sensation, making me feel like you are telling the truth."

I nodded and grinned. "Yes, that would be my angel's power to tell the truth from lies. She said this would happen."

"I thought it only happened in pure witch bindings."

"No. Her mother said the race didn't matter. Because of the blood bond, my access to it might be stronger, but we will both have it. Both powers will come in handy during the meetings with the humans." I glanced on to the bed, where our mate slept. "I wish this meant we could leave her here, where she is safest."

"As do I, but as we saw earlier, the others will get behind her before they will get behind us. And if she really is the Queen of the Witches, we need her to lead them."

I sighed and turned forward again.

"What else did the letter say?"

I grinned at my other mate. "Don't feel like waiting for her?"

Colton scowled at me, but the feeling I had coming from him was playful. Then suddenly changed to sadness.

"I don't want her to have to relive her mother saying goodbye."

I nodded and told him everything. He chuckled at the soap box parts, as did I. Our difference in opinion about morality was always a sticking point for the witches. We both sat in silence, lost to our own thoughts, for a time. The sun lowered, causing the room to darken where it could no longer reach.

It was odd. We hadn't sat next to each other, naked or otherwise, in silence, for so long.

Normally, we got distracted doing other things. Instead, we were content. We didn't feel the need to constantly remind ourselves that the other was there, that they chose to be with us. We didn't need that reassurance. We could feel it.

The love all three of us had for one another burned bright in my chest.

Fire runs through my veins, and yet, the burn from the bonding was the first time I had ever felt like I was actually burning on the inside.

I felt a flash of nervous energy coming down the hall. I looked over at Colton, who looked just as confused as I did. Both our eyes widened when someone knocked. He stood up slowly, giving me an eyeful, then slapped the back of my head when he felt the stirrings from me.

I mean, it was right there!

I just laughed. He flipped me off as he walked away from me. I could feel he was nearly where I was. That was something about feeling your mate's desire for you, it instantly sparked your own.

Colton opened the door, and we saw Bryant standing on the other side, hiding his nervous energy well. The older vampire guffawed.

"Do any of you ever wear clothes when you are locked in a room?"

Colton shrugged. "They just get in the way. Everything get settled?"

"Yes. The humans are in a suite on the third floor. They said they were fine sharing a room. Although, one of them is staying with the Nightwalker you brought home. I have a feeling they will be bonded soon."

Colton and I both laughed. We thought the same. Todd may have started out not liking certain things, but he got attached to Carter. It wasn't uncommon. Especially since Carter had provided more stability and affection than the boy was accustomed to.

At one of our stops, while Todd was inside with the others, Carter asked me how you marked someone. I was more than happy to tell my friend about the process. I just had to hope that Todd was ready for that. It wouldn't be a mated bond, since Carter was only a Nightwalker and did not have a soul to seal with Todd, but it would still tie them together. As long as they traded blood often enough, the tie would hold. If they ever decided to part ways, they would go through withdrawals, and discomfort. But in time, the tie would dissolve. I didn't see that happening though. Even if Todd started living a normal human life, I was sure they would maintain the bond.

"Thank you. Could you make sure enough food is supplied in the house for the humans? Our Queen has been craving strawberries frequently."

Bryant chuckled. "Yes, my Lord." He looked at Colton oddly. "Did you all do something? You seem different somehow." He leaned in and sniffed. "Your scent has changed, too."

Colton looked nervously back at me. I felt those butterflies in my stomach again. It wasn't until then that I realized it had been a while since Carrie had been that nervous. She had adjusted to our new life with the grace of the royal blood she was born with. I stood and walked over to the open door.

"My King." Bryant bowed again.

"Bryant? How strong is the scent change? Do you smell it on me as well?"

He leaned over and sniffed me. "Yes. It's as though your scents have been blended with the Queen. Are you sure him trading blood with both of you was wise? It might weaken your bond, and our Queen's body."

I sighed. "How noticeable is it? Will even the younger ones be able to tell?"

He shrugged. "Possibly."

"Alright, we weren't going to say anything, but I guess we will have to. No, he did not trade blood with us. Carrie was able to find the witch's spell for bonding. She and Colton used that. This way we are both bonded with her in one way or another, hopefully giving her the extra strength that her body needs. In the book you brought over for her last night, was a letter from her mother. There is no general timeline to follow. Carrie gestated for only four months, her father six. It all depends on the magic of the baby. Seeing as no one can remember a set time for vampire babies, I'm thinking we are much the same."

Bryant nodded, his eyes looking to the past. "That sounds like a good plan. Was that why you all have been hiding away all afternoon?"

I felt the strangest sense of protectiveness coming from the vampire in front of us. It felt like he was holding a shield over me. He often played the role of my grandfather when I was younger.

"Yes. We were anxious to do it as soon as possible. Just like with our own matings, there are side effects in the beginning." I winked at Colton, who turned away with a small blush.

Bryant laughed hard, his head tipping back. "Yes. That is something I will never forget. My Miriam and I didn't leave the bedroom for two days. Unfortunately, we don't have the time for you to soak it all in. I wish you did. I will see to the groceries and send for warmer clothes for all of the humans. We are due for snow fall soon, with December just around the corner. I'm surprised we had clear roads, I expected otherwise. Does the Queen have any preferences?"

"Skirts." I answered automatically. Colton choked on the laugh he was trying to hold back. "I didn't say *mini*skirts. Besides, she said it herself this morning. Her jeans are getting a little tight. She already has the slightest bump beginning. A couple pairs of sweats would be good too, loose ones."

Colton's impressed look irked me, which he found amusing. Not that anyone else could see most of that. But we both felt it from the other.

"As you wish, my King. I will send someone out immediately. Will she need dinner for the night?"

"No, she will be sleeping the rest of the night."

Bryant bowed one more time and walked away. His intent solely focused on accomplishing his tasks, nurturing, and fulfilling our needs.

Colton turned to me as he locked the door again. “Carrie is not going to sleep much longer, and she will be hungry when she wakes up.”

I walked straight over to the bed, lying down next to her. “I know. But she needs her sleep. If we are this tired, imagine how tired she is.” I slid my arm under her neck, then bit into my wrist. Even in her sleep, she greedily accepted it.

Colton sighed and sat at my feet. “She is going to be mad at you in the morning.”

I shrugged. “It never lasts.” I grinned at him. “Which do you think will soothe her more? Us, or the strawberries?”

Colton laughed and shook his head. It didn’t take long before her lips fell away from me. My blood increased the melatonin in her body so she was comatose and would be for the rest of the night. Nothing would wake her.

After sealing my wrist, I slowly lowered my nose and enjoyed the aroma of her neck. It was better than ever.

“Her scent has changed with ours.”

I took a long, deep inhale through my nose, enjoying the new blend. Then I sank my teeth into her neck. I moaned and my eyes rolled to the back of my head. She tasted better than ever too. It made me hungry to try Colton’s blood. Something that would have to wait until after our son was born, of course. We couldn’t take any risks right now.

Colton was ready and waiting for me when I finished. He knew well what her blood did to me. And from the feelings coming from him, he enjoyed watching me feed from our mate, nearly as much as I enjoyed doing it. Which made me feel better about him not being able to feed from her. I had always felt a little guilty about that. Carrie did as well.

It was hard, pun intended, on both of us that we had to wait until I finished. Especially tonight, we didn't want to risk the other effects.

After we both got what we needed, we kissed her growing baby bump, then snuggled in next to her.

Chapter 20

Carrie

I woke up to the wonderful soreness that came as a result of an afternoon of the good kind of workout sessions. I reveled in the warmth of my mates beside me, and the feeling of both of them in my heart. I could no longer feel the guilt I always carried with me. The guilt that came from worrying about Colton feeling left out.

I smiled, feeling both their contentment and joy. I giggled when I finally opened my eyes and saw them both asleep. I had passed out on the floor, but I knew, even then, that I would wake up in the bed.

I was just deciding to snuggle in deeper and enjoy the moment when my bladder woke up. I didn't want to wake either of them, they needed the rest as much as I did. But the need was real.

Should I carefully try to lift both their anaconda arms off me? Or just get it over with and wake them up?

What time was it anyway?

I mentally cursed, realizing we left all the others to do all the work and hid away in our rooms to play together. As soon as I was done in the bathroom, I was going to run down to see what was left.

I looked around the room, trying to find a clock. On the far-right wall, I spotted a beautiful wood analog clock. The numbers were in roman numerals and looked to be placed directly on the wall. It took me a minute for my still sleepy brain to translate the numbers into English.

I frowned in confusion. Seven? I glanced at the blinds, where the sun was already shining through. Was it always so bright at seven at night here, this close to Winter?

No. I sure bet it wasn't. I moved my eyes to the mate on my right. I was willing to bet it was seven in the morning. I knew exactly what had happened. Again.

Now that I was thinking about it, I even remembered dreaming about him feeding me.

That made my decision for me. I picked up Colton's arm slowly. It moved fairly easily considering the weight. I only had it an inch off me when it started moving on its own. I turned my head and his eyes widened, noticing, whether by the look on my face, or the feeling he got from me, I was ticked!

Both his hands shot back, in surrender mode. I just nodded slowly. I already knew he had nothing to do with it. Then the other snake around my waist tightened and I stiffened in response. I didn't even look at him.

"Colton, please help me up. I need to use the bathroom."

I felt the confusion from both sides, but Colton caught on faster. He grinned and jumped up.

"Sure, sweetheart. You feeling alright?"

“Fine, thank you. Just the effects of sleeping longer than I planned, mixed with a boy who seems to take after his father.” I turned to glare at the grimacing mate still on the bed. “Thinking he knows better than everyone else.”

“Angel…” Deacon called in a partial plea, as I walked away from him.

“I told you.” I heard Colton hiss right before I closed the bathroom door.

I already knew the reasons Deacon did it. It was the same as always. It didn’t matter how many times I told him to stop knocking me out like that, he still did it when he thought I needed more sleep.

Why did he think he knew my body better than I did?

I took my time washing my hands. I could feel both of their anxieties. I did feel a little guilty that Colton was going to pay for this too, but there wasn’t much I could do about that.

I stood at the bathroom door, my hand on the knob. I wasn’t ready to go deal with Deacon yet. Plus, he proved the other day just how much he hated the distance. So, I let go of the knob and walked over to the shower.

I took a very long shower. Alone. The hot water felt good on my sore muscles. I couldn’t quite tell the difference between their feelings yet. All I could tell was that one was sad, and the other was smug. I figured Deacon was the former and Colton was the latter.

Nearly an hour had passed from the time that I woke up to the time that I walked out of the bathroom. Wearing nothing but a towel around me. My blow-dried hair twisted over one shoulder.

"Bryant sent someone shopping last night. I told him to get you dresses and sweats." Deacon's voice sounded pitiful, like he was begging for something.

"Thank you." I didn't even look at him. I turned to face Colton.

"They've already been put in the closet and the dresser. We put everything away last night. Same places you had them before."

I nodded my thanks and headed for the dresser. Deacon tried to grab my hand, but I pulled it away. When I felt his flash of irritation I spun on him. With one finger in the air, pointing at him, I finally told him off.

"Don't. You have no reason to be mad at me. I've told you time and again to stop doing that. You know I don't like sleeping through everything. I have told you repeatedly to stop forcing me under like that. How many times have I told you in the past to stop pushing your will on me, Deacon?"

He opened his mouth to argue, but I cut him off. "I know most of it was for good reasons. But it should still have been *my* choice from the very beginning. If you think I need more sleep, *ask* me first next time. You don't get to make decisions about my body for me! You knew I would be upset, yet you did it anyway. Does my opinion matter for anything?"

He stepped forward, probably about to hug me, but I stepped back. I raised a hand between us and looked away. I didn't want that stupid fated mate bond to force me to forgive him yet.

"I need some space right now."

He nodded sadly and walked into the bathroom. I sighed, immediately feeling guilty.

Colton came up from behind me, wrapping his arms around me. "He meant well."

“I know. But he can’t keep taking my free will away from me.”

Colton kissed my head, and then followed after Deacon. I opened the drawer I used for pants, not really feeling like wearing sweats. But I also didn’t want to wear a dress in the cold. Or the jeans that were getting tighter.

I was relieved to see that the sweats weren’t actual sweatpants. They were actually leggings made out of fleece. Perfect. I found a light sweater to wear with them too.

They were both still in the shower by the time I was dressed. For once, I hated the fact that I could feel their feelings. Deacon felt bad, but not guilty. Colton felt torn and confused. At least, I was assuming those were each of theirs. It made the most sense.

It all just made me want to cry. So, I did. And, oh boy, did I.

It wasn’t long before a pair of arms wrapped around me from the side, pulling me onto his lap. There was no thinking involved, I just turned into him and cried into his neck. Stupid fate bond.

“I honestly thought the rest would be good for you and your body.”

I huffed in annoyance.

“I’ll ask first next time. I promise.”

I leaned back enough to look at Deacon. “There will be no more next time. What happens if we get attacked? I won’t be able to defend myself. And you two could already be off fighting someone else. What if I go into labor randomly, but I can’t wake up? What if the baby is crying and needs to eat, but you decided I needed more sleep because he kept me up the night before? What if a Witch or a Shifter comes and they need to talk to me, but you put me in a coma? There are too many possibilities, Deacon.”

His eyebrows scrunched up, and I could feel he was finally thinking about what I said. I let him hold me while he processed it all. I kind of needed it to. Stupid bond.

The moment lightened when my stomach decided to add its own reasonings for why I should not sleep so long. They both found that to be the funniest thing ever.

I pushed Deacon over and climbed off his lap, walking out of the room. They were both still undressed when I stepped out, but they were both fully dressed and by my side before I made it five feet from the door.

I still didn't talk to him much while he made me French Toast - in an effort to suck up - with extra syrup, and a bowl of strawberries on the side.

The teenagers joined us eventually. The twins caught on to my irritation with him and were giggling like normal. Everyone else watched us warily.

"I need to go call the human General. We need to know where they stand with everything." Colton stood up, a little later, from where they had sat with me at the table, kissing my forehead. "Be nice."

I scowled at him, and he laughed.

He turned to Deacon, kissing the top of his head. "Behave."

Deacon was the one scowling then, and I was the one laughing. Deacon's scowl dropped quickly, and I felt the fluttering from him. He loved it when I laughed, even if it was at his expense. Which sobered me up again rather quickly.

"Speaking of calls. I should call Clarise. She's probably ready to pull her hair out. It's been too long since I checked in."

Deacon pushed a lock of hair behind my ear, bending down to sniff my neck. "Do you need help?"

I stood up, pulling away from him. "Nope. I do recall how to dial a phone. And I'm sure you have royal duties you could be doing somewhere."

I ignored the ooh's, and other childish comments from the males in the kitchen. The twins, and Rachel, caught my eye, silently asking if they should come with me. I just shook my head and headed back to our room.

I found my old beat-up backpack. The same one I had packed for the bus trip from Phoenix to LA. It felt like a lifetime ago, not just over three months. I plugged my phone into the wall near the bed and curled up.

Clarise answered immediately but didn't speak to me.

"Miss Anna? Will you come cover me for a minute, please?" I heard her shout toward someone.

I slapped myself. Of course, she's at work. Most people were still living their normal lives.

"Two seconds, girl. Don't you dare go anywhere on me!"

I just laughed as I heard the phone move again.

"It's Carrie, finally checking in. Thank you for covering."

That was weird. Had they all been talking about me or something? I barely knew Anna. She was a few years older, and the school counselor. I really only knew her in passing.

"Take your time. Grill that girl good." Her voice sounded firm, and like there was an underlying message I wasn't getting.

A door closed, footsteps ran down a hall, and then I heard another door open and close.

"Okay. I'm in the staff lounge. What the hell, girl? Where have you been? I haven't gotten so much as a message from you in weeks!"

"I know. I'm so sorry. You would not *believe* what all has happened."

Clarise scoffed. "Try me."

The pregnancy hormones were having a field day with me today. I heard the challenge and accepted it.

"Alright, you asked for it. I've been keeping a few things from you."

"Yeah, I already knew that." She snarked.

"You want me to tell you everything or do you want to keep giving me attitude?" My eyes widened and my hand shot to my mouth.

The other side of the phone was quieter than the grave. Until it wasn't. I could practically see my best friend bending at the waist, slapping her legs, laughing so hard I was sure she had tears coming out her eyes.

When she finally regained some control, she spoke again. "What the hell crawled up your butt and nested?"

"Vampire sperm." I moped out.

Crickets.

Crickets.

Crickets.

"Clarise?"

“Say that again, Carrie.” She wasn’t laughing anymore. Far from it.

I cleared my throat awkwardly. “You remember my drop-dead gorgeous boss that saved me from the vamp chasing me?”

“Ya huh.”

“Turns out he is a vamp of another type.”

Clarise sighed with disappointment. “Please tell me you are not shacking up with a Vampire Born.”

I pulled my phone away from my ear, looking at the screen with confusion. Nope, it still said Clarise.

“How do you know about them?”

Clarise huffed once. “I may have kept a few things from you too. But, before you go getting all mad at me, remember, you never once felt like I was lying to you or had bad intentions. You are my best friend. You just weren’t ready to hear the rest yet.”

“What the hell are you talking about?” I yelled.

I felt concern spike in my chest. My mates were reacting to my roller coaster emotions. I took a few deep breaths, calming myself and them.

“Nu huh. You first.”

I growled into the phone. “Fine. I’m not just shacking up with one. Turns out Deacon is my fated mate, kind of like a soul mate. We also invited his best friend to be part of our mating. I found a letter from my mom in an old book that Colton, my other mate, brought from my house when he was there a few weeks ago. She apparently *saw* that I would have them both. Anyway, it's a long story.”

"Are you pregnant? Is that what you meant by vamp sperm?"

"Yup. And this sucker ain't following no nine-month schedule."

"Of course, he wouldn't. Not with as powerful as you are."

"Ya huh. Your turn."

"Our mothers were close friends. My mom was the coven healer. I have her gift. That's why you felt comfortable around me."

"Say what, now?"

"You are my Queen. A good portion of this school is in our coven. Your mom instructed the coven to give you time. She promised that you would come back to us and lead us. When you got trapped in LA, we all freaked. We are trying to figure out a way to get you out of there."

I giggled. "Well, you all can stop worrying about that one. I'm already out."

"What? When?" It was Clarise's turn to yell into the phone.

"I don't know, a week or two ago. It's been crazy, and hard to track time. Deacon jumped the wall with me on his back."

"Why? Why didn't you both just hide in there somewhere?"

"Because my fated mate isn't just any Vampire Born. He is the Prince. Well, was. His father was murdered by Curtis, the night we got out. Now, my mate is the King."

Clarise was silent for a few beats, processing. "So. What you're saying, is that you aren't just Queen of the Witches anymore?"

I huffed again and picked at my nail. "Nope. And it seems the shifters prefer speaking to me instead of one of my mates. Just call me Queen of the Freaks."

"Well, you've always held that title, sweetheart." Clarise sighed. "Where are you now?"

"Colorado."

"Okay. Send me the specifics. I will catch the first flight out."

I sat up in shock. "What? You're coming here? Why? Is it safe? Can you get it off?"

Clarise chuckled softly. "Chill, girlfriend. Like I said, this school is filled with coven members. Besides, I am your healer. You are pregnant. *And* my best friend. Do you really think I am going to let you go through this pregnancy, for however long it takes, without me? You are going to need a midwife, and that's me honey."

I hadn't thought about the birthing part yet. But I guessed it wasn't exactly like I could go see a human doctor here.

"Do you even know anything about vampire babies? It's been quite a while since one was born."

She gave me that "don't be so ridiculous" laugh. "A magical baby is a magical baby. Besides, you are going to need me to help bridge the gap between you and the rest of the covens anyway. Your mom did say that when you came back into the fold, it was going to be a doozie. That and I miss my best friend." That last part was both nonchalant and filled with love.

I sniffled and wiped my eyes. Stupid hormones. "Sorry. My emotions have been everywhere today." My voice cracked the same time my bedroom door opened.

Deacon had the door closed and was by my side seconds later.

Clarise laughed again. "How far along are you?"

"Maybe a month, maybe a little less. But I already have cravings, I pee a ton, and obviously my emotions can't be trusted." Deacon slid his hand softly over my stomach. "Awe, yes, and my clothes are already getting tight."

Clarise whistled. "Definitely not working on a nine-month scale here." Her voice sounded further away, like I was moved to speakerphone. "I can catch a flight in the next few hours. Cross your fingers they all let me come alone. You don't mind if I tell them, do you? Or is it safer if no one knows yet?"

I looked up at Deacon, momentarily forgetting that I was supposed to be mad at him. He just shrugged.

"How well do you think they will take it? I mean, it's not like I haven't been the black sheep of the coven, even though apparently I am supposed to be some Princess, Queen, person, that I knew nothing about before yesterday. And now I'm pregnant with the heir to the vampire throne. Oh, and my mother did say they have always tried to keep the line pure. Pretty sure I just muddied it up a bit."

And my hormones were swinging a whole new way now. This time they were headed down. Far, far down.

Deacon rubbed my back softly and tried to soothe me. And now they were swinging another way, one that had him sitting up straighter when he felt it. That stupid grin spread on his stupidly handsome face.

"Oh, honey. It's alright. They are going to be happy no matter what. We've all been waiting for you. Besides, it's a *vampire baby*. This is a big stinking deal."

Now Deacon was grinning for a whole new reason. Pride. I pushed him away with my shoulder. Or, rather, tried to anyway. He refused to move like he was supposed to, he only held me tighter.

Any chance the baby would imbibe me with some of its vampire strength?

I'd be willing to trade out the sense of smell for it.

"Alright, I need to go to talk to Mr. Sorenson, who is also part of the coven." I gasped, she giggled. "So much we need to talk about, girl. Don't forget to send me that address, or even better, send someone to get me. Make it a cutie too. I'm nowhere near the royal line. And I sure ain't pure. I've always wanted to try me a vamp on for size."

I laughed at the way she smacked her lips. Deacon nearly choked on the laughter he was trying to hold back.

"Thanks, Clarise. I can't tell you how much all of this means to me." And the waterworks started again.

"Psh, nothing to it. I've been itching for you to come back to the fold. And don't worry about the others. They will be so happy to put an end to our rescue plan, and hear that you are safe, they won't care about anything else. You are the Queen for a reason. Anyone who says otherwise can suck it!" She said goodbye and hung up.

"I take it your friend is coming for a visit?" Deacon smirked.

"Uh, yeah. Apparently half my school is part of my coven. And my best friend is the coven healer. She is coming to act as my midwife. With everything going on, I hadn't even thought about the doctor stuff. I guess part of my brain is still thinking about human pregnancies. How, with all this? I have no idea." I waved at my belly that should have still been the same size for a couple more months.

Deacon exhaled, sounding like a huge weight had just been lifted off his shoulders. When I gave him a questioning look, he filled me in.

"It may not have been on yours, but it has been on ours. It will make both Colton and me feel more comfortable if we have someone who knows what they are doing here. What is her power?"

I leaned against him and thought carefully. "She said she has her mom's gift, and she was the coven healer before. If I remember right, my mom always had a friend come over when one of us was hurt or sick. You can't help but feel calm in their presence. Like a warm blanket. Which may be why I trusted Clarise so quickly. I always felt comfortable around her."

"I am glad she is coming then." He closed his eyes and laid his head against mine. "I really am sorry about last night. I don't want to force you into anything. I never have. But Colton and I could barely walk after the bonding. We napped, unpacked, and then passed back out. I'm sorry I made you feel like I was being pushy again."

"I know. And feeling how bad you felt about it, made me feel guilty. And then feeling how Colton was torn between us, not wanting to take sides. It was all just too much for me."

"I get it. I could feel how upset you were, and how sad you were, and how guilty you felt. Which just made it all worse. I love you so much. I just want to do what's best for you."

"I know. But it's not your decision on what's best for me. That's my choice and my choice alone."

Deacon started kissing me softly, making it even harder to stay mad at him.

And then my stomach growled. We broke apart laughing.

"Would you like to eat?"

I frowned. "I just ate!"

Deacon laughed again and then stood up. “Yes, but my son has a voracious appetite… Just like his father.” He winked at me and pulled me toward the kitchen again.

Chapter 21

Colton

I now understood why Deacon backed away anytime Carrie and I argued before. Being stuck in the middle, between two people you loved, was not an easy place to be. And that was before we could feel one another so deeply.

I could feel what their fight was doing to both of them. I wanted to comfort both of them. But I didn't want to pick sides. At least our girl wanted space, so I didn't have too.

When I joined Deacon in the shower, I fully planned on giving him crap. I told him she would be mad. He blew it off like it wasn't a big deal. Ha! Joke was on him. Only, this was one bad joke.

Unfortunately, he already looked like someone had stolen his puppy when I caught up to him. I didn't have the heart to add to it.

"I never saw it as pushing her to do what I want. I wasn't trying to hurt her."

"I know. I think most of this is the pregnancy hormones. Just give her time."

If I thought the painful look on his face was bad, the stab of guilt when she felt it was worse. That was not how our usual mornings went.

The air around them was tense enough that everyone in the house picked up on it. Carter was right behind me when I left the kitchen for what I assumed would be my office.

"What the hell did Deacon do now?"

"It's nothing. Just a misunderstanding mixed with pregnancy hormones. It will blow over." Hopefully very soon. "Did you need something?"

Carter looked around like he was trying to find answers in the air, then sighed. "What can I do? I'm a little lost here."

I huffed and leaned against the empty desk. "For now, just hang around. We are all kind of in limbo at the moment. Have you been able to catch the news yet this morning?"

"Yeah. Looks like Curtis is hitting more cities. I swear I knew nothing about those. I thought we were just taking Cali for us. That was it."

I nodded. "I'm not surprised. Curtis has never been one to share his plans with the class. Go find Bryant, the head of staff, ask him if there is anything you can help with. No one has lived in this house for decades. It will need to be cleaned up. The other cabins too."

Carter scratched his chin. "Just how many of you are there, anyway?"

"Last I checked, over two thousand. At least in the states. Not everyone will come here. But many will. Mostly to see the pregnant Queen for themselves."

Carter nodded distractedly as he left.

I paused as I began to dial my phone. Carrie's emotions were all over the place. It was the buildup of anxiety that concerned me. I felt Deacon go on alert, then Carrie began to relax. She must have been having a pretty intense conversation with her friend. Deacon didn't seem to be relaxing all that much though. Not that I expected him too until they kissed and made up.

With a resigned sigh I put my phone to my ear. It was a few rings before a professional female voice answered.

"General McKay's office."

"Hello. I need to speak with the General immediately. Please."

"Who may I say is calling?"

"General Colton, of the Royal Born Army."

"I'm sorry, sir. I do not recognize your organization and he has asked to not be disturbed by anyone."

"Trust me, he'll want to talk to me."

She gave me a very audible, frustrated sigh. "Just one moment, sir."

It was two, and it wasn't her that picked back up.

"Why the hell would I want to talk to any of your people right now? I don't care what that King of yours says, a vampire is a vampire." I heard him spit on the ground. It was disgusting.

I growled at his disrespectful attitude. "If you think you are the only one losing leaders in this fight, you're wrong. King Dominic was murdered the night we left Phoenix. All because *you* decided to try and hold his son and daughter-in-law hostage to use against us."

"Well, now… see here. His death had nothing to do with us. And we had no way of knowing their relationship beforehand."

I sneered at him. "Had you told us that you had them, we would have told you. Instead, you kept them there, close enough for the Nightwalkers to see, until Curtis was able to catch up. Then he had his men follow us." I clinched my jaw, trying to pull myself together, and to keep from saying something that would make the situation impossible to work through. "We shouldn't be fighting. We should be working together. Now more than ever. Curtis is stepping up his game."

"We don't need you. We can do this on our own."

I laughed sardonically. "You wouldn't even be able to pick one of them out of a line up. Us on the other hand, we know them by sight and smell. Vampires are not the only magical species out there. Do you really want this turning into humans versus magic? It will not turn out well for you."

The line was quiet for a minute. When the General spoke again, his voice was low. "What do you mean more species? What else is there?"

"Two more. All things I would rather not discuss over the phone. We have representatives from each race willing to meet with you in a summit. You already know what we want. We know what you want. Now we need to find middle ground. But if you even think about double crossing us, this war will be over faster than you thought possible. And you will *not* be on the winning side."

I waited a few minutes, giving him time to process. "Talk to your new President. Get back to me. Oh, and this time, we meet somewhere in the middle. We will not come to you again. This is your last chance to make allies with those who have the power to end this."

I hung up in a hurry, dropping my phone on the desk. I gasped for air and hunched over and gripped the desk for support. What the hell was this?

I slowly sat down in the chair, trying to figure out what was going on. I felt anxiety and fear. But that wasn't what confused me. I also felt a deep depression. The fear of being unwanted, of being a castoff.

Was that Carrie?

I felt the rush of relief mixed with the rest, and then a slow calming of the others. Deacon must have gotten to her. I jumped to my feet and started walking out of the office, headed for my mates, but then my phone started ringing from where I left it on the desk.

I felt conflicted. Carrie needed us. I needed to see that she was alright. But I also needed to answer that call.

A warm, soothing feeling flooded through me. The flutter I felt from last night with it. I smirked. Deacon was telling me it was okay to stay. The dark feelings were gone now. Whatever had descended on our mate had already passed.

I picked up my phone just before it went to voicemail, feeling only slightly mollified. I needed to know what had happened and why. I needed to know how to keep her from feeling that way again.

"Hello."

A deep chuckle sounded from the other side. "Well, aren't you in a good mood this morning?"

I may have been a little snarky in my greeting, but the laughter on the other end wasn't as annoying of an interruption as it could have been, so I smirked. "It's already been a long one. What can I do for you, Alpha?"

“Wish I could say I was calling to cheer you up, but I’m not. The wall is back up.”

I sank into my chair. “More rubble?”

“No. It’s cemented over. I doubt even Deac would get over this one. I’ve spent the last 24 hours talking to the other bases. I waited until I knew you all were safe again before calling. Somehow, he finished nearly 500 miles worth of wall… overnight.”

I cursed and stood back up. I paced back and forth behind my desk, my speed getting faster with each pass.

“Have you heard from the little witch yet?”

“No. I’ve thought about sending her a message, but with her that close to him…”

“Yeah, I get it. We don’t want to accidentally blow her cover.” I growled out in frustration, my free hand pulling at the back of my head. “He has to have a witch on his side. One that can freeze time. There is no other way. When the little witch contacts again, see if she knows anything.” I smelled my mates nearby and turned to see them both in the doorway. Just the sight and smell of them had my nerves calming.

“If Curtis has a time freezing witch, we need to know. That puts us on a whole other playing field. The humans will be no help then.” I continued.

“Have you spoken to them yet?”

“Yes, just a few minutes ago. I told them this was their last chance. Whatever they decide though, we still have to keep going. I would just rather not have to fight two wars at the same time.”

Hill huffed. “You and me both. You’ll let me know?”

“Yes. And you let us know when you hear from the witch.”

"Always a pleasure speaking with you, Colton."

I gave a small huff as I hung up the phone and went straight to Carrie. "What happened? I felt your pain. I've never even imagined something like that before."

She looked like she had no idea what I was talking about.

"She was talking to her friend. Turns out, angel here has been surrounded by her coven all along. She got worried they would not accept her or our child." Deacon explained, wrapping an arm around her back.

I let out the breath I had apparently been holding since I chose to answer the phone instead of going to her.

"I'm sorry. I wanted to come, but..."

Carrie cut me off. "But you were needed here. I was fine. I *am* fine. Now, what is this about Grace?"

I kissed her head; grateful she was both feeling better and had forgiven Deacon already.

"Curtis finished rebuilding his wall the other night. All of it. California is officially sealed off from the U.S. by land." I explained both my calls to them.

"I'm sure the humans will change their minds once they find out about the wall." Carrie was such an optimist. "In the meantime. Feed me. This son of ours is a glutton already."

We all laughed and walked back to the kitchen together. It had only been a little over an hour, but things were back to normal.

Deacon made our mate a sandwich with the leftover French toast he had prepared not that long ago, while she told me about her call. I told Steve to go pick her friend up from the airport. I also asked Bryant to arrange one of the rooms on our floor for Clarise. If anything happened, I wanted her close by to help take care of our mate and son.

Just before dinner that evening, Steve opened the front door, holding a large suitcase, and looking happier than ever. Right behind him was a woman a few years older than Carrie. She had a little more weight to her, but she owned it. That woman had confidence in spades. And Steve looked even more pleased with it.

Clarise winked at him as she passed through the door. Then squealed and ran to Carrie.

“Girl. I missed you so much!”

Carrie laughed and held her tight. “I missed you, too.” She pulled away from her with a serious look that did not match the amusement I felt brimming inside of her. “Just be warned. We are supremely outnumbered when it comes to the men to women ratio. And they don’t care about who they are with or what they are doing.”

Clarise’s eyes sparkled. “Why do you think I wanted to come?”

Steve snorted and walked up behind her. “I think you and I will get along *really* well.”

Clarise’s head moved up and down slowly as she made a show of checking him out. “We’ll see.”

Carrie tried to keep a straight face but failed. “I almost forgot how forward you are. Maybe you should have been in that bar instead of me.”

“Nope.” Deacon and I said at the same time.

“I take it these are the mates, then?”

Carrie put an arm around both of us. "Yes. This is Deacon and Colton." Clarise licked her lips and checked us out slowly now. "Hey, none of that." Carrie put her foot out and tried to kick her.

Clarise just stepped back. We all laughed.

"Just messing with you. I must say though, they are both a step up from the douche."

"Yeah, yeah. Moving on. Are you hungry? Dinner is almost ready."

"Starving. But first things first. Lift that shirt, missy."

"Now that, I am all for!" Deacon laughed, grabbing her shirt, and lifting it up with unabashed enthusiasm.

"Not that high!" Carrie squeaked, pushing her shirt down to just under her chest.

Deacon just gave her his smug "I didn't do anything" look. Thankfully, she only rolled her eyes at him. I may have held my breath again.

Clarise dropped to her knees in front of her, and everyone who was in the room went quiet. The room filled with this peaceful feeling. Like all was right in the world. Carrie sighed and laid her head on my chest.

Her friend placed both of her hands on our mate's stomach and closed her eyes. We all watched, waiting. I wanted to feel anxious, but it was hard to do with that warm feeling covering us. Clarise moved her hands to different sides, tilted her head like she was trying to hear somebody better, and then, finally, she smiled.

"There he is. Oh, a big boy too. No wonder you are showing already." She slowly stood back up, her hands still there, her eyes open now. "Your sons are very healthy."

Cheers went up over the whole room, which had doubled in number over the last ten minutes. I pulled Deacon's head over our mate's, and kissed him, both of us laughing with joy. Clarise's jaw dropped, which made Carrie giggle.

"I told you." She told her friend smugly. Deacon spanked her butt. She yelped with a jump. "So, he is good then? All is good?"

"Oh, yes. Those two little boys are going to be powerful little men. I can feel it. I say you have three, maybe four months. Tops. What have you been doing to keep her strong?" She turned to Deacon.

"Hold up." I held my hand up, stopping Deacon from responding.

Carrie's jaw was on the floor, as what her friend said clicked for her as well.

"Did you just say *two* little boys?" Surely I heard her wrong.

Clarise looked at me like I was stupid. "Yes, of course. Carrie is having twins."

"That's not possible." Carrie whispered. "Check again, Clare."

Confused, Clarise moved her hands around. "Right here is one." She moved her hands slowly to the other side of my mate's small baby bump, her ear leaning in closer. "And here is another. Yes. You are having two boys. That's a good thing, yes?"

Carrie looked up at me, and then over to Deacon. Deacon looked to have checked out, so she turned back to me.

"Colton?" Her voice shook, taking the tone on that made me want to bend to anything she wanted. This time I had no clue how to do that though.

"I've never heard of a vampire having twins before. That doesn't mean it hasn't happened."

Deacon finally seemed to have come back to his own head. He grabbed Carrie by the back of the neck and twisted her around to kiss her. I laughed along with the rest. No one knew more than I how badly he had wanted a son. Well, maybe Carrie. But I was the one who had to witness it all for a hundred very long years.

"I will protect you." I reached over and smacked him in the head. He laughed. "Sorry, *we* will protect you. From the moment I saw you, I knew you were my angel. My everything." I kicked him this time, making everyone else laugh. His eyes came up to mine, the fire glowing. "Really going to be greedy right now?"

"Uh, yeah." I gave him a duh attitude.

"Oh, both of you shut up." Carrie half laughed and half snarked at us, while shaking her head.

"If this is as rare as you say it is, then we need to make sure you and the babies are blessed as soon as possible." Clarise told her. "We will get to that in a minute though. Deacon, what have you been doing to keep her strong?"

Deacon cleared his throat and blinked his eyes. "I feed her my blood. Our blood can strengthen our mates. A psychic witch we met told us to keep on the path we were on, and that was it."

"How often do you feed her?"

"Every night." Deacon had the good sense to feel at least a little upset. Probably remembering why, he had been in so much trouble this morning.

"Good. Keep doing it. If it is working, then we do not want to mess with it." She turned her attention back to Carrie. "How are your normal eating habits?"

"No change, really."

I choked on the snort I tried to hold back. Carrie elbowed me.

"Fine. A little more than normal."

"A little?" Carter smirked from a couch in the corner. Todd was standing next to him, grinning, his hand on Carter's shoulder. Carrie flipped him off.

My phone rang, so I stepped to the side, moving a little away from their teasing. Clarise finally let go of my mate's stomach, letting her lower her shirt again. I was paying more attention to them than the phone. I didn't even look at the screen before answering.

"Hello?"

"*General* Colton."

I straightened up from the deep and tense voice. Deacon and Carrie's heads snapped to me.

"General McKay. I'm a little surprised to hear from you so soon."

He huffed in irritation. "I was out voted."

I gave a half smirk this time. "Ah, democracy at its finest. What can I do for you?"

He let out a low growl, obviously not happy with having to make this call. "The Vi…the President would like to meet with you and your little friends. He agreed to your stipulation in finding common ground."

"Great. How about Durango? It's still a few hours from where we are currently staying, so we have no home field advantage."

He grunted again. "Fine. Monday, noon."

I chuckled. "That's fine. As we said before, the sun does not affect us. Any time works. I'll have a friend scout out buildings in the area and will send you the coordinates. See you soon, General."

"He agreed to a meeting?" Deacon asked as soon as I hung up.

"Yes. Monday." I turned to Clarise. "Is she okay to keep traveling? The shifters have already said they are more comfortable working with her, rather than us."

"Yes. But only if I go too. She doesn't go anywhere without me until after those babies are born. You lot aren't the only ones who need her alive."

"Agreed." Deacon's voice took on that of a command. Not that any of us would have argued.

"If you tell me where, I will have a few coven leaders meet us there. They can bless her then. Besides, if the shifters and the vampires have multiple representatives, the witches should as well."

"We welcome all the support we can get." I told her.

"Well, on that happy note. These boys are hungry. Let's eat." Deacon and I both frowned when Carrie grabbed her friend's hands instead of ours and left the room.

"I'm not sure I like this change very much anymore." Deacon pouted.

I chuckled and patted him on the back. "Come on." I kissed his head. "Twins, Deac. Can you believe it?"

He shook his head in disbelief. "Not really, no. She just got an even bigger target on her back from Curtis though."

"No worries, my King. When the word spreads that we have a Queen carrying twins, *every* royal will come to protect her. Whatever Curtis has promised to any turncoats will turn to ash compared to this." Bryant told us firmly, not betraying the emotion dancing in his eyes.

Chapter 22

Grace

I blinked my eyes at the bright sunlight coming through the open window. I smiled when I realized what the comfort of the bed, the brightness of the sun, and the real window (instead of a plastic window in a tent) meant that time had been restarted. Finally.

I lifted my arms above my head and rolled onto my back. Well, I tried to at any rate. I was met by a brick wall. The smile crossed my face of its own accord again. It grew even wider when the brick wall started to move. I rolled further and buried my face into him, sighing. Which then caused the wall to shake with laughter.

"Shush." I followed the soft command with a yawn.

The wall, of course, shook harder, soft laughter accompanying it. I poked him in the stomach, and the soft laughter soon turned to barking laughter. I didn't even open my eyes. I just closed them tighter and snuggled into him with another yawn.

Curtis slowly calmed down as he brushed his fingers through my hair and down my back. I'd like to say the purr was planned, but it wasn't.

"Are you still tired, love?"

"Uh huh. That was probably the longest night I have ever had."

He snorted. "No doubt. That one night lasted six months."

My eyes finally shot open, and I looked up at the scruffy face. "Six months?? Please tell me you are joking."

He scoffed that time. "You should know by now. I don't make jokes."

I giggled when I felt his hand slide further down, until it was able to grab a handful of me. My eyes closed and my head dropped back. The pleasure I felt when he pushed us together was interrupted by yet another yawn. And then a pout because he moved his hand off me.

I opened my eyes to scowl at him. Which he found hilarious. My scowl softened when his lips brushed against my forehead.

"Go back to sleep. You earned the rest." Curtis put his hand on the back of my head and held me close to him again, only in a sweet rather than spicy manner.

"What if I want something else first?" I made sure to lift my upper leg and wrapped it around him to emphasize my point.

His other hand grabbed my thigh and held me closer to him. I expected him to take it from there, but he didn't. Such a tease.

"Sleep first, play later. When your energy is fully back, we can play all you want."

All *I* wanted, huh? I believed I could deal with that. I discovered many things I liked doing during that six-month long night. Things I was quickly getting addicted to. And some things I discovered I didn't mind so much.

I closed my eyes, snuggling into him again, and started making a mental list of all I wanted to do with him… again.

Oddly, at the top of my list, was something I shouldn't want, but I did. I wanted him to drink from me again, and me from him. We'd never done it at the same time, always one after the other. Sometimes it was him feeding first, and sometimes it was me. Either way, it was pure ecstasy. I never enjoyed it when Carter, or any other vamp, had taken my blood before. I had to shut down and not let my mind spin when they sank their fangs into any part of me. Given it was easier when they drank from sensitive areas.

But with Curtis, my brain couldn't function at all. At least not anymore. The first time, yeah, it felt no different than the others. Now though? My body was so addicted to it, that it craved his fangs and his blood.

I was pretty sure he was getting just as addicted as I was too. At least he acted like it. Take just now for instance. He was laying with me, sleeping with me, holding me. Pretty sure it wasn't even my room. We may have only been here for a few days before he cast that spell, but he never once slept with me.

The next thing on my list was probably the rough stuff. Curtis was right, I did start liking it. I even started liking to hear Lucas' reactions on the other side of the tent. We were basically torturing him, and I loved it. I even heard him whimpering a few times. He was a jerk, he deserved it.

At one point, Curtis hollered out for him to go find one of the "toddlers" to take it out on. There were no kids with us, so I figured he meant the younger vampires. They often referred to them as though they were children. Lucas was much happier the next time we saw him.

I said *we* because Curtis almost never left my side during that entire time.

The fantasy running through my mind changed suddenly, and we were no longer in the tents. Instead, we were in Curtis' room. I was sitting on the bed, finishing dinner, and Curtis was pacing the room while on his cell phone.

He was getting worked up, clearly frustrated with whoever was on the end of the call.

"Have you heard from Ryder yet? He was supposed to check in by now... We don't have time to get distracted. In order for this plan to work, we need to stay on schedule... I don't care how you do it, get me that report!" Curtis hung up on whoever he was talking to and threw his phone on the bed.

I slid off the bed and sauntered over to him. I was wearing nothing but a black lace teddy he begged me to get during our shopping trip. I said begged because he refused to choose anything for me, it was all my choice on what I wanted.

I walked up behind him, his concentration set outside the balcony window, to the storm raging against it. Slowly, I slid my arms around him and started kissing his bare back. Little by little Curtis' body began to relax under my touch. Well, most of him was relaxing.

I slid my hand down his waist, and over the rim of his boxers. With one flick, I had them open and slid my hand inside to the one part that was not relaxing.

It wasn't long before both my teddy and his boxers were in shreds on the floor. And Curtis had me pinned to the bed. We continued for what felt like hours, the sun going down in the distance. My yells were louder than ever as his fangs sank into my neck. They were smothered however when his wrist locked over my mouth.

We had never drunk at the same time before, nor had we done it while doing… other things. Or for so long. It didn't matter how many times his phone rang, how hard Lucas banged on the door, not even when Lucas came in. We were both lost to the haze.

Neither of us could be satisfied, not until he collapsed and was barely able to move off me.

It took a minute or two, but he eventually rolled to face me, pulling me into him. He softly sealed my neck with his tongue, making my body shiver again. We both laughed. His laugh cut off first though. A look of confusion swept over his face. Slowly, he bent down and sniffed my neck. Once, twice, three times.

When he was sure of what he was smelling, a grin crept over his face. His hand went to my stomach and rubbed softly.

My back shot out of bed, my lungs gasping for air. I desperately looked around the room, but no one was there. The sun was still up, the skies were clear.

"What the hell?" I whispered.

The dream had been so real. I couldn't decide if it had been a dream, or a vision. I closed my eyes and focused. Nothing else was coming to me. No other path. Surely that meant it had only been a dream.

I whimpered as I laid back down. For a dream, it sure had some very realistic side effects. I jumped out of bed, deciding I didn't care. It was becoming unbearable. I had an itch that desperately needed to be scratched.

I ran to my room to get dressed, only to find my clothes weren't there. None of my things were.

Curious, I went back to Curtis' room and looked in his closet. Sure enough. They were all there. Even my old tennis shoes, mixed with all the new shoes I got. In hindsight, I may have gone a little overboard with those.

Giggling, because for some reason his actions in moving my things while I rested, for who knows how long, made me happy. I searched through a dresser on the same side of the closet as my things. I picked out a set of black risqué underwear, then grabbed a dress off a hanger.

The dress was styled after a men's white dress shirt, with a thin red belt that went around my waist. The dress was barely long enough to cover my butt once the belt was on. I had planned on wearing it with leggings, just not today. I was a woman on a mission today.

I paired the outfit with a pair of black heels, the strap wrapped around my ankles three times. I checked myself in the mirror, then left the room to go hunting.

I didn't have to do much in the way of searching, I had a feeling he would be in the conference room. The sun was barely beginning to set. He seemed to meet with his council at this time every day. I slowed down as I reached them, the doors sitting open.

Part of me knew I was supposed to be listening for things I could pass on, but there was a greater need I had at the moment. Instead, I was listening to make sure I wouldn't get in trouble for interrupting.

"I should be complaining that you are giving us extra work, but that's hard to do when you reward us so nicely." Lucas gleefully stated, followed by the sound of a slap against bare skin, and a grunt.

I couldn't see him, but I would recognize Curtis' laughter anywhere. And the sound that followed.

Not thinking it through, I walked through the door.

Yeah, just as I figured. Each of the six men in the room had a human in various positions, not all of them were girls either. In fact, that was my only consolation. Instead of one of the women, Curtis had a man. On his knees in front of him.

It still ticked me off though. I offered to do this very thing with him in the bedroom and he turned me down.

I had barely passed through the door when Curtis' head snapped to me from his spot on the couch. His eyes started at my feet, then slowly made their way up. His grin grew bigger as they moved.

Until he saw my unimpressed face.

Lucas laughed.

Without saying a word, I walked over slowly, almost at a saunter. Curtis gave a small, relieved sigh when I gave him a small smile. I reached down and slowly petted the back of the head of the man in front of him. Curtis' grin grew again, his eyes began glowing as he reached for me.

I swiftly changed my smile to a snarl as I fisted the man's hair and yanked his head back. From the way Curtis jumped back with a hiss, it obviously hadn't felt very good.

I roughly dragged the man to stand up, and pushed him toward Lucas' greedy, outstretched hands. I kept my eyes locked on Curtis the entire time. He was struggling, trying to decide if he should be ticked or turned on.

"Kitty's got claws." One of the other's in the room barked, causing them all to laugh.

Curtis lifted a finger and curled it, telling me to come here. Part of me was worried he would be upset, part of me was still ticked, part of me was confused why I cared so much as I knew going into this that he had a harem, but the biggest part of me was still aching for him. And for some reason, this little incident, and the fire in his eyes, was making that ache worse.

I separated my legs, while inching my dress up my thighs, and slowly walked over his lap. I let him help me place my knees on both sides of him. He tried to push me down, but I refused to budge. I could feel him, so I knew he could feel me. My shirt was unbuttoned enough on the top, that he had a good view as I leaned down to his ear.

“This Queen doesn’t share.” I whispered deeply in his ear. Followed by a lick.

The small whimper that came from him thrilled me. He swiftly caught my lips after that, and I relinquished control.

A few minutes later, I sighed contentedly as I laid on his bare chest. His fingers ran up and down the length of my spine. I didn’t even know where my dress was.

“Sir, the helicopter is fueled and ready to leave.”

“Thank you, Charles. Tell the pilot they are on the way. Please escort the pets back to their room”

“Yes, sir.”

I had been ignoring them, but at that comment I began to sit up. Curtis silently pushed me back down. Who was I to argue with that? I was comfortable.

While the others all filed out, leaving only Lucas, Curtis, and myself, I kissed the bottom of his jaw. My small sign of gratitude to him. Then got distracted making a path down to his neck while the others filed out. I wondered what the blood tasted like coming from his neck. Was it warmer? Thicker?

What the hell was wrong with me?

“Are you sure you want to cancel your trips to the other sections?” Lucas asked softly.

“Yes. I can supervise from here, for now. The others can organize and structure their own areas. With our timetable being pushed forward like it has been, my focus needs to be on the war. I didn’t expect Deacon to be able to convince the humans and shifters to join him. At least not this quickly. Have you heard back from our spies with the witches? Do we know where they stand, yet?”

"They mentioned something about the Queen finally stepping forward. They seemed a little excited about it themselves."

Curtis cursed softly. I was coherent enough to know I needed them to keep talking. So, I rocked my hips and nipped at his neck.

Lucas chuckled. "Kitty looks hungry."

I jumped when I felt a new hand rubbing down the back of my head. Both vampires laughed. The hand didn't stop until it was all the way down, ending in a smack. I yelped and jumped back. Curtis' eyes were glowing again, but not with anger at his friend for touching me.

"She is hungry, but I'm not sure if I should feed her. Kitty was very naughty today."

I frowned at him.

"Someone needs to remember her place, I think." Lucas added, his hand was back on me, rubbing between the cheeks.

My eyes widened when I realized Curtis was letting him. The chuckle coming from him this time was pure evil.

Something sparked in me, making me act crazy. That was my only excuse.

I snapped my head around to Lucas and snarled at him. He jumped back in surprise, taking his hand with him. Then I turned back to Curtis.

"What am I? Am I a pet? Or am I more? You want me to act like something more, then I will. But if you want to treat me like a pet, then I will act that part. You can't have it both ways."

Curtis' eyes faded for a moment before he threw his head back in laughter. When it came back down, he pulled me in for a kiss.

"I am so glad I took you from Carter. You were definitely meant to be my Queen and stand by my side."

My eyes widened just a tad. I cast a nervous look at Lucas.

Curtis slid a finger down my cheek. "No worries, my love. Lucas knows everything. He has been by my side since the beginning. I figured it would be easier for you to remember who you could and could not talk in front of if I made it everyone. You have done well with that."

I had no idea why that comment made me blush, but it did. They both laughed again. I ended up burying my face in Curtis' neck in embarrassment. He automatically went back to rubbing my back soothingly.

"Have you spoken to Ryder about the change in plans?"

My mind went on alert, but thankfully, my body remained nice and relaxed.

"Yes. He said the west coast will have a storm front moving in within the next few days. It will start in Washington and move south until it blows itself out. He believes that will be great cover for them to wipe out all the ports. They can move along with the storm. His only concern is the energy it will take for his men to move at that speed."

Storm? Ryder? Was that a vision and not a dream then?

Did that mean Curtis would be getting me pregnant after all?

Could I stop it?

It would be easy. I just didn't have to start anything with him.

On the other hand, he had obviously been dealing with a problem, and I thoroughly distracted him from it. If I let him impregnate me, would it save the lives of the people they were planning to attack?

“That won’t be a problem. We can send the shifters we have locked up at the Air Force base. Maybe some of the human soldiers too. In between ports, Ryder and his men can boost up.”

I could hear Lucas’ pout. “That will kill the shifters though.”

“We’ll find you another one. Don’t worry. I’d like to head to the base tonight. We can get them drugged and loaded onto the plane. Give Ryder time to get organized and stash them where they will need them.”

If I went with them, could I warn the shifters? Could I do something to help them get free?

My heart sank. This must be one of the hardships that dream witch mentioned. In order to save lives, I had to let him get me pregnant.

“Yes, sir. Will you need time to feed her first?” Lucas sucked at stifling the chuckle.

I was so focused on trying to make plans, I hadn’t realized what I was doing. Apparently, I was once again nibbling on Curtis’ neck.

Curtis laughed. “She does seem to be quite hungry today, doesn’t she? Why is that, little witch?”

I leaned back and looked down, feeling very embarrassed and shy all of a sudden. I was also a little scared at what I was going to have to do.

“I, um, had a very realistic dream. At first I couldn’t tell if it was a vision or not. It left me feeling… hungry. In many ways.”

“Well, now,” Curtis growled, “I must know what this dream was about.”

I shifted uncomfortably on his lap, then giggled as his eyes dramatically rolled to the back of his head.

"It started with you on the phone, talking to someone about a man named Ryder. There was a storm outside. And then, we, uh… were together on the bed for hours, feeding from each other. At the same time." Curtis' eyes kept getting wider the more I spoke. "By the time we were done, my scent had changed. You had your hand on my stomach, and that's when I woke up."

"That wasn't a dream, sir. The storm, Ryder. That is only a few days away."

Curtis' head tilted to the side, his eyes studying me. "I thought you said your visions came in snippets, like pictures."

"They do. That's why I thought this was a dream. It was so real, that it left my body aching for you." I bit the inside of my cheek. "Which is probably why I got so upset when I came in here. I needed you to take care of me, and you were being taken care of by someone else."

There, I said it. I confessed that I was jealous. And from the look in his eyes, he was eating it up.

"Sir?" Lucas broke the bubble we were in. "You have technically been feeding her your blood for months. It's possible that it not only strengthened her body, but also her powers. With time frozen, she would not have gotten any visions. But this is good. Now we know that during that storm, you two need to be making a baby."

Curtis' head swung to his friend as though he hadn't fully thought the vision through. His grin grew, and then it melted faster than butter on toast.

"We cannot trade blood at the same time. That would bind her to me."

Yeah, that probably wasn't a good idea. I had no interest in mixing my soul with his. Even still, I felt the pout pop out. The blood trading had felt so freaking awesome in the vision.

"What if she drank from me instead?" Lucas offered, a little more enthusiastically than necessary, in my opinion.

Curtis turned to face me. "Would that work?"

I obediently closed my eyes and thought about that path. It didn't take long. I jumped straight into the vision, realistic feelings, and all. My head fell back as I felt the fireworks burn through my body.

I was vaguely aware of them commenting about it. I mean, I was still connected to Curtis, so he was basically living the dream with me.

In the vision, Lucas sat on the bed next to us, thoroughly enjoying the show. At a signal from Curtis, he bit into his wrist and put it to my lips. I nearly got a headache when the vision suddenly jumped ahead.

I lost balance and felt Curtis grab me and keep me from falling over. I couldn't tell if it had been days or weeks. I was lying in the bed sobbing, curled in, my arms wrapped around my stomach. Curtis was holding me from behind, trying to comfort me.

The pain and sorrow I felt was so real, that Curtis was wiping the tears off my face as I came back to reality.

"I don't think I like this new power boost." I whispered, letting him pull me in and hold me.

"What happened? One minute you were obviously enjoying the vision, and the next…" For once Lucas wasn't laughing.

"If I take Lucas' blood, our baby will die. I couldn't tell how much time passed, but I don't think I even made it to a month. It was long enough that I was already attached to my child. Even though I knew it was a vision, I could still feel the pain it would cause me."

"Yeah, but you would survive, so you both could always try again." Lucas added, like an idiot.

My snarl at him this time was much deeper. He cursed as he jumped back even further.

"It will only work with Curtis' blood. Not your tainted half breed crap."

Curtis sighed, sounding as though it wasn't what he wanted but already suspected.

"Do we have to trade blood at the same time?" He was grasping at straws now.

"Yes, I think so. We drank for a long time. Long enough that it would have killed me if I hadn't been taking from you at the same time. I assume only me taking loads of blood from you would be bad for me?" I paused as he nodded. "If your blood is making me stronger, then my body must need it more at that point, to help sustain me as your seed tries to attach. Maybe, if my blood were purer, but I don't know. I know nothing about my witch heritage. I don't even know if it was passed to me by my mother or father."

I sank into Curtis again, the sadness still very much inside of me. The room was silent, Lucas keeping his annoying mouth shut for a change. Curtis' hand slowly started moving along my back again.

"If we keep it to just the one time that we trade at the same time, we should be okay. It shouldn't weaken me. It shouldn't weaken my power to freeze time. That didn't come from a blood trade." He almost sounded resigned.

Curtis pushed me back to sitting up, then lifted my chin to look at him. "We won't lose our son. I will feed you blood everyday if I have too. I will keep both of you healthy. Understand?"

I bit my lip and nodded. He sighed and wiped the tears streaming down my cheeks still and looked at Lucas.

"Get my chopper ready. Be ready to leave for the base in an hour." Curtis stood up, holding me in his arms. He grunted as we finally separated, then carried me down the hall, leaving our torn clothes behind.

Chapter 23

Grace

We spent the next hour locked in our bedroom. For once, Curtis stayed gentle and caring. He was trying to make me feel better. He gave me exactly what I had been wanting in that room, strengthening me. Then he had real food delivered for me. I only agreed to eat soup, not yet able to stomach the idea of anything heavier.

It wasn't just the pain of losing my son, which had been the worst feeling I could ever imagine. I was also nervous over what I was about to do. And I didn't just mean the bonding thing. That was starting to not bother me so much. Which did bother me.

No, my nerves were from the fact that I was about to take action against Curtis' plans. While my heart and body were softening to him, my mind could not accept all the deaths that would be on my hands if I didn't do something.

I chose to dress in a pair of designer jeans and a blouse for this trip. And a kick butt set of high heeled boots.

I didn't bother pretending to be asleep on the flight. Neither was I pretending to be putty in Curtis' hands. I only stared out the windows and watched as the cities went by beneath us. Curtis kept my hand firmly in his, the entire time. Every now and then, I felt soft kisses on my head, his reaction to my melancholy mood.

Once again, we landed in the desert not too far from Mojave. I should have paid attention to one of the signs, trying to determine where we were, so I could pass the information on. But my mind could only process two things. The loss of my son, and what I was about to do.

We had touched down in the middle of numerous hangars and buildings. A few were open, and I could see fighter jets inside. Further down the runway, was the largest plane I had ever seen.

"What kind of plane is that?" I asked in awe.

"That, my love, is a cargo plane. The military uses them to ship anything from tanks to hundreds of soldiers."

I turned to Curtis and smiled gratefully. He didn't have to answer my question, he didn't have to tell me anything. In fact, when I first planned all this, I assumed he wouldn't be speaking to me at all. At least not beyond commands and such. But those plans changed when I chose to go into that pool. When I chose to come alone, without my support system.

"And what are you planning to use it for, my King?" My smile grew as he growled and pinched my butt.

"I am using it to send a gift to my soldiers. They have a big battle coming, they will need all the help they can get."

I nodded, acting like I knew nothing about this battle. Which was ridiculous, seeing as I had been on his lap while he and Lucas discussed it just a few hours before.

"Come, I have a lot to do before it is ready to take off."

I let him pull me along with him, taking in everything I could. I noticed there were guards at most of the buildings and hangars.

"What are they guarding?"

Curtis paused and looked around him. He had been leading us toward someone who was walking in our direction. He must have decided we could wait for them to get to us, as we stopped moving altogether.

Curtis pointed at what looked like a couple of small, and boring, apartment buildings. "Those ones hold a bunch of humans we took from the shelters. They are still waiting to be relocated to either their new home, or a feeding center. For now, they are acting as donors for my men here. A few are working for me as well." He turned and pointed to a large hangar. "That one holds the shifters and some of the larger soldiers." His gaze softened as he turned to me. "Do I need to explain their purpose?"

I smiled and shook my head. "No. Testosterone."

He chuckled and kissed my head again. "Yes, exactly. We actually have to have a human take care of them. When it comes to shifters, they carry so much testosterone that it takes a great deal of effort to not fall to the siren call of their blood. Especially for the younger ones."

I bit my lip, acting shy. "I've never met a shifter before. Can I see them?"

His laugh was loud and boisterous now. "If I had time, I would gladly take you over there. But I have to meet with a few people and that plane needs to be gone by sunrise."

I frowned but didn't argue. He sighed and ran a hand down his face.

"Lucas?" He called to the side.

Lucas was talking to someone a few feet away but came over as soon as he heard his master calling. He was such a good little lap dog.

“Yes, sir?”

“Grace wants to see the shifters. Will you stand guard while she goes in?”

Lucas looked around, making sure no one was close by, then leaned in and lowered his voice. “Is that a good idea, Curtis? Your scent is all over her. They won’t take it very well.”

Curtis snorted. “They are all leashed up with silver. They can’t hurt her.”

Lucas licked his lips as he glanced at the shifter hangar. “I, uh, I don’t know that I can. When we rounded them up, I lost control with one and nearly killed him.”

Curtis nodded, probably remembering that. “Can you at least stand outside? Make sure no one goes in with her?”

His friend relaxed his shoulders, while giving a relieved sigh. “That I can do.”

“Good. Thank you.” Curtis turned back to me, pulling me into his embrace. “You aren’t the only one getting stronger off our blood. If you need me, yell. I will hear you, no matter where I am. If any of them tries to hurt you, tell me. I will make sure they pay.”

I went on my toes and kissed him under his jaw, which was all I could reach while we were both standing. “Thank you. You take such good care of me.”

He lifted a hand and ran his thumb under my lip. “Whatever my Queen wants, especially if it takes that look of pain from your eyes. It nearly killed me.”

Yep, I was screwed.

He kissed me softly, then released me into Lucas' care. We walked toward the hangar in silence, which was odd for Lucas. I waited as they opened the door. I could still feel Curtis' eyes on me, so I turned and winked at him. I heard him laughing as I stepped through. The door closed with a loud bang, making me jump.

The room was huge. Possibly large enough to fit that cargo plane. Instead of a plane though, it was filled with dozens of very large men lying on the floor.

I walked slowly closer to them, their eyes lifting to me, soon followed by their bodies. They were sitting at attention now. Each man was large, dirty, and had chains around their feet. Each chain was welded into the cement flooring.

"Who are you? Why are you here?" A man on the other end stood up and asked.

I sped up and kept my voice low. "I am looking for the shifter in charge."

His eyes rolled over my body, from top to bottom, then he sniffed and grimaced. "Why? What would a vampire whore want with shifters?"

I snarled at him. "You know nothing about me. You don't know what I have had to do to get here. I'd shut your mouth before you make me change my mind. Now, who is in charge?"

He snarled back. "Who do you think?"

I huffed and shook my head. I looked around at all the men on the floor, our audience.

"I am looking for someone who knows Captain Hill."

Well, that got their attention. More than two dozen of the largest men in the room managed to sit up straighter. Their eyes even darkened a touch.

"Quite a few of you then, huh? I guess I was right in my assumptions. He is a shifter."

The first man stepped closer. "How do you know Hill?"

I turned and watched his face carefully. He was eager, hopeful, concerned, and still a little wary. I closed my eyes briefly, looking to the future for a glimpse of the man I had not yet met, and probably never would at this rate. With a small smile, I opened them again.

"We have never spoken in person, but we do message frequently. I am a witch, or so I have been told. I see visions. Every time I message with Hill, I see a large man with black hair, usually laughing. Then I see a black wolf, possibly a slight tint of purple. I am fairly new to the magic life. But I am getting better with my power. He is a shifter, yes?"

The man in front of me was struggling, not sure if he should trust me. I would need to give him a little something to earn it.

"When the world turned to hell in a handbasket, I got a vision. It wasn't much, just a way for my foster brother and I to survive the vampire invasion. Then I got more visions. They led me on a path through enemy lines. Hill is my only contact to the outside. The plans for you and all these men have been changed. You are about to be shipped out of here. There is no time for him to come save you. And no way he would be able to reach you. Nor have I been left alone long enough for me to send him a message. So, I am doing it."

The man looked at me again, carefully. "How old are you?"

"Seven… wait. No. Huh. I must have lost track of the days. I turned eighteen today. Huh, oh well. Not the point. I may be young in years, but thanks to the curveball life threw at us, I aged faster. I'm sure I'm not the only one either. Now. Can any of you fly a plane?"

Half a dozen hands popped up from the men on the ground.

"Lovely. Then my plan should work well."

"Why should we trust you? I can smell Curtis all over you."

I rolled my eyes. "I guess I should be proud of the fact that you aren't taking anything at face value. I don't know how much time I have though. It took a lot of convincing for him to let me leave his sight. Now, as I was saying. They will be sending someone in soon to drug each of you, so you don't wake up on the plane. I assume that's because they can't exactly have you welded to the ground on a plane."

"She's right, they can't. If we can get a key, we can unlock the cuffs once in the air, and take over the plane." A man on the floor jumped up and stepped over to me. "Do you know where Hill is? We can go to him."

I put a finger up and closed my eyes. I thought hard about Hill. When he popped into my mind, peace flooded through my system. A peace I hadn't felt in a long while. As much as I wanted to revel in it, it wasn't the time.

"He is on a base that looks similar to this one. Surrounded by the mountains and snow." I scrunched my eyes, focusing on a sign in the background. "Grand something." I sighed and looked at the men again. "That's it, that's all I got." I shrugged.

"That's more than enough. I know where he is." The shifter in charge said, watching me carefully. "You said you keep seeing him? And you haven't met him?"

I shook my head. "Haven't even heard his voice. At least not in person. He is working with the Vampire Borns though. Prince

Deacon ascended the throne after his father's assassination. Deacon met his fated mate, a pure-blooded witch. She is pregnant. Hill is working with them. My last vision was of them rescuing some friends of mine in Mojave. They blew up the wall. Hill went in wolf form."

A bunch of jaws dropped. "The Alpha fought in wolf form? In public?"

I nodded. Didn't know he was an Alpha, but that did make sense. "Yes. From what I can gather, Deacon and Carrie are pulling everyone together to fight back against Curtis. Look, we don't have much time. Do you have any idea where we can find a key?"

"Ryan has one on him. He'll probably be the one to drug us."

"Whose Ryan?" I turned to the new voice coming from the floor.

"He's the human guard they assigned to us." Someone else said in disgust. "He brings us food and water every day. A fat, slimy man." The others chuckled.

Out of nowhere, the shifter in charge dropped to the floor. "Everyone shut up, he's coming. You, take a few steps away from us."

I didn't question him, I just went back to looking around the place, taking them all in. I ignored the door as it opened and closed again.

"Well, well, well. I knew the vamps said they would take good care of me, they've supplied me with many benefits since I agreed to help, but I never imagined they'd bring me *you*. Fate is a wonderful thing, ain't it, little darling?"

I grimaced and tried to hold back the gag as the voice drew closer. The last time I heard that voice, I was leaving him in his skanky office. Schooling my face, I turned around.

“Mr. Ryan. I’d like to say it is a pleasure to see you again, but then I would be lying. Why am I not surprised to see that you have turned traitor. Let me guess, they are paying you with young girls, right? As that is all you care about.”

At his deep chuckle, and shifting of his pants, many of the men - shifters and humans - growled.

“They did indeed. I was very saddened to see that you and your little friends snuck out of the shelter. I’ve been hoping you’d get rounded up like the rest of us. Tell me, little darling, have you been naughty lately?”

I laughed sardonically and shook my head.. “You have no idea.”

I took a step to the side, staying out of his reach, he was getting much to close for my comfort.

Mr. Ryan set the bag he was carrying down on the floor, a few feet from the men. One of them reached over quietly and grabbed it. I took a few more steps, making Mr. Ryan turn his back to them. The shifter in charge slowly shifted into a crouch before standing up behind him.

“Why don’t you tell daddy all about it? I’m sure I can find a way to set you straight again. I bet we can even find some rope around here somewhere.”

I pushed out my bottom lip and stepped closer to him. “I have been so naughty. More than ever before. See, I’ve been shacking up with a vampire.” I gave him a small, naughty grin. “But he has been oh so good to me.”

Mr. Ryan frowned and stopped moving. “Which vampire?” He took in my obviously not cheap clothes, suddenly realizing he may have been mistaken on my purpose here.

I leaned forward, closer to the scum of the earth, whispering in his ear. “Curtis.”

I leaned back just enough to see the look of horror cross his face. Then I lifted my knee and slammed it into his groin as hard as I could. I stepped back, giving the shifter space as he wrapped an arm around the human man's neck and held tight until he passed out.

"Please tell me you didn't kill him."

"No." He huffed. "Wanted too though. You wouldn't believe the stories he has told us."

I sighed and rubbed my forehead.. "Yes, I would. My friends and I had the privilege of being in a shelter he was in charge of. I'll spare you the details. They are going to be expecting him to come out soon. We need to give you all at least a tiny dose of that drug, that way the vampires will smell it in your system."

"What about him?" Someone asked, pointing at the unconscious cretin on the floor.

I kicked said cretin with my boot. "Easy, as soon as you all are lying down, playing dead, like good little pups," I laughed at their snarls, "I will scream bloody murder and Curtis will come running. Lucas first probably. Since he is right outside." I frowned. "I don't know why they let him in in the first place. No one was supposed to come in while I was here."

"They probably figured he was harmless since he was a human." One of them huffed.

I shrugged. "Maybe. Whatever. It'll be fine. Anyway, about those drugs…"

The bag was lifted to me, and I went around giving the smallest portion possible to each of them. Then I found a sink drain and dumped the rest. While I did that, the others searched Ryan's pockets for the key. The shifter in charge slid it into one of his many pockets.

“I still don’t see how they will believe you knocked the guy out and we all still ended up drugged.”

“No worries, I got this. Just lie down like the good little puppy you are.”

I giggled at his snarl.

“You still haven’t told me your name. How do I tell Hill who helped us?”

“I can’t give you my name. Curtis has spies everywhere. If someone around there heard you, and sent word back to him, we’d all be screwed. You can tell him that you were saved by Carrie’s sister. Pretty sure she’ll know what I mean.”

I made to walk past them, but he lifted a hand to my arm.

“Thank you. We’ll return the favor soon, I promise.”

I blinked back at the sudden onslaught of tears. “It might be too late to save me. I’ve gone too deep. I may not be worth it anymore. But thank you anyway. Just take care of yourselves. Oh, and in case I can’t get a message out soon, since my only way out of this is to put Curtis into possessive mode, tell Hill that in the next few days, a storm will be hitting Washington. The piers will get hit the most, and not just from the weather. The storm will make a path down every pier on the west coast. I don’t see them getting far without their energy boost though.”

“Will do. Good luck, and… don’t lose hope. We didn’t think we had a chance either.”

I let the stupid tears fall this time, they would help with my cover. I moved toward Mr. Ryan and sat in front of him. I waited until the shifter in charge was settled, until they all were.

One deep breathe in, and as loud as I could, I screamed. “Curtis!!!!”

One missis... Well, hello Lucas. Oh, look and there was the vamp of the hour.

“Curtis!” I whimpered from the floor, lifting my arms. He ran to me and lifted me onto my feet.

Lucas already had a gun over the shifter closest to Mr. Ryan and me. He was still awake, but he wasn’t showing fear.

“No, Lucas!” I shouted. “Don’t. He saved me. Don’t kill him.”

Curtis wiped a tear from my eye. “What happened, love?”

I hiccupped and pointed at Mr. Ryan. “That man tried to hurt me. He came in a few minutes ago. I knew him from the shelter. He was the reason my friends and I begged Carter to take us. Especially after he locked me in his office with him.” Curtis growled and placed a foot on the man’s neck. “I stayed away from him, I thought he would leave me alone. I told him I belonged to you now. He was giving the soldiers these shots and telling me what happened to the people we knew in the shelter. Next thing I knew, he was right next to me.” I shook and held Curtis closer to me, “he pushed me to the ground and started to get on top of me. He kept talking about tying me up. The shifter knocked him out. When they both hit the floor, I screamed. I was so scared, Curtis.”

“Sh, now, love. I got you.” He snarled and looked at Lucas. “Throw him in the feeding center. Tell them to make him suffer.”

Lucas grinned. “Can I do it?”

Curtis chuckled and turned me to the door. He lifted a hand and patted Lucas on the back. “Have at it, my friend. We’ll wait for you in the chopper. Load up our gift, I can smell the tranquilizer kicking in.”

I glanced down at the shifter in charge as we passed. He was lying on the floor, his eyes beginning to shut. A small smile on his face.

As soon as we walked through the door, I squeaked. Curtis swung an arm down, knocking my legs out from under me as he picked me up. Seconds later, he was setting me on the bench in the helicopter. He kneeled in front of me, one hand holding mine, the other on my cheek.

"Thank you for coming for me." I whispered.

"I told you I would. I was already on my way. Did you at least get to your fill of shifters."

I frowned. "No. I wanted to see their wolves, but they refused to do it. Honestly, if it wasn't for that one's help, I would have thought they were all kind of rude."

Curtis laughed before kissing my forehead. "They can't shift right now, love."

I tipped my head to the side. "Why not?" I put just enough whine into the question to show my displeasure.

"Because their chains are made of silver. Pure silver weakens their wolves. They cannot break through it the way they would with regular metal."

"Oh." I scowled at him, then pushed him playfully. He was off balance enough that he almost fell. "Why didn't you tell me that in the first place? I wouldn't have gone in there if I knew. Instead, I spent twenty minutes in a room full of stinky men." I made a disgusted face.

Curtis laughed harder as he moved to sit next to me. "So, you weren't just trying to get a look at a naked shifter?"

I looked at him, honestly confused this time. "They were all dressed. Why would I see them naked?"

His laughing fit started up again. I waited him out, not impressed with him for laughing at me.

He lifted me onto his lap as he calmed down. “I’m sorry, love. Sometimes I forget how little you knew before I found you. Shifters have to take their clothes off before they shift into their wolves, otherwise they shred them.’

I grimaced. “I didn’t know that. Why would you think I wanted to see any of them naked?”

“Many people do. They are strong and muscular. I have met many vampires that wanted to take one to bed with them.”

I wrapped my arms around his neck and pulled myself closer. “I don’t need to see any of them naked to know they are nothing compared to you.”

Curtis wasn’t laughing anymore. “Is that right?”

I nodded and licked his lips. He made a snap for my tongue, but I pulled back and giggled. I full out laughed at the way he growled at me. Before I knew it, I was on my back on the bench seat, my jeans on the floor. Once again torn.

“Is this why you insisted on me buying so much? I was only ever going to get to wear them once before you shredded them?”

He chuckled as he slid into place. “At the time, no. I just enjoyed watching you have fun. It is a benefit though.” My shirt soon joined the pile of material on the floor.

Chapter 24

Grace

We were in the coming down off the high side of things when Lucas arrived. I was lost to Curtis' soft kiss when the door opened.

"Ah shucks, did I miss the show?" Lucas laughed as he climbed in, closing the door behind him. He took a big sniff of the air. "Barely missed it too. Such a shame."

Curtis' lips were trailing down my neck when he responded to him. "Mr. Ryan?"

"Slept through the whole thing." Lucas patted his belly. "Very filling but left me with a sweet tooth."

Curtis moved to hover his face over mine. "What do you think, love? Should we reward him for taking out the trash?"

I lifted enough to kiss him. "If my King thinks he has earned one, then so be it."

“Ooo, yes please. I do love rewards.” Lucas piped in, sounding like a little boy being offered a cookie.

My eyes rolled back as Curtis was not so gentle this time. Lucas quickly moved to sit on the floor, sans his pants, getting the second-best view in the house. In his own little haze, he lifted a hand to my chest a few times. Which was immediately slapped away by Curtis.

He tried again, only lower. Curtis was either too distracted or he didn’t care. Shoot, I wasn’t either when I hit another high moment so fast. Curtis laughed, making me think he did know but wanted to see what would happen.

Lucas’ hand moved away, and I looked to see him licking his fingers. “So yummy.” His eyes lit up and his voice deepened to a growl.

Curtis pulled away from me with a sigh. Soon they were preparing to repeat my first trip, only I was wide awake this time.

“Sorry, love. I know you said you don’t want to share. But you did agree to reward him. I was hoping a small touch would be enough. I underestimated his reaction to you.” Curtis stopped talking when Lucas practically mauled him.

By the time he was finished, he was whimpering. Curtis laughed and told him to stand up. I didn’t know if he was laughing at Lucas’ ridiculous behavior, or the fact that I had my arm over my eyes. I had no interest in seeing more of Lucas than I already had.

Lucas dropped to the floor when he was done, a smile on his face. “Thank you, boss. I live to serve you.”

Curtis laughed some more as he pulled me back onto his lap. I grimaced when he kissed me. I could still taste Lucas on his lips. Which was probably the point. His laugh subsided fast when he remembered something.

"You still haven't been punished for earlier."

"I overreacted. I'm sorry. I just got hit with this surge of jealousy when I saw someone else with you."

"You may be my Queen, but that does not give you permission to disrespect me like that in front of my men. I will do my best to only come to you, but there are times when I will need a release, and you will need your rest." He glanced down at Lucas with a smirk. "And sometimes I use it as a reward. Although I'm thinking it's the taste of you he enjoys more."

Lucas gave him a thumbs up from the floor. Curtis smirked again.

"There needs to be a punishment. Normally it would be some kind of whipping but seeing as we need your body healthy and strong, I can't do that. And you like spankings too much."

I blushed and looked down, completely embarrassed. I really did.

"I can only think of one thing you will hate, mostly because you will hate yourself for enjoying it."

I yelped when he lifted me up and twisted me around, so my back was to him. He wrapped an arm around my shoulders and his other around my stomach, holding me tight to him. Lucas slowly pushed himself up, an evil grin on his face.

"No. Baby, I'm sorry. I am. Please." I begged Curtis.

He nibbled on my ear before whispering. "You need to remember your place, little witch. As much as I enjoyed seeing your fire, I did not enjoy it being in front of my men." His voice deepened enough by the end that it was little more than a snarl. Letting me know he had really not appreciated the way they laughed.

"C… Curtis, please. You said no one else would touch me."

“And they won’t, not without my permission. I’ve tamed him enough that he will not be as rough with you as he is with his own consorts.”

I jumped when Lucas’ hands grabbed me. One up top, and one down below. Curtis kept him restricted to hands and mouth only.

Curtis was right, that was the worst punishment he could give me. I sobbed the whole time. Lucas managed to inflict a lot of pain, and not the good kind, with just that much. He was allowed to keep playing until the helicopter landed, what felt like days later.

Lucas walked out of that helicopter happier than I had ever seen him. Without a word, Curtis lifted me up, and carried me to our room. He took me straight to the shower and washed me gently. Lucas had left more than a few marks on me.

Curtis left me in the bed, saying he would go get dinner for me. As soon as he was gone. I ran to the closet and dug into my shoes. But the phone wasn’t there. I started to panic, thinking Curtis found it when he moved my things over.

Then I remembered I had shoved it in between the mattress and box springs of the other bed. With a sigh, I ran over and pulled it out.

Me: 1 and done. I am sending you a gift, watch the skies. Oh, and C can freeze time. No idea how. The other night lasted 6 months for me. Gotta go. Good luck.

I quickly shut the phone off, putting my faith in the shifters to get away and to give Hill my message.

I turned off the phone and hid it back in my bed, before crawling under the covers and laying down. I had about one minute to catch my breath before Curtis was back. Talk about cutting it close.

“Grace? Where are you?” I could hear the control he was trying to use to not get mad, at least not yet.

I was pushing it. I knew I was. But it wasn't in my nature to roll over and take a beating. I shut my eyes tight, my back to the connecting door, and thought over what happened in that helicopter. Just as I hoped, the tears came.

"What the hell are you doing in here?" Curtis was trying to keep a string of amusement in his tone, but he was getting ticked and losing it, fast. He was going to lose it completely before I was done.

"What does it look like? I'm going to bed." I mumbled into my pillow, sniffing softly. I wanted him to think I was trying to hide the tears.

He sighed and walked over to me, sitting on the edge of the much smaller bed. When he laid a hand on my shoulder, I jumped and pulled away from him.

"Hey. What's wrong?"

"What the hell do you think is wrong, Curtis?"

The flinch when he growled at me was not an act. I knew I was walking a tightrope. I heard his neck crack behind me, and I could feel the tension in the air as he took a deep breath.

"Is this because of what happened earlier?"

I huffed. "Take your pick. It's been one awful night. One thing after the other."

He sighed and laid down next to me, trying to hold me in the way he had been lately. He kissed my shoulder softly, probably trying to soothe me. I was too ticked for that to work this time.

"My Queen…"

I pulled away from him rougher this time. "Don't call me that."

"Why? You are my queen."

I rolled over to face him, letting him see the tears running down my face.

"Am I? Or am I a pet you like to dress up as a queen? That's what you treated me like tonight."

He scowled and his body began to shake, but I felt a roll coming on and I didn't care.

"Seriously, Curtis. I need to know, that way I know how to act. A Queen doesn't let anybody touch her. A Queen is a leader, not a doormat. A pet is someone you can pass around to your friends as they wish. You use them as you wish. So, what am I? I would like to know so I can behave appropriately next time."

"You disrespected me in front of my top men."

I huffed and sat up, putting my back to him. Yeah, he didn't like that much. The growl was low and deep, but it was still there.

"No. I removed a pet and did my job. I took what I wanted, did what I thought you would have wanted. No one saw you as being disrespected except you. Honestly? I think you were looking for an excuse. An excuse to let Lucas play with me, an excuse to watch. You know I don't like him. You know how he is. I think you've missed playing with your pets with your friend. You got turned on when he kept trying to join. You noticed my body reacted when you let his hand slide in, and you wanted more. So instead of just saying that, you made up an excuse to punish me. That is not how you treat a Queen. That is how you treat a pet. A street whore. If that's all I am to you, then maybe you should move me into your little cage with the rest of them. I thought you actually cared about me. I thought…" I grunted and laid back down, burying my head in my pillow. "Never mind, it doesn't matter."

I knew he'd been trying to make me feel like I mattered to him. He acted like he cared, but that was all any of it was, an act. That was what I kept telling myself anyway.

Curtis didn't even hesitate. He put a hand over my shoulder and rolled me to my back, then moved over me. I kept my eyes closed and turned my face away. I wanted it to look like I was trying to hide the tears from him again.

I felt him sigh as he wiped my tears with his thumb.

"Maybe I did let things get a little out of hand with Lucas. I was keeping his hands away for your benefit, but my own desires took over. It felt good and I wanted to watch both of you as he did it again. I'm sorry, Gracey."

Dang stupid tears. Why did he have to call me that? It just made me miss my friends. How I wish I could see them, speak to them, hear that they were all safe.

How was Carrie holding up with the baby? Was she sick? Was she healthy? Were they sticking to the plan like I told them to?

"Baby, please, don't cry." Why did he sound like it actually hurt him when I cried?

"You hurt me, Curtis. Between that vision this afternoon, that incident with Mr. Ryan, and then you holding me down for Lucas like that. I… I…" I hiccupped and let a sob out. The whole night really had been the pits.

He growled again, only this time it wasn't in anger at me. It sounded more internal, like he was frustrated with himself. Curtis leaned down and kissed my temple. Then gently turned my face to him.

"Please look at me. I want to see your beautiful brown eyes."

I sniffled and opened them.

"I'm sorry, really, I am. You are my Queen, and I should have treated you like one. This is all new to me. I am way out of practice here."

"What is?" I whispered; unsure I wanted him to say what I had a feeling he was going to. Either his acting was getting better, or he at least meant part of what he was saying. It was getting hard to tell where the line was drawn between fake and reality lately. On both our ends.

"Loving. Caring. Thinking about others."

I bit my lip, like I was holding back a smile. "You care about me?"

He gave a short laugh. "Baby, I love you. When I heard you scream at the base, it about killed me. Seeing you on the hangar floor like that... I was ready to kill every man in that room, just to make sure I got the right one. Letting Lucas take care of that human was hard for me, but I didn't want to let you out of my sight again. The way I felt didn't dawn on me until Lucas was there. And it freaked me out, to be honest. It has been a *really* long time since I cared about someone else like this. And I screwed that one up too."

He lowered his face to mine, close enough that he could bump my nose with his, subtly telling me to tip my head back. Then he kissed me softly. It was softer than he had ever done before. It was more of a tease than anything else.

I pouted when he moved back, which made him chuckle. Curtis slid the back of his knuckle down my cheek and traced my jaw.

"Forgive me, love?"

"Never again?" I carefully placed my arms around his neck and brought him back down. He should probably be rewarded for apologizing; it might help him remember to do better next time.

He brushed kisses along my neck and dragged his hand down my thigh as he lifted it up.

"Never. Unless you want to, and then I am all game."

I jabbed a finger in his side, making him laugh. He then jabbed me with something much bigger and definitely not in my side. I had no idea when he got rid of the pants he had worn to get me dinner, but they sure weren't there now.

As he came down from his high, he softly kissed every bruise that Lucas left on me, apologizing with each one. After he finished with the bottom ones, he stayed to make it much better.

The pasta he brought me was cold, but I didn't mind. I was starving by that time anyway. He even let me feed him a few bites and we talked.

"One day, when our kingdom is stable, I am going to take you to Italy. You can eat the real deal Italian food. The whole place is more laid back then here. While they don't talk about it, many countries have accepted our existence. Madrid even has a restaurant with a back room that anyone can use, but the waitresses are the menu. People walk in and out, not blinking an eye. Eventually, all the restaurants in our kingdom will be like this. Only in reverse. The back rooms will be for the humans who don't want to be around it."

I listened as he told me about all of his favorite places in the different cities, excited for the day we could go. My heart nearly jumped out of my chest when that thought went through my mind. I shouldn't want that. I shouldn't want more time with him. What was happening to me?

Curtis suddenly stopped talking and put his palm on my cheek. "Why do I smell fear? What's wrong?"

I mentally cursed. Think quick, Grace.

"I, um. I don't know how to say it." I didn't know what to say.

Curtis picked up the empty tray that was still resting between us, moved it to the nightstand, then pulled me onto his lap.

"How about we start with what you were thinking about?"

I gave him a small grateful smile. I was grateful. I was grateful he was being patient and giving me time to come up with something.

"I was picturing us in Italy. I've always wanted to travel. I'm excited to go. But with the way things are, it could be months, or even years until that happens. And then I remembered the vision, our son. And then I remembered the pain." My voice cracked because that pain had been no joke. "The idea of losing him still scares me, Curtis."

"We won't lose him. Your vision showed us what to do. They are getting so much stronger. *You* are getting stronger. As long as we keep giving you my blood, you and our son will be just fine."

"And what about you? What if Deacon and his people get too close? What if they take you away from me? What if I have to protect our son from them? Surely they will not be happy when they find out."

He laughed arrogantly. "Is that what scares you?"

I nodded. Unfortunately, yes. That did scare me, not nearly as much as the fact that I even had those thoughts. I knew none of them would hurt my child. Nor would they look down on me for it. But the fact that I was even a little worried about losing Curtis terrified the snot out of me.

He pulled me forward, onto his lap, hugging me tightly. "Love, you have nothing to worry about. I have many friends in high places. I have been planning this for centuries. Everything is prepared. And we are perfectly safe behind my wall. Nothing and nobody can get through." He pulled my hips closer, bringing our chests together. "Plus, I have you as my secret weapon."

Huh? I pulled my head back to look at him with confusion and he laughed.

"Not only do I have a powerful psychic on my side, but one that will carry my son. The royals are suckers for babies, especially after not having one being born for hundreds of years. I am giving them everything they have wanted and dreamed of for nearly 500 years. And I have a witch who has the power to let me know when someone is coming. One who is loyal to me, and only me. Who loves me."

I felt my face flame up brightly.

He chuckled and kissed me. "What? You think I didn't know already?"

I nodded and tried to turn to hide my face. He threw his head back and laughed.

"I may have been a little iffy on where you stood with me, but the way you pulled the puppy off me earlier today proved it. And the way you called for me when you needed help. And the way you desperately need to be with me at all times." He swiftly moved us to my back, holding my leg up to his side, as he sniffed my neck. "How easily you respond to me." His voice dropped a few decibels, sending shivers down my spine. "The way you crave my blood as much as my bite."

He chuckled darkly, then sank his teeth into my neck the same time he sank something else in.

My brain malfunctioned as I took a fistful of his hair with one hand and dug the nails of my other into his arm. Spending an eternity like this really wouldn't be so bad. Would it?

Chapter 25

Carrie

I woke up with a start and shot to the bathroom. As had become our ritual, my mates followed close behind. Deacon held my hair, and Colton held a wet washcloth for me. They had almost become worse over the last few days.

I leaned against Deacon's chest, moaning with discomfort.

"Sweetheart, this is the third time tonight. Maybe we should call for Clarise."

I moved my eyes up to Colton, who had shrunk down to my level. "Why? It's morning sickness, nothing more."

"Let me at least help you sleep."

I turned and scowled at my other mate.

"It might not be a bad idea. You need your rest. Especially since we are leaving for Durango tomorrow."

Lovely, they were ganging up on me now. I ignored both of them and pushed myself to stand. They might have let me go further had I not gotten dizzy and started swaying. Seeing as Deacon was in the best position to do so, he caught me and carried me back to bed.

“At least let me feed you again. Let me heal you. Please, angel.”

If the tremor in his voice wasn’t enough, feeling both their worries and fears wore me down.

“Fine. But if I end up puking blood next, I’m blaming it on you.”

“As long as you are feeling better, you can blame whatever you want on me.” Deacon sat on the bed and held me against his chest.

He wrapped his arms around my shoulders, and he placed his split wrist against my mouth. No sooner had the first drop hit my tongue then my eyes rolled back. I felt Colton’s lips as he began leaving small kisses along my legs, moving up to my thighs. I held tight to his hair and arched my back against Deacon. It wasn’t long before Deacon’s fingers joined the party. They made quite the interesting mix down there.

It wasn’t what we had agreed to, but I wasn’t going to complain. I knew what they were doing. They were getting my blood pumping, forcing Deacon’s blood to spread through me faster. If it made them feel better, who was I to complain? I loved my mates. I would do anything for them.

Even if it meant letting them have their way with me.

Within minutes, my rolling stomach settled, and I felt the exhaustion begin to kick in. I started to push Deacon’s arm away, so he wouldn’t put me into a sleep coma. But I was already too tired, and he was much stronger than me.

He kissed my ear softly and whispered. “Blame me tomorrow, angel. I promised to protect you, even if that means protecting you from yourself.”

Deacon

“Why Deacon? Do you really want a repeat of the other day?”

“You said it yourself. She needs the rest. She has hardly slept the last few nights.” My voice shook from the fear that she and our sons were causing me. I stopped to clear it and felt the pity coming from my mate that was still awake. “We can’t let her get weak. She wants to be part of everything so bad, to do her part. I won’t let her do that at the risk of losing her, or our sons. I can deal with her anger. As long as she is here to be angry with me.”

Colton moved from her feet and came to sit next to me. He put an arm around my shoulders and held me tight, kissing my head.

“I’ll back you up. As will Clarise, I am sure.” Colton chuckled softly. “Just how long are you going to keep feeding her in her sleep?”

“When she is done, she will stop. I’ve never forced it on her. She wants this, her pride just gets in the way.” I smirked and looked into his eyes. “It always has.”

Colton leaned over to kiss me. “I can’t argue with that. I already knew how stubborn she was, but now I feel it.”

I huffed. “This is nothing. You should have felt her internal battle over you.”

We sat in silence until our mate released my wrist with a small, contented sigh.

“Have you felt when she has been ill?” Colton asked me softly.

"Is that what that is? I get this uncomfortable brick-like feeling in my stomach just moments before she runs. I wasn't sure what it was."

"As have I. I am fairly certain that it is coming from her. It started decreasing not long after you started feeding her again."

"Huh. You're right, it did. I hadn't thought about it. That's good to know. Now we can be prepared to help her. We will know when it is going to happen, or when she is being too stubborn to admit it."

"Are you ever going to lay her down?"

I looked down at my angel, sleeping contently in my arms. "I don't know that I can, Colton. I've been so scared, ever since Clarise announced we were having twins. I know what Grace said, but…"

"Hey, it's okay. I'm just as scared. You know that." He laid his hand on my chest, right over my heart. "You aren't alone in this. Carrie feels it too, why else would she be trying so hard to push through. Maybe we should be open with her and tell her how we feel."

"If she already knows, then why talk about it?"

"Because we are all ignoring it. We can read each other's feelings, not our thoughts. Which is probably good. We would never leave this room."

I laughed quietly. That was true.

"If we tell her why we are so scared, surely we can find middle ground somewhere."

"Yeah." I sighed. "Maybe. I guess it couldn't hurt."

"Lay her down, Deac. Let her rest comfortably."

"Are you saying she isn't right now? She looks plenty comfortable to me. I feel contentment from her."

"Deacon." Colton's voice was almost a growl. "Put. Her. Down."

I turned to look at him and was a bit surprised to see his eyes burning. I hadn't been paying all that much attention to his feelings, my focus was solely on my angel. Colton's hand was moving lower than it had been before too. I felt the fire in my eyes light up to match his.

Colton moved from my side and took Carrie from my arms, carefully laying her on the bed. Then he crawled over me. I groaned out a whimper when his body met mine, from lips to below.

The sun came up not much later. We took turns showering, making sure one of us was lying next to our pregnant mate at all times.

When it was time to go, we both just stood there, staring down at her.

"I think you may have over done it last night." Colton teased me.

I tskd. "Please. You were the one that started messing with her. And then with me." I turned at him, pretending to be shocked. "And here I thought I was the greedy one in this relationship."

I barked out a laugh when he spanked my butt. "You are. Still a greedy little prince."

"Admit it, you like it. In fact," I turned to face him, "I think I've even rubbed off on you."

Colton's eyes sparked when I said rub. I laughed harder.

"You can rub off on me whenever you like, my Lord."

We both closed the distance at the same time, meeting in a tangle of limbs.

"Seriously. Why did we take so long to do this?" I gasped out as he knelt down in front of me.

"We've done this many times in the past."

"You know what I mean. It's not the same. I can't help but wonder if we had been over thinking or under thinking it."

Colton didn't respond for a few minutes, not until my knees were giving out on me.

"Maybe a bit of both. We've said it was Carrie that brought us together. Maybe it's more that she opened our eyes, and our hearts, to what was already in front of us."

Colton tried to stand up, but I pushed him onto the bed instead. It was my turn.

"That's possible. We've been best friends, practically inseparable, for centuries. I was thinking about every time we were together in the past. I don't think either of us cared much for the women involved. I don't think we even paid as much attention to them as we did each other."

He pulled my hair from its usual pony and wrapped it around his wrist. "That's true. I've gone over them a few times recently as well. I remember only doing it because it was you. I don't think I touched another male after our first time either."

I collapsed next to him on the bed minutes later. "I always hated it when you would leave the bar. I figured it was because you were my friend."

"I hated leaving. I always worried about you. I figured it was because protecting you was my duty. Maybe it was more. As I said, Carrie opened our hearts to what was always there. I have no doubts that I have always loved you."

"And I you, my mate."

"Awe. You two are so adorable. But I'm getting a little jealous over here."

Both our heads snapped over to our mate, who was sitting up on the bed, looking down at us at her feet. In hindsight, I should have known she was awake. Otherwise, my head would have been on her knees.

In sync, as we have always been, Colton and I jumped up and moved to her. This time it was me climbing over her.

"How long have you been awake, Angel?"

She giggled as she laid back down like the good little mate she'd always been.

"Since Colton called you a greedy little Prince."

I scoffed. "And you just laid here."

She licked her lips, making a show out of checking us both out. "It was quite the show. You two were so focused on each other, it was beautiful."

"You're beautiful." I leaned down and kissed her softly. Then moved so Colton could do the same.

While he did that, I slowly pushed her leg to the side with my knee and took my rightful place. I mean our clothes were already on the ground from our own activities, and she was never more beautiful than when she first woke up. Colton kissed down her cheek, taking his time.

An hour later, we worked together to get her cleaned up and ready to go. Colton and I were both waiting for her to get mad at me, but it didn't come. It wasn't until we were finally leaving the room that I decided to relax.

And then she threw the hammer.

"Don't think you got away with last night. I understand why you did it. But you took advantage of my exhaustion. You will pay for that."

I grimaced and Colton laughed. She spun and pointed a finger at him.

"Don't you laugh at him. I know you were in on it too." She sighed and lowered her hand. "Please, stop making choices for me."

"Angel, it's not that we are trying to make them for you. We are just trying to help you. Admit it, you feel better after a good night's sleep. We were terrified last night. You haven't been resting, you've been so sick. Apparently we can feel it when you are sick too. Can you please lean on us and let us help you. Those are our babies too. Let's do this together. Please?" I wasn't far from dropping to my knees and begging her.

"I know it sucks, Car. And technically, yeah, a very bad move on their part. But I agree. You needed sleep."

Clarise stepped up to her friend and lifted her shirt to place a hand on her belly. She had been doing this multiple times a day over the last few days. You'd think my angel would have gotten used to it, but she hadn't.

Carrie yelped and jumped back, which put her in Colton's arms. He was more than happy to wrap an arm across her shoulders and keep her in place.

"I take it she had another bad night?"

"Yes. She threw up at least three times. We had to team up and convince her to let me feed her again. It seemed to soothe her and her stomach." I shrugged. "I put her in a coma after that."

We had already discussed all the intricacies of vampire blood and their mates or marked. Clarise was thirsty for anything we could tell her. If it had any chance of helping our mate, we would tell her anything she wanted to know.

"Good. Had you woken me, I would have said to do that too." Carrie's jaw dropped at her friend. "Suck it up, buttercup. You got two miracle babies in there. While I don't think they should force you to sleep every night, if it ain't happening naturally, then do what you can magically."

I lifted my eyebrows at my mate, gloating that I was right. She scowled back at me.

"That doesn't mean you can be a jerk and do it without her permission either. Her mental state is just as important as her physical state. They go hand in hand." She waved her finger at all three of us. "You all need to work on your communication. *Verbal* communication."

Colton was giving me the "I told you so" look now.

"Alright, that's enough with the lectures. We need to go." I was done with the lectures for the morning and getting irritable. I was the King. Nobody should be lecturing me.

Carrie stood in front of me and placed a hand on my chest. "I love you. And I appreciate you trying to take care of me."

And just like that, all my irritation was gone. Well, nobody but her. She could lecture me whenever she wanted. Pretty sure she did too.

"I love you, too. I'm sorry I made the choice for you. Again."

She giggled and kissed me. Then grabbed Clarise's hand and walked down the hall.

"Okay, see. Now this ain't cool. Why does she keep doing that?" I whined to Colton.

He laughed. "Don't you feel her amusement? She's messing with you."

I lifted an eyebrow at him. "You do know she picked the witch over you again too, right?"

"Whatever makes her happy." He paused. "As long as she doesn't invite her to join us. Sharing her with you is annoying enough." He turned and walked away.

"Hey!" I shouted, following him down the stairs at our own speed, beating the women in the elevator. "You got that backwards. You are the one who has to keep butting into my life and forcing me to share."

He stopped at the front door and winked at me. "Guess you have no one to blame but yourself then."

Crap. He got me with that. "You suck, you know that?" I pouted and started to pass him. He grabbed my arm and pulled my ear close to his lips.

"I do believe I already proved that this morning. And I don't recall hearing any complaints. Well, only one, about why we didn't do this sooner." He then licked my ear and rubbed his hand over my jeans. "I don't need to suck to get you off either."

I shivered when he took down the zipper in one of the passes. I popped out like a freaking Jack in the Box. He hummed with pleasure as he kept going. Neither of us cared about all the vampires walking around us, it actually made it even better. Not that they cared. It was kind of nice to have one mate who didn't shy away in public.

I ended up having to grab the door post to steady me.

“I’m beginning to think you two can feel *all* my pregnancy stuff right along with me.”

I opened my eyes and saw our mate walking down the hall toward us, grinning from ear to ear.

“That would explain why Colton can’t keep his hands to himself lately.” I kissed her softly.

“Was that a complaint?” He lifted a questioning eyebrow at me, while tucking me back in.

I laughed. “Never. But we should probably get on the road before I drag both of you back to that bedroom.”

Clarise let out a cackle as she passed us.

“Everything is loaded and ready for you, your highnesses. Including some egg sandwiches on French toast with a bottle of Strawberry lemonade. Clint said he would drive this time.” Bryant walked over, getting a smacked butt from Clarise. He gave her a playful growl. “I added a blanket for the Queen. In case she gets cold. It also comes in handy when they get handsy in public.” He bowed slightly, only somewhat hiding his grin.

Carrie laughed and kissed him on the cheek. “Thank you, Bryant. You take such good care of me.”

“Hey, what about us?” Yeah, even to my own ears I sounded childish. But that was twice in a matter of minutes she put someone else ahead of us!

Her eyes trailed down our bodies, staying longer where Colton was still holding me. He had tucked me back in but stayed with me.

“You two seem more concerned about each other lately.”

I pulled her to my chest and started kissing from her ear to her jawline, my hand started pushing her shirt up.

“Say it again, I dare you.”

“Or what?” Her breath came out shaky, and I grinned against her neck.

“Or I won’t bother using that blanket or taking you back to the bedroom. I will take care of you right here, right now.”

“Dude, seriously, get on the road.” Carter cut in. “You are already behind schedule.”

I cursed and let go of her. With the looks she was giving me; I could have finally had her in public! Just one time, that was all I needed. That was all it really took with Colton. One time to convince her how good it could be.

“Yes, you’re right. Thank you, Carter. And thank you for volunteering to stay and watch the house and the humans.” She told him nicely. Her tone didn’t display the relief she felt. But we didn’t need the tone to tell us. She knew how close she came to caving right then.

Carter winked at Todd. “My pleasure.”

I glanced at Todd and noticed the two marks sitting on his neck. The ones that were left as a warning to the other vampires in the world.

I laughed, then patted Carter on the shoulder. “We’ll see you both later.”

Colton and I each grabbed one of Carrie’s arms and held them as we walked to the car.

“What was so funny?”

“Carter marked Todd last night.” Colton answered her, as he helped her climb in before getting in beside her. “He’s been thinking about it for a few days. He wasn’t sure Todd would go for it.”

“With a house full of vampires and only a few humans, this was the best decision he could make. For both of them.” I finished for him.

I closed the door behind me, and Clint started driving. Clarise was already in the front passenger seat. We had a car filled with three more guards driving behind us. They had all been waiting on us.

“I thought Todd was only playing Carter though.”

Colton spread the blanket over Carrie’s lap as he answered her. “In the beginning, yes. But once Grace left him, Carter was all he had left.”

“He has the others.” She argued defensively.

“But it’s not the same. Carter basically took over where Grace left off.” I rested my hand on her knee, and she leaned on my shoulder, hugging my arm.

“Does Todd love him then?” Clarise asked.

“Maybe, maybe not. It could just be about comfort and stability. Carter will take care of him, and Todd knows that. In a world filled with so many unknowns, what else could you ask for?”

Chapter 26

Colton

I partially listened as Deacon explained markings and bonding to Clarise. My mind went back to what Carrie said before we left.

Maybe we were responding to her pregnancy hormones, to a point. I had mostly been responding to Deacon's needs though. He felt insecure about himself and his new position. He had been doubting himself since his father died. I didn't need the emotional connection to know that. I knew that before we bonded, the stronger connection just helped to solidify that knowledge.

I may tease him about it, but Deacon had never been all that greedy. Stubborn? Yes. He knew what he wanted, and he went for it. He never settled for anything less than that. It was one of the things I liked most about him. One of the reasons I stayed with him all these years. I wanted to enjoy the ride with him.

The idea of him getting lost on that ride always terrified me. I didn't have a name for it before. Now I did. I loved him. I loved our life together. And I wanted to prove that to him.

I would do what I had to, in order to help him rebuild his confidence. If Carrie's pregnancy hormones were pushing me to be more forward then normal, then so be it.

I reached my hand under the blanket to rest on top of her knee. I pushed a finger under the rim of the dress she chose to wear for the meeting and dragged my finger along the inside of her thigh. Through the corner of my eye, I watched as hers closed and her grip on Deacon's arm tightened.

Deacon had a small grin, knowing what I was doing, but did not stop talking to Clarise. Besides, I was proving his point from earlier, we weren't just focused on each other.

Little by little, I pushed her skirt further up. She bit down on her bottom lip, trying to keep herself from verbally responding. She had yet to show any signs of wanting me to stop though.

Clint was doing his best to stifle a laugh. The scent or her arousal was permeating the entire car. The only person who had no idea what was going on was her little witch friend. Which Carrie had to know, otherwise I was sure she would have stopped me.

I paused when I reached home base. I searched thoroughly, but there was no covering. The fact that she came bare about did me in.

Deacon gave me an odd look, feeling my confusion and building fire. I glanced down, telling him to feel for himself. With both our hands there, she dug her nails into his arm. His eyes burned as bright as mine.

We tried hard to make her scream over the next few minutes, but she wasn't having it. She did pass out on his shoulder though. So, we lowered her to lay across the seat, her head in his lap, her feet in mine. It seemed to have become our routine. One none of us had a problem with.

"I'm getting flashbacks." Clint said sadly.

"It feels like so long ago, yet it hasn't even been three weeks." Deacon's voice did not betray his feelings on the matter, but there was nothing he could do to smother the internal one. The guilt. The shame. The sadness.

I gripped Deacon's hand over Carrie's stomach and did my best to support him silently.

Three hours later, we pulled up to a small base near Durango. It didn't exactly look like an Army base, as I had been expecting. I'd seen a few over the centuries. This one was more spread out. It resembled a youth campground more than an army base.

Hill stepped out of the main building, a large cabin of sorts, dressed in a dark green pair of breakaway pants, and a black shirt. Clint pulled up and parked there. The other SUV pulled up to our left, putting us between them and the Alpha.

"Welcome." Hill spread out both hands.

I had this odd open feeling coming from him, a lightness. I wasn't sure that described it right. He wanted us there. I was sure of that.

How did Carrie learn how to understand all these odd feelings on her own?

I stepped out of the car, carefully sliding my pregnant mate's feet off my lap.

"Where are we? I thought we were meeting at an Army base?" I asked him, keeping my voice soft as I shook his hand. I called him the same night I heard back from the human General, and Hill suggested this base.

He lifted an eyebrow at my volume. I pointed at Carrie, who was still asleep in the car. He grinned and nodded, lowering his voice as well.

“Base, yes. Army, no. This is actually the home base for the Grand Lupine Army Pack. Any wolf who joins the army is loaned to my pack for the duration. This is where we live when we are not deployed. When a shifter’s enlistment is up, they can go home, or stick around for as long as they want.”

“Why wouldn’t they want to go back to their families?” Clarise asked, closing her car door behind her.

Hill looked at her, then me again. A question in his eyes.

“This is Clarise. She is a healer from Carrie’s coven. She will be accompanying the Queen wherever she goes.”

Hill nodded his understanding, the slight tension in his shoulders relaxed again. “Shifters are not all that different from humans. We frequently suffer from PTSD and have to adjust to a normal life again. Our pack is equipped to help one another. Similar to that of the Vet hospitals humans have. Here, our wolves can comfort each other. We are pack animals. We work best together.”

“And you, Alpha? Where is your home pack?” Deacon asked solemnly, having already stepped to my side.

“This is my home pack. I was raised here. My father was the alpha. The oldest remains in the Army pack, the others join the pack of their mates. Unless they want to go into the army. My sister is mated to a male in the Rockies pack.”

“Ah. Hence your connection to them.” I chuckled and shook my head. “How long until the humans arrive?”

“They should be here in about an hour. Would you like to move Carrie to a room? Carrying a pup isn’t easy.”

“She’s carrying two actually.” Deacon told him proudly.

Hill's grin was slow, like he was waiting to see if we were joking. "That's wonderful! Even among shifters, twins are very rare. I can't even imagine how it is for your family."

"Practically unheard of." I confirmed. "Which is freaking him out even more."

We all laughed when Deacon shoved me. For the first time in four centuries, he knocked me off balance. And he wasn't even using all his strength. Taking her blood daily was boosting him more than I thought.

"I take back what I said before. I don't want to be bonded to both of you anymore. Anytime you start messing with each other, whether teasing, or otherwise, I feel a buzzing in my chest. You worry about my sleeping so much, maybe you two should learn to behave."

We both laughed as we helped our mate from the car. She immediately walked over and gave Hill a hug.

"Have you heard from Grace?"

And she popped our fun boat, sinking it straight to the bottom of the lake.

Hill gave her a small smile. "I did actually. Just last night. Although, it didn't make very much sense. I have been going over it again and again. She said goodbye in the same message, which means she is turning her phone off right after."

"What did she say?"

"One and done. I am sending you a gift, watch the skies. Oh, and C can freeze time. No idea how. The other night lasted six months for me. Gotta go. Good luck."

"You really have been studying it a lot, haven't you?" Deacon teased.

"Yes. One and done means she can't talk. It has to be quick. Sending me a gift and watch the skies makes no sense. C typically means Curtis. But he is a vampire so I don't know how he can freeze time. I don't even know where to start with the other night lasting six months for her."

My mates and I shared a look. Carrie turned back to Hill.

"I do. It means at some point in time Curtis was bonded to a time freezing witch." Carrie said sadly.

I put a hand on her back, offering her support. "That's how he got the walls up overnight. She must have been with him. Six months to put up that wall was fast, but I'm sure he had shifts of people working."

Carrie looked at me sadly. "She has been with him for so much longer than we thought."

I pulled her to me, and Deacon held her from the other side.

"How was he able to sustain the spell for so long?" Hill asked, dumbfounded, looking at all of us.

When no one else offered an answer, Clarise cleared her throat awkwardly. "A witch's blood can heal a vampire, much like that of a vampire to his mate. I imagine he used your friend to sustain himself. And if she is still alive, then he was feeding her in return."

Carrie's jaw dropped, her lower lip wobbling. "That's six months of him feeding her. She will be addicted to his blood by now. It doesn't take much."

"Hey," Deacon rubbed her arm, "it goes both ways. I can tell you from experience how addicted he will be to her by now as well. He will most likely be fighting himself on it, pushing for the monster to come back. In some ways, she is in a better position because of it. He will be more possessive of her, more protective."

“But...” Carrie’s rebuttal was cut off when we heard another car turn down the dirt path.

“That’s not the government. Who is that?” Hill asked, a slight growl in his voice.

“Oh. That’s for us.” Clarise did a little cheer. “Did you guys not tell him?”

All eyes turned to look at me. I grimaced and closed one eye. “Can I claim pregnancy brain?”

Carrie huffed and smacked me in the chest.

“Care to fill me in now, at least?”

I gulped and Deacon shook his head, keeping his gaze down to hide his grin.

I caught Carrie’s hand and kissed her knuckles. “They are coven leaders. They came to join us and to bless our boys.” I mumbled against her skin.

“Ah. Well, the more the merrier, I guess. And whatever helps protect Carrie.” Hill let that irritation go faster than I thought he would.

“Thank you, Captain Hill.”

He waved Carrie’s thanks away. “Call me Andrew.”

We turned as Clarise squealed and ran to the person driving the large SUV.

“Mama! I didn’t know you were coming with them.” The woman who climbed out almost looked like a replica of Clarise, only older. Same curly blonde hair, same rounded face, and short nose.

“Of course, child.” She gave her daughter a hug. “I needed to see the girl for myself. I helped bring her into this world, after all.” She walked over to where we still stood, giving Deacon and I disapproving looks. When her eyes landed on Carrie though, they brightened up.

“You look just like your mama, our dearly departed Queen.” She gave a small curtsy, then drew Carrie up into her arms.

There were five others behind her. Three women and two men. They in turn gave small bows and curtsies, and then kissed her cheeks.

“Alpha? Do you have a quiet place filled with trees we can use for the blessing? I assume we have time before the humans show up?” Clarise’s mother asked.

“Uh, yeah. Follow me.” Hill spun on his heels, and we followed him around the main building toward a forest area.

Clint quietly instructed the guards from our other car to keep an eye on things from there, before following us. He would keep a closer eye.

“Alpha, would you shift? We have been giving this some thought. Clarise told us about the twins and that situation. So, we are thinking of a different type of blessing. Plus, none of us have ever blessed a part vampire child before. It has been done, just not in some time. We want to call on all the different types of magic.”

Without a word, the Alpha stepped behind a tree. Clarise pouted and Carrie laughed at her friend. They were so different. I couldn’t help but wonder how they became such good friends.

“Alright, now. We are going to create a circle with Carrie and her bondmate in the middle.”

Deacon and I both stepped forward.

She huffed. "Which one of you is bonded to her?"

"They both are, Kristine. I found mom's letter, and the ribbons that she left me. She told me how. She said it would make me, and them, stronger. For the babies and the struggle that we would be going through."

Kristine, Clarise's mother, opened and closed her mouth, then sighed while rolling her eyes. Judging by the intention rolling off of her, I suspected it was to hide the tears threatening to come down.

"Your mother was unconventional. I'll give her that. But she was effective. I miss her every day. Alright, both of you stand here. One hand each on her stomach."

I didn't know why she bothered giving us the verbal instructions, she pretty much moved us there herself. She placed Deacon and I partially behind Carrie, each of us had one hand on her stomach and one on her back. Kristine moved our hands a few times, finding the exact right spot on her stomach they should be. Deacon's ended up closer to Carrie's right rib, mine was somewhat centered in the front.

"Good, now, everyone else, create a circle around them. Yes, you two Mr. Skulky vampire in the back." We laughed as Clint frowned and reluctantly joined the circle.

"Good, now they will be blessed by all the magic in the world. Everyone hold hands, or fur, or whatever. Close your eyes, and keep your traps shut while we do this. You three don't have to close your eyes, just be quiet and don't move. No matter what happens, hold your positions." She was very adamant about that last part.

Deacon and I shared a concerned look. Carrie didn't seem bothered in the least. All I felt coming from her was peace and tranquility.

The five coven leaders started mumbling words I couldn't understand. Deacon and I had to stop looking at each other, it was getting too hard not to laugh. We both felt ridiculous.

After a few minutes of listening to their gibberish, things changed. A sudden gust of wind blew through our circle and Carrie gasped like she was coming up for air after too long underwater. Her body shook between our hands, not exactly roughly, but it wasn't minimal either.

I shook my head at Deac, who was fighting the urge to move his hands so he could hold her and protect her.

It was his turn to silently reprimand me when the winds started circling us. It didn't feel right, not protecting her from the harsh winds. We should have been blocking her from it, not just standing there! The winds didn't so much as blow a hair on the heads of those around us. It just stayed there, with the three of us, circling us like we were the center of our own little tornado.

I was glad that Carrie's hair was at least pulled back, so it wasn't blowing in her face. Although, her ponytail was practically parallel to the ground by this point.

As the winds began to die back down, two small lights appeared above Carrie, nearly on Deacon and my eye level, flashing a steady beat. Slowly, they lowered down until they were even with our hands on her stomach.

They just floated there, in the air. Part of me wanted to reach out and shew them away from our mate before they could hurt her or our boys. I had to control the jump when they shot like bullets, right at Carrie. One light each, shot through the back of our hands on her stomach, and right into Carrie.

She gasped again, followed by a long-drawn-out sigh.

Both our eyes widened when we felt two strong beats from inside our mate. They were slow and steady, right in sync with our hearts, which also seemed to be in sync. The lights began to fade after a minute, but they were still there, beating their steady beat. I only heard it, and felt it, if I paid attention to it.

A few small tears pushed their way out of Carrie's closed eyes. I still felt only happiness and peace coming from her, so I was thinking these were the good kind of tears. But I could be wrong. It wouldn't be the first time, when it came to guessing what she was thinking.

Back in the bar, when I first created my plan of double teaming her in front of the Nightwalkers, I thought she was just tolerating my presence. I thought for sure she would boot me the first chance she could. Boy was I wrong.

I had never been so happy to be wrong in my entire life.

I looked up at the coven leaders, who were smiling and crying as well. Kristina broke the circle first when she walked over to us. She put her palms on Carrie's cheeks and kissed her head again.

"Your mama is so proud of you. Did you feel her? And your father?"

Carrie sniffled as she nodded enthusiastically. "Yes. I felt them both."

"Wait. Was that what those glowing orb things were?" Deacon asked, slightly weirded out.

"Yes." Carrie did that laughing cry thing girls tended to do. "They blessed our babies. Both of them." She then fell into Kristina's arms crying some more.

"I hate to break up this lovely moment, but the government people are here." Hill was back in human form, only his breakaway pants on this time. He kept his voice soft, almost reverent, trying not to startle them.

“How do you know?” Clint asked curiously.

“Alpha thing. We know when someone is on our territory.”

“You didn’t know about the coven leaders coming on.” Clarise pointed out.

Hill chuckled and scratched his jaw. I laughed and pushed him.

“You were messing with me. You jerk.”

He lifted his finger and thumb up, creating a “little bit” sign.

We continued laughing as we walked back toward the building. Hill led us through a back door to the cabin. He led us through a large formal living room, down a hall, and into a conference room holding a table with over a dozen chairs around it. I signaled for Clint to go greet the guests.

We all took up position on the far side of the room, taking control of the meeting from the beginning.

Chapter 27

Carrie

Colton held a chair for me at the head of the conference table. Deacon took the one on my right. Clarise and Colton then took up positions behind us.

Andrew sat to Deacon's right. Two of the coven leaders sat to my left, Kristine and the rest added to the half circle behind us.

A few minutes later, Clint held the door open as half a dozen bodyguards walked through the door, taking up positions along the wall. Three men followed them. One was wearing a formal military uniform, the other two were in suits.

Clint closed the door behind them but stayed in the hall, he would hear us if we needed him.

Andrew stood up and greeted the human guests. "Welcome, General Brooks, President Clint, and Secretary of the Navy Glen Franks. May I introduce you to King Deacon of the Vampire

Borns, and his mate, Queen Carrie, who is also the Queen of the witches."

"Why are you out of uniform, Captain?" The very cranky looking General snapped.

"With all due respect, General. I am not here as a Captain in the United States Army."

"What are you here as? A vampire lap dog? Didn't think I noticed how chummy you all were at the last meeting, did you?"

Andrew stared down at the man, looking much taller and larger than he had moments before. His voice came out deeper, double layered like he did the last time we saw him, and his eyes darkened.

"I am Alpha Andrew Hill of the Grand Lupine Army Pack. I am representing the shifters in this meeting."

There was no denying his power. Out of the corner of my eye, I saw Clarise fanning herself. I could just hear "that was hot" rolling through her head.

"W…witches? Shifters? I thought we were only here to deal with rebellious vampires?" The new president asked.

I caught a whiff of something foul smelling. I scrunched my nose and had to swallow the bile climbing up my throat.

Deacon leaned over to me, whispering in my ear. "Are you going to be sick?"

"What is that smell?" I choked quietly.

Deacon rubbed his lips together to keep from laughing. "That's his fear, angel."

"It's gross."

Colton leaned down to my other ear. "Wait until someone lies."

"We are here to deal with them." Andrew struggled to keep a straight face, obviously having heard our little conversation. "This is a problem for all of us. The magical community, as a whole, has been in hiding for years. I'm sure you can all understand why. You do remember your history courses, don't you? A hundred and fifty years later, and people are still talking about the Witch burnings and trials. In order to keep the peace, we have all lived in secret for centuries."

"I get what a witch is, and what a vampire is, but not a shifter." Mr. Franks said. I only remembered his name because I was getting hungry, and a hotdog was starting to sound good.

Andrew looked at us, unsure of how to explain.

"Just show him, Alpha. It will make this easier. Besides, there are some things you have to see to believe." Deacon told him, a laugh in his voice.

Andrew sighed and nodded. "Glad I wore these pants then. I had a feeling I was going to have to do this today." He looked at Colton and winked. Then did a backflip, landing as a wolf.

Colton mumbled "show off" again. I giggled.

The humans in the room were not laughing.

"That, gentlemen, is a shifter. He can shift from a human to a wolf. At will. Alpha Hill is the leader of his pack, a governor if you will. The shifter culture does not have one King or President over the whole of their species. Not anymore at least. They live in packs, with an alpha in charge. He is the alpha because he is more dominant, stronger, powerful." Deacon explained.

Andrew's wolf head turned, like he was listening to something in the distance. When the humans opened their mouths to speak, Colton raised a hand and silenced them.

"Do you hear that, my Lord?" He asked Deacon.

"Yes. It sounds like a plane. Alpha, are you expecting any planes today?"

No. I am not. Andrew broadcasted the thought to all of us.

The humans screeched and jumped back. I giggled again. This was kind of fun.

My back shot up straight, realization dawning on me, drawing everyone's attention. "A gift from the skies. Deacon…" I didn't even continue, I just jumped up and started running.

Colton was faster of course, once again freaking out the humans. "No, my Queen. You must stay back. We don't know if it's from her for sure."

"But..."

Deacon came up behind me, wrapping his arms around me. "This is his job. And the Alpha's territory. Let them go first."

I slumped defeatedly into my mate's arms as Andrew's wolf followed Colton out the door. I half expected Andrew to get stuck, but then I realized his doors were slightly wider than average. Good call.

Deacon took my hand, and we followed them, at a much slower pace. From the living room window, we watched as a large cargo plane landed. We were soon joined by the others, everyone watching as the scene unfolded. A large door at the back of the plane lowered down, making a ramp for the passengers. It actually kind of reminded me of the butt flap on long john underwear.

Before they were even out, Andrew's wolf started yipping, howling, and running circles around a laughing Colton.

I gasped right along with the humans when two dozen more wolves ran out of the plane. All of them were barking and laughing. After a minute, the new ones lined up in front of Andrew and lowered their noses to the ground. I vaguely noticed a few human soldiers stumbling off the plane behind them, looking weary and just done with it all.

"What are they doing, Deacon?" I asked, somewhat reverently. The moment just seemed to call for reverence.

"They are bowing to their Alpha. These must be his pack members he thought were lost."

I clapped with glee and tried to run out the door. Deacon stopped me again.

"I know you are anxious for word, angel. But give them a minute. Their Alpha has been very worried about them for many months." I frowned. "They will also need clothes."

My frown swiftly transformed into a grimace, and he laughed.

Colton came back a few minutes later, a grin on his face. "Sergeant Morris will be joining us soon."

"Where are they from?" I asked, biting my nails.

"They have spent the last few months chained up and kept prisoner by Curtis. Last night, a woman visited them. She claimed to be your sister, Carrie."

I clapped again and jumped for joy. "So, she is okay?"

Colton's face fell. "That they're not so sure about. Morris promised to get her out next. She told him she wasn't worth saving anymore, it was too late for her."

“Like hell it is!” I shouted, stomping one foot. “I will go in there and drag her out by her hair if I have to. That girl is coming home!”

Clarise stepped forward and placed a hand over my stomach. “Calm down, Car. Deep breaths. The babies need you to stay calm.”

“But... But…”

“We will find a way to get our sister out, I promise.”

“I made a promise to that girl, and I intend to keep it.” A deep voice bellowed from the door. “I take it you are the sister.”

I nodded and wiped a tear from under my eye. “How was she?”

“Tired. But strong.” He looked around the room carefully. “No offense, but she told me to be careful who I spoke in front of. Curtis has spies everywhere.”

“I beg your pardon!” Franks shouted. “We are from the United States Government, not one of us would work for a mad man.”

I couldn’t keep the gag back that time. Thankfully, my mates were faster than me. By the time the bile made it up my throat, Deacon had a trash can from somewhere.

“Sorry.” I croaked in apology.

“You don’t need to apologize, angel.”

“Yes, I do. I slacked off. I got so excited about the plane. I wasn’t paying attention.”

Both my mates looked at me oddly. “Pay attention to what you feel right now. Do you feel that prick, like someone is tapping on glass. Trying to break in?”

“Yeah.” They responded at the same time, a little on the wary side.

“That’s the intent to spy. That itch you felt, right before I puked, that was the warning of a lie. I’m assuming the smell was that as well.”

Colton cast a look to Clint, who was behind Franks a second later, holding his arms behind his back.

“What the hell are you doing?” The human General yelled. “We came here with an understanding of peace.”

“As did we. But your secretary here did not. He is a spy for Curtis. As we said in the beginning, my mate is a witch.” Deacon told him. “Her powers are to tell lies from truth and people’s intent.”

“What because she threw up?” Franks scoffed. His two companions eyed him warily, then looked back at us.

I scoffed. “No, you idiot. I threw up because I am pregnant, and your lie stank so bad it made me puke.” I looked at Clarise with unabashed desperation. “How long until my sense of smell goes back to normal? That was awful. I much prefer the annoying itch.”

The others all laughed. Well, the magical people did anyway. The humans were still confused, except for the one who was outraged over being manhandled by a vampire. Vamphandled?

“We are going to need more proof than the word of a witch. No offense, ma’am, but we don’t know you.” The General at least tried to soften his tone that time.

Colton scratched his jaw for a second, thinking. A small grin crossed his face. He walked slowly over to Franks and Clint. Franks flinched.

Colton yanked on both sides of the man’s shirt, sending buttons flying everywhere. I covered my gasp with my hand when I saw it.

"If you look right here gentlemen, you will see the bite marks of a vampire. These specific ones are the sign that he has been claimed by one. Someone on Curtis' payroll marked him as their own. In other words, they own him."

He came back to me, taking Clarise's spot that she vacated for him. The President and General stepped forward, taking a closer look at their friend's chest area.

"Well, I'll be." The General mumbled.

"Why, Glen?" The President asked, his voice showing his disbelief and sadness. "Why would you take his side?"

Franks shrugged and relaxed his limbs, giving up the fight. "I was young. I was broke. I was ambitious. We made a deal. At the time, I thought of it as like going to a blood bank. Then all this happened, and he asked me to spy for him. I no longer had much of a choice. He opened doors I never would have found. He paid for my college education."

"Do you have somewhere to keep him, Alpha?" Colton asked.

I spun, not having even known that Andrew had rejoined us. Without a word, he turned and walked down another hall. Clint and Colton followed him to a basement, taking Franks with them.

I studied the other two carefully. They studied me back warily. I closed my eyes, giving myself a short moment to relax, then turned back to the Sergeant.

"They're good. You may speak freely."

"Last night, a young woman came to us. I didn't trust her at first, seeing as she had Curtis' scent all over her. Much in the way you carry the scent of your mates on you. She started talking and mentioned the Alpha. She said we were going to be drugged and sent off as a gift to vampires in Washington. She had no time to send a message to the alpha. And he had no way of getting to us, so she was going to have to do it herself. The human who was assigned to work with us came in. He recognized her from the shelter. I believe she said that he was the shelter manager."

I cringed and closed my eyes. I remembered meeting that creep before, and what the twins told me about him.

"He was very excited to see her, even thought she was a reward from the vamps. Anyway, she let him get close, then she knee'd him good. I knocked him out after that. She gave each of us a small amount of the tranquilizer, so the vamps would smell it in our blood. We took the key to our silver chains out of his pocket. Once we were situated, she sat on the floor and screamed bloody freaking murder. Those vamps came running faster than I thought they would. Curtis was really concerned about her. She spun the story of the human trying to hurt her, after he drugged us. They thought it was one of my men at first, but she told him he saved her. Curtis led her out and Lucas took the human to dispose of him."

"Did she say anything else?"

"She refused to give me her name, since she wasn't sure who would hear my message. She only said to tell Captain Hill that she was Carrie's sister. Although, you don't look anything alike."

I huffed. "We are sister witches."

He nodded like that made all the sense in the world.

"She did have one more message. She wasn't sure she would have time to tell the alpha. After the way Curtis was acting last night, I'm thinking it was because she knew he was going to keep a closer eye on her."

"What was the message, Sergeant?" Andrew asked as he reentered the room, again.

"She said a storm was going to be hitting Washington in the next few days. It would hit the ports the hardest, before moving south. I'm not really sure what that means."

Clarise pulled her phone out and did a quick search. "Tomorrow. A huge storm front will be hitting the Seattle area first and is expected to move South until it burns out. They think it will get as far as San Diego."

"How would that affect the ports most though?" I asked.

"Because they are going to use it for cover. Curtis is taking out the ports, cutting off the imports and exports. I expect they will do the same to the other coasts soon too. With the help of the storms, they are not limited to just the nights. The Nightwalkers would need to move fast though, to stay within the storm. Hence the need for the shifters and the other soldiers." Colton explained.

"Why would they need them? Surely they wouldn't have been helping?" The President asked in disgust.

"No, but their blood is filled with testosterone. They would have been used like chargers for the attacking vampires. Keeping their energy levels up. Vampires, Nightwalkers in particular, cannot create the basic chemicals in their bodies, at least not enough of it. Shifters on the other hand have an abundance of testosterone. Good soldiers, too."

Deacon popped in. "Curtis was sending them as a gift, to help keep them going."

"So does that mean they won't attack now?" The President asked.

"No." The General cut in. "Curtis is the big bad, right?" We all nodded to him. "Curtis will still have his men attack. These…" He flung a finger wave at Morris and Andrew, "shifters were probably meant as an incentive and an extra ammo dump. The attacking vamps can still get what they need as they go, but it will take them longer."

“What are we going to do to stop this then?” I looked up at Deacon, pleading with him to help.

“Simple. We are going to send people to Washington ready to fight back.” Andrew answered. “We know their plans. We can get into position and take them out before they cause too much damage. Sergeant? I assume you and your men would like to have a little payback. You get to fight in wolf form now, too.”

The sergeant’s eyes changed to a flat back, causing the humans in the room to jump a little.

“Thank you, Alpha.” His voice was deep and gravelly, a bit animalistic, as he bowed to him. “We will make them pay for what they have done. We lost a few strong wolves in the beginning. The younger vamps, even a few of the older ones, were not prepared for the call of our blood. We would like to pay them back.”

“Go prepare your men, then. Take a nap, eat a meal, go for a run. Whatever you need to do.”

The sergeant spun on his heels and walked back out the front door.

“We have a few men in that area right now. We will send them to you.” Colton told him.

“Well, looks like we came to at least one agreement today. I will make sure we have a unit at your disposal, Captain. Just name the meeting place.” The General added.

“And for the future?” I asked.

“One step at time, young lady. Let’s see how well we work together first.”

I scoffed. “You’ve been working with all of us for years. I’m a kindergarten teacher.” I pointed at Deacon. “He’s a bar owner.” I pointed at Andrew, “he’s a Captain in your army. We’ve all been together for years. You just didn't know what we were. Nothing has changed, except your eyesight."

"Vampires have killed thousands of people in the last few months. They have proven they aren't trustworthy."

"And with one call, you commanded Deacon and I to be held hostage, and me tortured to keep him in line." The General's eyes widened. "Oh yeah, that was us. And look, here we are. Willing to work with you. My own people were hunted and slaughtered for their beliefs. And yet, here we are. How many human armies have started wars over the fact that they wanted more land, more taxes, or just because they didn't like the color of someone's hair? Humans have caused more destruction to the world than anyone in the magical community *ever* has. All we are asking for is the same rights you have given to everyone else. The right to believe what we will. The right to live how we want. The right to live, period!"

The room went silent after my little tirade. I would have felt self-conscious about it all, but I could feel the pride coming from both my mates.

And then the silence was broken by my growling stomach. I blushed and buried my face in Deacon's shirt. Both he and Colton laughed. The others soon joined.

"I hate you all. Now feed me."

Andrew stepped forward, still laughing. "The kitchen is this way. A few of the females in the neighboring pack brought a spread of food by this morning. Their way of supporting what we are doing here."

"Females?"

Seriously. How did this guy get into office? I mean, I knew he only got to be President because the last one was murdered, but how did he get to being Vice President?

"Yes. There are female as well as male, shifters. We have children, families, jobs, all of it. Many of the small towns you drive through are actually pack territories. We stick together. Wolves are pack creatures. We do not like to be alone. And there is safety in numbers. Help yourselves." Andrew opened the door to the kitchen, and I giggled with joy.

Deacon escorted me to a chair, while Colton started making me a plate. Deacon then went and filled a cup with juice for me. The apple flavoring smelled heavenly after the smells of fear and lies.

Clarise sat across the table and watched them both. I felt the envy coming from her.

"You know all you have to do is say the word, and you can have your pick of any of them. And however many you want."

She sighed. "So, tempting."

Chapter 28

Grace

Curtis woke me up with him the next evening, watched me dress, then took me down to the kitchen. It was the first time I had eaten somewhere besides the bedroom.

Charles had a plate of pancakes, bacon, and eggs ready for me. I thanked him and dug in. Curtis sat on the chair next to me, one hand rested possessively on my thigh. I teased him with feeding him bacon, and he acted more like a shark trying to catch it and my fingers. We were both laughing when Lucas walked in.

It only took one look at him for my anxiety to spike and Curtis to lose all humor.

"What happened?"

"Washington never got your gift. The plane took off as scheduled, but it never landed."

Curtis cursed and stood up to leave. He barely made it five paces before he stopped and turned. He silently lifted a hand toward me.

I grinned and took it, and his whole arm. I held tight to him. I just had to hope that any fear he smelled from me he would assume was for different reasons. I planned to push it onto Lucas' presence if he asked.

After the helicopter incident, it was viable. I never had been all that afraid of Lucas - I just didn't like the twerp - but Curtis didn't need to know that.

"Do we know if it crashed or if it got diverted?"

"No. But I don't think it crashed. I think they somehow took over the plane."

We stepped into a new room; it looked like an office. There were shelves full of books, trophies that obviously did not belong to Curtis, and a large desk sat in the middle. Curtis pointed his chin at a leather couch, that was pushed to the side of the room, and released my hand. I took the hint and sat down, praying they forgot all about me again.

"The last transmission we received from the pilots said they heard movement outside the cockpit. A few curse words, a small screech, and then nothing.

"Those tranquilizers have never failed us before. Why would they now?"

"I don't think they did, my Lord. We have no proof the shifters were even drugged in the first place."

Curtis shook his head. "I could smell it on them. The whole place reeked of it."

"What if someone only gave them a small dose, and dumped the rest? Even going down a drain would have spread the smell throughout the room. Then, even while our men moved the bodies, they would have still smelled it enough to tame their base instincts."

Curtis looked at me. “You said you saw the human inject the shifters, yes?”

I nodded, pretty sure they could both smell my fear now. “Y… yes. I think so at least. I was mostly trying to keep a few of them between him and me.”

I blinked when Curtis was suddenly kneeling in front of me. “He scared you that bad?”

My smile was naturally wobbly. “I told you. We don’t have the best history from the shelter. In the hangar, he kept going on and on about his deal with you, and how he had unlimited access to young girls. I’m sorry, I wasn’t paying close enough attention.” I licked my lips nervously. “He did make a stop by a sink before coming to me. I just figured he was washing his hands. That's what doctors and nurses do when giving shots, right?”

My whole freaking body was shaking. Curtis was going to know I set them free.

He was going to kill me.

Or worse, hand me over to Lucas.

The tears were hot and flowing fast.

Contrary to what I expected, Curtis mumbled a curse, picked me up, and sat on the couch holding me.

“I’m not going to hurt you, love. You did nothing wrong. It wasn’t your job to monitor him. I should have remembered that he was going in there. I should have never let you go in alone.” He grunted and looked at Lucas. “If they weren’t given a full dose, that would explain why that one shifter was able to save her after getting the shot, and why some were still awake when we came in. They should have all been out within seconds of getting it. We must have been too distracted by what the human tried to do, to realize that yesterday.”

"That's true enough. You were distracted taking care of her, and I was distracted taking care of him." Lucas' lip curved up just a bit. He felt no remorse for where his attention had been. "But how did they get out of their cuffs?"

"Who knows? They could have picked the lock… or they could have taken the key off the human." Curtis clicked his tongue and only half shook his head, turning it away. "They weren't trying to save Grace. They used the opportunity to their advantage."

I laid my head on Curtis' shoulder, not having to fake my relief. This whole spy thing was stressful. I needed a vacation. At least a mental health day. Our foster mom used to lock Todd and I in our room, claiming she was taking a mental health day.

"At this point, we have to assume they found their way back to their pack."

"Will it affect your plans?" I asked softly, a little afraid I would get in trouble for asking.

He shook his head. "No. They would have been a benefit, but that is all. The shifters were locked up on day one. Even if the human was helping them, he wasn't privy to any information either. Don't worry," he smirked at me, "I told you. I know what I am doing. We are safe."

I gave him a small smile and closed my eyes. Holy crap that was close. This keeps up, I would be one of the rare cases of teen heart failure.

Lucas cleared his throat. "There may be one other problem." Curtis turned his attention back to him. "Franks hasn't checked in. He was attending a peace meeting with the American President and an Army General this afternoon. They were meeting with Deacon."

I pressed my lips together to hold back the hungry moan when Curtis' chest shook from his low growl. Yep, I had definitely lost all sanity. Maybe they should just lock me in a padded cell when this was all over.

“Do we know for sure he has been caught? For all we know they are still locked in a room arguing.”

Lucas squinted and tilted his head to the side briefly. “Not for a certainty, no. But he is usually good about checking in every two hours. Those were his instructions.” He licked his lips before rubbing them together. “My witch spies were able to gather information on the new witch Queen. Carrie’s powers took a back seat for a while, she went through a rebellious phase as a teenager and pulled away from the culture. Seeing as she was the only heir to the throne, everyone was aware of this. But the older ones all knew her powers had originally manifested as a toddler.”

“That is young, even for a royal witch. I take it, that it has come back now?”

“Yes.” Even I could tell there was more. Lucas just wasn’t sure he wanted to say it.

I watched the movement in Curtis’ throat as he swallowed back either fear or frustration.

“What is it?”

“She has the power to not only tell when someone is lying, but their intent. They don’t even have to be speaking for her to know what their intent is.” Lucas sounded like he was walking on eggshells now. He knew the volcano was about to erupt. I just didn’t know why.

Curtis’ voice was strained. “She has *two* powers?”

Lucas widened his eyes at me, trying to send me a message, which I thought was a little odd. Good thing I already knew what I needed to do. I carefully turned to straddle Curtis, slowly sliding my hands up his shirt, and began nibbling on his neck.

I didn't need their odd sense of smell to know that even Lucas was scared right now. His voice was giving him away. Considering I had never seen him fear Curtis, that had to be a very bad sign.

"Y… yes, my Lord. I've been questioning some of the men in town about Deacon's bar. One of them told me a story of Deac's little mate, who was able to warn them about someone who was going to cause problems."

Curtis shook under me with anger, and I moved up to his ears. I lowered one hand to his jeans and flipped the button. He didn't respond to Lucas while I worked to calm him back down. It kept me calm too.

I screeched and then laughed when my sweater fell to shreds around me. The leggings encasing my legs soon followed. I should have been scared with how rough he was being. I could feel the danger and the fire burning through him. I was stuck on deciding if it was a good thing or not, because instead of scaring me, it just turned me on.

I knew Curtis wouldn't hurt me. I also knew how good it would feel. And not just because of what he did to me. It made me feel good that I could calm him down and distract him like this. I loved the power I had over him.

Lucas just stood there and watched, for once keeping his mouth shut and his hands to himself. I thought it would be worse after last night. It wasn't though. For all I knew, it helped.

Or he was just that afraid of Curtis right now.

"Why did we not know this before?" Curtis' bark was slightly softer, as he was in the midst of taking his aggression out on me.

Lucas shrugged. "I don't know. We were asking more questions about Deacon, then we were about her. Most anyone had said was how good she smelled. I think Deacon was trying to hide who she was, about as much as he was hiding who he was."

Curtis was sporting many holes in his shoulders from my fingernails before he spoke again.

"I think it's safe to assume that Franks has been caught. Let Kyle know. He had grown fond of him after all these years. Did your witch spies have anything else to say regarding their new Queen?"

Lucas looked at the ground. "No, my Lord. But I did get the feeling that they were impressed by her power level."

Curtis gently stroked my neck - slowly pushing my head to the side in the process - ear to shoulder. Excited butterflies flew from my stomach to my chest. "I wouldn't blame them. Many witches prefer to follow those with the most power. That was how I got them to my side in the first place. Keep an eye on them, we need to be prepared to intervene if they try to switch sides. They *do* know too much." He leaned down and licked my neck.

"Yes. My Lord. On the positive side of things, Ryder has everyone ready. They have a plan and are just waiting for the clouds to roll in."

"Good, good."

I giggled. Curtis didn't sound like he was paying attention to Lucas anymore. I seriously loved the effect I had on him. My eyes rolled back as he held my lower cheeks so tight that he nearly broke my skin with his short nails. At the same time, he broke the skin on my neck.

He didn't take much. It was just enough to finish soothing the raging beast inside him. His eyes were on fire when he came back up with a groan.

"You taste heavenly right now. The last bit of the fear was still warming your blood, mixed with the dopamine from what I do to you. It was the perfect mix."

"Then why did you stop?" I whined.

He chuckled as he leaned down and slowly sealed my wounds shut with his tongue.

"I would love nothing more than to take more from you. But in 24 hours, I will be taking a good deal. I do not want to risk weakening your body before my seed has a chance to take hold." He slid a hand over my stomach. "I only took some this time because your blood has a calming effect on me. There is something familiar about it."

His voice lowered to a whisper and Lucas finally showed some decency in pretending not to hear him.

"I said that I would do everything I can to ensure the safety of you and our son. That includes now, before he is there." Curtis sounded so sincere, and the words were so sweet, they hit me hard.

I threw myself around his neck and attacked his lips.

Chapter 29

Grace

I was torn inside. I wanted, and knew I needed, to get to my phone and message Hill. I needed to make sure they understood the message from the shifter in charge. I needed to make sure they found each other.

But Curtis also wasn't letting me out of his sight.

After his impromptu meeting with Lucas, he took me back to the room to get dressed, again. He laughed when I chose a dress this time. Not just any dress, but one that would in no way keep me warm outside. It was a basic, slip-on white summer dress. No zipper, no buttons.

The top was made of one string that tied around my neck. The other end of that tie held up the two triangles that covered my chest. The waistline was placed high, almost to my chest. The skirt itself ended just above my knees. It was a perfect beach day dress. I assumed it was anyway. I hadn't actually ever done that though, so I could only go off what I had seen in movies.

I teased Curtis that maybe now we could go a few hours without him destroying another outfit. When he didn't respond, I looked up from where I was sitting on the bed, putting on a pair of heels. The whites of his eyes were glowing as he watched me bend over.

I giggled and finished, then stood up to walk over to him. They somehow turned darker as he slowly took me in. I looked down and laughed. Yeah, dark red underwear wasn't usually worn under white for a reason.

I laughed harder when my back hit the wall a second later. At least he learned why I chose a dress, and I didn't lose another outfit.

Curtis dragged me around all night, from meeting to meeting. Vampires came and went, all needing to talk to him about whatever it was they were responsible for. My favorite was when Lucas came in again, Ryley in tow behind him.

Curtis got this evil smirk on his face, then placed me on his lap, facing out. While he spoke to them, he left small kisses along my neck and shoulder, grazed my neck with his fangs, and traced the outline of the triangles on my dress. He pushed the rim further and further down, until my blood red lace bra was all that was covering me.

Ryley whimpered the entire time.

I was on the verge of hyperventilating.

Not from nerves. Nope. He had just worked me up that much. They hadn't even left the room before Curtis had me practically kissing the table and my skirt on my back.

We slept a good portion of that night away, preparing for the long day ahead. Curtis wouldn't let me get out of bed much. He insisted breakfast be brought to me. He also chose my outfit - the black see-through teddy from my vision. I hadn't told him that part.

A few hours after the sun rose, storm clouds could be seen on the horizon. Soon after, lightning streaked across the sky. Curtis watched it through our balcony window, concerned.

“This storm came faster than I expected.” He mumbled to himself, pulling his phone out.

“Have you heard from Ryder yet?” He barked into the phone. “He was supposed to check in by now… We don’t have time to get distracted. In order for this plan to work, we need to stay on schedule… I don’t care how you do it, get me that report!” Curtis hung up on whoever he was talking to and threw his phone on the bed.

He walked back to the balcony window, seeming to forget I was even in the room. I could ignore what was supposed to come next, but I was hoping by distracting Curtis, it would give Deacon and the others more of a chance to fight back. So far, Curtis was only worried the storm was moving too fast. He didn’t know for sure there was another problem.

If there even was another problem.

I had to believe there was.

I had to believe this wouldn’t be for nothing.

Steadying myself. I slid off the bed and sauntered over to him. Slowly, I slid my arms around his thick chest and started kissing his bare back. He was wearing nothing but a pair of boxers. He knew what we were supposed to be doing tonight as well.

Little by little Curtis’ body began to relax under my touch. Just as he always did.

I didn’t need the memory of the vision to tell me what to do next. But the memory was helpful in keeping me motivated.

I was scared about the bonding thing, about getting pregnant with his child. Neither of those things had been part of my plan in the beginning. My friends and I were only supposed to be his harem. I was going to sneak into meetings, hoping he would be too distracted to care that I was there.

As Curtis moved us to the bed, it finally dawned on me what the real sacrifice was. The dream witch told me this was going to be the harder path to take. That my sacrifices were going to be different then I planned. I thought that meant physically, not emotionally. Not mentally.

I wasn't prepared to become addicted to him. To care for him. To *want* him.

In the background, I heard the soft sounds of his phone ringing somewhere on the bed. Curtis began to move away from me, searching for it with one free hand. I wrapped my legs around his waist and pulled him back down.

"Now, Curtis. The baby. I need your blood. I need you to take mine. Make me strong enough to conceive our son. Make me strong enough to bear you an heir. Make us both strong enough to survive, so I can be with you, my love. So, I can give you many more heirs. Make me yours, Curtis."

A random tear slipped out when a small flash of Hill's wolf standing inside of a shipping container in a storm went through my mind. It was an odd time, and it confused me why that hurt my heart.

With a hungry groan, Curtis bit into his left wrist and placed it over my mouth. Then he bit into the left side of my neck. Wave after wave hit us. Neither of us paid any attention to the phone ringing nonstop, to Lucas' shouting outside the door, or his banging.

I was vaguely aware of the door being busted open and Lucas cursing when he saw us. He knew of the vision. He saw the blood trade. He knew what we were doing. With a loud growl, he ran back out the door and down the hall.

Even when Curtis tried to pull back from me, I pushed his head back down and bit onto his wrist harder. We weren't done. I didn't know how I knew that. I just did. And the longer he stayed distracted, the more time Deacon and the others had to wipe out as many vampires as they could.

After an incredibly long, yet satisfying time, something solidified in my gut. I knew that was it. I was now forever tied to Curtis, in more ways than one. I released his wrist, and he slowly pulled his fangs out. He kissed the spot softly but did not seal it. A minute later, he collapsed next to me, barely having the strength to keep from squishing me like a pancake.

It took a minute or two, but he eventually rolled to face me, pulling me into him. He softly sealed the wound on my neck with his tongue, making my body shiver. We both laughed, mine was a bit more nervous. I didn't feel the wound close like it normally did, but it did stop bleeding. Even after all that we had just done together, it was kind of funny that my body reacted to something so small already.

His laugh cut off first. A look of confusion and hope swept over his face. Slowly, he bent down and sniffed my neck. Once, twice, three times.

When he was sure of what he was smelling, he grinned from ear to ear. His hand went to my stomach and rubbed softly. Then he slid over me and down, kissing my stomach before looking up at me.

"We did it. We made a son. How are you feeling?"

I snorted. "My thighs are sore."

He chuckled and kissed my stomach again. "I guess it's too soon for anything else. We will have to monitor you closely, make sure we are being extra careful."

He laid one more kiss on me, then pushed to stand on his knees. Still grinning like the cat that caught the canary as he looked down at me.

"You are the most beautiful creature to walk this earth in a thousand years."

I blushed and covered my face with both hands. He laughed and slowly lowered back on top of me. I shivered again when his lips kissed the still sensitive part of my neck.

"Part of me wants to show you how happy I am right now. But another part wants to let you rest." He lightly brushed his hand down my neck and to my chest.

I gulped. "Well, technically, we should be celebrating. Right?"

He laughed and lowered his lips to somewhere that wasn't my stomach this time. He at least kept in mind what I said about being sore while he showed me how happy he was.

A little later, I was snuggled into his arms, completely exhausted. Curtis kept one hand on my stomach, the other around my back. He softly kissed my head and I sighed into him.

"Thank you for giving yourself to me. Thank you for giving me a son." His voice was soft and soothing.

His words were immediately followed by a flash that sent a knife through my chest.

I saw a black wolf, his fur showing a purple tint in the moonlight. It looked somewhat similar to my hair. He was howling at the moon in sorrow and pain. The most depressing sound ever made.

I made a mistake. I overreacted. But by the time I realized it, it was too late. I was too weak to do the right thing at the time, but, maybe, with a little bit of help, I can make things right again.

With every curse, there must be a way to break it. It's all about balance.

Read how it all started, and how it all ends, in the last book of The Cursed Ones Trilogy – The Witch's Curse.

THE WEIRD WORLD OF TJ LEE

The Cooper Family Chronicles

- Love, Devotion, and Trust...with a side of Brownies (Levi & Callie)
- For Ellie (Emma & Freddie)
- For Emma (Emma & Freddie Cont./Rick & Rachel)
- Forgive & Forget (Tim & Alicia/Zack & Zoey)
- Avenging Angel (Mitch & Charity)

Dark Protectors (frequent crossovers with the Coopers)

- Daughter For Sale (Eli & Vanessa)
- Heartbeats (Alyssa & Ryan)
- Sins of the Mother (Trixie & Ty)

Million Dollar Duet (Crossovers with the Coopers)

- Million Dollar Angel (Elizabeth & Antonio)
- Million Dollar Screw Up (Stacey & Ricky)

Standalone novels (still have crossovers with the others)

- Finding My Sunrise (Samantha/Sarah & Jackson)
- 2 Doors Down (Rose & Ryan)
- Last Christmas (Trish & Noah)

The Yin & Yang Collection (you guessed it, slight crossover here too)

- Oil & Water (Mia & Theo)
- Scalpels & Staples (Jeremiah & Sheila)

The Silver Moon Collection

- Ivory Snow (Snow White - Shifter Style)
- Now Until Forever (Jessica & Jake)
- Fate vs Choice (Cassie & Ricky)

The Cursed Ones

- Revolution
- The Birth of a Queen
- The Witch's Curse

ABOUT THE AUTHOR

TJ is an avid reader. Reading was always an escape for her in her crazy messed up world. She's always had a vivid imagination. It wasn't until she was locked in her house for a year and a half, with only her two young kids, and two dogs to talk to, that she finally started writing. She found an even better escape.

TJ is a High School English teacher and a single mom. She holds a Bachelor's degree in Cultural Anthropology and Master's in Cultural Responsive Education. Her life motto, one she says with her students regularly, is to "fly your weird flag high!" She wants everyone to learn to be true to who they are. Accept yourself the way you are. Love yourself the way you are.

www.ingramcontent.com/pod-product-compliance
Lightning Source LLC
Chambersburg PA
CBHW060601310726
48982CB00008B/1201/J

* 9 7 9 8 9 8 9 9 9 8 8 5 2 *